"That way!" shouted the commander to his pilot. "Get that man!" The pilot maneuvered the boat around until it was next to the man's floating, facedown body. With one movement, the commander reached down and dragged the human on deck, almost losing his seat and falling overboard in the process.

The commander carefully rolled the man over to see if he still breathed. He did, coughing immediately on the water he'd inhaled. "Lucky devil!" said the commander, wreathed in smiles and gently shaking the survivor. "Another few seconds, and you'd . . . you'd . . ."

Still coughing, the man squinted up into the commander's blue, wide-eyed, hippopotamus face, and the latter gasped.

"By the Great Captain's blunderbuss!" bellowed First Colonel-Commander Herphan Gomja, Commander in Chief of Base Security, Port Walkaway, Ironpiece. "You're Teldin Moore!"

———————— ————————

THE CLOAKMASTER CYCLE

• • •

BOOKS

The Maelstrom's Eye

Roger E. Moore

THE MAELSTROM'S EYE

First Printing: May 1992
Printed in the United States of America
Library of Congress Catalog Card Number: 91-66503

9 8 7 6 5 4 3 2 1

ISBN: 1-56076-344-2

TSR, Inc.   TSR, Ltd.
P.O. Box 756   120 Church End, Cherry Hinton
Lake Geneva, WI 53147   Cambridge CB1 3LB
U.S.A.   United Kingdom

To everyone in the Milwaukee Aikido Club,
who put up with my absences for the
sake of this book, and
to kender everywhere—
thank you

Chapter One

• • •

The beholder's yellow central eye still bore the gleam of fanaticism, even in death. Its wild gaze, undimmed by the passing of years, looked down at Teldin Moore as he walked past the guild hall where the beast's spherical body was mounted over the main doors. Teldin's mouth went dry when he saw it, and he couldn't help but stare.

A thick wooden beam ran through the back of the beholder's round body for support; the ash-gray creature was wider than a man's reach with both arms. The dozen eyestalks on its top were cracked in places, some revealing the iron rods that supported the fist-sized eyeball at each stalk's end. Teldin tried to imagine what the ugly beast had been like in life, before it had met its final opponent and was turned into an advertising sign.

"That's Graffin the Gray," said the big, blond-haired warrior at Teldin's side. Aelfred Silverhorn gave a lopsided grin at the stuffed monster. "He's been there as long as I can recall. Quite a looker, isn't he? He used to attack shipping near the Rock. It took three shiploads of men to kill him, and he disintegrated one of them before the other two finished him off from behind."

"Interesting," said Teldin, finally looking away to watch the thick street traffic around them as they walked on. He pulled his royal blue cloak closer around his shoulders. "I wouldn't like to meet one of those here."

"There is one good thing about beholders," Aelfred replied, his eyes sparkling. "Given the choice, they'll kill each other long before they'll kill us. But they're not going to give us any trouble here, old son. There's one beholder who does live here, but Luigi's all right. He's a bartender. The Rock of Bral's just a calm, run-of-the-mill place."

As he spoke, the big man made way for a pair of grunting, red-haired gorillas in rainbow-patterned robes, each sorting through fruit in a streetside bin. Teldin tried hard not to stare as he and Aelfred walked past them, but Aelfred never gave them a second glance. "The Rock isn't very big," he continued sagely, scratching his broad chest through his loose black shirt. "Still, damn near everyone in the Known Spheres comes here eventually. Politeness is the rule. You might have your pocket picked, but the picker's in more danger than you are." Out of long habit, Aelfred let one hand stray to the money pouch on his thick brown belt, then dropped his hand when satisfied of the pouch's safety.

Teldin nodded blankly, looking back at the red gorillas for a moment. Each wore two huge swords in crossed scabbards on its back and probably weighed as much as three adult men. Their huge chests and thick forearms were an effective promise of their talents. By contrast, Teldin's work-hardened frame looked weak indeed.

Aelfred raised a thick-knuckled hand and pointed up the street. "The Greater Market's right ahead, around the corner, where that cyclops is going—the one with the head horn, not the bald red one."

Teldin Moore looked in Aelfred's direction and started to say something, but the sight of two cyclopes at once among the crowd caused his thought to trail away. He'd never seen a cyclops before, much less discovered that cyclopes came in different sizes and shapes. His blue eyes widened at the sight, but he was slowly becoming accustomed to being surprised.

"The market can be a rough place," said Aelfred, warming to a memory. "I heard a story about a goblin here who tried to cut the purse on this merchant, only to find out that the merchant was an illithid. The illithid mind-controlled the little guy, then made the goblin take its dagger and cut out its own—"

"Aelfred," Teldin said abruptly. He was already able to visualize the rest of the gruesome tale. "You told me you'd heard that the elven Imperial Fleet was here, but you didn't say anything about exactly where it was. I haven't seen any elves wearing that silver fleet armor you described."

"Oh, the elves are here, all right. The first mate on the *Drunken Kraken*, in the dock next to ours, said that his sister, who's a helmsman on a freighter out of Toril, once met this gnome who said the elves had an admiral or two here on the Rock. Their embassy is just a small one, up in the forest I pointed out when we were coming in. The elves had the trees imported to make a little bit of home for themselves. The forest is just beyond the Greater Market, a little ways up toward the prince's palace over there." Aelfred pointed in the same direction as before, his finger elevated toward an illuminated tower shining against the black, star-filled sky.

They walked on together in silence, Aelfred's tale about the unfortunate goblin thankfully dropped. Hundreds of white, gull-like birds—Aelfred called them gullions—wheeled and cried above them, sailing against the starry darkness like winged ghosts. In a few moments, the two men rounded the corner and came to a stop.

"The Greater Market," Aelfred said.

Teldin gaped, then closed his mouth. For perhaps a tenth of a mile ahead of him lay a shifting sea of humans and other beings, their voices filling the open square like roaring surf. Teldin rubbed his bristly mustache as he surveyed the rolling chaos before him.

An arm's length away, a huge giff in a green military uniform drank from a great pewter tankard as he walked by, his normally blue hippopotamus face now a warm purple. A brown, waist-high halfling with curly black hair and a bright yellow outfit argued vehemently with an overweight albino human, the latter in a black robe belted with a live white serpent. A shoulder-high elf wearing only deerskin trousers and moccasins, his face and chest tattooed with fine green whorls into patterns of trees and leaves, examined the wares of a leather-goods booth. Behind the booth's counter was a sad-eyed, winged baboon-woman in a toga of white silk, whose two hairy children shouted creative insults at passersby. A stone's throw to his right, seven colorfully dressed aperusa, human gypsies whose handsome, tanned skins shone with sweat, entertained the crowd for coins. The men played mandolins and tambourines as the women danced and laughed. On and on went the sights, across dozens of races, scores of languages, and hundreds of beings stretched over the whole of the marketplace.

Teldin smelled the heavy, sweet perfume of the aperusa women, the scent mixing with that of curried meats from a nearby food vendor, the citric odor of a pulpy green fruit crushed on the paving stones, and the smell of potent beers and ales. It was a place once beyond his imagination.

"Doesn't look like much is going on today," said Aelfred, surveying the crowd with a bored gaze. He shrugged and glanced at Teldin. "You want to find the elves on your own, or you need a hand?"

"I . . . I'll be fine." Teldin recalled with an effort the details of his mission to the Rock. "Let's meet at the *Probe* later. I could be quite a while, so I can't say when I'll get to the ship."

"Take your time," said Aelfred. "I'm going to look up some old friends and get another cask or two of sagecoarse for the saloon." He gave Teldin a nudge in the ribs with a rock-hard elbow. "Maybe you can find a trinket for Julia. Women love that, even the warriors—sometimes especially the warriors."

Teldin clenched his teeth, but he kept calm and looked away. This wasn't the time to start thinking about the copper-haired woman back on the *Probe*, Aelfred's sharklike hammership, but Aelfred insisted on poking at the topic of Teldin's love-life at least once a day.

"I'll look around for something," Teldin said vaguely.

Aelfred grinned. "That's the idea. Good luck, then. Don't let the elves put you on a waiting list." Aelfred slapped Teldin on the shoulder, then strode away and was lost in the crowded market within seconds.

Teldin pushed the conversation out of his mind and tried to make sense of the madness around him. It struck him that he was being introduced to some of the limitless and alien possibilities of wildspace civilization and commerce, and he was content to soak it in for a moment before moving on. He wondered again if he should have commanded his cloak to disguise his features, changing him into another person entirely, but again he decided against it. There was no point in trying to fool the very people whose help he needed most.

Teldin knew he was not especially remarkable in appearance, being of average height, weight, and looks for a human male of thirty-three years from his now-distant homeworld of Krynn. His tanned face and hands were lined from years of farming and soldiering, more recently scarred by fighting in wildspace. His sandy brown hair had grown longer; he kept it brushed back and trimmed, but the feel of it was more pleasing now than the short-cropped style he had once favored. He'd even grown a mustache and had been pleased with the result, though he still shaved the rest of his beard whenever possible.

His clothing—except for his cloak—wasn't particularly striking, either. He'd always liked quiet tones. Today he favored a well-worn blue cotton shirt and long, stone-gray trousers belted with dark leather. The brass hilt of a short sword stood out from his left side, strapped to a second leather belt. Two worlds ago, Teldin had found a comfortable pair of high-topped boots, simply done, made from the rust-colored hide of an alien beast whose name Teldin couldn't begin to pronounce. In contrast to Aelfred's careless but often dashing dress, Teldin looked quiet and somber, not one to attract attention. Given the events of late, he was quite happy to be seen and forgotten.

Grandfather would have loved to have seen this, Teldin thought, and he smiled. Old Halev had always wondered what, if anything, lay beyond the moons of Krynn. He'd dearly loved tales of mystery and adventure, but Teldin suspected the old man would never have believed a word of what had happened to his grandson in the last few months. Still, he would have loved to hear the story.

Teldin pulled his long blue cloak close around his shoulders again as he started uphill into the noisy crowd. This little world certainly looked big enough when you were walking on it, he thought. Teldin had looked down at the Rock of Bral with the other crewmen as the *Probe* had flown in for docking. From space the Rock had looked like a mile-long potato covered by a city, complete with streets, buildings, and trees. Aelfred had had the ship dock at the small end of the Rock; the bigger end, uphill from the docks, was given over to the estates of the local prince and a narrow lake where gullions congregated by the hundreds. While the crew was unloading the cargo, Aelfred had offered to give Teldin a quick tour through the city. Teldin had been grateful for the help, but he was happier now that Aelfred had found other things to do.

Being on his own was Teldin's natural state. He knew he would have lived out his natural life on Krynn, hoeing crops and caring for his animals, needing only occasional company. It was easier to get things done by himself. Nowadays, it was safer, too. It wasn't wise to trust many people, thanks to his cloak. It had become the ultimate scavenger-hunt prize to the worst sort of foes.

Teldin scanned the crowd for any sign of Aelfred's face, but he could see nothing of the grinning warrior. He almost felt relieved. Teldin was all too aware of the dangers he presented to everyone who traveled with him, and he knew his few living friends were aware of the risks, too. Aelfred, Julia, and a handful of others had suffered terrible injuries because of him, and uncounted numbers more, friends and enemies alike, had died in awful ways. If he weren't looking for the elves, he knew he probably would have disguised himself using the cloak, or at least would have shrunk the cloak until only the silver clasp, chain, and a tiny bit of cloth showed, concealing its true nature. Removing the cloak was impossible and always had been. He couldn't unfasten the cloak's lion-headed catch, and the cloak held unpleasant surprises for those who tried to cut it or remove it from him by force.

Teldin slowed, seeing a knot of beings ahead of him. Some Oriental humans were arguing politely with a horse-sized creature that looked like a brown praying mantis, apparently about a payment of some kind. None of them spoke any language Teldin had ever heard, but he understood them anyway—another benefit of the cloak, which often, seemingly at whim, translated unfamiliar languages for him. For all its faults, the cloak had its benefits, too.

As he made his way around the arguers, Teldin thought about his past. How would he tell Halev about it, if the old

man were still around? Just half a year ago, Teldin was an em-
bittered war veteran, scratching out his life on a farm in a little
valley. He knew his homestead would be a mess now. Neighbors long ago would have found his home burned to the
ground, with the ruins of a ship, of all things, right in the
middle of it. The burned or butchered bodies of his closest
neighbors and several unknown people, including an alien
woman of a race called the reigar, would have been dug up
shortly thereafter. Unless they traced him across the continent
of Ansalon after the fire, the few people left who knew Teldin
would have assumed that he was dead, too. Almost everyone
else who knew of his troubles after the ship fell out of the sky
and crushed his home was now dead. His new enemies had
killed them all.

Teldin shrugged. Like his grandfather, the neighbors would
not have believed the rest of the story either. Teldin was given
his strange cloak by the reigar woman before she died of her
injuries from the crash of her space-flying ship, called a
spelljammer. Teldin and an alien soldier named Gomja—a
huge blue, hippopotamuslike humanoid—had crossed the
lands of Ansalon, pursued by a murderous, wicked, spiderlike
race called the neogi, who wanted the cloak he now wore.
Aided by the gnomes of Mount Nevermind, Teldin had escaped into wildspace and had survived treachery, piracy, and
murder as he searched for clues to the cloak's purpose.

Once, Teldin gladly would have left the cloak with anyone
who had asked for it. Now, he didn't dare let it out of his
grasp. Pirates, vile neogi, hideous mind flayers, blue-skinned
humanoids called the arcane, and others wanted his cloak very
much. The neogi in particular wanted it badly enough to torture and murder everyone they met. They had hinted that
they could enslave and decimate whole worlds if they came
into possession of the cloak—just how, Teldin hadn't a clue,
but he wasn't sure he wanted to know.

On the advice of Vallus Leafbower, an elven wizard who had
once been the helmsman for the *Probe*, Teldin had decided to
contact the admirals of the elven Imperial Fleet. He wanted
answers. Who had made the cloak? What was the cloak's purpose? What were all of its powers? Why couldn't he take it
off? And why were so many forces willing to kill for it? The

dying alien woman had told Teldin to take the cloak to "the creators"—but who or what were they? He shook his head as he walked. It was a crazier universe than Grandfather Halev ever could have imagined.

Teldin stepped around a group of steel-armored dwarves, all examining a faded parchment in a tight circle. They barely glanced up at him before returning to their whispered conversation. It would be nice one day, he reflected, to be able to take the cloak off and walk around like a normal human being. With as many enemies as he now had, though, perhaps even that was unwise. The cloak had an assortment of magical powers that Teldin had painfully discovered by accident and by trial and error. He could hardly afford to lose its protections now.

Teldin passed and ignored a pair of babbling, fishy-smelling penguins, each dressed in red-and-green plaid shirts and ridiculously waving their flipperlike wings at him from the blanket on which their wares were laid out. Aelfred had already warned him about the dohwar, and their squawking pleas faded behind him. He did give a long look at a towering gray giant sitting cross-legged ahead of him. The giant wore purple-and-red striped breeches and a dirty white shirt. He stroked his braided beard as he quietly spoke with a motley collection of children of every race Teldin had ever heard of. Even sitting, the being was twice Teldin's six feet in height and almost as broad across the chest as Teldin was tall. A spacesea giant, he thought, recalling Aelfred's lessons on wildspace inhabitants.

It was because of the spacesea giant that Teldin didn't see the girl, and they thumped solidly into each other in front of a rug merchant's stall.

"Oops!" the girl squealed, a startled look on her face. Barely a teenager, she came up to Teldin's breastbone. It struck Teldin next that the girl was also very beautiful.

"Paladine! I'm sorry. Are you all right?" Teldin instantly reached out to steady the girl.

The girl giggled and reached up to her black hair with a golden-bronze hand. A bright magenta kerchief was tied around her head, and a high, thick ponytail fell like water down her back. Teldin was vaguely aware that she wore a flowery perfume and a color-splashed dress that reached to her toes, but he was not able to look away from her huge, dark eyes. Flecks of gold swam in them like distant stars. She would be a stunner when she grew up.

"I wasn't paying attention either," the girl said, still smiling. "It's hard to get around in a place this crowded. I've been here a few days, and I'm still trying to find my way. Are you new here, too?" Her voice was songlike. Something about it and the way she looked tugged at Teldin's memory.

"Uh, yes." Off guard, Teldin gestured behind him, downhill. "My ship docked about two hours ago. I was, ah, taking in the sights." *That's all she needs to know,* he thought. *No need to involve anyone else in my problems.*

"Great!" she said easily, as if she'd known him all her life. "Then we can explore the Rock together! Have you had something to eat since you got here?"

Things were getting out of hand. Teldin looked uphill for a moment, then deliberately let his gaze wander away and around the city. "I was going to explore a bit on my own," he said slowly. "I . . . need to see some people about business. It could take a while."

"Oh, but you have to eat, right?" the girl said brightly. "My name's Gaeadrelle Goldring. Gaye is fine. I saw this weird little tavern near the Burrows, sort of half-sunk into the ground. Halflings run it. It smelled like they serve some kind of chicken dish. Let's try it. If it's awful, I'll pay. C'mon!"

"What about your parents?" Teldin asked, uncomfortable with the thought of having her tag along after him. She wasn't acting like a teenager, yet she was like a child in a way. "Wouldn't they—"

"My *parents*?" cried the girl, putting a hand on her chest in mock surprise. "Give me some rope! I'm not a kid! I've been walking loose on deck for years! I'm just shorter than you are, that's all. C'mon, let's take a walk. I don't bite much, and I'm starving. We've got to see a bit of the Rock before you get serious. This chicken place, now . . ."

Before he was fully aware of it, Teldin was walking beside Gaye as she led the way through the Greater Market. Still talking, she headed perpendicular to Teldin's original course.

What in the Dark Queen's name am I doing? he thought. *I*

have to find the elves and see what they know about this cloak. My life and many others depend on it. If the neogi find me again, they'll cut me to pieces and pick the cloak out of the gore, and then—

Gaye abruptly turned toward him and gave him a wide, happy smile. Her eyes were like wildspace itself. "So, are you hungry enough to try it?" she said.

Well, he reasoned, Gaye was charming, but she still seemed too young for anything other than polite company. She was very self-possessed, but she couldn't be more than sixteen, eighteen at the most. He sighed and looked away, weighing his decision. This was an armed asteroid, and there were no neogi about. He'd been here only two hours. Another hour or two wouldn't make any difference. He hadn't eaten in almost half a day, thanks to his nerves over seeing the elves. Gaye could probably do worse in choosing a male figure to whom she could attach herself; he could at least look out for her, even if Aelfred felt the Rock was safe. Aelfred was seeing it from his own point of view, not from a teenaged girl's.

Halflings were supposed to be great cooks, too, or so he'd heard. There were no halflings on Krynn, and the halfling deckhand on the *Probe* wasn't trusted in the galley yet. Maybe Teldin had been missing something.

He wondered if he'd pay for this with more than money.

"Sure," he finally said. Gaye looked ecstatic.

If I'm missing anything, he decided, it's common sense.

*   *   *   *   *

Lunch (or had it been supper? Teldin had no sense of time on this night-sky worldlet) had been excellent. Afterward, he and Gaye had wandered through the Burrows, the surface-and-tunnel community of the local halflings, then through orderly Giff-Town, with its quaint and long-winded signs. They'd even gone into the Lesser Market, a filthy street bazaar where the silent, meaningful gazes the local men sent in Gaye's direction led Teldin to walk close beside her with one hand on his sword hilt. (So much for Aelfred's opinions of the Rock's safety, he thought in disgust.) Gaye had been oblivious to potential danger, stopping at several ramshackle tables to inspect peculiar cups, ornaments, rings, and other items.

And Gaye had never once stopped talking. She had extensive, if superficial, knowledge of numerous worlds, cities, races, and ships. So far, Teldin had heard some of Gaye's experiences with, and opinions of, gnomes ("delightful!"), elves ("nice, but a little snooty."), dwarves ("so serious!"), wildspace ("it's *big*, isn't it?"), and some place called Kozakura, where she'd studied art of some kind. She'd arrived at the Rock on an aperusa ship about eight days earlier, admitting that she'd been here longer than she'd let on earlier. The aperusa men had been unbearable, she'd said, and had always tried to get her alone somewhere. Teldin felt his blood rise at that, but Gaye thought little of it, aside from saying, "I don't know how the women put up with it."

The details were jumbled up, but Gaye had apparently been roaming on her own for ten years or more. The issue of her exact age was becoming more confusing all the time, but Teldin wasn't ready to ask about it.

Three hours after they'd eaten, they were somewhere in the Dracon Enclave, near a semitropical grove of palm trees, sitting on the short-cropped grass. Before them was a large collection of reptilian beings of every sort, from centauroid dracons to manlike lizard men.

"I used to think that a lizard was a lizard, you know," said Gaye, "but then I saw that there were as many types of them as there are of people like us. I met some trogs once, not very friendly ones at that, and, wow, did they ever stink. It was incredible. Then I met dracons, saurials, sithp'k, and, of course, the wasag, like that little blue guy over there." Gaye pointed at a halfling-sized reptilian humanoid about thirty feet away, which looked over at them with a blank expression.

Teldin leaned back on the grass and looked at the wasag, which flicked a thin, forked tongue in his direction, then he looked off to his left at one of the Rock's huge hexagon-base defense towers, bristling with siege machines aimed into the starry sky. The tangerine sun hovered low over the city skyline ahead of him. Aside from the sun's presence, he had learned that night was no different from daytime on the Rock of Bral. The air envelope around the asteroid wasn't thick enough to create a colored sky, so it was always dark above. Street and shop lights kept the city lit even when the sun was shining on the Rock's other side.

Things were becoming stranger still. The Rock had seemed large earlier, but after wandering around he had discovered that the horizon was so close that he thought he was on a mountaintop. It was hard to get used to. He suspected that the scenery could get monotonous, but at least the locals never had to worry about bad weather. And the steady stream of visitors from other worlds kept things interesting.

Gaye said something that ended in the word "Krynn," then stopped speaking. Teldin looked at her. She was giving him a big-eyed look, waiting for a response.

"What about Krynn?" he said.

"I asked if you were from Krynn. You said the name of the god Paladine when we met, so I assumed you were from Krynn, like me."

Teldin's mouth fell open. "I *am* from Krynn," he said in amazement. "I had a farm in Estwilde, south of Kalaman. You're from Krynn, too?"

"I don't believe it!" Gaye shrieked. Every reptilian being within earshot turned in their direction. "Is this a pocket-sized universe, or what?"

Teldin was on the verge of asking her where she came from when he noticed a group of elves, probably diplomats or nobles, walking down the street toward him. He remembered something important then.

"Damn," he said, and got to his feet. "I've got to find the elves." He cursed himself then for letting her hear that.

"The elves? You have to see the elves? Was that your business here? I know where they're at. You should've just asked me back at the Greater Market. They're right in the middle of the Rock, on the edge of the High City." She pointed to Teldin's right, uphill.

Teldin belatedly realized how far they had been wandering in the last few hours. "We've got to get going," he said quickly. "I mean, *I've* got to get going. I have to go see them by myself." He quickly brushed off his pants. His magical cloak never got dirty or wet, so he didn't bother with it.

"Let's go, then," Gaye said brightly. She hadn't heard his last two sentences very clearly. "We'll go this way, around the dracons and down to the arena and up by the festival grounds. We'll reach the elven forest in a few minutes."

"But—" Teldin started, then had to run to catch up to Gaye's quick pace. As they passed the dracons and lizard men, the reptile-folk stopped hissing and croaking at each other and gave them both cold, unblinking stares until they were well down the street. *I wonder if they think we're good to eat,* Teldin thought, then shoved the question aside. He let go of the brass sword hilt and focused instead on keeping up with the girl with the color-splashed dress and anthracite hair.

Gaye chatted on as they went, now talking about the lore she'd picked up about the festival grounds. Something was pulling at Teldin's memory about Gaye. Had he met her before? He doubted it. Then why did she seem familiar to him? She didn't have much of a Krynnish accent, but the way she spoke, her appearance, her fearlessness, her face—what was it? He found himself staring at her magenta kerchief, where it covered her ears.

They had just passed the Rock's arena and were heading up the boulevard past the festival grounds when Gaye, in her happy rambling, started talking about Krynn and how she'd first made her way into wildspace.

"It was really the craziest thing. I'd just finished seeing some relatives in Kendermore when this big gnomish side-wheeler came right out of the sky and crashed, just smashed itself into little—"

"No," said Teldin, slowing abruptly and staring at Gaye with the beginnings of astonishment and horror. The childlike face. The endless talking. The nonstop traveling. The unremitting curiosity. The lack of fear. Great Paladine.

"What?" Startled, Gaye looked up at him and slowed down, too. "What's wrong?"

"You're a kender," he said.

Gaye's dark eyes widened to enormous size. Her mouth fell open, mocking Teldin's expression. "Reorx's Hammer, do you really think so?" she said, stopping. "Is that where I got these?" She reached up and pulled off her kerchief.

Gaye's ears were pointed on the tops, just like the ears of all elves—and the ears of all kender. She saw his expression and grinned like a devil.

I've been traveling with a kender, Teldin thought with dismay. *She's probably robbed me blind.* His hands strayed to his belt purse, which was still strapped shut. That meant nothing, he knew; she could have gotten into it a dozen times by now. Krynnish kender were born thieves, magically descended from humans despite their superficial elven looks. Gaye's height had fooled him; most kender were willowy and only three and a half feet tall. Gaye was almost four foot six with the build of a human teenager, more muscular than he would have expected of a human girl. She could be almost any adult age. Kender lived longer than humans—and they made life hell for everyone around them, every day of their lives.

He had to ditch her before he saw the elves; they'd never let him near them if they knew anything at all about kender. She could keep the money she'd stolen from him, too. It would teach him to look before he leaped.

"Listen," he said abruptly. "I have to do some very important things, and I have to go alone. I've had a great time, and I appreciate your showing me around the Rock, but I do have to go."

"You have to go?" repeated Gaye, her grin fading somewhat. "Well, when you get back, we can—"

"I'm going to be a long time. I'm sorry. I probably won't see you again." He hated to be cruel about it, but this was best stopped now. He'd been a fool long enough.

Teldin looked up the street. The tops of some broadleaf trees in a densely forested region were now visible above the pavilions and booths at the end of the festival grounds' boulevard. It had to be the elves' forest. He turned back to Gaye and stuck out his hand. "Thanks again."

Gaye looked blankly down at his hand. She then took it in her own small hands, gently and carefully, and simply held it. Her touch was very soft and warm.

"Maybe we'll meet again anyway," she said hopefully, a trace of a smile coming back.

"Maybe," he said, and pulled away. *In a million years, if I'm lucky,* he added to himself.

Without a backward glance, Teldin set off for the forest. It was only with great difficulty that he could push the image of the wildspace eyes out of his mind.

Chapter Two

• • •

The first screams began at sunrise, only slightly muted as they entered through the frosted windowpanes of the old elven citadel. General Kobas Hamarka Vorr flipped a page as he finished reading another report at his oversized stone desk. He was in early today, hoping to plow through the mound of paperwork before him. The only interruption so far had been from his goblin aide, who had shuffled in bearing a wooden tray with an assortment of spiced meats, rice, fruit, and water for breakfast. The rest of the day, excluding meals, would be the usual ritual of reading, noting, signing, and moving on.

The only entertainment would be that provided by the elven prisoners, taken when their homeworld had been conquered by a humanoid naval fleet and the general's scro and ogre marines. Every hour, after the abrupt cessation of one elf's cries, a new voice would ring out its agony. This timing had proved helpful, and the general usually let the screaming set the pace of his work.

The present system of handling elven prisoners was a great improvement over the old one, the general reflected as he paused in his work. Many of the troops still preferred the dusk-to-dawn mass rituals now permitted only during religious holidays and military celebrations, when prisoners were many, but that system ate up too much time and required too many troops to manage the captives; it was simply wasteful. Now only three or four soldiers and a war priest could handle affairs, and the limited pool of subjects was stretched considerably. The timing also allowed for normal sleep, and the new ceremony still satisfied the legions. Best of all, it had a profound effect on those prisoners awaiting their turns on the red-stained granite block in the citadel's withered garden, and they offered up the most remarkable secrets in the hopes that they would be spared. That was always the most amusing part, thought the general, as he started the last of one batch of reports and took another bite of his meat and rice.

Sometimes the general would stop and listen to a particularly interesting cry a victim would make. He thought he could make out individual words in Elvish, most being pleas for mercy, but he was never sure. His hearing had only recently recovered from the day when the main gun on the *Groundling Scythe* had blown up in front of him during the landings on this curious little world, which the elves had named Spiral. The blast had otherwise merely bruised and cut the general in numerous places, thanks to his thick armor and innate fortitude, but it had also killed eighteen marines and his previous goblin aide, the third he had lost in only a year. Aides were damned hard to train properly, and getting along without them was inconvenient at best. He hoped the current one would last a while.

The morning sun's red light was supplemented by magical light globes set up around the room, and the general had no trouble reading. The air was still cool, not yet up to the dry oven heat that would come in the afternoon. The food was well prepared, and the water cold and fresh. It must have been the tedium of the reports, then, that caused General Vorr to let a page drop from his fingers to the desktop. He rubbed his bald gray pumpkin head with both huge hands, his eyes closed. It was hard to concentrate, and he wasn't sure what was bothering him. He'd gotten used to the low ceilings in the elven buildings, barely two feet above his eight-foot frame, and Spiral's sun didn't bother his eyes the way the brighter stars did. He paid no mind to extreme temperature changes. Even his steel-banded, black-trimmed armor was as comfortable as leisure clothes could hope to be.

It couldn't be a lack of exercise, either. Despite the end of direct combat action in these last few weeks, the general was careful to maintain his Herculean musculature with heavy lifting and stretching exercises every other day. His pale-gray skin had a healthy shine, and none of his many old injuries were bothersome these days.

Something was wrong. After a moment, the general knew what it was, and he knew also that there was no immediate cure for it. He sighed and looked down at his paper-strewn desk, noting the heavy, red-iron tarantula paperweight his troops had cast for him, then the thick mithril-steel globe the elves had long ago made of Spiral, showing the strange, winding rivers that flowed from its polar seas to its equatorial ocean and back. He felt no inspiration there, and that was the trouble. Spiral was already conquered.

Looking up, the general found himself staring at the immense clawed hands mounted to either side of the oaken double doors of his expansive office. The green, four-fingered husks went well against the white walls, mute testimony to the broken might of the elven ground forces. The zwarth that had once wielded those claws had been a real titan, a thirty-five-foot undead insectoid monster crewed by eight elves. General Vorr wished again that he had seen the expressions on those elves' faces when the zwarth had bounded out from ambush and fired its rapid spray of magic missiles directly at him while he was directing the landings on Spiral. By the Tomb of Dukagsh, that had been a fight, a damned good fight. Cutting the hands off the smoking green wreck afterward had been especially satisfying. Sometimes those elves knew a good trick or two, for all the good it did them in the long run.

General Vorr sat back, listening to the hoarse, distant cries of the fifth prisoner of the day. The garden ceremonies were good, but they were losing their morale value. This group of elves had been only farmers, after all, not warriors captured in battle. The last of the fighting for Spiral had been too long ago. Little Spiral's orange sun now rose and set across a world controlled by the Tarantula Fleet's ground and wildspace forces. With the local military ground into blood and bones, the troops lacked an appropriate outlet for their aggressions. Hunting down elven refugees in the deep caverns and mountains was a job for orcs and goblins, not highly trained marines like the general's black-armored scro and ogres.

We came here to kill elves, the general thought darkly, not to settle down, play games, and squabble among ourselves. Somewhere in this vast crystal sphere there were more elves, possibly even elements of the Imperial Fleet, but hunting for them would stretch the resources of the Tarantula Fleet too far until the scro had time to build more ships on Spiral. This was the third sphere the general had seen since the War of Revenge had begun, and the once-mighty fleet had been reduced by over two-thirds in constant, glorious, challenging, savage, righteous battle. All of the beautiful mantis ships were destroyed; hastily repaired derelicts and hijacked ships had been pressed into service. They had to rest or perish.

That was the whole problem, of course. General Vorr hated just sitting here, knowing his troops were rotting from within. We should be back in wildspace again, he thought. We've been grounded for five hands of days now, and the reports are filling with summary executions for fighting among the troops. That energy should be directed at the Imperial Fleet, not at fellow soldiers. It was the accursed politics behind it all, of course.

The general's eyes wandered around the room, taking in the crude array of tribal, religious, and unit banners crowding the walls to either side of the doors, past the zwarth's claws. The Tarantula Fleet admiral's policy of letting common orcs into the ground legions only fed the problem. Orcs had boundless hatred for elves, but they also had equally violent hatreds for almost every other sort of humanoid, including orcs of rival tribes and cults and even the orc-descended scro. Other humanoids were like that, but few as much as the orcs.

In their favor, the orcs and minor humanoids were useful for assaults on the gigantic, space-going dwarven citadels, where they could absorb the initial losses from traps and ambushes before the highbred scro and their allies took over and battered their ways through to the forges and redoubts. Rabble could be spared for rooting out survivors on conquered worlds like Spiral, settling down in the meanwhile to create their own colonies. Otherwise, they were just a nuisance.

Whether he liked it or not, Vorr knew that Admiral Halker and the admirals of all other fleets now at war with the elves were doing what had to be done, following the words and plans of the Almighty Dukagsh, the Scro Father. Only by uniting all humanoids into the War of Revenge could the elves be driven from wildspace like sparrows in the claws of a gale— and driven they now were. In the year that the war had been underway, the general had seen the Imperial Fleet forces in two crystal spheres destroyed; elven worlds and fleets in other spheres were rumored by scouts and spies to be under attack or to have fallen as well. The war was vast, and Vorr knew he saw only a small part of it. Few elves had escaped the butcher's cleaver, and little word had spread so far to alert other spheres of the coming of the blade. Spiral itself had fallen so rapidly that it was unlikely any other elves in this sphere knew of it yet. The elves, who had once ground the humanoids under their silver heel, had grown careless and lazy. They paid for it now with their lifeblood.

Still, Vorr reflected, if orcs and lesser vermin were to come along for the elf slaying, they'd have to pull their own weight. General Vorr carefully bled off his supply of naive orcish auxiliaries with every opportunity, sending them without qualm into deathtraps and ambushes. If Halker noticed the high losses among Vorr's orcs and goblins, he said nothing. Halker was a full-blooded scro himself, and it was likely that he understood and approved. Vorr never saw the need to bring the topic into the open and risk finding out differently.

A low knock sounded at the double doors, interrupting his thoughts. General Vorr's left hand casually dropped beneath the stone desktop, blunt fingers fitting into the leather grip of the weapon there. He'd been fooled once by a half-elven rogue on a suicide mission; he'd not be fooled twice. "Enter!" he called briskly, his voice booming through the room.

A lock clicked, and one of the half-ton doors swung silently open. The still air stirred to brief life. The door was held by the steel-armored arm of an ogre elite guard. The ogre, named Gargon, was unusually big, a head taller than the general himself, and he made a fine wrestling and sparring partner. Gargon never spoke, thanks to an arrow through his voice box, but Vorr considered that an asset.

A scro platoon officer strode with efficient precision through the doorway and into the broad office, his black leather armor squeaking pleasantly. Stopping well across the room from the desk, the only piece of furniture present aside from the general's thick wooden chair, the sergeant raised a black-gloved fist, forearm vertical and upper arm straight forward, the back of his fist directed at the general. A thick red spider emblem was clearly visible on the back of his glove.

"The Tarantulas remember!" the sergeant shouted, his flat, porcine snout raised with pride. He spoke in perfect Elvish. "Almighty Dukagsh hail my general!"

General Vorr grunted. "Speak." Tell me something different and new, he added mentally. It was time for a change. Fate would be his guide.

"Sir," said the sergeant crisply, switching to the scro's Orcish dialect. "Sergeant Hagroth bears news from Admiral Halker, who reports the sighting of a large flying vessel of unknown type approaching the camp along Victory Highway. The ship has signaled a desire to talk. We have scorpion-ship escorts with it now. The base is being brought to half alert. Admiral Halker requests your attention within the hour to meet with representatives of the intruders, dealing with them as is deemed best."

Fate actually listens to me, General Vorr thought with mild surprise. Tell Fate that you are weary with boredom, and it sends a cure. Was I better off being bored?

Vorr let his hand drop from the grip of his concealed weapon and looked down at the green-skinned humanoid standing at attention across the room. Sergeant Hagroth's black armor was cleaned and polished; the steel studs on the leather gleamed in the orange light from the tall windows. A scro marine's marine. The armored scro showed nothing but supreme confidence.

Far away, the elven voice arose to a shriek—then silence filled the room instead.

"Describe the intruder, Sergeant." Vorr had seen more than his share of unknown ships; it couldn't be too weird.

"Sir, the ship is built of stone blocks in the shape of a ziggurat. There are no visible doors or openings. It has four triangular sides and a square bottom, which it keeps facing the ground as it flies."

Fate was being too generous. The description fit the design

of the pyramid ships used by certain undead human wizards, the sort that brought nothing but trouble. General Vorr abruptly shoved back his chair and stood to his full eight-foot height; Sergeant Hagroth barely reached past his chest. He carefully sorted and put away his papers, his well-oiled armor making no sound.

"Sergeant Hagroth," he said, "tell my staff to bring all the marines to full alert, but in secret. Show no outward sign of our preparations. I want the Fifth Leg Battalion in assault gear at once, war priests in the lead. Attach two wall-breaker ogres to each company." He paused, considering. "Battle bonuses and honors to the first company to get inside the pyramid, if it comes to that. No attacks are to be made unless I give the order. Death to anyone who fires before then. Inform Admiral Halker of my plans. Anything more?"

Sergeant Hagroth's face twitched as he fought to contain his excitement. He, too, must have felt the lash of boredom for far too long. "Sir, nothing more," he said, then stepped back one pace and raised his black-gloved fist in a final salute. "Vengeance is ours!" he shouted in Elvish.

"Get on it," returned the general in Elvish, looking down again at the stacks of paper on his desk. He heard the door shut and the faint sounds of someone hurrying away, then silence. He hesitated for a moment, wondering what was wrong. Oh, he thought, no screaming. The elf must have died already. That was odd because they usually lasted much longer than that. Vorr wondered what the elves thought when the scro administering the ritual tortures spoke to them in fluent Elvish; it must be torture all the more. The orcs and scro had remembered the victors of the Unhuman War too well for the victors' own good.

General Vorr had just finished stacking his reports and was preparing to leave when another knock sounded. He looked up, wondering what Fate could possibly be cooking up for him now. His hand again fell below the desktop and clutched the weapon's grip. "Enter!" he barked.

One of the steel-and-oak doors across the room opened gently. An emaciated Oriental human in flowery silken robes stepped through, a serene smile half hidden behind wisps of a white beard. A withered hand covered by paper-thin skin carelessly pushed the weighty door shut behind him. The old man appeared relaxed and calm.

"Greetings, General," said the old man in a strong voice, bowing once. His dark, almond-shaped eyes gleamed. "I pray that I am not disturbing your work."

Vorr eyed the intruder speculatively as his hands relaxed and let go of the weapon's grip. "We have visitors, Usso. I trust you've heard."

"Yes. When the gates open, the flood comes through." Without explaining the remark, the old man approached and raised his right hand as he reached the desk. Where his hand had been empty, a sheaf of papers now soundlessly appeared as if by magic—which, of course, it was.

"My spies have been busy," Usso said, almost cheerfully, setting the papers in a neat stack on the desk and turning them around to face the general. "I trust their reports will make entertaining reading." The old man's hands pulled back, then began to fingerspell words rapidly against the desk's surface. The general appeared to study the new reports while reading Usso's message.

Elf and human guerrillas here. Three groups. I have warned unit commanders. Some seek you.

General Vorr considered the news soberly. "Nothing interesting here," he growled, thumbing a report page absently. He kept up the charade in case the guerrillas had the ability to scry on their meeting with spells, magical mirrors, or crystal balls. "Any other news?"

"The pyramid ship has halted two miles outside the base's northern gate. It shows no sign of hostility. It is also invulnerable to scrying, so I cannot say more about it." The frail old man looked toward the windows and grinned mirthlessly. "We should be so fortunate. The air is itself a window for the ants, if not for those insects that fly."

We're being magically spied upon by the intruders on the base and possibly by the flying pyramid's inhabitants, Vorr interpreted. "Do, um, the ants and bees travel together these days?" Vorr asked. He felt foolish trying to speak in riddles so those scrying on him couldn't make out his intent. Usso was so much better at deception, making it an art.

Usso pointed a narrow finger at the top report. "The answer

lies here," he said, and his fingers began working again. *No. Pyramid from other world. Elves from Spiral. Bad timing. I go. Stay alert.*

Vorr sighed heavily, his huge hands resting on the cool stone desk. Then he straightened and busied himself with filing papers in a desk drawer. "Work to be done, then. I will see to greeting our visitors from the pyramid—and I'll be watchful."

"I shall stay watchful as well. A little fresh air would not hurt you, so I'll leave your door open."

Usso meant for reinforcements to get to the general rapidly if necessary, Vorr knew. A closed door would not stop magically armed commandos. "Fine," Vorr said, still storing papers. "I'll be on my way in a minute."

The wizened man bowed formally, though the general ignored him, and turned to walk back to the closed doors. "Call if you need me," Usso said as he left—but his voice had changed. It was now a very feminine one, seductive and young. After opening a door and motioning for Gargon to leave it ajar, Usso was gone.

Vorr had most of the paperwork put away in a wall safe behind his chair and was about to take the last of it with him when a loud thump came from the double doors. He turned around. The door that had been open was now closed. After a startled pause on the other side came the sounds of heavy, pounding fists, followed by regular body slams against the wood and steel.

A locking spell. That was quick, Vorr thought. He had no time left. He was on the wrong side of the desk and couldn't go for his weapon. Vorr dropped his papers and reached for the only two solid objects on the desktop: the steel globe and the red tarantula statuette. He spun, scanning the room.

An elf stood before him, having appeared out of nowhere just thirty feet away in front of the double doors. It was a female with silver hair and no armor, her staff sparkling with spell power. The coiled emblem of the massacred House of Spiral blazed from her fiery diadem.

General Vorr threw the steel globe in his right hand with all the force he could summon. The impact of the sphere against her upper chest flipped the elf completely over in the air, her staff spinning away. She struck the wall behind her, then fell in a crumpled heap, her wide blue eyes staring at the ceiling.

More teleporting images came into view. A tall human in a covered helm and plate armor appeared to his far left. Teeth bared, Vorr flung the forty-pound red spider with his other hand. Solid iron crashed into the knight's upraised shield, knocking the attacker into a dwarf who had appeared nearby. Both fell cursing into a heap.

Eyes of Dukagsh, Vorr thought, they must want me badly. The room was still filling with teleporting intruders. Out of nine attackers so far, six were still on their feet. All stood at least twenty-five feet from the general. Several were making spell-casting motions. He knew instantly what was coming and almost relaxed to enjoy it.

The spy reports from Usso!

Vorr turned and snatched the last stack of papers on his desk, flinging it at a short male elf in a glittering green cloak. The elf sidestepped the papers, which sailed out of harm's way. The elf pulled something small from his necklace—a golden bead, it looked like—then flung it at the general with a snap of his wrist. "For Spiral!" he shouted in the world's Elvish, his face filled with cold rage.

The tiny bead burst into a flaming yellow streak that struck the general's chest—and vanished with a sputtering hiss that a flame would make when doused by water. Almost immediately, Vorr saw a second fireball and a stream of shining magic missiles streak toward him from his right, where other wizards must have appeared, but these spells vanished with equal speed when they struck him.

The floor then exploded in a hurricane of fire beneath his boots, the concussion of the flames hammering his body as it took him by surprise. He instinctively stepped back and raised his arms to ward the fire away from his face, though he knew he was safe. The magical flames died away almost at once.

The air was filled with ash and smoke. His desk and the floor around him were now covered with black soot, and his once-comfortable chair and the tribal flags and banners on the wall behind him were engulfed in yellow flames.

Vorr, however, was unharmed and still on his feet. The attackers gasped when they saw him. The general used the seconds he gained to vault over his desktop. His left hand found the grip on the weapon under his desk, and he tore it free of its leather harness.

The human knight, now weaponless and on hands and knees, produced a small, golden object from a belt pouch and hurled it clumsily across the room. The other attackers held back. The object clanged on the floor just a dozen feet away from the general. It was a statuette of a lion. "Lord of Cats!" shouted the knight in a hoarse female voice. "Slay the humanoid!"

The golden figurine abruptly expanded and changed shape, growing a mane and numerous two-inch fangs within seconds. Its meowing cry turned into a full-throated roar. Vorr raised the metallic double-barrel device he'd tugged from under his desk, aimed from the hip, and pulled both triggers.

He never heard the blast, but he felt its punch; it was too close and too loud. While he had braced himself as best he could, the recoil slammed Vorr hard in the gut, and he staggered back a step before he caught himself. A deafening whine filled his head for a few moments before his hearing recovered. Through the sulfurous smoke, he saw the thrashing shape of an enormous lion with two three-foot-long spears of barbed steel sticking out from its shaggy mane. Bright gore splattered the floor around the beast as it writhed in agony and shivered, then collapsed and moved no more.

"Hammer time!" shouted a male human. "Then torch him!" The attackers were still holding back but were in the act of drawing more weapons—throwing weapons.

"No! He is fireproof!" an elven male called out in Elvish. "Strike Plan B! We must—"

The elf sounded like a leader. Vorr whipped the discharged harpoon-bombard overhand and let go. The weapon crossed the room in a whirling, circular blur and smacked the elf in the face, then went on to clang against the wall beyond, splattering red droplets across it. The elf fell backward when he was hit, his sword flying, one arm raised uselessly to ward off the blow.

As the elf fell, everyone else in the room stepped forward and threw weapons of their own at the general, who shielded his face with his foot-thick arms. A twisting, magical rope slapped around his legs, but fell limp to the floor. Something thumped against his chest, cracking a rib with a stab of pain. A hatchet blade punched through the banded armor near the base of his neck, leaving a tingling and burning sensation. Poison. Vorr had no time to strip off his armor and wipe the wound to keep it from hurting, but no matter what poison it was, he could afford to wait and withstand the pain.

Reaching for his belt, the general pulled out a three-pronged device like a black fork with a long central tine. He then lunged around the desk at the knight, the nearest of the attackers, who had drawn a gray long sword and was charging in for the kill.

The sword had begun its downward arc when Vorr's iron fork caught it, turned it aside with a fluid sweep, and jerked it out of the knight's grasp. Vorr spun in place, the butt of the fork coming around to slam the knight in the back and throw the human forward. The spin gave Vorr a chance to glance around the room. He then sidestepped and kicked at the axe-wielding dwarf who came at him next. The axe cut through Vorr's leg armor before it and its owner were knocked rolling more than a dozen feet away.

The fighting became a jumble of sharp, violent images. An elf thrust in with his sword, only to be caught and thrown into the desk, breaking his spine. The snarling dwarf came at him again with a broken nose and a bloodstained beard, long daggers in his red hands. Two chanting priests, human and elven, lost their attack spells when Vorr rushed and leaped up to body-slam them both. Glowing blades tore at his armor and flesh, licked out for his face, stabbed for his back, cut down for his neck. Streams of lightning and energy came at him and were snuffed out as they touched him. Shouts and screams filled the air. He lost track of all time in the madness of dodging and fighting, the crackling flames and smoke, and sprawled bodies and slippery blood.

At some point, he saw that the elven leader was crawling aimlessly across the floor. A bubbling, whimpering noise spilled from the mask of red where his face had been. He was in the way, so Vorr straddled him and grasped his head. The elf's neck snapped when Vorr wrenched his huge hands backward and sideways, and the elf fell with a clatter of armor at last.

Vorr pulled back and looked around quickly. Across the hazy, body-littered room, only one opponent remained. It was the knight, missing her helmet. Vorr blinked, startled to see a female warrior confront him. She was a tall, blond-haired human, reasonably pretty by their standards. Strands of curly, wet hair were plastered to her forehead and neck. She gripped her recently recovered sword with both hands, crouched and facing Vorr, ready to move in any direction. Vorr saw a faint aura around the woman's slim gray blade. No telling what it could do, but it mattered little now.

If the woman knew her doom was sealed, she never showed it. She followed Vorr with unblinking eyes. Her mouth was open just a bit, as if she were concentrating on a knotty problem of philosophy. The tip of her sword hovered in the air like a hummingbird.

Not what you'd expect from a human, the general thought, his mind clearing from the battle. He moved right; she rotated, sword up, and coughed once on the foul, smoky air. He kept the three-pronged fork ready in his right hand, pointing down at the floor. His left hand, nearer the knight, was aimed down at the knight's feet with fingers extended, ready to grab, strike, block, or distract. If the knight didn't strike, he could try a feint to get within reach of the sword and take it away from her. Or he could throw something to wear her down. This circling around would get old quickly, and it wasn't becoming to true warriors. Better to drive in and be done with it.

He started forward. The knight adjusted her distance, shifting the grip on her sword to compensate. She coughed again and cleared her throat, but the point on her weapon was still steady and confident. Vorr readjusted his thinking about his foe. She looked to be far better than he had thought. If he lunged in, she could probably evade and thrust at least as well as he could. Her armor didn't seem to slow her down, so it was probably magical. During the mad melee earlier, she had turned aside one of his strikes and danced back before he could strike on the return swing, and she cut him in the side as well. She must have learned something when he knocked her sword away the first time. This was a real fight. He felt strangely pleased and anxious. Anxious to win.

"I asked you to call if you needed help," said a petulant

voice out of the haze. The voice was silky and feminine, the same voice that Usso had used before he had left.

General Vorr licked his lips. The blond warrior had not moved a muscle while the voice spoke, but now she turned her head slightly, obviously straining to hear anyone approaching from her flanks or rear.

"Let me have her, Kobas," said the voice. "I want to play, too."

"Get out of here," Vorr said in a low, steady voice, his lips barely moving. He noted a pool of blood to the knight's right and slowly edged backward and to her right to draw her toward it.

"I don't want you out playing with other girls," said the disembodied voice with an unmistakable bite to it. Vorr noticed something forming in the air behind the swordswoman. It looked like a glowing rod—no, a sword, floating in the air. One of Usso's deadlier spells, probably from a prized scroll. The swordswoman did not notice the sword, though she noted that Vorr was looking behind her. She would have to decide now if it was a trick.

"Usso . . ." Vorr warned, still maintaining his calm but feeling the strain wear his patience away.

The sword rotated in the air, aiming point-first at the swordswoman's back.

Damn that magic-casting, shape-changing slut, Vorr raged. This was a warrior's fight. He hurriedly stepped back, anticipating Usso's imminent attack and trying to get the knight where he wanted her. The swordswoman followed, stepping into the pool of blood.

With a bellowing shout, Vorr lunged at the knight, iron fork coming out and up to strike at her face or catch her blade if she made another roundhouse strike. She didn't. The woman kept her balance, having apparently been aware of the bloodied floor, and crouched, stabbing directly upward. The blade bit like a viper through a chink in Vorr's steel armor and deep into the muscle of his forearm. Vorr roared and jerked back in bright pain, but he kept his grip on the fork. He struck down in figure-eight arcs to keep the knight back while he readjusted his stance to regain his initiative and attack with his other hand.

"Game's over," said a cold, flat feminine voice.

Something punched the knight hard from behind, nearly throwing her forward onto her face. She was suddenly supported awkwardly in the air, bent back like a marionette on a single string attached to her armor's breastplate. Vorr saw the blood-covered tip of a glowing sword blade thrust out between two plates of the knight's abdominal armor. The blade continued to push out of the armor, twisting and cutting upward, until two feet of it showed. The knight's face was hideously contorted with agony, her mouth open wide. She made a strangled, gasping sound.

Falling from nerveless fingers, the knight's sword clanged loudly against the floor. The glowing sword behind her abruptly vanished. The knight crumpled backward with a metallic clatter and thump, relaxing against the floor.

For a few seconds, General Vorr could only breathe heavily and stare down at the fallen warrior. He lowered his arms.

"Damn you," he said through his teeth. He looked up at the ceiling and roared aloud. "The lords of the Abyssal Deep take you and keep you! *Damn* you for interfering!"

The disembodied voice made no reply. She was probably off sulking somewhere. Bitch.

He slowly slid the iron fork back into his belt, then held his wounded arm and put pressure on it to aid the regeneration. Fate had been especially kind to him at birth; Vorr was not only immune to all magic and poison, but his wounds healed at an astounding rate. Vorr often wondered if either his orcish father or ogrish mother had also been part troll; in either event, he was grateful to them for that, if for nothing else. He checked the wound and noted that the bleeding had stopped, though not the pain. When he looked up again, he noticed with surprise that the fallen woman still breathed.

The knight had been a brave one and a good fighter. She hadn't been a talker, uttering stupid threats like some warriors did. The general hesitated, then undid a flap on one of his small belt pouches and pulled out a tiny silver vial. She deserved an honorable death, at least.

The knight was unarmed, but Vorr doubted she could have lifted a weapon if she'd had one. Bubbles of blood formed on her lips, the bright red running down to her neck. Her breathing was labored and irregular. Her eyes were partially open, but she didn't react when Vorr loomed over her, his round gray face solemn and heavy. He knelt down beside her, keeping one hand free. She might have one trick left.

Vorr unscrewed the cap on the vial, then gently slipped his thick fingers behind her head and lifted it from the cold floor. "Drink this," he said in a quiet, deep voice. She tried to put up a hand to ward the vial away, but he ignored her feeble strength and put the vial to her bloodied lips. "Drink this," he repeated. "It will ease the pain."

Blue liquid poured from the vial into her mouth. She almost gagged, then swallowed reflexively. For a moment she resisted, struggling weakly—then the knight relaxed, the wind easing from her lungs in a long, slow sigh. She looked almost sleepy as the poison took effect, deadening all her pain. She would go out with peace and honor, with the best of the general's foes.

Her eyes rolled back in her head, then rolled down again and focused as she turned her head toward the general. Her red lips worked as the final sleep took hold.

"I . . ." she whispered. "I would have . . . won."

She smiled, then her head sagged in his hand, her pale eyes closing. After a few moments, Vorr let her head down gently, then recapped the vial.

"Very touching," came Usso's voice, echoing in the still room. "Do you do this kind of thing with all the girls?"

Muscles knotted in his neck, shoulders, and jaws. Vorr got to his feet and replaced the vial, then picked up the knight's sword and laid it across her chest.

"Next time, Kobas, I'll save you the trouble and just kill all the pixies before they—"

"Shut up! Damn you to the Pits of the Nine Hells! *Shut up!*" Vorr roared. "Get *out* of here!"

Silence answered him. He no longer cared if she watched him. They'd settle this later.

He tried the double doors and found them immobile. Whatever spell the attackers had used on it before their entry into the command room had welded the doors together; his antimagical touch was of no help. The smoke was becoming a problem now since he had breathed so much of it, so he broke out the windowpanes to get more air. He next collected the scattered spy reports that Usso had brought in just before the attack. Only a few of the papers were damaged, but all were legible. Many of the unit banners and flags were burned to crispy rags, however; even one of the zwarth hands had been damaged, though not badly so. It was a shame.

There was a shout outside the double doors, followed by a thundering of feet. General Vorr stepped out of the way.

One of the half-ton doors split and danced free of its hinges with a thunderclap explosion, then both doors were smashed to the floor. Two hulking ogres, fully nine feet tall and covered in thick leather and armor plate, crashed into the room, hauling a huge wooden pole between them as their ram. The ogres' feet crushed and scattered the bodies around them. Behind the ogres came wild and frenzied shouts, and a force of armed ogres and scro poured into the room, swords and axes held high, led by Gargon himself.

For the first time in weeks, General Vorr felt like laughing, but it was entirely too much effort.

"You're late," he said. "Just clean this place up."

* * * * *

"You're late," Fleet Admiral Halker said with the trace of a smile, "but I understand you were busy."

"It's over with, sir." In newly cleaned armor, General Vorr bowed and stood at attention before his superior's cluttered desk. His arm had healed, but his shoulder still burned from the poisoned axe; he ignored it. "Two other guerrilla groups came in with the assassin team, directed at the prisoners' barracks and the war priests' armory, but all have been neutralized. We've taken only light casualties. Four ogres and seventeen scro died at the armory, and eight scro and eleven orcs at the barracks, among them a war priest on the torture team for the day. Our wizard Usso destroyed those attacking the armory, then assisted with mopping up those who had attacked me."

"The vermin of Spiral still have some fight in them, then," the old admiral said with some surprise, leaning back in his cushioned chair. He scratched at the thick gray fur on the head of the worg that sat at his side; the huge wolf panted, eyes closed in pleasure. "Any idea of where they came from, their main base?"

"None, sir. All those who personally fought me are dead now. The war priests will interrogate their spirits within the next few hours. I'll have them see you for their reports."

The admiral nodded absently. His heavy black robes shook as he patted the worg's head, the red spider emblem across his chest partially hidden in the folds of cloth. "I take it that there were no survivors among the other groups of intruders?" he said wistfully, with a pale gleam in his green eyes.

"Two, sir, from the group at the prisoners' barracks. They're conscious and ready for interrogation."

"Ah." The old scro gave a toothless smile, his snout wrinkling with satisfaction. "It is always good to have a chance to chat with the enemy. I will enjoy my work this evening, once we've settled things with our other visitors. Speaking of which, the one in command of the ziggurat is here now. He claims to have an interesting proposal for us."

Vorr bit back on his next remark. This must have been visible to the admiral, as the old scro waved a lazy hand. "Speak freely. The room is sealed with lead mesh, and no one can spy on us here, or so Usso has informed me. The pyramid ship's commander is in the waiting room with a few of his bodyguards—under our own guard, of course. The war priests are monitoring him—or it—for spying spells and such. I'd like to have Usso here, but he seems to have business elsewhere."

The general took a deep breath. "Sir, pyramid ships are usually controlled by undead humans. I was involved in a boarding action against one in the Glowrings Sphere, before I came to this fleet. A lich in command there destroyed seventy-two boarders just by itself. Other pyramid ships are reported to be commanded by others of the living dead, working together to bring about an empire of the dead throughout wildspace. I advise the greatest caution in dealing with whatever being claims to command that ship. I put my marines on full alert because of it."

The old scro nodded again, his lips sucking in over his hardened gums. "Our visitor then lacks subtlety, General, as he has already revealed himself to be a lich, of human origin. He claims not to threaten us and further claims to know the location of, as he says, 'a treasure to fight for gladly you will.' His speech is curious, probably archaic. Anyway, he's said nothing about undead empires so far."

The admiral was lost in thought. His flat, yellow-green face lacked the scars that marked many other military leaders, but Admiral Halker had climbed the ranks with his own kind of power, rooted in magic, charisma, and a genteel sadism that made even other scro uncomfortable. He pushed his chair back from his desk and stood. The worg licked its lips and watched, then settled down to lie on the floor. Halker adjusted his belted black robes, belt weapons, wheel-lock firearm, and magical paraphernalia, pampering his appearance.

"Unless you have any objections, General," he said, motioning to the door, "let's go downstairs and see our guest to discuss this 'treasure to fight for.' " The admiral then looked up quizzically at his imposing subordinate. "Purely out of curiosity, how did your boarding force deal with that lich in the Glowrings Sphere?"

Vorr looked him in the eye. "I killed it," he said.

The admiral stared at him a moment, then laughed. "Of course! Forgive my asking. You're a dream come true."

Being here is a dream come true for me, too, Vorr thought as he agreed modestly and headed for the door. I thought I'd never get away from the hell pit I grew up in. Sometimes, though, I've wondered if there wasn't a reason for things to be as bad as they were early on—a reason to suffer blow after blow, breathing the heavy fumes from Father's breath, or lying awake with Mother's demon-haunted shrieks ringing in my ears. I was already at the bottom of the pile for having a low-born orcish father and an insane ogre for a mother. I had to kill three scro before they would let me into their military school, no matter that I was stronger than any of them had ever been and healed ten times as fast. The Troll, they called me, and laughed—but rarely to my face. Then they discovered that I was immune to magic and poison, too. After that, they let me do anything and said nothing about it.

So, maybe there *was* a reason for things to be as they were. I've fought all my life, but I'm stronger now for what I've withstood. My own parents could not break me when I was helpless before them, but they were helpless enough later when I came home from military school and killed them.

The admiral had finished speaking as they reached the door. Vorr had no idea what the old scro had just said. It didn't really matter.

"Shall we be off, sir?" Vorr asked politely, opening the door and stepping aside.

Chapter Three

● ● ●

"You may go in," said the elven guard politely, opening the door before Teldin's astonished eyes.

Teldin had no idea of what to say in return. He had prepared himself for an argument or for the kind of disdainful dismissal that he had once received from an old elf on whose ship Teldin had sought passage, many months ago on distant Krynn. But the guard had merely listened impassively when Teldin had asked for an audience with representatives of the Imperial Fleet, thought for a moment, then . . . Saying nothing, Teldin walked carefully through the door.

There was bright light beyond the front door of the elves' embassy building, bright enough to remind Teldin of daylight. Brushing against the doorjamb was a sword-leaf plant, waving in a breeze from inside. Elves must like house plants, thought Teldin, a moment before he realized that in walking through the doorway, he had stepped into a clearing in a forest. In shock, Teldin looked around and saw a brilliant golden sun in a clear blue sky above and a wall of tall pines encircling the clearing, which was perhaps a hundred feet across. Elves in pale robes stood in the clearing, a short distance away, but Teldin hardly noticed them. Tall grasses and plants brushed his trousers. A cool breeze, laden with the smell of fresh earth, wildflowers, and evergreen trees, caressed his face.

He whirled around, looking for the door, but instead stared straight into a flat rock face a dozen feet high.

Momentarily panicked, Teldin put his hands against the cool rock, searching for an exit. The rock was hard and rough and solid. It looked as if it had been there forever.

"Teldin Moore," said an even, strong voice behind him, "you have come a long way to find us."

Teldin turned quickly, his blue cloak whispering around his legs. There were five elves in the clearing with him, standing in random places in the knee-high grass. The closest one was thirty feet away, a male who came up to Teldin's chin. He had thick, autumn-brown hair, the color of rich, polished wood, and a richly embroidered robe of pale gold and white.

Teldin wondered if he was being toyed with, and the spur of anger got him going. "I am looking for the Imperial Fleet," he said, his voice not as strong as he would have liked. "I need advice."

"We are with the fleet," said the elf simply, looking at Teldin with clear gray eyes. A slight breeze passed through the clearing, rocking the daffodils and grass tops.

Teldin risked one more look behind him at the rock face, then turned back and cleared his throat. "I was told that I should find the fleet . . . you, that is, by one Vallus Leafbower, an elf who was the helmsman for a ship I've been traveling on." Teldin stopped, frowning. "How did you know my name?"

"Did you not identify yourself to the watch at the door?" said the brown-haired elf. Teldin couldn't tell if the elf was serious or making fun of him.

"Yes, I . . ." Teldin hesitated. They must use magic to spy on people at the door, he realized. It made sense. "You just caught me off guard," he finished. "You said you were with the Imperial Fleet? I might be a little suspicious, but—"

"We are with the fleet," repeated the elf calmly. "I am Uliananor Cirathorn, Admiral of the Sphere." The elf gestured behind him at the other figures in the clearing, never taking his eyes from Teldin. "With me is my personal staff. You have our full attention, Teldin Moore."

Teldin eyed his surroundings again, noticing that two of the admiral's staff were women. "I want to know where we are," he said.

"We are still on the Rock of Bral, in a safe place," said the elf. "Our magic protects us. You will not come to harm here, and your words are held in secrecy." Cirathorn raised his chin slightly. "If you have something important to tell us, please do so now."

Teldin swallowed, feeling out of his depth and feeling some resentment, too, at being told what to do. He knew the admiral had a point, though. He had wasted enough time with that kender earlier, and he was wasting it now. He debated about where to start. There was so much to tell.

"I am being hunted by the neogi, among others, because of the cloak I am wearing," Teldin began. He felt a little more confident now, but he had no idea if the elves would even care to help him. "The neogi have murdered many people to get this cloak, and I don't know why. I need some kind of advice on what this cloak is and what it's supposed to do. And I want to know why the neogi want it so much. Vallus said that you— I mean, the elves—had made this, so you might know of it."

The elf's gaze dropped to take in the bright blue cloak that waved in the faint breeze. "What do you already know of this garment?"

"Not a lot," confessed Teldin. He considered describing its powers, but it was a little early to spill everything he knew. "It's magical."

"Magical . . ." The elf put a slight emphasis on this word. "We need more, Teldin Moore." Showing no reaction to his near pun, the admiral became expectantly silent, looking into Teldin's eyes with mild impatience.

Teldin gave up. He'd never get anywhere unless he told all. Or almost all—he still wanted to keep some of the cloak's powers a secret, like its ability to change his shape. Sometimes it was a good idea to have a few secrets left.

"The cloak has a strange history, and I've been swept along with it," Teldin said. "A reigar woman handed it to me as she died, her spelljammer burning on the ruins of my home and farm on Krynn. . . ." He went on, telling a much-shortened version of the tale of his journey with the cloak. It still took about twenty minutes to get it all out. He hadn't always been good with stories, but a story was all he had to offer.

As he spoke, Teldin watched the elves for their reactions. Several of the robed elves in the background gradually moved closer, their alert faces showing considerable interest. Admiral Cirathorn, on the other hand, merely watched and listened. When Teldin told the theory of the mind flayer Estriss, that whoever made the cloak had also built the enormous and legendary spelljamming ship called the *Spelljammer*, a muscle twitched in the elven admiral's cheek. Teldin guessed that this revelation might be the key he needed to get the elves' help, for good or for ill. Indeed, the admiral moved closer after that point, though he came no nearer than two dozen feet. Paranoia, perhaps, thought Teldin, but he didn't blame them. They were military people, after all.

Teldin finished his story with his arrival on the Rock of Bral, leaving out only his meeting with the kender, Gaye. He paused, then added, "I have little to offer you for your help, but the lives of many depend on what I do about this cloak." Now it was his turn to wait. He was not accustomed to speaking for so long, and he felt drained. His throat hurt, too. If the elves turned him away, he decided, he would simply leave and find help elsewhere—but he didn't know where.

"You came to us," said Cirathorn, breaking the silence, "because one of our people directed you to us. It is known among our people that a meeting with the staff of the Imperial Fleet is not a light matter. There are many of our people who would go to any length to avoid it, preferring to administer their own solutions to matters, whether we approved or not. Why would this Vallus Leafbower have sent you here? What did he think we could do to help you, Teldin Moore?"

Teldin blinked in astonishment. "I haven't the faintest idea what he thought you could do!" he snapped, feeling his self-control slip away. "Didn't you hear what I said? The neogi want this cloak! They've slaughtered more people for it than I can count, and they're determined to have me dead as well." Stirred by his anger, Teldin reached up and undid the button loops on his shirt front, exposing his bare chest—and the dozens of deep, fiery-red scars that crisscrossed it. The eyes of several elves widened with horror.

"I got these from the neogi," Teldin spat. "I was on their meat tables. I've escaped from mercenaries, draconians, and pirates. I've been attacked and betrayed because of this cloak, and I've seen dozens of people slain for it. The neogi said that if they got this cloak, they could destroy or enslave worlds with its powers—elven worlds among them, I would think. I don't know what you can do for me, but you could do a lot more for me and for your people than you are doing now."

With a violent effort, Teldin bit off his next words. He quickly regretted what he had said, but he was still too angry to care much. If they wanted to throw him out, at least now they had a good excuse for doing it. He'd never liked dealing with most officers and authority types, even when he had been in the army during the War of the Lance. They were fools more often than they were true leaders, except for a few who were either just and fair or too cynical to be anything other than honest.

Cirathorn's gaze had become distant while Teldin spoke. He said nothing when Teldin finished, though some of his staff members moved close together to whisper to each other. A new breeze ruffled cloaks and hair.

"I remember Aerlofalyn," Cirathorn said, without emotion. The other elves fell silent at once. "It is a world you would not have heard of, Teldin Moore. Aerlofalyn was a garden world in another sphere, a world of wind and air across which great islands and continents drifted like leaves on the bright surface of a river. My father's father was from Aerlofalyn, and his father before him, and every ten years my family would meet on the island estates for a feasting and celebration that would last for a hundred days. My father's father was married there, and all his fathers before him. It was paradise."

The other elves stared at the admiral as if they were statues. Cirathorn looked at Teldin but did not seem to see him.

"You have heard, I have no doubt, of the Unhuman War," the admiral continued. "It is called that among your people because humans felt it had so little to do with them. The depredations of goblins across the spheres had little meaning for the human masses on the ground. Do not be too offended, Teldin Moore, if I say that an attitude like that is typical of your kind. Humans rarely care about the fate of others."

Teldin's face flushed, and his fists clenched tightly. He was on the verge of calling the elf a liar and worse when Cirathorn started to walk toward him with a slow tread.

"A war fleet of the enemy fell upon Aerlofalyn in my

father's father's time. My father was sent away with his sisters at the last hour, aboard a secret vessel that escaped to another sphere, where they stayed with relatives. He returned to Aerlofalyn in seven years at the vanguard of a war fleet of his own. He landed upon the island where he had been born, where he had learned to speak, where he would have taken his wife. There he buried the bones of all who had remained behind. He buried bones that were burned, bones that were broken, bones that were gnawed upon. He buried a world and a family line. The name Aerlofalyn is rarely spoken by our people, except in our memories and when we gather to remember the dead and all that has passed."

Cirathorn stopped. He appeared taller now, though it could have been only a trick of the light. "I have been to Aerlofalyn, Teldin Moore. I know about murdered worlds. Every ten years now, I go there, just as my father took me, and for a hundred days I mourn."

Teldin and Cirathorn stared at each other. Suddenly the elf roused himself and saw Teldin as if the man had just appeared before him. "We have been poor hosts, and we ask your forgiveness. Please join us for our next meal. We will eat in peace together and speak of your cloak and your concerns." Without waiting for Teldin's answer, Cirathorn turned and called behind him, at the forest. "*Siol tath, alwe doe maith*," he said. As he turned back to Teldin, the sky grew darker, as if a cloud were passing over the face of the sun.

"Forgive our fantasies, too, Teldin Moore," said the elf, as the entire forest around them faded into darkness. Teldin looked wildly around as the elf continued speaking, unperturbed. "We have become creatures of the past, bound by our memories. This forest was how my father's father's home once appeared, given birth again through the magic of illusion. It is a weakness in which I indulge for the sake of impressing company."

Now, Teldin saw dim, distant walls arching over his head in place of a sky, as if he stood beneath a vast, overturned bowl whose ceiling was studded with tiny starlike lights that gave off light of increasing brightness. Teldin could see great patterns carved into the ceiling itself, weaving around the unfamiliar constellations displayed there. The rock face behind him had faded and become a wooden door, which he could now tell was banded with iron and painted with symbols.

"This is our reality," said Cirathorn, sweeping a hand around him. "We are sheathed in old rock beneath the surface of the Rock of Bral. The doorway on the surface brought you here by our magic, a teleporter of sorts. You may speak and rest in safety, as I have said. My staff will show you to a room where you may bathe and don new clothing if you so choose. You are our guest."

Teldin's voice found its way back to him. "I could probably use a bath," he said. "My ship is in the docks for the next few days. I don't think I'll be missed right away." Even as he spoke, it dawned on him that he sounded as if he was inviting himself to stay here. It wasn't quite what he'd meant.

It seemed to make no difference. Cirathorn, his robes whispering around him, had already turned to leave the domed hall, gesturing for one of his staff to stay behind and the rest to follow him. "We are pleased to have you, Teldin Moore," the admiral said on his way out. "Your visit should be very educational for us all."

*   *   *   *   *

A slim young female elf with gleaming black hair showed Teldin through a vine-covered stone corridor, away from the domed hall. Light spilled from hand-sized glass figurines mounted in the ceiling, each one made to resemble a flying bird. Pushing open an oaken door at the first bend in the corridor, the elf showed Teldin the room beyond. It was the size of the largest inn room Teldin had ever seen, and it contained a sunken bath, a bed, several tables and cushioned chairs, some slim books and rolled scrolls on a shelf, and a wardrobe filled with clothing of every size.

The young girl looked uncomfortably like Gaye in certain respects, but she was interested only in explaining how the bath pump worked, where he could find the dining hall, and where the sanitary facilities were. She nodded and left when Teldin said he needed nothing more.

The memory of Gaye reminded him of something else, and Teldin checked his belt pouches and pockets to find out what, if anything, the kender had "borrowed" from him. To his astonishment, he still had everything he had started out with when his ship had docked. No kender he had ever heard of had resisted an opportunity to pick a pocket. He went through his inventory twice, but he was missing nothing. He shrugged and decided a bath was in order before changing.

An hour later, he was standing near a glowing swan lamp, examining a volume of woodcuts showing landscapes and portraits, when the door opened again. It was Cirathorn. Teldin didn't recognize him for a few moments, as the elf had changed clothes, too. He was now wearing a suit of silver-bright plate armor over which a black tabard was hung, bearing a complex design of a many-colored butterfly against a starry background. The elf wore no helmet, but he wore silken black gloves and high, star-speckled black boots.

"Is everything satisfactory?" asked the admiral.

Teldin flushed. "Actually, I wasn't prepared to be served like this." He quickly shut the book and put it on a side table. He could read only with great difficulty, and he was too embarrassed to admit that he had only been looking at the pictures.

"We will be having dinner with other guests in two hours," Cirathorn continued. "You may rest comfortably until then. With your permission, however, I would like to examine your cloak. I wish only to look at it in the light here, without attempting to remove it from you. Would that be possible?"

Others had touched the cloak without incident. "I think so," Teldin said, feeling a little nervous. "Don't try to cut it, though. The cloak will shock you if you do."

Cirathorn spread his hands as he approached. "I have no intentions of harming either you or the cloak." He reached out and carefully took hold of the fabric at Teldin's right arm. Nothing happened. The admiral pulled up the cloak and moved toward the nearby light. Teldin obliged by standing closer to it as the elf began his examination, watching the elf's narrow fingers probe gently at the silky inner lining with its complex geometric pattern. For a moment, Teldin was reminded of Estriss and the movement of the mind flayer's long, four-jointed mauve finger as it pointed out the subtle pattern of a three-petaled flower in the weave of the lining.

The admiral made no comment during the long minutes he spent looking at the cloak. Teldin looked at it as well, wondering what, if anything, the admiral was able to see in it that Teldin or Estriss had not. After a time, the admiral slowly released the cloak and let it fall again.

"Did you find anything?" Teldin could not resist asking.

"It is authentic," said Cirathorn in a distant voice. "I must go back to the library and speak with the loremaster again. I will tell you more later, at dinner." He suddenly turned to leave, looking back once as he opened the door. The admiral's gaze lingered on Teldin's cloak. He then left, pulling the door shut behind him.

The time crawled by so slowly that Teldin believed he would go mad. He was lying on the bed, trying to relax enough to get rid of a headache, when the door opened again. Another young elf, this one a blond male, motioned for Teldin to follow him. "Dinner is about to be served, good sir," the elf said.

"I could have waited a while longer," muttered Teldin, pulling on his boots. He decided that maybe he could nibble a few items, just to be polite.

The hemispherical dining hall was smaller than the starry hall, but much brighter and more comfortable-looking. A circular table surrounded by soft chairs took up the middle of the room. No other furniture was present; the entire floor was covered with a carpet, too, Teldin noticed. Bowls of fruits and finger-foods were scattered around the table. Glowing globes and figurines hung from the ceiling, spilling bright yellow light everywhere. To Teldin's surprise, living vines crawled up the walls, encircling carved wooden figures of elves, many with wings, that graced the decorative pillars. The air inside was cool on his face and smelled fresh, as if it had just rained.

Perhaps a dozen elves were already seated at the table and chatting softly and animatedly when Teldin was escorted in. They all looked in his direction, but they never stopped their conversations or made any move to welcome him. He looked about, pulling his cloak around him, and took a place to the right of one of the staff members Teldin remembered seeing earlier in the forest illusion. While he didn't understand Elvish, Teldin found he was able to make out the gist of what the elf was saying—all gossip about the goings-on around the

Rock, he realized. He was almost disappointed, though he wasn't sure what he had expected. Teldin sighed and ate a small piece of fruit, trying not to look as out of place as he felt. Why were the elves ignoring him? Was he just some kind of groundling peasant to them?

It was then that he heard a scratching noise, and he turned to his right and noticed a gnome two seats away. He was too short to be seen over the top of his chair. The scratching noise came from the movement of the gnome's pen across a folded-up page of parchment. Like many gnomes Teldin had known, this one had brown skin with short-cut, silky white hair; a large bald spot showed on top of his head. A pair of gold-wire spectacles perched halfway down the gnome's broad nose.

Teldin smiled. What was the Gnomish word for hello? There was a phrase that the gnomes with whom he had traveled into wildspace had always called to each other while they were aboard ship. The cloak hadn't bothered to translate it for him. How did it go?

"*Woda ganeu!*" Teldin said, leaning toward the gnome and waving a hand in greeting.

The gnome started and looked up, blinking in surprise. "What?" he said in a high, nasal voice. "Why should I get out of your way? Am I blocking your view?" The gnome looked to his right for anything Teldin might be trying to see.

Teldin winced. So *that's* what the gnomes had been saying! "No, no! Just forget it," he said hastily. "I'm Teldin Moore. Pleased to meet you." He scooted a little closer to hear the gnome better.

The gnome stared at him for a moment. "Teldin Moore?" he asked, his voice rising in puzzlement. "Teldin Moore. You're the one with the magical pants?"

"Cloak," Teldin corrected, picking up an edge of his blue garment. The gnome squinted at the cloak, then sat back, raising his pen and obviously looking to end the conversation. "Ergonomic fabric design was not my life quest," he muttered. "Useful, of course. Got to have clothes. Good business." His bushy eyebrows knitted together in deep concentration as he was absorbed again by his scribbling.

Teldin rubbed at his mustache with frustration. He had a momentary urge to simply get to his feet and leave, but he told himself it was just a question of making his patience last. All upper-class people, elven or human, must be as bad as these elves were. Only a few minutes passed in boredom before footsteps and a faint metallic sound issued from the hall outside.

As one, every elf in the room stood. Teldin clumsily got to his feet, one of his legs having fallen asleep, just as Admiral Cirathorn entered. He was still wearing his silver armor and tabard. The elves bowed and curtsied as he entered, but he took no notice of them. Cirathorn strode directly over to a place across from where Teldin sat, taking an empty chair there. Here he clapped his hands, and two elves sprang to their feet and left the room.

"Teldin Moore," said Cirathorn, settling himself in his chair, "we welcome you to the embassy of the Imperial Fleet, the web of light that binds together all known spheres. You have endured much to meet with us. We offer our hospitality, our rooms, and our food for your physical nourishment and rest. And we offer you our guidance and advice in resolving your most pressing questions."

Regardless of the admiral's words, Teldin still felt a curious coldness in the room. He noticed that none of the other elves were looking directly at him.

Cirathorn went on. "Our library is poor, but our loremaster was able to divine some of the past of your cloak. There is not much that is known, and what is written about it is subject to question. Nonetheless, I will share it. Would you please rise, Teldin Moore?"

Flushing slightly, Teldin did so. What now?

"Sisters and brothers of the spheres," said Cirathorn, looking around the room. "We have sung the songs of the past, when the hands of light first forged the great crystal spheres out of deepest darkness, and we have chanted the hymns to the blending of earth, fire, air, and water, for the birthing of worlds of every kind. We have read the poems of those first few who stepped out into the wild dark and called it their home. We have only the fragments of that first sailing, faded legends of that awakening. What was history is now mere dream.

"You know that among the legends on which we were nursed as children are those of the Star Folk, the race that is said to have first crossed those vast reaches within the crystal spheres and without. Of the identity of the Star Folk, we have no clue. Yet before us, about the shoulders of this man, is one of the last known surviving items of their handiwork. Our dreams are proven to have been reality, after all."

The elf turned to look directly at Teldin. "Our guest wears the Cloak of the First Pilot, the favored being who took the helm of the largest ship in all existence, that which we call the *Spelljammer* and after which we have named all devices and ships that sail the spheres. Of the First Pilot little else is known, though some legends have it that he and his ship and its crew vanished on its journey to reach the edge of the cosmos, hoping there to meet the creator or creators of all. The truth of this, no one can know now."

No one spoke for several long seconds. Teldin tried to swallow, but his throat was too dry. So it was true that his cloak was connected to the tale of the *Spelljammer*, just as Estriss had long ago guessed. But Teldin had never suspected that he wore the same cloak that this First Pilot, whoever or whatever he was, had worn. He looked down and fingered the hem of his cloak, feeling its alien smoothness. Could these Star Folk have been the Juna, the aliens of which Estriss had spoken? Estriss had said the Juna lived millions of years earlier. . . .

A thought came to him, and he cleared his throat, hoping his interruption would not be taken badly. "I was told," Teldin said slowly, "that this cloak was made by the elves. An elven helmsman named Vallus Leafbower asked me to bring it to you—to the Imperial Fleet, rather—because you would know what to do about it." He decided not to mention then that he had also been told that the cloak had been made by the blue-skinned giants known as the arcane; after all, an arcane had told him that, and he might have had ulterior motives in doing so.

"It would not surprise me if the elves had indeed made it," said Cirathorn. "We know nothing of the identity of the Star Folk, and perhaps they could have been elves. Here and there across the spheres, our fleet has found strange ruins or ships, perhaps one in every ten spheres, which are each unaccountably old and bear symbols in a trifoliate pattern—three leaves, three-pointed stars, and the like. These ruins are filled with danger, with magic so powerful and old that it has lost its meaning and now strikes out in its madness at all who trespass. A few more fragments of our past we have found in those ruins and wrecks, but no sign of the Star Folk, and no trace of their fate. Your cloak, Teldin Moore, as you probably know, also bears that trifoliate pattern."

Everyone in the room stared at Teldin, which made him acutely uncomfortable. "It's a flower, I believe," he said.

The admiral nodded agreement. "Indeed it is, as I have seen with my own eyes. We wish to copy that pattern for our histories before you leave us. Of the Cloak of the First Pilot, only a few rhymes and tales remain. One speaks of the 'shining garment' the First Pilot wore. Another says that the First Pilot was given a necklace before he set out on his mission, and he wore this gift, though some authorities refer only to the cloak. The most extensive fragment, the 'Song of the First Pilot,' is a short set of verses that tells of the gifting of the cloak and the First Pilot's enthusiasm for the voyage. Little else is known to us. Long have our people thirsted for knowledge of every sort, but of the distant past, of the origins of all space-faring peoples, we have found little to whet our tongues. You honor us all, Teldin Moore, with your visit."

Teldin was embarrassed. "I'm honored, but I still don't know why this cloak has become so attached to me."

"You've previously told me how you came to possess it, though you kept your story shorter than it needed to be," said Cirathorn, settling back slightly. "Perhaps you could tell your story in full. We have no end of time to listen."

Relieved that things seemed to be going his way, Teldin did exactly that. It took forever to get the story out, and sometimes he went back to correct something he'd said earlier, but in time he had brought everyone up to the moment when he walked up to the sentinel at the embassy. He decided to give them all the details on his cloak and what it could do, down to its color-changing habits, though he demonstrated only the cloak's power to change its size and turn into a sort of necklace—which explained the confusion in the old tales, Cirathorn said aloud. Teldin left out only the details of the past year that he felt had nothing to do with the cloak, the confused elements of his personal life since the evening when his farm had burned and his life was thrust into chaos. Once he asked for water, and the admiral merely clapped his hands for an elf to hurry away to get it.

Teldin had no idea of how long he had spoken, but his voice was cracked and hoarse by the time he had finished. If I have to do this again, Teldin thought, I'll have to hire someone to write it all down so I can just give the questioners the notes.

None of the elves left the room during his story. Many had not even touched their food. When it became apparent that Teldin was done, Cirathorn stroked his bare chin, staring through Teldin as if he were not really there.

"The cloak may have its own agenda," said the admiral. "I do not believe it is intelligent, but it is likely to be responding to certain commands cast into it at its creation. The cloak probably stays with you because it was meant to always stay with and protect the master of the *Spelljammer*, and you were merely unfortunate enough to put it on and be mistaken for that master. It is my fear that you still have far to go before you learn the truth. Forgive me for asking, but where had you planned to go next, Teldin Moore?"

Teldin considered. "I really hadn't the faintest idea, Admiral. You and the Imperial Fleet were my last hope of finding any clues about the nature of my cloak and what exactly I should do with it. Wherever it goes, I may as well go. I've no home left, and my only friends are those who travel with me on the *Probe*. I've come so far now, I'd rather just keep going to the end of it all."

Cirathorn looked at Teldin with wistful eyes. "If the cloak would permit it, I would have asked you to let us take it and solve its mysteries. Our lives are long, as you know, and any one of us would have joyfully pursued its secrets to the ends of the Known Spheres. It would appear, however, that this burden has fallen to your shoulders."

Teldin snorted. "Don't think I'm happy about it."

Cirathorn almost smiled. "No, I don't believe you are. You must forgive me, but your decided lack of experience, knowledge, and skills does make you an inviting target." Teldin bristled and was on the verge of making a sharp remark when the admiral cut him off. "If you are to solve these mysteries at all, you must solve them with haste. Given the legends and tales that link your cloak with the great *Spelljammer*, you would do best to find that ship and let the course of destiny be fulfilled. What direction that course will take and what other powers the cloak may grant you, neither I nor any other creature could say. Except perhaps one."

The admiral paused, considering something. "It would be advisable for you to seek out this one before you search for the *Spelljammer* itself, if you are minded to do that. You are poorly armed with knowledge, and you are in need of the best weaponry your mind can carry. I would have you meet with the falmadaraatha who calls itself One Six Nine, whose *tcha* lies somewhere in the sphere that our world-scouts call Herd-space."

"Meet what?" asked Teldin. "I don't know what that is or where it's supposed to be."

"Ah." Cirathorn raised a hand. "Forgive me. A falmadaraatha, which most other beings call a fal, is one of a race of sages whose lifespans are greater even than our own. They adore peace and knowledge, and love solitude only slightly less. For a gift or service, they will answer any questions you might ask them. If there is an answer, they will know it." The admiral smiled. "If you were an elf, your meeting with the fal would go all the easier. Sometimes they are said to be quite slow in deducing the answer you need, and it has happened that months or years will pass while the fal meditates on a proper and accurate reply."

Gods, thought Teldin, I don't think the neogi would let me have that much time. "Why couldn't my friends and I just start hunting down the *Spelljammer* now, instead of having to wait around for the fal to make up his mind?" he asked. "We can take on supplies and leave right away."

Cirathorn frowned. "You have no idea of the dangerous course you are proposing, Teldin Moore. What do you know of the *Spelljammer*?"

The elf's dark expression convinced Teldin to tell the truth. He was obviously missing something here. "Not much," he admitted. "I've heard it is the largest ship in the universe, and that it drifts randomly from sphere to sphere. Most tales about it say that it's a ghost ship, crewed by the dead, but some say it's completely abandoned."

"If you listen only to tales," said Cirathorn without humor, "you will be fatally unprepared when you find the queen of ships. We have heard tales, too, of the *Spelljammer*: that it was built by goblinkind or devils, that it is overrun with beholders who fight among themselves in endless wars, that it is willful and intelligent, that it is the toy of an evil god, that to even see it will cause death or blindness or a sickness of the spirit. It is said to be the abode of the most monstrous beings in the cosmos.

"We trust in the information within our own archives most, which were painfully built from guesses and luck, supplemented by visits to One Six Nine, who has spent a thousand years studying the lore of wildspace. Of late, we have not troubled One Six Nine with questions about the *Spelljammer*, as these queries are slow to produce an answer and we have had more pressing business to attend to than the chasing of a rogue ship. One of our own sages spent eight years waiting for a minor detail on its structure and received only a sentence. Knowledge we value, that is true, but there are fewer dreamers among us than there once were. Only a dreamer would chase the *Spelljammer*." The elf leaned forward. His dark gaze pierced Teldin's own. "Are you a dreamer, Teldin Moore?"

The word "no" hovered on Teldin's tongue. I don't believe in dreams, he thought, not since the war. We crushed evil and left poverty in our wake. Men with dreams, those were the Knights of Solamnia, who left all their dead behind to be buried by us, who followed their bloody footprints. They killed to save the world, but they left only ruin behind them. Hard work in peacetime was not a part of their dreams.

Ever since I was given the cloak, I've had no goals left but to find out what it is and what I should do with it. All of my options have been cut away. I have no dreams left except to follow the cloak's path.

Strangely, for a moment he thought of Cwelanas, the beautiful elven seafarer he had met just before he left Krynn, and of the copper-haired Julia, waiting for him on the *Probe*. Did he ever imagine now that one or the other might be a good traveling companion on the way to the *Spelljammer*? Instantly his jaw tightened, and he looked down. As long as he had the cloak, he was more deadly a partner than any lover deserved.

The one time he had trusted enough to take a lover, it had been Rianna Wyvernsbane, who had betrayed him to the neogi and tried to kill him, only to die horribly herself. Love was a nightmare now, not a dream. He dared not think about it.

Teldin roused himself. The admiral stared at him with cool patience.

"I will find the *Spelljammer*, whatever it takes," Teldin said.

"My question is unanswered, then, but no matter," Cirathorn said. "If you would go hunting, you would do well to learn the lore of your prey. Will you seek One Six Nine's advice before you set out?"

"It doesn't sound like I have much choice."

"You have every choice there is, but few wise ones. We cannot give you the current pathway through the phlogiston to the sphere we call Herdspace, but on a small worldlet in this sphere, only three days from here, you can find the answer. The gnomes have a colony on that planet, which they call Ironpiece, and they were the last to have visited One Six Nine, only a year ago. I do not know the result of their query, or even what it was, but I doubt that what they would ask of a falmadaraatha would interest us. We will give you whatever supplies you need for your journey."

Cirathorn looked to Teldin's right. "Indeed," he continued, finding the subject he was looking for, "we might even be able to find a traveling companion for you, if you have room. Have you met Dyffedionizer Artifactos Jammermaker?"

Even before he turned to look, Teldin knew who was being talked about. Only a gnome would ever stand for a name like that. He immediately saw that he was right. The pudgy gnome stared in shock at the admiral and other elves, his hands still clutching his pen and paper.

"What did you want? What are you saying?" asked the confused gnome in his nasal voice. "Where am I going?"

"Dyffedionizer Artifactos Jammermaker," continued Cirathorn, unperturbed, "is unrivaled in his understanding of spelljamming theory and construction. Dyffed long ago completed his work on ship design for the Imperial Fleet, and had requested that he be given passage back to his home on Ironpiece. Unfortunately, his subsequent studies have distracted him, and he has missed every voyage back to Ironpiece for the last eight years. If you offered him room aboard your hammership, he might well offer you able assistance on your quest for the *Spelljammer*, as I believe that ship is of special interest to him."

"The *Spelljammer*?" mumbled the pop-eyed gnome, his face covered with amazement. "Now, you don't mean just any spelljammer, do you? Or do you mean the big *Spelljammer*, the really big one? The one-and-only *Spelljammer*? Or is this a joke? I can never tell with you elves. You must mean some other kind of—"

"If you will bear with him," said Cirathorn patiently, "you will find his advice most helpful, though you may have to remind him when he should eat, and perhaps when he should bathe as well. We will—"

"Wait!" yelled the gnome in a panic. "No one's told me if you're talking about the one-and-only *Spelljammer* or not yet, and besides I did take a bath not long ago. You elves think you know everything, and if you're doing this just to trick me, well, I'm not just anyone's fool, but first tell me if you really mean the one-and-only *Spelljammer* or not so I know what you're talking about, because if you really mean the one-and-only *Spelljammer*, well, that's another kettle of lug nuts, because I wrote an article on the *Spelljammer* for *Spelljamming Week & Wildspace Technology*, which will see publication in just five years, once they get their printing presses working again after the last explosion, but more to the point—"

Teldin glanced at the admiral. Cirathorn's head bobbed slightly in rough rhythm with the gnome's pressured speech. "You will become accustomed to him, as have we," the elf said softly, turning in Teldin's direction again. "Trust me that it will be worth the trouble."

Teldin shrugged his shoulders. "It depends on the *Probe's* captain, but I don't think he'll have a problem with one more passenger. If he can help us when we find the *Spelljammer*, it will be worth any amount of trouble." *Almost* any trouble, he added to himself.

"It is settled, then." Cirathorn sighed and rose to his feet, stretching his legs and ignoring the gnome's continued rambling and questions. "Let us rest for an hour, then return here when all have been refreshed. You have given us much to consider, Teldin Moore, as well as much wonder and entertainment, which I am sure was not your purpose. Please remain with us in our embassy until we reconvene. We will present you with our papers on the *Spelljammer* as soon as possible, then will see you on your way."

"That will be fine," said Teldin, but it wasn't as fine as all that. He would have to see if someone else could translate the papers for him, especially if they were in Elvish or used unnaturally long words, which he feared would be the case. Maybe Aelfred could translate them. Anything would be better than having the gnome try to explain them.

Something else bothered Teldin. It was great that Cirathorn was being so helpful, but why? Teldin had been betrayed and attacked so many times that he found it impossible to believe that anyone would help him out of pure goodness. What was the admiral's take in all of this? Or had Teldin merely become too cynical? He had to clear this up before his ship left. Elves weren't inclined to be blunt like humans, but he had to know the truth.

Cirathorn motioned with his hands toward the door, and the other elves stood and left the room in twos and threes. All of them stared at Teldin and his cloak from a comfortable distance. No one tried to touch it—or him.

The admiral remained behind with his two aides as everyone else left. Teldin went out with the gnome, who was still babbling away, accompanied by an elf who would show them what supplies could be offered.

As the footsteps faded, one of the aides leaned close to the admiral. "Your forgiveness, Your Grace," he said softly, "but you were less than forthright with our guest. That you said nothing of your own research on the *Spelljammer* I can understand, but confusing the song-told madness of the First Pilot with 'enthusiasm' could only have been delib—"

One of the admiral's hands came up and pressed itself lightly against the elf's chest. The aide stopped speaking at once. Cirathorn's eyes were fixed on the doorway.

"We live in interesting times, Alsilor," whispered the brown-haired elf. "Have my battlewizard, watchmaster, and

loremaster report to my chambers at once. The captains of the
Leaping Hart, *Free Wind's Fury*, *Unicorn's Wing*, and *Emerald Hornet* are to put their ships at ready within the hour, under the code of the leopard—no sound, no sign. Signal the
Empress Dorianne that I will be aboard soon, but cannot say
when. It, too, is to be readied for flight under the leopard's
code. Go and do."

Paler than he had been a moment before, the elf hurried
away, accompanied by the other aide. The admiral stood in
silence, alone, and listened to them leave. He sighed deeply,
his gaze dropping as he pulled off his gloves. On the middle
finger of his right hand was the signet ring of his family: a
golden eagle in flight against a burning sun. An arrow pierced
the eagle's heart—his father's addition after the retaking of
Aërlofalyn and the laying to rest of the old, wronged bones.
Cirathorn had long debated with himself over what changes, if
any, he would make to the crest.

A sword, he decided, clutched in the eagle's talons. A dying
eagle with the blood of its slayers upon it. It was worthy of
thought. There would be time enough and plenty to decide.

"Go and do," he said, though no one was present. He
pulled the glove back on and set off for his chambers to prepare for his meeting.

*   *   *   *   *

"The *Spelljammer*!" exclaimed the gnome for the dozenth
time. "You know, certainly, that elves are notorious for not saying what's really on their minds, and their love of metaphor will
one day be their downfall, mark my words, and they will give
way to those who say what they mean, like the gnomes—ah,
and humans, of course—who are many times more clear in their
speech, so when that elf said you were going to find the one-
and-only *Spelljammer*, I was taken aback for a moment, because I've read everything there is about the *Spelljammer*, with
the possible exception of the sources kept at the libraries of
Doth B and Zphidnin, and maybe the Academy at Lirak's
Cube, but, as I was saying, you could have knocked me over
with a size-four gear wrench when I understood that he actually
meant the one-and-only *Spelljammer*. Where are we going?"

"What?" said Teldin, who had not been paying attention. The two were past the Greater Market now, on the way downhill toward the warehouses and docks. He had trouble believing his good fortune. The admiral had given him access to a warehouse full of supplies. Undoubtedly, it would be too much to carry aboard the hammership, but still—

"I said, where are we going? You'll have to forgive me, but I haven't gone outside very much in the last few years, and I'm not very familiar with the city here, since I was working in the libraries in the embassy—"

"We're going to the ship that brought me here," Teldin said, cutting him off. "Then we're going to take you to Ironpiece, get the maps to Herdspace, and go see the fal for more information." Teldin chewed on the inside of his cheek. "Afterward, I suppose we'll find the *Spelljammer*, and . . . do whatever we need to do there." Just what *did* he mean to do at the *Spelljammer*? Teldin realized he didn't have a clue.

"Ah, that's just excellent," said Dyffed with obvious relief. "I have a suspicion that the careful study of the *Spelljammer* could produce a revolution in every kind of science, most especially in the field of cold dweomerfusion, which as you know is the most up-and-coming field of energy research, possibly to replace even hydrodynamics, given a century or two and some successful field trials. . . ."

The rest of the gnome's monologue was lost in the ruckus of a shouting match between two red-faced dwarves, both stinking with ale, outside an equally noisy tavern. Teldin hurried by before blows could be exchanged. The docks appeared down the street ahead. Barely a minute later, he waved his arms at Aelfred, who leaned against the ship's railing on the *Probe*'s forward castle, directing the unloading operations on the main deck.

"About damn time!" roared Aelfred in a good humor, noticing Teldin at last. "Did you get lost, or did the elves have you seeing one flunky after the other? And who's the dwarf? You want me to hire this one on, too?"

"I'll tell you in just a moment!" Teldin shouted back. "This is Dyffedionizer . . . ah, Dyffed. I'll explain everything later. Why did you ask about hiring him?"

"'Cause I hired the other one. I was going to ask you why

you sent her over, but I guessed that you knew what you were doing, and she's working out fine."

Teldin was trying to imagine what Aelfred was talking about when a dreadful possibility came to mind.

"Aelfred," Teldin called, his voice rising with tension, "who did you hire?"

"*Hey, Teldin!*" screamed a young girl's voice. With a jolt of sudden horror, Teldin looked toward the ship's stern, where someone small with long black hair, a colorful dress, and a magenta headband waved at him with both slim arms. "*Teldin, how'd it go?*"

"Paladine save me," Teldin whispered. From what, Teldin didn't want to imagine.

Chapter Four

• • •

As he placed his hand on the waiting room door, General Vorr took a moment to touch his sword hilt and reassure himself of its weight. Vorr had long ago discarded any worship of the uncaring gods, except perhaps for the hero-ancestor Dukagsh. Vorr placed his faith instead in his strength, skills, and willpower. Still, if he never admitted to having fears, he sometimes felt doubt, and getting the feel of a weapon before a battle was as close as he would ever come to praying. He did not fear the undead, but he did not like them either. Victory was the healthiest antidote for doubt.

His previous injuries were now largely healed, thanks to his regenerative powers, but his right arm still ached deep in the bone where the knight had stabbed him, and his left shoulder still burned from the poisoned axe. With Admiral Halker waiting impatiently behind him in the hallway, he opened the door and stepped into the cool air of the room beyond.

The room, in a building adjacent to the one in which Vorr had his headquarters, once had been the spacious stone chapel of a local elven deity. After the fall of Spiral, it had served as a prisoner-holding station and was now just a room where scouts and other visitors were quartered before meeting with high officials. Enthusiastic orcs, scro, goblins, and others had demolished or stolen everything of value in the area during the assault, leaving the chapel as barren as if it never had been inhabited at all. Only the great brass lanterns, hanging on long chains from the vaulted ceiling, remained of the elves' original furnishings, their magical glow illuminating the room despite the battering they had taken from debris hurled at them by bored visitors.

Vorr did not know what to expect when he entered, except for the lich. Indeed, standing in the room's center, by the faceless and almost unrecognizable statue of an elven god, was a skeletal human in dark velvet robes. From its thin rope belt hung a single gray pouch. At Vorr's entrance, the creature turned from the statue with a startled movement to face him. Its bony hands came up with its fingers spread in an obvious spell-casting movement. The stench of long-dead meat assailed the general's nostrils almost immediately.

It was then that Vorr saw the four huge creatures standing farther back in the room, their black carapaces gleaming in the light overhead. The monsters turned as one to face the general, then raised their great clawed hands and widened their yard-long mandibles in anticipation, hurrying forward with a lumbering gait to pass the lich and plant themselves before him.

Vorr immediately blocked the doorway with his huge body and threw a hand out to stop the admiral's advance. "Umber hulks!" he shouted as he drew his sword. Then he saw that the room already had perhaps two dozen ogre guardsmen lining the walls, weapons at the ready. He also saw that the umber hulks' dangerous magical eyes were shrouded with torn strips of black cloth, preventing their mind-destroying vision from affecting the ogres already in the room. He hesitated, sensing that he had reacted too quickly.

"Halt!" The lich's rasping voice was strained and barely understandable. Striding forward between the huge monsters, the undead being placed a gentle, skeletal hand on the thick arm of one of its wide-bodied beasts. "You must slower walk, and less loud be, or difficulty with my servants I will have," the lich said, cold yellow-green light burning within its eye sockets. "Their eyes tightly bound are, but guarantee your safety I cannot, if them again you startle."

"This is my fault, I'm afraid," said Admiral Halker. He stepped past the general and entered the room, casually wiping sweat from his forehead. "I was careless and did not mention that your bodyguards were umber hulks, Skarkesh. I hope I got your name right."

"Skarkesh, it is." The lich dropped its fleshless hand from the umber hulk's arm. "Apologize for their presence I must. Trust in all things I lack, having this lesson in unfortunate ways learned. Like pets to me now they are."

Vorr sheathed his broadsword after another look around the room. Thanks to the eye shrouds, his ogres were not affected by the terrible madness that seized anyone who looked into an umber hulk's eyes—anyone but himself, of course, since magical effects couldn't touch him. The ogres, who had tensed at Vorr's arrival, relaxed slightly, keeping their pole axes and huge swords at the ready. Vorr was pleased to see their courage in the face of the lich, whose magic usually drove its foes mad with panic before it. Vorr frowned suddenly, sensing that something was wrong.

"To you two plainly I must speak," rasped the lich, turning to walk back to the battered statue. "At my news with excitement I am seized, but with you to speak alone I had hoped. Too many guards we keep, and my news best in quiet surroundings is given. Possible this is?"

The general and admiral carefully exchanged looks. "There is a small room in the back of this one, where we could discuss things," said the admiral, looking back at Skarkesh, "if General Vorr feels it would be safe enough."

This could be tricky, thought Vorr. Even two dozen ogres would be hard pressed against four umber hulks, and he knew damn well that the hulks' first action in combat would be to tear away those flimsy eye coverings. Vorr reached for the nearest ogre and waved him over. Pulling a small card from a pocket on his thick belt, the general handed it to the ogre and motioned at the door. "Take that to your company commander," he said softly. The sweat-streaked ogre grunted, sheathed its weapons, and left, pulling the door shut behind him. "We can talk now," Vorr finished.

"Enjoy tricks I do not," said the lich sharply, its voice rising in pitch. "What trick have you done?" The umber hulks shifted in agitation, their long mandibles clacking softly together like vast ivory claws.

"I sent him to tell his commander that if we were not back

in two hours, he was to bring his entire force here to find out why," said the general in a matter-of-fact tone. "Trust in all things we lack, too, having learned that lesson in unfortunate ways like yourself. You and your big pets have as much safety as your behavior allows us to grant you."

The lich made a curious wheezing noise. "As you want," it said finally, "but unpleasant my gratitude will be if treachery for dinner you serve." General Vorr noted that the stench of carrion in the room was now stronger. Odd, he thought, looking at the lich. It's completely bone, with no trace of flesh. Could it have rotting meat under its robes? There was also the reaction of the ogres—or, rather, the curious lack of any reaction among them to confronting the lich. It didn't make sense. Things had gone quite differently, years ago in the Glowrings Sphere, when Vorr had been the only warrior who dared come within striking range of the undead sorcerer.

Admiral Halker stepped forward, waving a hand to the back of the room. "Let's get on with our talk. Skarkesh, if you would have your bodyguards remain here, we shall do the same with ours. They look like they should keep each other in good company." The admiral rubbed his flat nose briefly, undoubtedly not enjoying the stench the lich was giving off but still putting up a pleasant front.

"Agreed I am," whispered the lich, and uttered a series of harsh syllables at its bodyguards. The umber hulks shifted their huge clawed feet, forming a defensive square to watch all sides of the room, and appeared to await further instructions.

Admiral Halker took the initiative and led the way to the back of the room. The little room at the rear had been for the elven priests, in all likelihood, as the scro had slain several minor clerics and their followers there in a massacre after the landings. The old scro stepped aside to allow Vorr to enter the little room first.

The room was about ten feet square, with a ceiling low enough to force the general to stoop. Its imported sandstone walls were once covered with bas-relief work and paintings, all now destroyed. Vorr examined the room briefly, seeing only the two heavy tables normally stored here and a few wine bottles and pots lying broken in one filthy corner; low-bred orcs or goblins held their parties here, no doubt. The floor was still stained brown from the massacre after the invasion, and the stale air bore the stink of old blood. It would get a lot worse with the lich here as well, Vorr thought.

Motioning the other two inside, Vorr stepped back. The admiral came in first and stood along the wall nearest Vorr. The lich came in only after peering inside carefully, then motioning the general away from the door. Once all were inside, Vorr reached over to shut the door.

"Wait!" hissed the lich, hands out suddenly, pointing with pale white finger bones at both admiral and general. "Cursed you will both be if any tricks you try! In any circumstance, escape I shall, and wild my unhappiness will be! This clearly you understand?"

General Vorr briefly considered ways to call the lich's bluff and dismember it. He hated undead things and he hated this whole meeting, and the lich's paranoia was making it worse. He did not worry so much for his own safety, but having the scro promote another admiral would be time-wasting and bothersome, especially after he had spent the last few years getting used to this admiral's quirks.

"I understand," said Vorr, gently closing the door, "but wild our unhappiness will be if more threats you utter. I am not known for my patience. You would do best to start discussing your reasons for wanting to see us."

"Which involved gaining some great treasure, as I believe you mentioned," said the admiral smoothly, his arms folded across his robed chest. The admiral's steel chest protector did not show beneath the thick black fabric, the general noted. Nor did the admiral's weapons show at all in their leg sheaths. Good; it was better for the general's weapons to draw the lich's attention. If worse came to worst, the admiral might even be able to lend a sword in the fight, though his skills at diplomacy were a dozen times better than his meager sword-fighting techniques.

The lich's finger bones curled, and its arms fell toward its sides. "Greater than your brains can dream the treasure is," the lich said hoarsely. "Beyond my grasp it is, and dislike that I do. Dreamed of this treasure I have, long dreamed I have, and within my grasp it will one day fall. An army I need, and found it is. If in this treasure you are pleased, me will you serve to gain it?"

"We are not for hire, Skarkesh," said the admiral, raising a hand to scratch at his broad snout. "We have our own mission to perform, and we are deeply involved in it. You may have missed the signs, but we are at war."

"Yes, yes," hissed the lich, waving its arms in dismissal. "A war nice is, with toys of ships and a thousand toys of soldiers. Yes, it nice is. But nicer it is with bigger toys, and nicest with biggest toy of all ships. To find this biggest toy I wish, and the key now in this very sphere is. Knowledge of this big toy, the *Spelljammer*, you have?"

Neither general nor admiral spoke in reply. "Well?" hissed the lich more loudly. The carrion smell was noticeably stronger. "Of the *Spelljammer* you know? Or beyond your reasoning powers does it lie?"

"The *Spelljammer*," said Admiral Halker carefully, "is a mythical spelljamming ship the size of a small world. It's supposed to be shaped like a manta ray. Its coming is said to be an evil portent, as it brings destruction and chaos in its wake. No one can destroy it or command it, not even a god. It drives its captains insane. That's what the myths say."

"Mythical it is not!" the lich said heatedly. "Across centuries have I chased it, and for its secrets a thousand foes dead now are. Its secret buried in a sunless asteroid two years ago I found. The key to its power in a block of ice was frozen, and my lordservants, my umber hulks, to free it without harm could not." The lich's eyes glowed more brightly now. "Then! Then my captain-servant the block from me stole, he into black wildspace flew, coward thieving spew of lowest slave meat!" The lich was nearly screaming, its body shaking with rage. "Coward the block of ice from me stole, and chase him and kill him I did, but gone the block was. It lost had been, its worth unknown, to a reigar cow!"

For perhaps half a minute the lich rocked, then the shaking slowed quickly and stopped. "A reigar cow the cloak had stolen," it rasped tonelessly, pulling its hands back from the table to fall at its sides again. "Away in her ship, the *Penumbra*, she flew, by I and my servants pursued. She through the void we chased, and then . . ."

The lich broke off. Vorr heard a scratching sound and noticed that the lich was rubbing its finger bones together, over and over. He glanced at Admiral Halker, who appeared calm but watched the lich with narrow eyes.

"Then . . ." prompted the admiral.

The lich looked up and stared at them with cold light before it spoke, so quietly that Vorr had trouble hearing it clearly. "Then my servants . . . to kill me tried. Poison they tried. Hard I fought before escaping them. My little masters a *yrthni ma'adi* wanted, but gone then I was, and they a new one chose, no doubt. Gone I was . . . but back now I am. Different now I am, too. Better, you see." The lich raised its hands and spread its fingers, peering at them as if it had not seen them before. It looked up at the two who faced it, raising its hands to the ceiling. "Better, yes, better the cloak to find again, and it to wear and the *Spelljammer* to control!"

General Vorr understood almost nothing of the lich's last remarks. Every muscle in him was tensed to attack. It would be a snap. He would have to break out through the door to slay the umber hulks next to avoid losing his ogres to them, but the door wouldn't withstand more than one blow. If that ogre he'd sent away returned in the next few minutes with the company of ogre and scro reinforcements that the general had requested on the preprinted card, the fight would go a lot better. Admiral Halker wasn't the best judge of fighting strength, and Vorr was used to doubling the admiral's estimates of the size of the marine force required to accomplish any particular mission.

"I'm having some trouble following what you are saying," said the admiral quietly. "You say that you found some sort of cape or cloak that will allow you to control the *Spelljammer*—this nonmythical, mightiest of all ships—but one of your servants stole it. You chased down the servant and killed him, but a reigar had stolen it by then, and your other servants tried to murder you after that. You've since . . . well, changed into your current form, and now you want us to help you find and seize this cloak from the reigar."

The lich had watched the admiral intently as he spoke. "Little trouble with my words you have had," it said at last, "but reigar the cloak has not. My not-servants to slay her did succeed, but the cloak missing has been, by a human stolen away. This human I know where is. Clever he is, as all not-servants now not-alive are. With other ships and companions this human travels, ahead of me always. Now in this sphere he rests, on the Rock of Bral on this sphere's far side. Of this body you know?"

"It's an asteroid city of mixed population," said the admiral easily. "We have it charted. It's of no interest to us. Our quarrel is with but this one small world."

"Good news that is. With me you will serve then, this cloak to find?"

The admiral frowned with annoyance. "I think we've said that we are not for hire, Skarkesh. Besides that, you're implying that you, not we, will gain this treasure, the cloak. Just what could we gain from following you?"

The lich said nothing for a while. General Vorr fidgeted, the strain of waiting to attack beginning to eat at him.

"The universe," said the lich.

There was a pause.

"I'm sorry?" said the admiral, leaning more closely.

"The universe," repeated the lich. "The benefit you as my servants would gain. Need you I will, when the cloak is to be found, and need you I will, when the *Spelljammer* later is found. Need you I will, when the universe beneath the wings of the *Spelljammer* is held, and all the worlds in existence mine will be. Need you I will, my riches to count and share."

The admiral looked at the lich without comment. His arms slowly unfolded, and the old scro rubbed his hands together before him, as if to warm them in a cold wind.

"What proof do you have that anything you have said is true?" asked Halker.

The lich tilted its head halfway to one side. "Proof?" Slowly, the lich reached for its side, dipping a skeletal hand into the lone pouch on its belt. "Proof?" it asked, and pulled out a heavy, round disk on a short chain. It set the disk and chain on the table before it. The disk appeared to be cast from bronze and was greatly worn. A few deeply carved geometric patterns remained on its weathered surface, forming a three-pointed star design.

"Proof," said the lich. "To examine it you are allowed." The lich stood back with careless grace.

The general and admiral stared at the item without moving for it. "What is it?" asked Vorr, more out of curiosity than anything. He still craved an excuse to destroy the lich.

The lich gestured toward the disk. "Pick up you may."

The admiral weighed the risks, looked at General Vorr, then sighed heavily and reached for the disk. He touched it—and froze in midmovement. His eyes took on a glazed, unseeing look as he stared off into space.

"Admiral?" asked Vorr, glancing away from the lich. Seeing that the black-robed scro could apparently make no reply, Vorr tugged his sword from its sheath and took a heavy step toward the lich, who retreated. "If he's been cursed," Vorr said, his voice thick with promise, "you're garbage."

"Your admiral unharmed is," hissed the lich, eyes bright with angry green flames. Its hands rose, fingers spread. "But if closer you come, on your flesh the worms will feast tomorrow. Prepared for your treachery I was, gray orc meat, long before my ship here landed."

"What is happening to the *admiral*?" The words came out as Vorr moved in on the lich, his voice starting soft and growing in strength until he was almost shouting. His sword arm swung up, the tendons standing out on the back of his huge, hamlike fist as it gripped the pommel.

"Stop," said Admiral Halker flatly. Vorr froze, sword poised and ready to cut off the lich's hands. He held his position, waiting for more.

"Stop," said the admiral again. "Cease. This . . ." Vorr heard the admiral swallow. "This thing is speaking in my head, and I . . . I don't want to miss what it is showing me."

The lich slowly stepped back, almost out of General Vorr's range but now backed up to the wall. The three of them held their positions for what seemed like an age, with the general's sword arm lowering slightly.

There was the sound of something being laid on the table. "General Vorr, put away your weapon. Now."

Licking his lips and feeling that he would regret this, the general did as he was told. The lich waited at the wall a little longer, its gaze focused on Vorr alone.

"Tomb of Dukagsh," said the admiral. Vorr looked at him sharply and saw that the admiral was a pale yellow now. "The things I saw. What is that?"

The lich moved from the wall, but not by far. "It by the hands of the ancients was built," it said. "Through the eyes of the *Spelljammer* it lets you see, world after world. Buried in the dark asteroid with the cloak this was, under the ice. This alone I kept when my servants then traitors became. Weak now this relic of old is, and not long to last. It my last clue to the *Spelljammer* is."

General Vorr suddenly reached down for the disk and chain himself. He picked it up in his thick fingers as the other two looked on. After looking it over for a few moments, he held it to his head, then put it down.

"You, too, through the *Spelljammer*'s eyes see?" said the lich. "What revealed to you was?"

Vorr hesitated. He'd seen nothing, of course, being immune to the influences of magic. "Impressive," he said, and glanced at the admiral, waiting.

"It was startling, to say the least," said the old admiral, quickly covering for Vorr. "I saw a small green world below me, and there was a voice in my head that said the world was called Torus. The world was round but had a hole through it. It was so clear when I saw it."

"Sufficient proof now you have?" inquired the lich, edging closer to the table where the disk and chain lay. "Now my servants you will become, my cloak to rightfully rescue from the touch of a groundling human?"

Vorr felt something inside him snap. "We're not servants to any being but our own kind, Skarkesh," he said, his jaw tightening. "You'd best drop that word from your vocabulary before it gets some of your thin, little bones broken."

"Brave the gray giant's tongue is," retorted the yellow-eyed lich, stepping back and raising a hand toward him. "Will so brave the tongue be if in flames it is wrapped?"

Vorr's hand went for the hilt of his sword.

"Stop it!" bellowed the scro admiral. He slammed a fist onto a wooden tabletop. "By the Holy Tomb of Dukagsh, you will both cease this damned bickering! If we are to work together, then we are *going to start now*!"

The admiral pointed a withered hand at the lich. "Skarkesh, you threaten us once more, and not even a wishing ring will save you from us. I won't tolerate that kind of crap from anyone, especially not a dead wizard. If you want slaves, you can get them dirt cheap at any marketplace, and you can treat them however you want. But if you want a wildspace navy to back you up, you're going to pay through your eye sockets for it, and you're going to cut out this krajen dung about us being your servants. If we decide to help you—and I mean *if* we help you—you're not going to become our little brass god. If you don't like it, you can load your big rock-diggers out there back on your ship and get your bone-white ass off our planet. Do you understand me?"

General Vorr waited, watching the lich. His hand still hovered over his sword hilt. The next time he pulled it out, he'd use it, the admiral be damned.

The lich made no immediate reply, but the yellow-green light in its skull burned furiously. It lowered its hand quickly, reaching some decision. "Money and gems you may have," it said, its voice devoid of emotion. "Magic you may have. Slaves you may have. The cloak, not. For the cloak much I have suffered, too much to see in other hands it held. To me the cloak must go. Agree you must."

The old scro tilted his chin up. "We'd have no use for a gods-damned cloak. It's yours, but we'll have to work out the basics of what you're going to pay us. Trust me that it will be a king's sum, but if we accept your mission, we'll make it worth the cost."

"Then agreement we have?" asked the lich, appearing to have no trouble with those terms. "You my serv—my helpers on this quest will be? Soon we must leave if so, on to the Rock of Bral."

"General Vorr and I need to talk first," the admiral said, his anger appearing to dissipate. "But we need to talk alone. Will you excuse us?"

The lich was taken off guard, but it recovered quickly. It reached down and snatched up the bronze disk and chain, then sidestepped to the door. With a last look at the two, it pushed the door open and stepped outside.

With a nod from the admiral, General Vorr reached over and shut the door lightly, allowing them to hear any noises in the other room. The general trusted his ogres to raise a shout and attack if the lich made any hostile move. They wouldn't be able to do much to stop it, but once Vorr came out, the fight would be over. The ogres would have to handle the umber hulks on their own, but Vorr had faith in them.

Halker leaned against a table and massaged his pale, watery eyes with a thumb and forefinger. "Paranoid bastard, isn't he?" he remarked.

Vorr said nothing, still feeling the raw heat of his anger, but he nodded.

"I think our undead friend is insane," said the scro, looking up at the general, "but I also think he's telling the truth. I can't describe what happened when I touched that medallion. The vision I had was so real that . . ." He raised his hands helplessly. "The damned thing convinced me. Maybe he enchanted the medallion to do that, just to fool us, but I don't think so. He has nothing to gain. I think he needs us."

"I can believe he needs us to get the cloak that will let him control this *Spelljammer*," Vorr said in a low voice, "but that he needs us afterward to count his riches—I doubt that very much. All the tales I've ever heard about the *Spelljammer* were terror stories for infants. Every soldier and sailor in wildspace has heard them. They're all skavver crap. But if a tenth of what's said about the ship is true, and if Skarkesh were to get his bony little hands on it, he wouldn't need us. If he could rule the universe with that one ship, we'd be only flies to him. Everyone swats flies when they get in the way."

"Mmm-hmm," mumbled the admiral. He rubbed his wrinkled chin with thin fingers. "Certainly. Unless . . ." He left the thought unfinished.

The two commanders looked at each other in silence.

"I don't believe it would be the first time for you, would it?" said the admiral at last.

"I'd love the chance," said the general, "but I couldn't do a thing with the cloak. You know that."

"I'll need someone like that," said the admiral. "Someone I could trust to handle things. If a spell-casting lich can use the cloak, then perhaps a spell-casting scro admiral can, too." He raised both his hands, fingers apart. He didn't smile. "We'll need all the information we can get on this *Spelljammer*, and I don't mean baby tales. If we can use it against the elves, we might just win the war by ourselves."

Vorr's interest was rising by the second. He was starting to imagine leading his marines into action again. It would be good to fight after so long a peace. "We'd still have to follow his lead for a while," he said.

"That's another thing," said Halker. "He claims he can show us the way to the cloak, though I'm damned if I know how he could. Does he have a crystal ball, a seeing pool, a spell, or a helpful godling? I want to know *how* he knows. Usso could help us there, and maybe he could get a little more intelligence on the pyramid ship, too.

"One more thing. Skarkesh wants us to fly to the Rock of Bral, which, the last time I heard, has its own little navy. We could crush it, but we'd be wasting our strength on humans, not the Imperial Fleet. I'd like to avoid that unless absolutely necessary, no matter what the lich wants. Maybe a marine raid, in and out, something like that. You'd know what to do. Then we'd have the cloak."

Vorr nodded again, looking at the door as if he were looking through it. His face was set in stone, broad teeth showing between his drawn lips.

"Later," said Halker. "First, the cloak. Then . . ." He tilted his head toward the door.

Vorr considered that and smiled, showing all of his teeth. It was the first time the admiral had seen him smile since the landings on Spiral, when a zwarth had attacked the general's command post. "Don't want to forget the elves," Vorr said.

"I haven't," said the admiral.

"Then we're agreed to help him?"

"Mmm-hmm. But first have Usso check him out, just to make sure he's not pulling us along for something else. If his story is clear, then let's get on with it."

"Agreed." The general reached for the doorknob—and stopped, deep in thought.

"What's on your mind, General?"

Vorr shook his head briefly. "I was just wondering what route the lich took into the building."

Halker raised an eyebrow. "He and his bodyguards walked in. They came up through the goblins' quarter of the camp. The 'hulks wore those eye shrouds, and none of them gave us any trouble. Why?"

"Just curious, sir," he said. That tears it, he thought. If goblins wouldn't run from a lich, something was wrong. The truth was suddenly undeniable.

Skarkesh was not a real lich.

The general grunted, then opened the door. Together, they went out to greet their guest.

*   *   *   *   *

When General Vorr got back to his office late that night, he found his charcoaled chair replaced by a less-comfortable one. Fortunately, he'd been told that scro carpenters were at work on a replacement, though it would take a few days. A single light globe illuminated his command room. It looked a lot tidier now, but it still smelled of smoke and death. The breezes that blew through the broken windows would clear even that out in time. It being long after hours, the general wore only a military kilt and shoulder straps for small weapons. With the doors firmly closed and the guards properly warned for privacy, Vorr sat in his chair and waited for Usso's report.

"You called?" came the invisible feminine voice.

"I'm not in the mood," Vorr said bluntly. He leaned forward, resting his elbows on his desk. "Just get it out."

He heard Usso snort. "Short of temper, are we? You wanted to know about the lich, or whatever it is? Well, it isn't a lich, I can tell that. You nailed that right. It lacks all the basic lich parts. A lich is a lot more than a bare skeleton in a robe. I couldn't break its disguise without it knowing, but it does show up as undead, as an organized evil being—which liches aren't particularly—and as thick with magic, especially illusion. It also has no personal history, so it isn't who it says it is. I'd guess it was another undead creature that for some reason wants to look like a lich. It's not lying about the cloak, anyway. It wants it so badly it could just about fall apart."

Vorr thought it over. He could end the charade by touching the lich, but he felt like playing along for now. "Can we trust it not to kill us if it gets the cloak?"

"Kobas," said the silken voice, "if you had your big hands

ready to grab the universe by the neck, would you think anyone could trust you?"

Vorr grunted. "Recommendations?"

"Leave the ground troops here, the orcs and goblins, but
get the fleet up for a spin. Hit the Rock of Bral if the human's
still there. When you grab the cloak, break some bones—
Skarkesh's. And when you do get it, toss the cloak to me, not
to that senile orc-dog you take orders from."

Vorr looked up sharply. "You are out of line."

There was faint laughter in the air. "Use that tone with me
again, Kobas, and you can sleep by yourself."

Vorr felt his face darken. "If you play games with me," he
said evenly, "I'll see that you go hungry for a month. You
know I can do it. You know what that feels like. You know you
can't escape me."

In the silence that followed, Vorr heard a presence stir behind him. A small, soft hand appeared on his left shoulder,
sliding over his rough gray skin.

"You were joking with me, weren't you, Kobas?" said the
sweet voice, a trace of anxiety behind it. "You know I hate to
joke about that. I don't like to go hungry."

Vorr reached up, his broad hand swallowing hers whole. He
slowly turned in his seat and looked into the long-lashed al-
mond eyes of a human woman with long black hair. Her
yellow-brown skin was paler than when he had last seen her;
she must be quite hungry already. It had been three days since
she'd fed last, on an elf prisoner who'd lasted only a day.

Vorr knew all that lay behind those eyes. If he gave Usso the
cloak, she would be only marginally more trustworthy than
the false lich. He'd have to watch her closely from now on and
warn the war priests and the admiral if she showed signs of
treachery; she'd be dangerous right up to the end. It was a
good thing Usso couldn't read his mind the way she could everyone else's.

"Mad at me?" asked the woman. She ran her hands over
the sides of his face. "Will you feed me soon?"

She'd love to have the *Spelljammer*, Vorr knew. She could
pick her meals from any populated world she chose. She was
almost as bad as a vampire. Vorr remembered seeing Usso for
the first time, a prisoner from an Oriental human-built dra-

gonship. She'd looked human enough; in fact, she'd looked like an old male wizard. The old man's skills and charisma had impressed his captors, and soon he was adopted into the Tarantula Fleet. Only the general knew the truth about her. All he'd had to do was to touch the old man, and the shape-shifted form had melted away. Vorr had kept Usso's secret, but he had named a price for it.

"Maybe," he said. "Maybe later tonight."

Her long white robes stirred in back; she had wagged her tail in her excitement. *Hu hsien*, she had called her race, fox women with spells and an endless hunger for human life energy. "I wish you could find a human for me, Kobas. I'm getting tired of those elves, but anything's better than a goblin. Could you find a human for me?"

"I might find one for you," Vorr said. Still holding her hand firmly in one of his own, he reached out and caught her under the chin, forcing her to look at him. "But you owe me, Usso, for ruining my fight today." His grip tightened as he pulled her closer, and she winced, her eyes tearing up with the pain. "You owe me a lot."

"Careful," she said in a quavering voice. "You get rough sometimes. Be careful, Kobas."

"Of course," he said.

It was a very good thing, the general thought again as he pulled her face to his, that she couldn't read his mind.

Chapter Five

● ● ●

The door to the captain's cabin had barely closed when the argument started.

"Aelfred, you've got to get rid of Gaye."

The warrior looked up in shock. "You're kidding me."

"Tell her we're overbooked. Tell her you have an unlucky number of crew aboard. Just get her off the ship."

"Old son, you're not making any sense."

"Gaye is a kender. You don't understand what kender are like. They're pure trouble. We're just begging for—"

"Ptah's black beard, Teldin, do you hear what you're saying? You served on this ship when it was commanded by a mind flayer, and just a minute ago you asked me to hire on a gnome, but now you're having a fit over a girl who—"

"A *kender*! Aelfred, kender will steal you blind without even thinking about it. They're not evil—that's not what I'm saying—but they can't help themselves. They steal, they wander off and bring back trouble, they—"

"No!" shouted Aelfred. He raised a thick finger and jabbed it an inch from Teldin's nose. "You stupid son of a bitch, we are *not* going to start a fight here about a kender, whatever the hells a kender is, and we aren't going to start up about this one. She was aboard just an hour when she caught two thieves trying to make off with one of our silk crates. We caught 'em both because she was so fast and quiet that she got five of us after them before the thieves had even cleared the docks. *Then* she fixed the rear catapult's trigger lock. *And* she says she can cook. There's no shame in having a woman cook aboard ship once in a while, and if she wants to do it, I'm all for it, so cut out this crap. What's eating you?"

Teldin dropped his gaze and rubbed a hand over his face. He could see it wasn't going to work. "She lied to you, Aelfred," he said, feeling tired and frustrated. "I didn't send her over here. She's just a—just a gypsy, some homeless kender I ran into in the Greater Market. I couldn't get rid of her. I'm just—"

Aelfred slammed a fist into a wall. Teldin started and looked up. "So, she lied! Who in the Nine Hells cares? I lied to get aboard my first spelljammer. I didn't know what I was in for, but I wouldn't have cared if I had, you know that. I had people after me. I can't hold it against every person who tells me a lie just to serve on a ship, as long as he or she's got skills worth having!" Aelfred paused to clear his throat, then suddenly gave Teldin a crooked smile. "If nothing else, she's a long sight better looking than you are. We've needed some color around here, and she's just in time."

Teldin frowned. "She's just a kid, Aelfred," he said, even though he wasn't quite sure of that.

Aelfred snorted and suppressed a laugh. "Gods, Teldin, there are no kids in wildspace. She can handle herself. I'm not saying that looks mean everything, but it sure brightened up my day to have her on board." He stared at Teldin hard. "You never came out with so much jettison before. Did the elves throw a hate-kender spell at you, or what?"

Teldin said nothing in return. His gaze dropped under Aelfred's own. Strangely, he found it hard to pinpoint what had set him off. He'd been angry with Gaye's intrusion, and he had never trusted the few kender he'd known. Something else was eating at him about Gaye. He couldn't say what.

"Speaking of the elves," Aelfred said, his voice growing warmer again, "how did things go? What did they have to say about your cloak?"

After a few moments, Teldin went along with the change in topic and related everything that had happened since he had left the *Probe* hours earlier. Aelfred whistled when he heard the news about the connection between the *Spelljammer* and the cloak, and he grimaced when Dyffed's passenger status was explained, but the document that Teldin produced giving them access to Imperial Fleet supplies in the Rock of Bral's warehouses made his jaw drop.

"I've never heard of the Imperial Fleet giving anyone anything if that person wasn't also in the fleet," he said, staring at the paper as if it had just given him kingship over a planet. "I can't believe they'd just do that."

"Cirathorn was going to give me some papers on their research into the *Spelljammer*, too, but he said they needed time to get their notes together. I don't know why I didn't trust them." After a moment, he let his breath out slowly. "No, I do know why. I have a hard time trusting people these days. It just seems like . . ." He ran a hand through his hair. "Every time people get a look at the cloak, things change."

Aelfred watched his friend carefully. Teldin was on the verge of saying something more, but didn't. They both knew what wasn't being said. Other faces and names joined them in the room, with memories of betrayal and blood. Teldin had given up counting those who'd died in the wake of his cloak.

"Hey, old son," said Aelfred quietly, "We've got to use this writ before it expires on us. I've got a ton of stuff I need to get if we're going to run through this sphere. Let's sit down and make out a market list."

Teldin nodded. He was still angry, but tired now, too. "I didn't mean to get so upset about Gaye," he said suddenly. "She's probably a good kid, but she . . ." He fought for words, then gave up. "Just put a lock on your door."

Aelfred grinned. "I never lock any woman out." He took a light punch at Teldin's shoulder, but as he did so his grin faded and he looked away. "Speaking of which, Julia was looking for you. . . . She wanted to say good-bye, Teldin."

Aelfred continued as Teldin's expression slid from one of surprise to resignation to depression. "She came to me for permission to leave the crew. Said she'd gotten a commission on another ship. She left you this."

Teldin took the folded scrap of parchment offered him. He opened it to find the words "It's better this way" hastily scratched across it and few locks of coppery hair caught in the crease.

Aelfred cleared his throat, obviously uncomfortable, then headed for the cabin door. There he paused. "Listen, we'll write down what supplies we need to get while we have a drink, and then we'll get our gear from the elves. It'll be like Midwinter Festival back home."

Teldin nodded mechanically. The big warrior's joking change of subject hit a raw nerve, but Teldin wasn't willing to fight about it. Thinking of Julia made him think of the traitor Rianna, since she had nearly killed both Julia and Teldin before he and Aelfred had killed her. Sometimes, when he wasn't careful, he still saw Rianna's bloodied face, her feral grin, the spear that pinned her to the deck. If he was very incautious, he remembered other things that had passed between Rianna and him, things he wished had never happened. Julia's departure had to be for the better. What kind of death would she have suffered to be his companion? he wondered. Without thinking, Teldin reached up and fingered the silver chain that held his cloak. It took time to come back to reality when that period passed.

* * * * *

Writing down the supply list took five tankards of ale, only one of which was Aelfred's. Teldin nodded off as he finished his last ale, and Aelfred walked him back to his cabin. The big warrior left Teldin asleep in his hammock.

Gaye was topside, talking with a deck hand about repairing a broken railing on the main deck. Aelfred motioned her over. They walked back toward the stern castle stairs, where they leaned on the railing and looked together at the flapping gullions and the empty dock to starboard.

"He's taking a rest now," said Aelfred, supporting his weight on his elbows. "Meeting the elves wore him out. Got a lot on his mind."

"I thought he did," said Gaye, chin resting on her folded hands. "He was really tense when we met. We ran around, then he had to see the elves. Is he okay?"

"Ah." Aelfred waved a hand. "Fine. Well, sort of. Our second mate took off, and he was a little down about it. I think he liked her. He's also sort of worried about you."

Gaye blinked. "Oh. I thought he was angry with me."

"Well, he's got this thing about—well, kender. He was afraid you might get into trouble. He says he's known kender who steal things."

Gaye chewed her lower lip. "Some do."

"That's probably it, then," Aelfred said, as if the knowledge solved everything. "Stealing things wouldn't go over well here. It would cause a lot of trouble."

"Yeah." Gaye watched a particularly large gullion wheel in flight nearby, over the docks. "I can understand that."

"That's good." Aelfred suddenly sounded much more cheerful. "Anyway, Teldin should be fine in a few hours. Didn't sleep well before we got here. Too keyed up."

"Can I stay? On the ship, I mean."

Aelfred looked into her wildspace eyes with a crooked grin. "Are you kidding?" He pulled away from the railing. "I owe you a drink. I always buy a new crewmate one free drink." He suddenly stopped and looked directly at Gaye. "Say, forgive me for asking, but just how old are you?"

Gaye looked up at him, thought carefully, then told the truth. "Forty seven."

Aelfred went limp. He stepped back, mouth open. "No."

Gaye gave Aelfred a slow smile. "Yeah. Isn't it incredible?"

"Damn." He stared at her for a long moment, then suddenly began laughing aloud, slapping his thighs. Other crewmen stopped working to stare at him with astonishment. When he could contain himself, he just shook his head. "Come on," he said with a wide grin, motioning her to follow him to the saloon. "You're old enough for a *real* drink."

"I'll be there right after I visit the head," she said brightly. Aelfred waved and headed off to get started.

She put the compass, the three coins, the earring, and the belaying pin back where she had found them—more or less—before she ran down to the saloon.

* * * * *

Getting the supplies from the Imperial Fleet two days later proved to be absurdly simple. Its crew safely aboard and ready for the journey to Ironpiece, the *Probe* slid backward from its

dock, drew away from the end by half the ship's hundred-foot
length, then dropped toward the Rock's invisible gravity plane
only a few more feet below them.

"Turn us over," called Aelfred from the forecastle.

The hammership slowly began to rotate on its long axis, as if
rolling over in a storm. Teldin felt a now-familiar sense of ver-
tigo. His stomach churned, and his palms grew sweaty. Finally,
he looked away from the vast stony bulk of the Rock spread
out before him, letting his stomach settle as he stared out at
the turning stars in the empty blackness of wildspace. That
wasn't so bad. He couldn't help thinking that the Rock was
flipping over, and everyone on it would be crushed.

The elven Imperial Fleet maintained storehouses for its naval ships at the sprawling naval base on the reverse side of the
Rock of Bral. The *Probe* very slowly cruised up the side of a
great rocky face from which dozens of windows and batteries
of ballistae and catapults peered. Up one hundred, three hundred, maybe five hundred feet, the lip of the cliff came into
view. The weapons batteries were numerous, and among them
were many unfamiliar but discomforting weapons. Weapons'
crewmen sullenly watched the *Probe* pass by, hands resting on
crossbows or the release levers of loaded siege engines. There
were even a few huge versions of the smokepowder pistols that
the giff Gomja once had carried with him. Teldin shook off the
depressing memory of Gomja's death, earned by battling
neogi and umber hulks on their own ship when it crashed into
a mountain lake on Krynn.

The *Probe* reached the cliff ledge and rose over it. Ahead
was a flat plain of smooth rock marked in a grid pattern with
huge white stripes and dots. Lights shone from tall poles on
the edges of the plain. Red-brick weapons' towers abounded,
far and near. Teldin saw two wasp ships, each hovering just
twenty feet above the plain about fifty feet away, one to port
and one to starboard.

"We have clearance," sang the lookout. Teldin glanced forward and saw a bright yellow light shining directly ahead from
the base of another great cliff face, perhaps five hundred feet
away. The light was directly over the rightmost one of three
titanic gray doors, each capable of swallowing the *Probe* and a
dozen like it at once.

"Slow ahead," said Aelfred. "Let's take our time."

The *Probe* glided forward over the plain. Teldin now saw that the plain was a sort of naval landing field or dry dock. Huge wood-and-iron doors were set into the rock at various places, for purposes Teldin couldn't begin to guess at. Sealed boxes and short stacks of lumber were visible here and there across the rock flats. Even a few walking figures were visible, but for the most part the field was clear.

The monstrous gray door toward which they glided led into a dark hall illumined by hundreds of lights in its high-vaulted ceiling. Teldin saw a man carrying a box from which a red light suddenly glared toward the *Probe*.

"All stop!" barked Aelfred. The ship groaned slightly as it came to a halt only thirty feet from the hangar doors. A single silver-armored figure, smaller and thinner than an adult man but with a straight-backed bearing that marked him as a military officer, stood next to the doors.

The figure, Teldin realized, was Admiral Cirathorn.

The elf slowly waved in greeting. "Your supplies can be loaded aboard your ship using our portable cranes," he called in a pleasant voice. "All you requested is yours."

"We're grateful to you," Aelfred called back from the forecastle railing. "I'm Aelfred Silverhorn, the captain of this ship. I'm honored to meet you."

"And I, you," Cirathorn returned. "The loading should take less than an hour. I ask that you and your first mate join me for a moment."

Aelfred turned and looked at Teldin, shrugging. "I assume that's if you don't mind," he said.

"I trust you more than I do anyone else," Teldin replied. "It's your ship, and you may as well hear what I hear."

They rode to the ground in one of the ship's boats, where they had the helmsman of the tiny craft wait for them. Cirathorn greeted them with a smile that looked remarkably bloodless in the intense blue-white lights spilling from beyond the hangar door. His eyes were narrowed against the light, but they were friendly enough anyway.

"I hate to be nosy," Aelfred said after they greeted each other, "but how did you manage to get the Rock to let you store Imperial Fleet goods here?

"The prince of this world and city was kind enough to allow the Imperial Fleet to lease a portion of this naval base," Cirathorn said. "We may store supplies, berth our lesser ships, and maintain contact with the numerous elven colonies in this sphere. In return, Prince Andru and his government benefit from our strength. Our presence brings additional trade from elves who would rather land where the fleet lands as well. If there is cause to defend this port, we aid in that defense, though we have little here on the Rock with which to fight. As the prince would say, it's the thought that counts."

"A nice arrangement," agreed Aelfred, "though I've heard a few stories about the prince that weren't too complimentary. Wasn't he involved in some way with his brother's—"

"The wise do not question their allies too deeply," interrupted Cirathorn, as if he were discussing the weather. "None of us is as others see us, and every field bears the seeds of disappointment. Prince Andru is our ally, and a good one he has been—but we have digressed from my reasons for meeting you here."

The admiral untied a leather tube from his belt and passed it to Teldin. "I believe you may find these notes of some help, limited though such may be. They are written in the common tongue of Ansalon, for your ease. This is the sum of our lore about your goal. You will find this material contradictory at best, as most of it consists of second-hand tales told around a tavern fire by those who would know the least about their subject. Nonetheless, you may find a reference or two of use."

Teldin uncapped the tube and noted that it contained many sheets of rolled papers. He recapped the tube and held it tightly rather than tying it to his own belt.

"I don't know how to thank you," Teldin said, looking with relief at the elf's angular face. "I'm afraid I didn't know whether to trust you or not. I've had a difficult time since I picked up this cloak. It's never gotten better."

"Until now, I would hope," Cirathorn said. A smile brightened his pale features. He extended his right hand. Surprised, Teldin took it and gave a cautious but firm handshake. Cirathorn shook Aelfred's hand as well, then stepped back. "I am needed at a long dinner honoring Prince Andru," he said. "I am fashionably late as it is, but it would be best not to keep everyone waiting past the appetizers. Thank you again for honoring us with your presence, Teldin Moore. May the gods watch over your journey."

The two men bid the elf good-bye, then headed back for their boat. They had lifted away for their ship when the admiral reached the hangar doors. The elf turned to look back in silence, noting the billowing of the now maroon-red cloak. He walked on again only after the hammership had been loaded and had begun its slow glide back over the landing field, and the red cloak could no longer be seen.

Cirathorn's walk took him to an unlit supervisor's room. He closed the door behind him, paused in the darkness for a moment, then walked over to a writing desk and opened the lowest drawer on the right. From inside it he pulled out a key. Reaching up, he let his fingers pass along the wall until he found a nail stuck there, then moved up three hand widths from the nail to find a nearly invisible slot in the wall. He inserted the key in this and twisted.

A panel slid soundlessly aside in the wall to reveal a closet-sized room with a faintly glowing circle of amber on the floor. The admiral returned the key, then entered, closing the door behind him, and stepped into the center of the circle with the clinking of mailed boots against the stone floor.

"The embassy," he said, and vanished into thin air.

Moments later, he stopped in the doorway of his office below the embassy structure. A row of elven faces turned. His staff and officers came to their feet.

"It has been ages," he said, "since we last hunted together. Now is the time. Let us hunt."

*　*　*　*　*

The Rock of Bral became a giant potato again, covered with miniature streets and houses. Sunlight glinted from green copper spires and painted rooftops, all slowly receding from the *Probe*'s bow. Gullions slowly whirled and spun over the city, becoming flecks of white against the endless starry night beyond. The potato shrank into the endless night until it was just a bright star, then shrank again until it was lost against the reaches of space.

"Learn anything from those papers the admiral gave you?" Aelfred asked at the end of the first day out, in the privacy of the officer's saloon. The captain was pleased to see that Teldin had taken only a small mug of ale; whatever had bugged him earlier no doubt had passed. It was probably Julia's leaving.

Teldin stared thoughtfully at his mug. He'd had a devil of a time with the scrolls; the writing in many places was beyond his abilities to read, and he was too proud to ask for help. Still, he had gotten the basic idea. Dyffed, the self-proclaimed expert on the *Spelljammer*, had added a few thoughts of his own, but surprisingly little more of use than the papers had given him. The gnome had collected only trivia on the *Spelljammer*, not useful facts.

"The elves wrote down everything they'd ever heard concerning the *Spelljammer*—rumors, tales, lies, everything," Teldin said. "None of it fits together or makes sense. People say the *Spelljammer* has been blown to pieces, smashed into asteroids, driven into suns, and exploded in the phlogiston, but it still reappears, looking like new. It's been commanded by elves, men, goblins, and creatures called orcs, which I assume are like the hobgoblins and goblins we have on Krynn. It's been overrun with mind flayers, undead wizards, and priests, and those things like, um, Graffin the Gray, I think you called him—"

"Beholders," said Aelfred. His smile vanished.

"Beholders." Teldin nodded. "And a few other things that I've never heard of." He hesitated, then reached down and unstrapped the leather tube from his belt and handed it to Aelfred. "You may as well see for yourself. You're just about the last person left alive that I trust, and it's your ship."

Aelfred took the scroll case with a look of surprise, but handed it back. "I'll pass. I have more than enough to read, and you're in this up to your neck. It's better that you keep your eyes on this while I run the ship. What else?"

Teldin took a swallow of his drink first. He'd hoped that Aelfred, who was better at reading, could have told him more. "Lots of other things. Dyffed knew something about it, too. The *Spelljammer* looks like a gigantic manta ray with a city on its back. It moves faster than any ship that size should. It goes wherever it wants. Half the races in wildspace claim to have built it or owned it. Several legends talk about people or monsters who went on quests to command the ship. All of them failed. They missed some key or important bit of information, or they were killed by the creatures living aboard the *Spelljammer* itself. Some say the ship cursed them, and some say the ship ate them. It's all lunacy. It's one of the oldest elements in space mythology, Dyffed says. Of course, it would have to be the very place I have to go to get my life sorted out, assuming that we even make it there."

Aelfred reflected on this. "Are there any races who *don't* have a claim on the *Spelljammer*? Anyone who doesn't really care about it?"

Teldin laughed without humor. "*Everyone* cares about it. The only race that doesn't claim to have built it is the gnomes, but they'd like to take it apart just for fun."

"Ah. Speaking of which, Sylvie caught our little friend Dyffed on the forward bridge," Aelfred said, referring to the half-elven helmsman. "Dyffed was taking measurements of the helm chair and was next planning to take it apart. He had the usual idea to rebuild it better than before. I'm beginning to think that all gnomes on this ship should be locked in the hold until we reach port."

Teldin looked past the broad-shouldered captain, his gaze traveling out the huge window into the star-filled deeps. "Do you know anything about Ironpiece?"

"Sylvie and I looked it up in the books and charts a few hours ago. It's a little world, a few hundred miles across and shaped like a coin. It's an old gnome colony with a naval base, nothing important." His grin returned. "I don't know how I feel about landing there. We may have to fight them off with pikes and knives if they try to get aboard and 'fix' things."

Teldin remembered the Krynnish gnomes of Mount Nevermind, and how one had come up with the idea of removing Teldin's head and keeping it alive in a machine as a prelude to removing his cloak. He genuinely liked gnomes and counted some of them as his friends, but they were still gnomes. "Save a boarding pike for me," he said, a trace of a smile coming back to him.

Aelfred grinned. "That's a good son," he said proudly.

A thought drifted into Teldin's mind. He wondered why he

hadn't thought of it before. "Have you ever heard of anything called a falamath . . . well, a fal?"

Aelfred grunted, looking away at a wall. "Fal. That's the sage the elves wanted you to see, right? I thought 'Fal' was the sage's name."

"No, the sage *is* a fal. It's a race of some sort. The fal's name is a number, One Six Nine."

The two men stared at each other in thought, resting back in their chairs.

"Sylvie might know," Aelfred said at last. "She's studied wildspace a lot more than I have—the book parts, anyway."

"Well, then," said Teldin. He took a last drink from his mug, draining it before he stood up. "Let's ask."

"We could also ask Gaye," Aelfred said. "She seems to have gotten around. Or we could try the gnomes."

"Sylvie it is, then," said Teldin, pointedly ignoring the last suggestion.

Aelfred led the way out of the saloon and down the companionway to the hatch leading down to the cargo deck, where the helm room was. Sylvie had her back to the door when the two men entered. Her slender form was bent over the chart table, a penlike implement and a drafting tool in her hands. Long silver hair spilled over her shoulders down to the map like a woodland waterfall. She wore an outfit she had picked up several worlds back, a sleeveless black blouse with a dark blue pair of billowing pants that looked almost like a dress. She had lost none of her natural grace and beauty.

Teldin sighed and looked away from her at the charts and maps covering the walls. He remembered walking into the chart room before the ship had arrived at the Rock of Bral, as Aelfred and Sylvie had been leaning across one of the maps. Aelfred's hand had rested across the half-elf navigator's shoulders in a way that spoke volumes for a relationship that Teldin realized he had completely missed ever since he had been brought aboard the *Probe*. Despite all of Aelfred's talk about the women he had known and loved, Teldin realized that Aelfred had been quite inactive in seeking the opposite sex for as long as he and Teldin had been friends—which was at least as long as Sylvie had been aboard the ship. Aelfred never spent any time in the chart room unless Sylvie was there, plotting out courses. They were rarely seen together on the ship otherwise, but Teldin knew from his own experience at dating the daughters of local farmers, back on distant Krynn, that not being seen together meant nothing.

Without a word, Aelfred stood behind Sylvie to her right, waiting for her to finish her calculations. She made a rapid series of notes, turned her head, and saw the two of them waiting for her in the doorway.

"What's the matter?" she asked. "Admiring the view?"

Teldin was suddenly aware that he and Aelfred were staring. He flushed with embarrassment and looked away.

"Hey, don't kid yourself, woman," said Aelfred in a mock-cavalier tone. "I've seen millions of better ones. Listen, we were curious if you've ever heard of a being called a fal. You read a lot about wildspace. Anything ring a bell?"

"A what?" Sylvie asked. "A fal?"

"That's the one," said Aelfred. "What about it?"

Sylvie blinked, looking at the two men as if they were small boys who had rushed in to ask what the number five was made of. Her eyes smiled even if her lips didn't. "I haven't the faintest idea," she said. "Is this something you made up? Where'd you hear about it?"

"The elves recommended that we meet a fal to learn more about Teldin's cloak," Aelfred said, his shoulders sinking. "We thought you might know about it."

The pen rotated in Sylvie's fingers. "Why not ask the elves?" she said.

"Well," started Aelfred. "We sort of—"

"I forgot," said Teldin.

The pen stopped, then began to rotate again, more slowly. The navigator nodded at this piece of news. "Well, I'm only part elf, so I'm afraid I can't help you," she said, "but you might ask the gnome, Dyffedionizer. He's an interesting little guy, if you can get him to shut up about irrelevant things. He knows a lot about wildspace. On the other hand, if I catch him taking apart the helm once more, he's going overboard."

Teldin and Aelfred bade their farewells and left Sylvie hunched over her charts. They considered their options in the hallway outside.

"Teldin, I'd sooner stick my head in a beholder's mouth

than ask that gnome anything," Aelfred said. "That will be your project. You're good with gnomes. I'll ask Gaye if she knows anything. That way, we'll split our forces."

Teldin scratched his head, hearing a door open down the hall. "I can't believe I didn't ask the elves when I was there on the Rock. Sylvie must think I'm an idiot, and I am. How could I forget to ask such a simple thing?"

"Ask about what?" came an all-too-familiar voice. Teldin nearly stumbled over the waist-high Dyffed, who had appeared out of nowhere right in his path. The gnome was trying to carry a stack of books down the corridor, but he couldn't see over the top of it. "I might be persuaded to answer a question for you, though my expertise in the medical field is necessarily limited, since I took my graduate degree from Lirak's Cube in spelljamming theory and applications and tested out of the undergraduate courses in biology and anatomy, which were such a bore, as you can imagine, but—"

"No, no, no," Aelfred said, cutting off the gnome and trying to quickly move past him to get to the stairway leading up to the main deck. "Teldin's just trying to figure out what a fal is."

"What? A fal? A falmadaraatha?" called the voice behind the stack of books in excitement. "Oh, well, beyond the usual, I'm afraid I don't know a lot about them, as I missed that course at Lirak's Cube, too, though my colleagues and I at the Ironpiece naval . . . ah, um, yacht club, yes, that was it, yacht club, my colleagues and I used to go off to talk with one of them, old One Six Nine, yes, the one the admiral mentioned when we were at the Rock—a fine old fellow, that One Six Nine—many times in the last six decades. Um, I meant that we'd gone to see him many times in the last six decades, not that One Six Nine has been a fine fellow only within the last six decades, which would be amusing, see, since they do live so long, the fal do, about two hundred decades, give or take a few centuries, of course, and One Six Nine—I believe my colleagues at the naval—I mean *yacht* club—call him 'Thirteen Squared' as sort of an inside joke, you see—anyway, One Six Nine has been a fine fellow for much longer than that." The stack of books turned uncertainly to face a point directly between Teldin and Aelfred, who had stopped short in the companionway. "You did get the joke about 'Thirteen Squared,' didn't you? So many people don't, and that's quite sad, really, but that's what you get when funding for mathematics is cut in favor of things like 'Introductory Troll Slaying' or 'Treasure Appreciation' or some other rot."

"So what is a falama—a fal?" Teldin asked. He already had a mental image of an elflike being with a wrinkled face and a cluttered office, or perhaps a superhuman sage like the cold, all-knowing scribe Astinus, whom Teldin had met once on his homeworld of Krynn.

"Oh! Well, a fal is . . . I say, Teldin, you said you were a farmer once, from Krynnspace, correct?"

Teldin nodded, then realized the gnome couldn't see him through his stack of books. "Yes," he added hastily.

"Well, you've seen garden slugs, true? Little tiny black squishy things that get on your tomatoes and on your boots and have no function in life except to emit slime?"

Aghast, Teldin felt his image of a race of reasonably humanlike sages crumble.

"Well," continued Dyffed jovially, as a book on top of his stack started to slide toward his head, "a fal is pretty much like a slug, except, of course, for having two mouths and sensory antennae and those marvelous eyestalks and a most remarkable petrophagic capability. Bright and pleasant fellows, too, the fal are, especially old One Six Nine. Did I mention that?"

"A slug," said Aelfred. He stared at the gnome as if Dyffed had grown eyestalks himself. "The elves want you to talk to a slug? I guess I've heard stranger things." The way Aelfred said that made it clear that he had never heard anything stranger in his life.

The whole idea was so ludicrous that Teldin found he was unable to grasp it. "How will we keep from stepping on him and smashing him?" he asked, thinking that things could not possibly get to be more unbelievable.

"Step on him? Step on him?" The gnome was suddenly seized by a fit of laughter that was cut short only when the topmost books slid off his stack and struck him on the top of his bald head. The whole stack spilled across the floor immediately after that. Teldin and Aelfred helped the gnome pick up his books, though the gnome had trouble picking them up himself because he was unable to stop laughing.

"My, my, I really am going to have to remember that one. That was very good, just excellent!" Dyffed gasped, wiping away the tears. "When I get to Ironpiece, I'm going straight to Admiral Maxineutonarisprago to tell him, and the old boy will simply rupture himself."

"What's so funny?" Teldin asked, dreading the answer.

"Oh, you know that—no, wait, of course you don't know, you couldn't, which makes it all the funnier, you see, because a fal would just barely fit into the cargo hold on this ship, with no room left over for its luggage, if it had any to carry with it. Not to mention any of our luggage. Stepping on it and smashing it—now, that was quite the funniest thing." The gnome sat on the floor and wiped his eyes again. He occasionally chuckled or shook his head in amazement.

Teldin sat back on his heels. The *Probe*'s cargo hold, he recalled, was about sixty feet long and a quarter of that wide. "A *giant* slug," he said dully.

"I guess it makes as much sense as anything that's happened to us since you came aboard, Teldin," Aelfred said, picking up the last book and setting it on the gnome's stack. He got to his feet and ran a hand through his close-cropped curls. "Well, fine, we eventually have to look for a giant slug. I'm tempted to go back to the saloon and think about this for a while, but I'd never come out again—not under my own power, anyway."

Teldin had nothing to add as he came to his feet. In the months since the reigar's ship had crashed on his house, he had managed with some success to keep his head above water as he learned more and more about the grand design of the cosmos. Once in a while he had to tread water harder than usual. This time, he felt he'd gone under.

"I'll be in my cabin," he said at last. "I've got some reading to do." He started upstairs with Aelfred, leaving the gnome struggling with the stack of books below.

"It could have been worse, old son," said Aelfred sagely, clapping a thick hand on Teldin's shoulder. "The fal could have been another gnome."

Chapter Six

• • •

"Ship ahoy!" rang out a distant cry on the third day. Teldin started awake. He raised his head and blinked, his head encased in thick fog. After a moment, he realized he was seated at the table in his cabin, with Cirathorn's papers on the *Spelljammer* pressed under his folded arms. He had been struggling through the papers for hours, cursing his inability to grasp the meaning of any word longer than six or seven letters, and the frustration and exhaustion had claimed him at last. He rubbed his eyes. He was aware that his clothes smelled of old, stale sweat, and his skin felt grimy. It was long past time to see about washing up and changing clothes.

He heard the bell on the main deck clang loudly, fast and hard. It didn't stop.

"More ships! Low to port, just forward!" came a call from the direction of the forward bridge. Teldin froze, then jumped up from his chair and hastily stuffed the papers back into their scroll tube, sealing it and tying it to his belt with fumbling fingers. He then crossed the room in quick strides and flung the door open. As he ran aft down the companionway toward the door to the main deck, he heard frantic shouting from other crewmen.

"It's a fleet, by the gods!"

"There's a big one, like a pyramid! To the left!"

"Crew on deck! Battle stations!" Aelfred's voice rang out from above, probably from the forecastle near the ballista, as always. "Get the damned lead out!"

"Captain, ten ships! Eleven!"

"Scorpions! Those are scorpion ships!" screamed someone in disbelief. "And viperships!"

Teldin ran onto the main deck and into chaos. Sailors ran for their stations, every face drawn and white with fear. He slammed into a half-elf gunner who was heading for the forecastle ladder, never feeling the pain, then nearly bumped into a waddling Dyffed before he got to the port railing. A solid line of a dozen crewmen was already there, cranking back heavy crossbows and stringing longbows with tight-lipped speed. He looked down over the rail and slightly forward.

A dozen or so specks of light moved against the infinite backdrop of constellations. Two of the specks were especially large; one even had three points, like a triangle. Teldin couldn't imagine how far away they were or how fast they were going, but he could see they were moving in the same direction as the *Probe*. The specks of light were quickly getting larger, too. He could now tell that they were irregular in shape, some of the smaller ones being long and thin.

"Intercept course, Captain!" bawled a sailor from the forward bridge, hidden from Teldin's view. "They'll be ahead of us in a few minutes!"

"Clear the deck and strike the sails!" Aelfred roared out. "Get cover, but prepare to fire when we hit tactical speed! Helmsman!" Aelfred was shouting into a tube that went down to the lower bridge. "Maintain course, all ahead full! They can't turn and catch up if we drive straight through them! We'll run their gauntlet!"

"Almost down, and now this," muttered a crossbowman standing next to Teldin, staring anxiously at the drifting specks of light to port. "I've rarely seen so many ships together in my life. Ptah send us luck with his wisdom."

"Almost down?" Teldin said, not comprehending. He leaned over the railing and looked toward the bow. A huge, bright oval was fixed in space ahead of the hammership. The shape was painted with tans, greens, and blues, and wispy clouds streaked its face. Ironpiece, he thought, maybe named after the Krynnish coin, and he saw with astonishment that the world truly was shaped like a flattened coin seen from an oblique angle. This coin was hundreds of miles across at least. The world was so close that the *Probe* was only an hour or less from landing. He must have missed the approach as he slept.

"More ships behind the first wave!" screamed the lookout. "At least a score more!"

"Teldin!" It was Aelfred. "Get your ass up here!"

Teldin immediately bolted for the stairs up to the forecastle. Aelfred was at the rail, watching the approaching ships with his brass spyglass. His lips pulled back from his teeth in an ugly parody of a smile.

"Know what those are?" Aelfred asked conversationally. He suddenly handed the spyglass to Teldin, who took it and sighted it on one of the irregularly shaped ships below.

It took a moment to find the ship among the star field's distant glory. A yellow-legged thing swam into view, upside down in the glass. Teldin immediately thought of a large insect with a tail coiled over its back.

"A scorpion?" he asked.

"I've never actually seen a scorpion ship before, except in a scrap yard," said Aelfred, "but they used to be everywhere before the Unhuman War. The elves wiped them out—or we thought they had. Orcs used them. See the claws?"

"Yes." Paladine's blood, Teldin thought. The claws on the ship he was watching had moved. The pincers were opening and closing. The scorpion's deck was crowded with figures wearing black leather and holding polished steel.

"If they get hold of us with those things, we can hang it up," Aelfred said. "They'll tear the ship apart. A deathspider's arms have nothing on them."

Aelfred took the spyglass back and took another look. "All the gods be cursed," he said under his breath. "What did we wander into?"

The answer came to Teldin easily. It was perfectly simple. "They want the cloak," he said as he looked down over the railing, hands gripping the wood so hard that it hurt.

"How do you know?" Aelfred demanded, lowering the spyglass. Then he grimaced. "Of course. Everyone else does. Why not the orcs? Why in the Nine Hells not?" Aelfred turned and yelled right at Teldin's face. "*But how did they know it was here?*"

Without waiting for a response, he turned away and shouted to everyone on the ship. "Prepare to fire, on my command!" When he looked back at Teldin, there was no trace of the crooked smile that was his hallmark. "Old son," he said softly, "if you've got a good card in your deck, you'd better play your hand now. We've got one chance to get through their formation when they drop us to tactical speed. I don't know what they'll do with us if they catch us, but I have no intention of finding out. We've got to get down to Ironpiece."

What can I do? Teldin thought in anguish. He looked around and saw a half-crouched crewman beside him raise a heavy crossbow and sight on a ship. "Let me take that," Teldin said, reaching for the weapon. The crossbowman looked surprised but gave up the device without a word.

Teldin raised the heavy weapon and cradled it in his arms, fitting his right hand over the wooden stock and trigger. He looked down the notched metal sights, took a deep breath, and blew the air out of his lungs. Now's the time, he thought, and willed the cloak to use its powers to help him.

On Teldin's first trip into wildspace, he had discovered quite by accident that the cloak could change his perception of time, sharpening his concentration in the process. He had then been able to aim and fire a crossbow with unbelievable accuracy, killing a pirate gunner with but one shot. Would he be able to do anything now?

The oncoming scorpion ship in his sights was only half the size of a small coin held at arm's length. What could he do to stop it? He couldn't even see any creatures on it! He stared at the ship until his eyes watered.

Nothing happened.

Biting down on his fury, Teldin closed his eyes and lowered his head. He then handed the crossbow back to the sailor. He felt Aelfred's eyes burning into him, waiting for some miracle to happen.

"Give me a few minutes," he mumbled in despair.

"We don't have a few minutes, Teldin," Aelfred said quietly. "If you're going to do something to pull us out of this, do it now."

"I don't know what to do!" Teldin screamed, balling his fists and turning to look at the orcish fleet, now closer and farther forward than before. The *Probe* was about to drive directly into them with only a minute remaining.

Aelfred stared at him, white-lipped, then turned away as if Teldin had vanished. "Aim on that scorpion with its back to us, the one just off to port there!" he shouted, pointing. "There's a catapult on its tail! When I tell you, get that and the ballista crew on its back!"

Helpless, Teldin looked over the side to forward. One of the long, thin viperships ahead of them suddenly produced what looked like a glimmering cloud from its stern. The cloud became a hundred tiny flecks of light, expanding as it came on toward the *Probe*.

"Jettison!" yelled someone from the forward castle. "It's dead on—"

Teldin had jerked his head back when he heard the word "jettison." Scarcely a second later, hundreds of rocks, spikes, bolts, and deadly debris slammed into the hammership in a spray. He heard glass shattering and screams from forward. Suddenly he thought of Gaye. Where was she? Terror took hold of him. He didn't know where to look for her.

The deck rocked under his feet at the same moment that the sound of snapping boards and screaming metal rang out. Teldin clutched at the forecastle deck railing. He saw board fragments spin wildly away from the bow.

"Helm down!" someone cried out in a hollow voice over the speaking tube. "We've been hit! The helm is down!"

"Damn it!" Aelfred bolted for the stairs, running crouched, taking the steps three at a time down to the main deck. Teldin ran after him, his mind reeling from the news. How could something have punched through the metal-plated hull that surrounded the lower bridge? It struck him then that Sylvie might be there, in the chart room next to the helm. He felt his chest tighten as he hurried after the captain. The helmsman on this watch would be Garioth, a bearded minor priest that Aelfred had hired two worlds back. Teldin ran from the foot of the stairs, across the main deck, to the forward companionway door, then through it and down the companionway to the stairs. At the bottom, he turned left, then forward to the open door into the lower bridge.

Red-splashed bodies lay on the floor among scattered charts

and books. Part of the port hull was smashed through. Wild-space and stars beckoned through the hole. Aelfred had shoved aside a dead crewman whose green clothing was stained and glistening from a dozen awful wounds across his legs, chest, and face. Another crewman, a white-faced assistant navigator, staggered past Teldin, a foot-long spear of wood sticking out of his left side. An arm hung slack over the arm of the helm, framed in the doorway in which Teldin stood. He couldn't see the priest in the chair, but he saw Aelfred grimace and pull back from the helm, his hands dark with the helmsman's blood.

"Catapult got us. Let's get out of here," Aelfred said, heading for the door again. Teldin stood aside as Aelfred pulled the door shut. The captain then ran back to the main deck. Teldin started after him.

The companionway wall to his right was suddenly flung aside into Teldin's face. Shooting stars filled his vision. There was a roaring sound in his head. He came to lying on his back, numb and disoriented. Someone was screaming far away. He blinked, looking at the paneled wall that hung at an angle over him. For a few moments he gaped at the woodwork that was revealed at the top of the wall. This ship was solidly built, he thought stupidly.

His head began to clear. "Paladine save me," he whispered, trying to get up. He couldn't move because of the pressure on his legs. Looking down, he saw that the door to the galley, which had been to his right, had been blown off its hinges and now lay across his legs with the greater part of the door frame and wall around it still attached. He looked up and saw a gaping hole in the ceiling as well. Beyond the broken timber lay blackness and many stars.

The galley's gone, he thought, the port "eye" of the hammership. Completely gone, and it tore away part of the port side when it left. Far away, men were shouting. Teldin tried to pull himself out from under the door and frame, but his legs were caught and the door had wedged itself into the starboard companionway wall and the door to the helmsman's quarters.

Shivering panic ran through his bones. "Help me!" Teldin called out. "Somebody!" He clawed at the companionway floor for the stairs, where Aelfred had gone. No one was coming.

The floor shook again as a cracking burst sounded from the ship's stern. "Fire away!" he heard Aelfred roar in the distance. "Fire for all you're worth!"

Teldin tried once more to pull out from under the door, but he couldn't move. My cloak, he thought dully. Why doesn't the cloak do something? Why doesn't it help me? Why, why, why? He was feeling tired and overwhelmed. So suddenly, everything was gone, all because of the cloak. How many dead now? How many dead?

The floor rang again. People were yelling about the aft helm. Teldin closed his eyes. I wish, he thought, I wish, by Paladine, that we were out of here.

Time slowed down.

*   *   *   *   *

A warm feeling spread down his back, through his legs, through his arms, into his face. Sharp agony stabbed him in his knees and thighs, then receded. His thoughts were strangely clear and light. Teldin felt a tug, that being the only word he knew for it, and he pulled free of himself.

The next thing he knew, he was hovering over the forecastle ballista. A half-elven gunner gripped the loaded weapon, aiming at a nearby scorpion ship. To Teldin's surprise, Gaye was there, too, the kender ready to crank back the weapon after it fired. There was no sound. Everything had stopped dead.

Teldin looked around, down at the main deck. The bodies of several crewmen lay with their faces turned to the wooden deck or staring open-mouthed at the sky. There was Old Hok, an ex-slave of the neogi, who used to call Teldin "Talon." Near him was a cargo hand, Mamnilla the halfling, who now lay curled around a pool of dark crimson. The survivors stood by the railing, poised to fire their bows and crossbows, their faces set as they looked at their last battle.

Teldin drifted back from the forecastle deck over the ship. It felt perfectly normal to move this way. It was all a dream anyway, wasn't it? The killing had stopped. Nothing would hurt his ship and his friends.

He hadn't thought about it, but he headed for the spare helm room, on the main deck to his right, beneath the stern castle. He looked through the open door and saw a new hole in the port wall, where a ballista bolt had passed through. The bolt was now embedded in the helm, the helm's wood split through where the flat-headed bolt had struck it. Two men were trying to pull the bolt out. Teldin saw that their efforts were wasted. The secondary helm was destroyed.

The *Probe* had no power.

Teldin left the sight and hovered over the stern castle. The star-filled space before the hammership was filled with yellow scorpion ships, green and blue vipership, and even a long, cherry-red squid ship with a ram. All bore insignia and flags of black, on which a fat red spider stood out. To port, Teldin could see another wall of ships lined against the distant stars. A huge stony ship, shaped like a pyramid, hovered perhaps only a quarter of a mile away. The nearest enemy vessel was dead ahead, a vipership perhaps a few hundred feet distant.

The *Probe* could no longer be saved.

So I will have to save it, thought Teldin. It was the most logical thing to do.

Time was going to start up now, he knew (without knowing quite how he knew), so he would have to hurry. I will become the ship, he thought. And he did.

He was now the *Probe*. Painlessly, he felt the great holes and tears in his hull, the shattered wood beams, the missing left eye of the hammerhead shape, the torn-away spanker at the tail. The ship's spine still held, however.

We're getting out of here, Teldin thought. Right *now*.

Time began.

* * * * *

Spiral was lost behind them. Before them was a shattered hammership. The fight was over as quickly as it had started. The admiral had wasted his time in bringing all that smoke-powder, General Vorr reflected. But it was just as well. The old scro was entirely too fond of the stuff.

"Prepare for boarding!" Vorr shouted to his scro marines. The *Venomous Hullcatcher* would be the first marine vessel to reach the hammership, but Vorr's ship would be close behind it. Vorr would have preferred the first boarding go to a more experienced crew on another scorpion ship, particularly the *Eyecutter*, but the scro of the *Venomous Hullcatcher* could use the experience, and it was, after all, the closest marine ship. If the crew on the vipership *Hellfang* held back on its jettison fire, the operation would be over within a matter of two or three minutes.

The whole thing was rather a waste of time, Vorr thought, given the way the hammership was so overwhelmed. He should have taken out just six ships at most, maybe four, and made it a challenge. He still wondered how the false lich was able to know that the cloak-wearing human had taken a ship to Ironpiece from the Rock of Bral. He'd have to check the lich's equipment over after he killed it; maybe Usso would get a present out of it.

"The pyramid is signaling, sir," the scro at his right elbow observed. General Vorr looked across the black gulf to the lich's pyramidal spelljammer. Bright light flashed out from each of the four corners of the pyramid, spelling out a short message in scro pulse code. The lich—or whatever that skeletal, robed thing was—had been remarkably efficient at installing the magical lights and at learning basic scro codes. The undead thing had admitted to being quite taken with this method of communication; it gave the lich ideas, the lich had said.

"The commander of the pyramid asks you to cease fire, to prevent harm to the cloak," the scro read.

Vorr nodded, having seen the same message. "Signal to him that we are about to board," the general muttered. "We will cease fire." He looked back at the ruined hammership and again thought about the joy he would have, wrapping his thick fingers around the lich-thing's skull and shattering it into a thousand—

The hammership moved. Rather, it shot forward so fast that Vorr could barely follow it. He saw its bow slice through the upper deck of the vipership ahead of it, then its mast smash against the lower hull of a scorpion ship farther ahead, splitting the scorpion almost in two. The hammership's main mast snapped off only ten feet above its forecastle deck, the pole carried away in the collision. Then the hammership was through the whole formation and was fading from sight on a course dead-set for the flat world of Ironpiece.

Vorr simply stared. Precious seconds slipped by before he regained his thoughts and voice.

"Go after it!" he roared. "Signal all ships! Get that damned hammership!"

The scro at his elbow grabbed at the signaling switch on the railing before him and prepared to knock out the message, but he was distracted by the flashing of another ship's lights, from the hammership *Chain Master* just to starboard. The scro read the message, then spun around and looked up and aft.

"Armada, by Dukagsh!" he yelled, pointing. "Elves!"

Vorr turned, eyes wide. From out of nowhere, out of nothing at all, a titanic orange butterfly had appeared. It was right behind Admiral Halker's elephant-faced flagship, an ogre mammoth called the *Thundertusk*, easily within weapons' reach. This the gigantic elven ship proved by opening fire at point-blank range, above and aft of its huge, oval target.

Fireballs and lightning bolts exploded across the *Thundertusk*'s upper deck. Vorr saw ogres and scro hurled like cornhusk dolls into space from the mammoth's back, their black armor aflame. Shattered and burning planking burst in all directions, backlit by a stupendous fireball that punched into the rear of the reconditioned mammoth like a god's sledgehammer. A flaming wood-and-metal shield, a section of the mammoth's starboard ear, was thrown whirling into space.

"All units! Attack!" Vorr shouted at the top of his lungs. The admiral would have to save himself, if saving he needed. The scro hastily flashed Vorr's message as his own ship's catapults came to life, flinging two-ton loads of stone up at the gigantic wings of the elven warship above them. The first shots were off, but the gunners were already adjusting the sighting.

By the Tomb of Dukagsh, this was a fight! the general thought with a mixture of shock and excitement. An armada, an elven capital ship! But how could it have just appeared there? Were the rumors of cloaking devices on elven ships true? Could the elves hide entire battleships right up to the moment of attack?

"We'll know soon enough, when we peel your skin off," the

general said aloud. The scro next to him wisely said nothing. "It shouldn't take long. Twenty-seven ships to one seems fair enough to me." Vorr smiled.

At that moment, he saw a second elven ship, a man-o-war, appear out of nowhere and open fire on a vipership. The smaller vessel immediately burst apart in flames, its back broken.

Another man-o-war then appeared and went for its prey. Then a third and a fourth one came out of nowhere.

Ten minutes later, the gnomes arrived and shot at everyone.

* * * * *

Teldin wondered when the dream would end. He felt very warm and light-headed. He still couldn't move his legs, but they felt fine now. Numb, but fine.

In one way, Teldin could still see the companionway around him, with the buckled port wall and the hole in the ceiling where the galley had been. In another way, he was looking ahead of the *Probe*, as if he were still hovering above it like a guardian spirit. The curve of Ironpiece's distant edge now filled the forward view. The near edge of the world was below them and falling sternward rapidly. The ship was going right where Teldin wanted it: down to the ground.

I need a lake, he thought, as he watched one pass far beneath the ship. The *Probe* has to land in water. There must be water ahead somewhere.

"Teldin."

Teldin wasn't surprised. He had vaguely noticed Aelfred coming down the stairs from the main deck. Aelfred was followed by Sylvie, who had a torn strip of cloth wound around her bloodied head. It was a strip from Aelfred's shirt, he noticed. Aelfred seemed uninjured.

"Teldin, what are you doing?" Aelfred appeared to be afraid to get any closer than the bottom step. He was just a few feet from Teldin's outstretched left arm. He spoke very quietly but clearly, like a child, staring at Teldin's cloak.

How odd, Teldin thought. My cloak is glowing. It's pink, like a sunrise.

Teldin licked his lips. The dream still held. "I'm saving the ship," he said in a barely audible voice. He tried to clear his throat. "We're going to Ironpiece."

Aelfred looked around the corridor. "How? We don't have a helm, Teldin. Both of the helms were destroyed." His voice was different, as if he were afraid of something. Maybe it was the cloak, the way it was glowing.

"I know about the helms," Teldin said. He tried to think of how to explain it, but couldn't. "Don't worry about it, Aelfred. I won't let us get hurt."

Aelfred knelt down, looking over the bright-pink glow of the cloak and the door covering Teldin's legs. Sylvie stood back, her eyes as large and round as plates. Aelfred was sweating, though it wasn't very warm in the hallway.

"Should I move this?" the big warrior asked. "Can you move your legs?"

"No, and no," Teldin gasped. "Oh, there's water."

"What?" Aelfred was confused. He looked up and around, trying to follow Teldin's blank gaze.

"Water," said Teldin. "We're going to land soon, very soon. There's a city on the far end of the lake. Get the crew ready."

"What about you?" Sylvie asked, her voice strained.

"I'm fine," said Teldin, though he thought he might be mistaken. He felt nothing in his legs. "Get the crew ready. We're coming down."

Aelfred got to his feet. His face was as white as a ghost's. A low, throbbing sound was starting to build through the ship. Aelfred recognized it as the sound of atmospheric reentry. With one backward look, he started up the stairs, catching Sylvie by the arm and pulling her after him.

It was easier to concentrate now that Teldin was alone. He became aware of the loud, throbbing howl building all around the ship. The decks were filled with men and women, all trying to get firm holds on the railings or bracing their backs against forward walls. Teldin could see light playing in through the ruined ceiling, a dark blue sky forming all around as the hammership fell through the air of Ironpiece. He watched the long, narrow lake ahead of the ship grow slowly. Clouds flew past. The pink of his cloak grew brighter. The ear-blasting howl was shaking the whole ship. Treetops and dirt roads raced by below; now they weren't so far away. The near edge of the lake grew wider. Down a bit. A bit more. To starboard. Down more. Down. Starboard.

Waves were visible on the lake, marching in perfect order. The wind howled in a fury all around the *Probe*, blasting down the ruined corridor from the ceiling and whipping Teldin's face. He felt nothing but warmth. He was bringing the hammership down to safety. His friends would be fine. The marching waves were coming up now. Closer. Closer. Closer. He was at peace. A hundred feet.

Fifty. Now—

The *Probe* struck the lake's surface with a thunderclap and skipped upward. Everyone on the decks screamed and clutched at railings and each other, momentarily weightless. Teldin barely heard them over the crash of the landing. The hammership dropped back and the thunderclap sounded again, nearly shattering the hull. The ship skipped up again, traveling at incredible speed. *I need to slow it down,* Teldin thought. *We're going too fast.* The ship slowed at once, fell and struck the water with a terrible sound, and everything slammed forward toward the bow, including Teldin and the door frame on his legs. Teldin could not hear the screams over the explosion of water against the hull, the shaking and battering as the ship sliced through the waves. Then cold water poured down through the ceiling in a torrent. Teldin choked, and the dream ended, and he screamed and screamed as the water rose all around him until it covered his head.

* * * * *

"It's down!" boomed the security commander, watching from the shore. He swung his huge bulk to his left and pointed. "Squadron Twelve, fire your engines!"

Gnome pilots pulled down their goggles, flipped the starter switches on their machines, and grabbed for the leather-covered steering levers that stuck up in front of their belted seats. One by one, the giant steam-powered fans mounted in the back of each wide, flat boat thundered to life. The security commander quickly found his seat on his own boat, especially built to accommodate his immense size, and leaned toward the pilot. "Take us out!" he yelled.

The gnome pilot tugged on a cord, and an ear-splitting whistle sounded from the rear of the boat. The fan-powered vehicle lurched forward, then picked up speed as it crossed the lake's surface. The security commander fidgeted, realizing that his seat was less solid than he had hoped. It might not even be bolted down; perhaps his own weight alone kept him in place. He'd have the maintenance teams out in droves on every ship after this run, he promised himself.

His gnome pilot was waving an arm over his head. The security commander looked up and saw that the hammership had slowed but was starting to list to starboard. It had been badly damaged in some space battle. It was a miracle that it was even here at all. The forward helm room appeared to have been holed, and the port hammerhead eye was gone, ripped completely off. Human men and women were leaping into the water now, clutching at boards and debris, waving their arms wildly for rescue.

The fan boat crossed the wake from the ship's crash, slamming through the waves with several bone-jarring jolts. When the fan boat was close enough, the commander reached forward and poked the pilot hard in the back. The pilot immediately flipped the engine switch and cut the fan's power. Now, the commander could hear the voices of the hammership's crew crying out for help. He was close enough to read the ship's nameplate, too—the *Probe*.

Other fan boats behind the lead one were cutting their engines now. Gnomes were hurling every sort of buoyant object on their fan boats' decks into the midst of the swimming humans. Some humans were badly wounded and were being pulled from the water, screaming in agony. As the lead fan boat rounded the port side of the hammership, the crashed ship settled down into the water. The commander noticed one more survivor clamber out of the huge hole in the upper hull where the hammership's port "eye" had been, a man in soaking rags who could not use his legs. Exhausted, the man fell forward into the water—and disappeared.

"That way!" shouted the commander to his pilot. "Get that man!" The pilot snatched an oar and maneuvered the boat around until it was next to the man's floating, face-down body. With one movement, the commander reached down and dragged the human on deck, almost losing his seating and falling overboard himself in the process.

The commander carefully rolled the man over to see if he still breathed. He did, coughing immediately on the water he'd inhaled. "Lucky devil!" said the commander, wreathed in smiles and gently shaking the survivor. "Another few seconds, and you'd . . . you'd . . ."

Still coughing, the man squinted up into the commander's blue, wide-eyed, hippopotamus face, and the latter gasped.

"By the Great Captain's blunderbuss!" bellowed First Colonel-Commander Herphan Gomja, Commander in Chief of Base Security, Port Walkaway, Ironpiece. "You're Teldin Moore!"

Chapter Seven

• • •

"The helmsman on the *Unicorn's Wing* has ceased to speak with us, my admiral," said the battlewizard. Her hands dropped from the crystal globe in her lap. Her face was streaked with tears, but her voice was calm and even. "I fear the smoke and flames have overcome her."

Admiral Cirathorn said nothing. He stared out the broad, high windows of the *Empress Dorianne*'s bridge at the yellow and red fires in the distance. He could see the *Unicorn's Wing* ablaze now, about two miles distant and receding swiftly. It was moot whether anyone else had survived the close assault the humanoids had staged against the man-o-war. The gnomes had arrived just as the *Wing* was being boarded; its captain apparently had mistaken the gnomes for more humanoids and had ordered his gunners to fire on them as well. It proved to be a costly error. One of the gnomish vessels caught fire, but three others unleashed their weapons at the man-o-war and humanoid ships, damaging everything in view—including, if reports were to be believed, one of their own ships.

That had been only a small slice of the action. The battle, all told, had taken about four hours. The most severe fighting had come in the first hour, when the elves sighted and recognized the fleet before them as humanoid in nature, then crept in for the first strike. This was followed by cat-and-mouse games played out by vengeful, blood-hungry elven and humanoid captains. Cirathorn had secretly hoped that Teldin would require rescue, placing him and his cloak with the Imperial Fleet, but that had proved unnecessary. If there were any winners, it would be the gnomes, who had driven all others away from their world.

A distant star of yellow and white bloomed among the almost-invisible wrecks. A few moments later, the star grew in ragged brightness, then grew larger again. One of the humanoid ships had blown up. It must have been the ogre mammoth, the one to which the marines from the *Dorianne* had teleported. A good move, that, to decapitate the ship's command and helm with one strike, just before decloaking and setting the mammoth ablaze. Orcs and ogres had crewed the mammoth's bridge, fighting surprisingly well for otherwise slow-witted scum.

"What word do we have of the *Probe*?" Cirathorn asked, still peering out the windows.

The battlewizard answered promptly. "It has either landed or crashed on Ironpiece by now, my admiral. It appeared to have been damaged by the initial assault before it pulled away. It was traveling at five times the basic speed a spelljammer can attain when it left."

Cirathorn hid his surprise. "Did you observe any activity aboard the *Probe* that would account for its speed?"

"No, my admiral. Its flight was completely unexpected."

The admiral stared out the windows in silence. The exploding vessel had come apart in a thousand pieces. The air envelope around the remainder of the hull was visible as an expanding gray smudge against the endless stars.

Teldin had used the cloak to help the *Probe* escape from the humanoids. Cirathorn knew this for a fact. Only the cloak might have the power to serve as its own helm, and so powerful a helm at that. Perhaps it had even overridden an active helm. It would hardly surprise the admiral now to hear it. The Cloak of the First Pilot was said to have been an artifact, after all.

What was there to do now? The humanoid fleet was massing again in a position trailing Ironpiece by about five to six million miles. Did the humanoids have reinforcements following them? Where had they come from originally? Was this the start of the long-rumored and long-feared second Unhuman War? Were the humanoids allied with the undead, given that a pyramid ship—long known to be an abode for mummies, liches, and other perversions—traveled in their fleet with them?

There were other awful possibilities. Did the humanoids have a base in this sphere? The battlewizards said the humanoids were largely made up of powerful-looking orcs who appeared to have been recently armed and supplied. Could the orcs have invaded and conquered a nearby elven world? They reportedly had an elven wizard on the ogre mammoth's death helm, who had to be slain in his madness by the *Dorianne*'s marines. The death helm warped the mind and spirit of its doomed helmsman, causing him to fight all attempts at rescue while it drained its victim's life force. The helm was a perversion that only humanoids would cherish; its possession by any being in civilized space was normally punishable by death.

There were many small colony worlds here, not a few of them elven, and most were widely scattered or socially isolated. Some elven worlds had been settled by renegades, officers cashiered from the Imperial Fleet for disobeying orders or causing trouble, and these worlds did not welcome any contact with the Imperial Fleet as yet. Had pride led a small elven world like Numeliador, Spiral, or Minial's Arch to turn down a chance to call for help to the fleet's forces at the Rock of Bral?

If the answer to the last question had been yes, then it had been a foolish, if not suicidal, error. Four elven man-o-wars and an armada had invisibly trailed the Rock of Bral for the last two years, their presence permitted by the Rock's bribe-hungry Prince Andru. One man-o-war was an odds-on favorite in most ship-to-ship battles; four could strike genuine terror into the commander of a small space fleet. An armada was avoided by all but the most desperate of warriors. The force could have turned the tide of an invasion and spared another world the fate of lost Aerlofalyn. That an elven world would be conquered in Cirathorn's own assigned sphere without his knowing of it—the thought was devastating.

The elves had taken no prisoners in this fight, there being so little time and coordination of efforts among the elven ship captains, but the orcs and their allies could have taken several prisoners during their boarding and firing of the *Unicorn's Wing*. Intelligence on the humanoids was thus minimal, though the battlewizards were working on the problem. Further reconnaissance of the sphere would have to be undertaken, meaning the fleet's presence here would have to be reinforced. Any delay could spell doom for the other colonies. Cirathorn was an elf, and he knew well how the Imperial Fleet worked. If this sphere had any salvation, he alone was that salvation for the foreseeable future.

He had only three man-o-wars left now, two of them—the *Free Wind's Fury* and the *Leaping Hart*—with minor damage, and they had the apparent hatred of the gnomes of Ironpiece. As inconsequential as they were in the grand scheme of things, the gnomes certainly had their usefulness. It was a poor start.

Nonetheless, the elves had an armada, nearly undamaged. They had cloaking helms. They had magical weapons and superlative wizardry, though the pyramid's master might prove itself an equal if it were an undead monstrosity. The elves had punished the orcs badly in the first round, killing their capital ship.

The elves also had the report of the helmsman and wizard Vallus Leafbower, made to the Imperial Fleet at Evermeet, on Toril. That report on Teldin Moore and his cloak was worth at least as much as any other advantage.

"Mirandel," said the admiral, turning and walking from the windows to the battlewizard's chair. The battlewizard's eyes were drying, her mourning for her sister's death at the *Unicorn's Wing*'s helm set aside for now. The admiral reached for the heavy crystal ball in her hands, and she carefully gave it to him. He raised the globe and studied its depths. He had used one of these once.

"I cannot use the crystal again this day, my admiral," the battlewizard said. Her green eyes were framed by her long white hair. "Contact with the other ships during the battle has exhausted my talent for now."

"I did not mean for you to use it," said the admiral, walking away with the ball. "I mean to use it instead." He picked up a stool, then returned and placed it a few feet from the battlewizard, sitting so as to face her. He looked into the crystal ball with a thoughtful gaze.

"I am about to reveal some things to you that have been kept secret by the Imperial Fleet for some weeks now," the admiral began. He looked up from the globe and at his battlewizard, who sat in expectant silence. "You are aware that I have developed an interest in a human named Teldin Moore, who arrived on the Rock a few days ago on the hammership we were trailing. You were present when I spoke of the history of his cloak and gave him directions to Ironpiece and places beyond to aid his search for the *Spelljammer*. I believe our battle has proven that there are others who are also interested in the cloak of Teldin Moore, and those forces are as dangerous as any we could hope to meet."

"My admiral," interrupted Mirandel. "Is it not possible that the humanoids were already on their way to attack Ironpiece, and we were merely in their way?"

"No. The humanoid fleet has neither transports nor landing craft for armies. There are few worlds known to be inhabited by orcs or other lower humanoids in this sphere, and none of them have achieved spelljamming ability. The humanoid fleet originated from outside this sphere, but it is probably supplied from a base within. Its presence on an intercept course with the hammership *Probe* could not have been coincidence." Cirathorn smiled. "I cannot believe that more than two dozen humanoid ships would waylay a hammership out of a sense of common piracy. I cannot prove it, but I believe they were after Teldin's cloak, too."

"How can you be sure, my admiral?"

"The cloak is valuable to many others already," said the admiral, looking down at the heavy globe again. "The lying neogi, several groups of pirates, and the mind flayers of the world Falx also seek this cloak. If some reports are to be believed, perhaps even the arrogant reigar are seeking it. All such forces have been able to locate the cloak, through either spies or some other means." He gently tapped the crystal ball with a fingernail. "This is the means."

The battlewizard frowned and appeared confused. "My admiral, if seeking the cloak were merely a matter of looking into a crystal ball, I would think the cloak would have been discovered many centuries ago."

"I agree, but there was one element missing. The key was

discovered by an elven wizard named Vallus Leafbower, who was once the helmsman of the *Probe* before it landed on Toril. Vallus had once been allowed to touch and examine the cloak. With the assistance of another elven wizard in the city of Rauthaven, he found that, after scrying for the cloak in a magical mirror, he was able to find it and its wearer with ease, without the need for a spell or device. The key was to touch the cloak before divining its location with magic. Some connection is made by the touching, and it lasts beyond normal magical limits once the scrying contact has been made. Vallus knew, without failure, where Teldin Moore was at any time, and he was even able to track the man while he was disguised by the powers of the cloak. Vallus delivered a warning to Teldin to go to Evermeet and speak with the Imperial Fleet there. Teldin Moore chose to ignore that advice, instead fleeing into wildspace."

Cirathorn looked at Mirandel with cold eyes. "I do not know if scrying upon the cloak involves any sort of risk. Vallus Leafbower's discovery was felt to be important enough to deliver to as many Imperial Fleet regions as possible, using every sort of spell and ship available. The admirals of every sphere were warned to look for a human of Teldin's description, one who always wore either a cloak or a silver necklace. If Teldin should appear, and if his story matched in some part the events that Teldin Moore related to us at that dinner, then we were to give him every assistance to his goal, with the encouragement to allow the Imperial Fleet to transport and protect him.

"You recall that some weeks ago I warned you and the rest of the staff to look for such a person. The sentry at the embassy door had explicit instructions to admit anyone who answered to this human's description and asked for the assistance of the fleet. I took a chance that if Teldin Moore were to appear on the Rock of Bral, he would come without disguise and would be in need enough to give us his trust. The gods blessed us, and that is why we are here now."

The battlewizard licked her bloodless lips. "Is it the will of the gods, or merely your own, my admiral?"

The admiral gave her a faint smile. "Am I so transparent, my eyes like windows to your own? I do want that cloak, though I will not stoop to bloodshed to obtain it. Surely you know of the old poems, Mirandel, of the Cloak of the First Pilot, and the legends of the *Spelljammer*. Why do you think I want the cloak?"

She swallowed. "Power," she said quietly.

"Exactly," said the admiral. "The cloak grants control over the *Spelljammer*—the largest, most powerful, and most dangerous ship in existence, a ship that some legends say once belonged to our people, Mirandel. A ship against which no evil could stand. A ship with which we could bring the Imperial Fleet's rule to all worlds in all spheres."

The woman's face was very pale. "My admiral," she said in a small voice. "There are tales of the *Spelljammer*, which you must have heard as well, of the curse it casts over all who try to take it, and the evil that befalls those who even see it."

"We have already fallen into evil times," the admiral said bluntly. "We will have worse times to come. The neogi have almost certainly handled the cloak in the recent past, as so many of their ships are now following the cloakbearer's trail. The mind flayers are probably using spies. Some neogi may have been captured by other forces and are being forced to lead their new masters to this ultimate treasure. Vallus Leafbower reported that pirates off Krynn were able to locate the gnomish sidewheeler on which Teldin traveled, and no one knows how they were able to find him. Now, with these humanoids, we will face enemies beyond counting, foes who have many reasons to hate us just because we are elves. I assume they are on Teldin's trail, too."

The admiral looked into the green eyes of his battlewizard. "We could turn away from Teldin Moore and his cloak," he said. "Our people have always been willful and have done as they pleased. We could save ourselves and say the Imperial Fleet be damned, and only I would suffer for it, and perhaps not even then. Who could say?"

"You read my thoughts clearly, my admiral," said the battlewizard softly.

Cirathorn smiled more broadly. "I know you, my wizard. I know and understand what you think of this, but I cannot be turned away from the hunt now. When Teldin Moore falls, we must be there to snatch up his body and his cloak, and spirit both away from all other takers. We face destruction without salvation from a growing pool of foes, but the bright prize beckons to me. The *Spelljammer* is power, but it is the power to save as well as to destroy."

Cirathorn reached out a hand, resting the crystal ball in the other one, and took hold of the battlewizard's cold fingers. "Mirandel, you stood with me over the grassy graves of all my ancestors on Aerlofalyn. You heard me swear to the stars and the gods and the spirits of all our people that this would be the end, that I would not permit this to befall us were it in my power. You swore with me that you would aid me on this quest, to the ends of our lives. Will you aid me now?"

"Yes, my husband," said the battlewizard, with only the slightest pause. Her hand did not tremble. Cirathorn noticed this and was pleased.

"You are my strength," said the admiral. He released her cold hand and looked down at the crystal ball. "If Vallus Leafbower is to be believed, then I should be able to find Teldin Moore, across all spheres, and we shall bring to the Imperial Fleet the very strength that it now needs so badly."

The admiral stared into the crystal ball. Within moments the glass darkened until it was of the deepest black that either had ever seen. The ball cleared again with amazing rapidity— and Teldin and his surroundings appeared. For several minutes, the two elves watched a scene unfold.

"I know of that one," whispered Mirandel suddenly. She pointed a delicate finger at the ball and tapped the glass. Even as she did so, she knew she had genuinely cast her lot with her husband, and she would share his fate, for good or ill. So be it. She took a deep breath. "I have a plan, my admiral."

* * * * *

The scro looked out into the starry darkness over Vorr's head. "Sir, we've lost the mammoth flagship, three scorpions, two vipers, and two wasps. The remaining ships have varying damage but are able to move on their own. The other ships are pulling survivors, including Admiral Halker, from the wrecks and will rendezvous in two hours with the pyramid, just that way, sir." The scro pointed over the general's shoulder to a distant, flashing light. "The pyramid appears to have been only lightly damaged."

"And the enemy?" Part of the general's question was answered as he saw a distant burning object like a great butterfly, low to port and toward the stern.

The scro stood a little more erect. "We got one of the man-o-wars, sir. No prisoners were taken. We have a confirmed kill on a gnomish sidewheeler and six of their little one-crew spellfighters, with up to a half-dozen more assorted craft as possible kills. The elves may have hit more. The armada and two of the remaining man-o-wars appeared to be lightly damaged when they disappeared again. I believe cloaking devices are in use aboard them."

Vorr grunted. "I want a round-the-clock watch out, looking in all directions," he said briskly. "All ships' weapons are to be cocked and loaded. Send the same to all ships. The moment you see an elven ship, fire at it. A full rank with pay to the first one who hits an elven ship; an officer's commission or two officer ranks to the first one who sets foot on it. We're going to redecorate our ships with elf heads."

"Sir!" The scro's face was outwardly stonelike, but his voice betrayed his joy. He gave the general the fist-up salute. "Death to the elves!" he shouted in Elvish, his voice full of battle glee.

"Death to them all," the general agreed. He made his words a promise.

"Sir?" called the captain, as Vorr was heading through the main deck door to his cabin. Vorr turned, and the captain saluted and went on. "The pyramid ship is signaling again. Skarkesh says he has located Teldin Moore on Ironpiece."

Chapter Eight

• • •

"You can't imagine what went through my mind, sir," said Gomja, seated at the foot of Teldin's polka-dot-sheeted bed. "When I pulled you out of the water, I thought that you looked familiar, but I couldn't believe it until I rolled you over. Then . . ." The giff's voice trailed off, and he sighed with happiness. "You just can't imagine, sir."

In the afternoon sunlight pouring through the infirmary window, Teldin could see tears of joy still running down the giff's wide cheeks from his tiny black eyes. This was only the fifth time Gomja was repeating the tale of his reaction to rescuing his old friend, but Teldin was too weary to care, and the bed was too comfortable to make protesting worthwhile.

No one else was present in the little white room. The single window opened out to show a forest-covered slope and the lake beyond—Lake Crashsplash, the gnomes called it, with painful appropriateness. If Teldin turned his head, he could see part of the lakeshore but nothing of the sunken *Probe*. The lake was quite shallow, only twelve feet deep where the hammership had gone down, and he'd been told earlier that gnome salvage crews were already at work trying to refloat it and transport it to the dry dock at the wildspace naval base bordering the lake. Whether there was anything worth repairing would be determined there. The helms were just so much firewood now. As for the rest of the ship—he wasn't sure it was worth much more.

Teldin blinked, focusing on the huge, happy giff. Gomja hadn't changed much in the half year or so since Teldin had last seen him. He was still a seven-foot-tall, broad-shouldered blue-gray hippopotamus—a manlike hippopotamus, at that. Gomja had put on more muscle, which Teldin found difficult to believe. The giff's bright red uniform, covered as it was with gold trim, tassels, and an assortment of medals across his chest, did nothing to hide his oxlike strength. As Gomja wiped at his small black eyes, now red-rimmed and watery, great cords of muscle stood out on his biceps and forearms.

Nevertheless, Gomja's huge flared nostrils were running and his chest shook as he breathed. This was the first meeting the gnome healers had allowed between the two since a water-logged and exhausted Teldin had been brought to the infirmary two days ago. The giff was still in shock.

"Gomja," Teldin said. His voice sounded scratchy and rough. "I doubt that you could imagine what went through my mind when you pulled me out either." No words were ever truer, he thought. He still wasn't sure he believed anything at all that had happened since he had awakened aboard the *Probe.*

Feeling for something in a side pocket in his uniform, Gomja gave up and pulled a large, ragged towel from a table near the foot of Teldin's bed. The giff noisily honked into the towel, wiped his nose, then carefully folded the towel and placed it back where he found it. "I've been embarrassing myself, sir," he said apologetically. "I'm not usually like this, you'll recall, but you just can't imagine what went—"

"Gomja, I know. Look, just tell me how in the name of the Dark Queen you got here."

"Oh, of course, sir." The giff sniffed and perked up a bit. His shoulders straightened as he spoke. "Well, as you remember, sir, my first platoon and I had some trouble with that neogi deathspider over Mount Nevermind."

"Trouble?" Teldin gave the giff an incredulous look. "The last I saw of you, the deathspider crashed in flames into the lake on the mountaintop. I thought you were . . . well, gone."

"Frankly, sir, I didn't think I was going to be around very long myself. My platoon and I had fought our way into the bridge, where we disposed of the neogi and their lordservants—the umber hulks—and broke their command. We couldn't do anything right away for the poor soul in the lifejammer helm"—Gomja grimaced, remembering—"as we couldn't move him without crashing the ship."

"Which you did anyway," Teldin mumbled. On seeing the stricken look on Gomja's face, he hastily added, "Bad joke. Just forget it. Go on."

Gomja nodded somberly, then his chest swelled. "Well, we broke out into the corridor leading to the rest of the ship, and my platoon was doing an excellent job of driving back the slaves the neogi were sending toward us, when an umber hulk came right through the enemy's ranks with a little present for us: a cask of smokepowder with a burning fuse. It would have been sufficient to stop our advance dead, as they say, if I had not taken the liberty of removing the cask from the beast's claws first and tossing it behind us into the bridge. I tried to shut the door and block it, but the umber hulk had my attention by then, and the explosion knocked all of us down, friend and foe alike. I'm afraid the poor soul in the lifejammer had no way to escape. The ship lost power, and we went down. We braced ourselves as well as we could, and most of my platoon made it out. The deathspider didn't sink right away, luckily for us. Gnomes from the shore got to us rather quickly, all said and done. I even had a tattoo placed on my chest to commemorate the victory."

Gomja retrieved the towel, vigorously blew his huge nose once more, then replaced the towel as before. Except for the red circles around his eyes, he now looked quite buoyant. "The best part of it all, sir, was that the gnomes were able to retrieve the helm from the deathspider and modify it. We also took several neogi prisoners, though I'm afraid they didn't last long in the gnomes' hands. Research committees in the Healers', Zoologists', and Military guilds wanted to examine them, and the results were quite ghastly. The umber hulks, those that hadn't drowned, had to be slain, except for one that went to a research committee." Gomja shivered. "Many of the neogi's prisoners were freed, though they had no idea of what to do with themselves. I believe they were turned over to the local human authorities for care."

"This still doesn't tell me how you came to be here," Teldin reminded him.

"Sorry, sir. Anyway, the neogi helm was repaired and revamped, and a new spelljammer was built, a galleon-type based on a merchant sailing ship that the gnomes had on hand for some reason. I was offered a chance to ride the ship into space, though some of the gnomes wanted me to remain on Mount Nevermind as director of the Military Guild. I felt it the wiser course to, um—" Gomja lowered his voice, glancing briefly toward the open window "—to seek gainful employment elsewhere, if you understand my drift, sir." Teldin nodded knowingly.

"So we took off," Gomja went on, "and over the next few weeks we consumed a great deal of time fighting pirates and a rather nasty squid ship full of zombies. I earned three more tattoos as a result. I tried to get work with the elven Imperial Fleet, but without success. Eventually, we were directed here by a gnomish sidewheeler-trader, and here we, ah, landed. In fact, our landing was not unlike yours and was in nearly the same spot. The gnomes even renamed the lake on account of us. It used to be called 'The Big Lake.'" Gomja grinned, his ears straight up and his thick, blunt teeth showing.

Teldin shook his head in amazement. It was still too much to believe. "When I saw you last," he said, remembering their parting, "you were Sergeant Gomja. I heard one of the gnomes outside call you colonel-captain something-or-other."

The giff sat fully upright in his heavy wooden chair, his great chest swelling and stretching the fabric of his red uniform to new dimensions. "I am now First Colonel-Commander Herphan Gomja, Commander in Chief of Base Security, Naval Port Walkaway, Ironpiece. My sire would be proud of me if he knew. I am but seventeen years of age, a youth in the eyes of many, but I now have six hundred seventy gnomes, twenty-two humans, and fifty individuals of other races as my subordinates. No other giff in my memory has gained such a command so early." For a moment, his blue face glowed as he spoke.

Teldin tried to suppress a grin but couldn't stop it. Obviously, the giff didn't understand just how ridiculous he sounded. Gomja hadn't changed a bit. The giff saw Teldin's smile and returned it, no doubt thinking that Teldin was pleased for him. "By the way," Teldin asked, "why do they call it Port Walkaway?"

"That, I believe, came from a human's remark to a gnome about the best kind of landing to make with a spelljammer. Her words went something like, 'Any landing you can walk away from is a good one.' I don't believe they actually got the joke, sir."

Teldin groaned. "One thing that you haven't explained," he said as he reached for a cup of water on a bedside table, "is how you got your command so quickly. You can't have been here longer than a few weeks."

Gomja shrugged. "Eight weeks, actually, sir. The security commanders were on strike when we arrived here. There was some disagreement about the appropriate length of unit mottos, I believe. The colony secretary-general hired me to replace the striking gnome commanders, and that was it. It struck me as out of the ordinary for any race but the gnomes, I confess, but I decided not to question an opportunity such as that. After I reorganized the security and marine forces, the gnome commanders asked to sign back on, and I took them as my subordinates. If I may be allowed to wave my own flag, things have run very smoothly these last two months. Your arrival was the first call to action that we've had."

"If I could have warned you, I'd have tried," Teldin said, smiling. "What I don't understand is why you'd take a job here leading gnomes when you were offered the very same position back at Mount Nevermind."

Gomja rolled his small black eyes. "Oh, that. I'm afraid the research committees had begun to take an interest in me, sir, and rather than risk a turn in their examination room and—"

"Stop." Teldin could picture it all too well. "I'm glad to see you, Gomja, however it came about."

"I'm glad to see you, too, sir," Gomja replied with a wide grin, his pert ears giving a wiggle on top of his broad hippopotamus head. "You can't imagine what went through—"

"—your mind, yes." Teldin sank back into his pillow. Suddenly he felt very tired. "Gomja, if you don't mind, I think I need to rest for a while."

"Certainly, sir!" the giff boomed, coming to his feet and

thoughtfully retrieving the towel he'd used. The floorboards creaked in protest. "I'll make sure everyone is kept out for a while. The surgeon says you should be up on your feet in another day or two. We've been helping you along with healing spells, as you may be aware, and you're almost as good as new! I'll be staying downstairs in the infirmary here, in room number eight. Call for me if you need anything, sir." The giff threw Teldin a sharp salute, then turned on his broad footpads and opened the door. He hesitated, then looked back just before leaving. "Sir," he said, flushing a darker shade of blue, "I just thought I should say that even though I am First Colonel-Commander now, the best promotion I ever had in my life was when you made me a sergeant at Mount Nevermind. I've never forgotten that."

Teldin wasn't sure quite what to say in reply, but he was deeply touched. "I've never forgotten it either. I knew a good soldier when I saw one. Carry on!"

"Right! Good-bye, sir." Beaming, the giff closed the door behind him with a solid thud.

"Good-bye," Teldin said to the door. He closed his eyes. Life had been getting only stranger and stranger since this entire adventure started.

"Psst!"

Teldin started and looked at the open window. A small, elfin face surrounded with gleaming black hair looked back at him with a joyful expression. Bright wildflowers rested in Gaye's hair. She appeared to be hanging onto the outside window ledge by her fingers and elbows.

"Is he gone?" Gaye said in a loud stage whisper.

Teldin wanted to close his eyes, but pushed himself up on his elbows instead. "What in the lower blazes are you doing there?" he whispered fiercely. "This is the second floor!"

"I thought you'd like some company!" she whispered back, pulling herself fully into the room. The dark-haired kender was wearing a short purple dress with a red sash and no shoes. "I would have brought some fruit, but the gnomes said you weren't to eat anything but creamed soaked grains until you were released."

Teldin's stomach knotted at the thought of facing another bowl of that tasteless gray sludge. He was being fed five times a day now, and he hated every moment of it.

Gaye wiped her dirty hands on Teldin's bedsheets. "Anyway, now that I'm here, we have some time to talk!" she said brightly, seating herself on the bed. She was wearing a new sort of flowery perfume. "Aelfred said you brought us down when both the helms were knocked out," she said, leaning toward him excitedly. "Is this another power of your cloak? I don't mean to be nosy. Aelfred was trying to keep it a secret, but I overheard him yesterday talking to the navigator. I hope I'm not getting him into trouble or anything by saying that."

"Well—" Teldin began.

"I guess I should first say thank you for saving us," Gaye continued quickly, "but that seems so inadequate. That big blue guy with the nose, General Gomma whatever, said you almost drowned when we splashed down, but he pulled you out. I was really grateful he did, too. We've only known each other for what, five days, and here we are, crashed on a flat planet with no ship left, and who knows what's lurking in wildspace for us, trying to get your cloak. That's what Aelfred was saying, but not to me. That was to the navigator."

"I don't—" Teldin said.

"Oh, don't worry, none of that's important," the kender went on. "None of us can predict the future, so we'd all better eat our desserts first. That's what everyone says, anyway. I like your mustache. So, what have you been doing with yourself lately?" She waited expectantly, her dark eyes shining.

Teldin opened his mouth to answer.

There was a knock at the door. "Teldin?" came Aelfred's muffled voice from outside. "Teldin, mind if I come in?"

"Oops," muttered Gaye, bounding to her bare feet. She looked hurriedly around the room, then dropped to her knees and crawled under Teldin's bed. "Don't tell!" she whispered with a wink, and was gone from view.

"Teldin?" came the voice at the door again.

"Come on in," Teldin said in defeat. "Why not."

The door opened silently. Aelfred had a new gash over his left eye, but it had healed already. He moved unsteadily, favoring his right leg. The big man gave Teldin a lopsided smile as he limped over and reached out to shake his hand. "Good to see you alive, old son," Aelfred said, taking a seat on a stool he pulled close to Teldin's bed. "Hope you don't mind a visit."

Teldin snorted. "Gomja was going to keep people out for me, but you must have missed him. Don't worry about it. How are things going here?"

"Well," Aelfred started, leaning forward to rest his elbows on his knees, his hands clasped together in front of him. His crooked smile faded, then was gone. "I've got some bad news, some good news, and some more bad news."

Grimacing, Teldin tried to prepare himself. "What?"

"The first bad news is that we did lose a few people," Aelfred said, not looking Teldin in the eye. "Asinwilk, the stern castle catapult crewman, he drowned, and Bor Oxeman and that new priest, Garioth, they were killed in the lower bridge by that catapult shot. We haven't found five others: Varisot, Mamnilla, Old Hok, Mithko the Elder, and Yishi Narsh, the cook. They could have fallen off anywhere in space or in the lake. We just don't know. Yishi was probably in the galley when it was hit."

Aelfred looked down at his interlocked fingers. His eyes saw nothing there. Teldin remembered Mamnilla and Old Hok, lying on the deck as Teldin had hovered over the ship in his dream, or whatever state the cloak had produced. Mamnilla had had a warped sense of humor for a halfling. An empty place formed in Teldin's stomach. He tried not to take it personally, but he knew he was the cause of all these deaths—he and his cloak.

"The good side," Aelfred went on, "is that the rest of us survived, which comes to thirty-nine people that you saved. The gnomes have their healers—real healers and priests—working on the crew, and we're getting back on our feet. They told us we should be at full strength by the day after tomorrow. Now, we go back to the bad news again."

Aelfred paused, not looking at Teldin, and swallowed. "The *Probe*'s just scrap, I'm told," he said, no emotion in his voice. "The orcs, or whatever they were up there, did for us pretty well. You got us out of there in time, but the ship's going for kindling." Aelfred gave Teldin a rueful smile. "At least I got to be her captain for a while."

"I'm sorry," Teldin said. He was blanketed in misery. He

knew more than ever that his presence threatened everyone he had ever cared about. "It's my fault," he mumbled. "I shouldn't have stayed and put you and everyone else in so much danger. The neogi, the mind flayers, the orcs, they want this cloak"—he gestured at the silver "necklace" at his throat, the cloak being kept small so it was out of the way—"and I couldn't even give it to them if I wanted to."

Aelfred made a short gesture as if brushing away a fly. "Don't talk like that. You're not getting anywhere with self-pity. We chose to be with you even though we knew it would be hard going. We stuck together, and you pulled our roast out of the cooking fire when things balled up." Aelfred rubbed at his face. "The point of all this is that my crew has nowhere to go, and some of them are thinking about staying here. They're not that crazy about gnomes, but they'd rather either settle down here and work or else wait for the next freighter that stops by and sign on her, no matter where she's bound. I released them all of their duties as of this morning, and paid them off with what the gnomes salvaged from the currency locker in my cabin. Everyone's staying here at the infirmary for now, but soon they're going to start going their own ways." Aelfred hesitated. "And Sylvie and I are going our own ways, too, old son."

I'm going to miss you, Teldin was ready to say, feeling even more depressed and responsible for the whole mess.

"So," said Aelfred, rising to his feet and stretching his right leg gingerly. "As soon as you get off your lazy ass and get some real food in you instead of this scavver dung they've been feeding us all, you and Sylvie and I are going to see this sage the elves want us to see. And if I have any luck at all along the way, I'm going to make some space orcs damned unhappy that they shot up my ship."

Teldin stared at Aelfred with an open mouth. The captain leaned down and gave Teldin a healthy punch in the shoulder. "I've also got to teach you about landing ships if you're going to spelljam them, if that's what you did to get us down. A blind-drunk liar bird would have done better. And I haven't forgotten that other problem you and I were going to work on, either. We can't do anything about it here, since all they have available are gnome women—unless you *like* that type—but we'll work on it." With a crooked, knowing grin, the blond warrior waved and headed for the door, letting himself out.

"You old dog, you," Teldin said, staring at the door. I can't believe you still want to travel with me, he thought. I just can't believe it. For the first time in ages, he felt a sense of lightness inside him.

"Hey!" came Gaye's voice from under the bed. "What kind of problem are you having? And why did he say you couldn't do anything about it here because of the gnome women?"

Teldin closed his eyes for a moment. "Gaye," he said wearily, "it's none of your business."

The kender, now covered in dust balls from her black hair to her tanned legs, scrambled to her feet. "They don't sweep very well in here," she said conversationally, brushing herself off beside Teldin's bed and scattering dust clouds everywhere. "Well, if you don't want to talk about your deep, dark problem, then maybe you'll talk about it later when we get to the fal. Aelfred told the navigator that a fal was like a snail, only a zillion times bigger. Is that true? Why are we supposed to go see a snail, anyway?"

"You know," Teldin said irritably, "I don't recall that any invitation was extended to you or to anyone else for a chance to go on this expedition."

"Really?" Gaye said, unfazed. "We were all going there anyway until we crashed here. What's the difference?" She wiped her hands off on Teldin's sheets again. "Anyway, I've already been talking with the gnomes. I told them you were looking for the *Spelljammer*, and they were quite excited about helping us out. So get some rest." Gaye patted Teldin's shoulder. "You've been a big hero, but you need a little more nap time. Then we'll visit the big snail and find the *Spelljammer* and tell all our friends about it."

The kender padded over to the window and hoisted herself onto the ledge with youthful grace. Turned so that she faced out, she leaned back and gave Teldin a last wave.

"I'll ask Aelfred if I can help with your problem, whatever it is," she called, then swung herself off the ledge, disappearing from view.

"No!" Teldin cried, half sitting up. He waited with terror

for the awful crash that he knew would follow as the crazy kender hit the ground.

No crash came. Wind stirred the tree leaves outside the window. Some very loud machine could be heard in the distance, probably a fan boat rumbling across the lake.

Teldin swung his feet off the bed, wadded up the now-filthy sheets, and carefully made his way over to the window. Thanks to the gnomes' healing magic, his legs had outwardly recovered from their injuries on the *Probe*, but they ached abominably with every step. Limping to the window, he peered down to find a trace of the kender.

There was nothing on the ground but grass, running right up to the infirmary walls. Gaye was nowhere in sight.

Stunned, Teldin looked down at the wall itself. There were no handholds, no pipes, nothing at all that she possibly could have used to climb up the wall to his window. He looked up, and it was then that he saw the last bit of a piece of rope flick over the roof's gutter, pulled up by unseen hands, Gaye's. Teldin felt a stab of admiration with his relief.

He was heading back to his bed when he heard short footsteps outside, marching up to his door. As he swung his feet under the sheets again, shaking the dust off as well as he could, Teldin heard a rapid, continuous knocking sound from a spot low on the door.

"I'm busy," he said, too worn out to see anyone else. He figured the knocker had to be a gnome, and his legs were still aching from moving around. He fell back on the pillow and stared at the ceiling.

Half a minute passed before the knocking resumed.

Maybe if I tried real hard, Teldin thought, I could choke myself with this cloak and save the neogi and everyone else the trouble. Maybe then I could get some rest.

The knocking went on and on.

"Come in!" Teldin shouted in surrender. "Just come in!"

"I'm not bothering you, am I?" came a voice outside his door. It was Dyffed. "I wouldn't do this, you understand, but some matters have come up since we landed here, and I felt that I should probably discuss them with you when you had a free moment, and I didn't think you'd be doing anything right now, so I thought I'd come by and—"

"Come in, come in, come in, come in, come in!" Teldin shouted, too tired to throw something at the door.

"Ah, then I'm glad I'm not bothering you," said Dyffed cheerily, letting himself in. Sporting a thick bandage on top of his bald head, tied down with a strip of white cloth, the little gnome also wore a new set of gold-rimmed spectacles, probably having lost his previous pair in the ship crash. He was dressed in maroon pants, a white shirt with a round, stiff front made of white paper, and a gaudy green-and-gold jacket with at least eight pockets visible on the front. His short beard was neatly trimmed, and Teldin could tell that the gnome had probably had a bath, his first in a while.

"You're looking splendid, if a bit pale," said the gnome, beaming up at Teldin from the side of the bed. "They've gone and put you in the humans' ward, too, so the doorknobs are all at your height and the water closets don't bump your ankles and you can sleep without feeling you've been stuck in a bookshelf. Simply splendid. I must tell you, your joke about One Six Nine is quite the rage around the yacht club, and even First Commodore Smedlookinblakburdincan was quite beside himself, laughed until he nearly vomited and had to be taken outside and given water. Marvelous sense of humor, but that's not why I'm here. Just sign these." The gnome pulled a stained sheaf of papers from an inside pocket of his jacket and spread them out on Teldin's chest. He then produced a short, black stick with a coppery point on one end. "You can use my portable hydraulic transcription device if you like," he added, "but mind the ink. Refilling it takes four hours."

Teldin made no move to take the black stick. He valiantly resisted the urge to punch the gnome in the nose. "What are you talking about? What are these?"

"Ah," said the gnome, pointing a stubby finger at various sections of the papers as he spoke. "This is a legal statement giving me permission to accompany your expedition to the *Spelljammer*—not just any spelljammer, of course, but the one-and-only *Spelljammer*—purely for scientific purposes. This is a release form that absolves you from any responsibility for all accidents, illnesses, or injuries, to include death and/or dismemberment, that I might suffer while in your company. This is a release form that absolves me from any responsibility for all accidents, illnesses, or injuries, to include death and/or dismemberment, that you might suffer as a result of anything that I do for research purposes. This is a waver that grants—"

Teldin snatched the papers out of Dyffed's hands and almost wadded them into a ball. Instead, with the greatest single effort of willpower he ever recalled using, he carefully handed them back to the gnome. "I am not signing anything," Teldin said with finality, "and it doesn't matter if you want to go or not. We have no ship. We're stuck here."

"Oh, but we do have a ship," Dyffed corrected him. "The Board of Admirals has given us an excellent ship from the naval ya—um, um, yacht docks, silly of me—an excellent ship from the yacht docks, ready for its trial run. Within a few days, we shall be off to see One Six Nine."

The charade about the "yacht club," on top of everything else, managed to push Teldin's temper to its limits. "Why do you persist in calling this a yacht club?" he demanded. He half sat up in bed again, feeling his face flush with anger. "This is a naval base for spelljammers, isn't it? Gnome spelljammers?"

"Shhh!" Panicked, Dyffed waved his hands in front of Teldin's face. "Careless vocalizations produce maritime disasters!" he hissed, glancing fearfully at the open window.

"Damn it, everyone *knows* this is a naval base!" Teldin protested. "I knew that when Gomja brought me ashore on his boat! All the gnomes wear uniforms, you have huge catapult and ballista towers surrounding this valley, you have a military dry dock, and even your security commander told me it was a naval base!" As he uttered those last words, Teldin instantly wished he could take them back. He had undoubtedly just sunk Gomja's whole career.

"First Colonel-Commander Herphan Gomja has a security clearance that allows him to say it's a naval base, but you don't!" Dyffed retorted, unfazed. "As Colonel-Commander Gomja says, the void holds many foes, even if that's not logically correct because a void should be empty and hold nothing. Regardless, we ask that you please not refer to this base, the lake, or the airspace above it, out to a fifty-mile altitude, as anything other than a yacht club. If our enemies knew that we were working on a coherent-beam, synergized thaumamplifier here, they'd—" The gnome froze, his face filled with horror at his words. "No! I meant, if they only knew we were working on a secret birthday party for the admirals here, they'd be all over us. It's the nature of space monsters, always crashing birthday parties." Dyffed drew a shuddering sigh, his face pale. "I've been working on this weapons project for so long, I almost forgot the code words."

Teldin thought about this latest revelation. Whatever this secret weapon was, he didn't want to be around when it was set off. "Forgive my asking," he said, "but were you working on this, uh, birthday party at the Rock of Bral?"

"What? Oh, yes, I was. Their library was of considerable help, too, though I don't think they understood a scrap of what I was doing there. Elves!" The gnome rolled his eyes. "Wonderful people, of course, but absolutely no concept of real science. The admiral and I got along quite famously, though, thanks to his interest in the *Spelljammer*—that's the one-and-only *Spelljammer*, of course, not just any spelljammer. We used to talk about that for days. He must have asked me a thousand questions about it. That's the sort of thing that happens when you get a proper schooling, none of this 'Everything I Needed to Know I Learned on Dungeon Level One' nonsense. That was why he had me go with you, so I could perform a scientific analysis of the *Spelljammer* when you found it, then answer all of his own questions about it later."

The gnome paused for breath, and Teldin broke in. His worst suspicions were dangerously close to being confirmed. "What kind of questions was Admiral Cirathorn asking about the *Spelljammer*?"

Dyffed hesitated, lost in thought. "Oh, the usual things, of course, that a scholar of history might ask. How big was it, what kind of weapons would it carry, how could you control it, where would you find it, what sorts of military things might you do with it if you had it, would your cloak have any effect on it, that sort of thing. Natural curiosity."

Natural curiosity, hell, Teldin thought. I should have known. Why in the name of the Abyss do I keep trusting everyone I meet and hoping they won't stab me in the back with the first chance they get? I never thought the elves would do it, but I've not been seeing this in perspective. The *Spelljammer* is more valuable than gold; it's real, raw power, and no one can turn away from it, not the neogi, not the mind flayers, not the pirates, evidently not the orcs who attacked us, and apparently not even the elves. Possibly not even the gnomes.

"At any rate," Dyffed went on cheerfully, "my research assistants and I shall accompany you when you leave to find the *Spelljammer*. We're going to find out what makes the *Spelljammer* squeal, as they say, but first we'll be off to see dear old One Six Nine. I've communicated with him only by parcel for the last sixty years. He was quite a help to me on the, uh, um, birthday party. We'll be bringing it with us, by the way. It should be a marvelous trip."

* * * * *

Night fell across the face of Ironpiece. Watches changed at the naval base, and spelljammers began landing in the evening, the last of those returning from the battle that had been joined after the *Probe*'s escape. Teldin heard from various nurses and technicians that the humanoid and elven ships had fought each other mercilessly, but both sides had been driven away from Ironpiece by the gnomes' dreadnoughts, deathglories, spellfighters, and other craft. Confusion had reigned at first as to whether the elves were allies or enemies, but the matter was resolved on a practical level when an elven man-o-war opened fire on a deathglory. From that point on, it was every side for itself. As usual, the gnomes took the greatest casualties from their own experimental weapons. Once the humanoids had retreated and the elves had simply vanished (minus one of their man-o-wars), the gnomes had mopped up and gone home. Teldin went to sleep with a certain amount of satisfaction at the news.

The infirmary's inhabitants slept. In the dark corridors, a handful of gnome attendants snored on their stools or wrote medical notes by candlelight. One of them was in the middle of listing a series of proposed experiments to determine the best design for a new lighting system for the infirmary—one that would not burn the place to the ground, as the previous natural-gas system had done sixty years earlier. She finished with another page, admiring the simplicity of her design—to have giant, refillable wicks installed in the walls—and set it on the ever-growing pile beside her.

"*Somnoluncia, parafar, nombilbulum*," came a whispered voice from the darkness down the hall to her left.

Startled, the gnome looked up—and immediately started to yawn. She leaned back, a quill pen and a stack of unblemished paper sliding from her lap as she fell off her stool. A soft thump sounded as she hit the floor, accompanied by the sound of an upended ink bottle rolling away across the floor to empty its contents in a widening puddle.

Out of the darkness came a darker thing, floating soundlessly up to the snoring gnome. The figure observed the slow rise and fall of her chest, then moved on to the door on her right. There the figure took a last look around—then it simply moved through the entry as if the door did not exist.

Beyond the door the darkness was broken by faint light from a window. After an appropriate wait to assure that the rhythmic breathing from the bed in the room was genuine, the figure silently drifted closer. A lone being slept there, curled up like a baby. The sheets were bunched up at the foot of the bed. Peace was written across the sleeper's face.

The dark figure raised a finger of white jointed bone and pointed it at the sleeper's head.

"*Obedia noamei, prejarki noh*," it said quietly. The rhythmic breathing from the victim immediately became heavier and deeper. The sleeper's eyes opened and stared at the wall, seeing nothing. The dark thing felt relief. The controlling spell had worked on the first attempt.

"Much from me this spell has cost, but much need I have of you, live meat," the dark thing whispered. "Much for me in the weeks to arrive you will do. The cloakmaster to approach I dare not. Dangerous he is, and because of him my not-servants exist not. But you in my service will be, hidden slave with hidden master, you by all trusted, yes. My words now attend you will, much to learn, and my dreams to fulfil. Power everlasting mine will be, the cosmos to hold."

The dark figure spread its arms wide, covering the window and the light, and began the next enchantment.

*   *   *   *   *

The following morning, before Teldin forced his own release from the infirmary, Gomja visited him and announced
he, too, would be going with Teldin to find the *Spelljammer*.

"I don't understand," Teldin said. He stopped rubbing his
knees to ease the aching in them. "Why would you leave your
work here? You've got everything you've ever wanted."

Gomja sighed, sitting on a heavy crate and looking at a spot
on the floor. "I know, sir, but the gnomes decided that they
need a marine commander aboard the ship they're taking to
the *Spelljammer*, and they felt that I was the best choice. The
commanders that I replaced wanted their old jobs back, too.
It's all for the best." He looked uncomfortable and dropped
his voice as he looked up. "Besides, sir, not a lot has been going on here, and I've been hoping for a little more action. I'm
also worried that you might need a strong arm at your side,
given your current goals."

Teldin grinned and shook his head. "I can't deny that,
Colonel-Commander. It seems as if I'm going to have
company with me, whether I want it or not." His smile faded.
"To be frank, after the fight just before we crashed here, I'd
almost decided to go on to the *Spelljammer* alone. Anyone
who goes with me is in danger. I don't even think I can trust
the elves on this one. They're as eager to get their little hands
on this cloak as everyone else."

Gomja said nothing, but still stared at the floor. Teldin
leaned forward and slapped the giff on the shoulder. "It will
be good having you with me again," he said with feeling. "I
need someone I can trust. I don't have many these days, and
you, Aelfred, and Sylvie are about it."

The giff looked up into Teldin's face for a moment with an
unreadable expression. "Thank you, sir," he finally said. The
floorboards groaned as he eased himself to his broad, round
feet. "I'll get my things then."

"Do that," Teldin said. "I'm getting the hell out of here
right now myself." He waved as the giff left, then went back to
collecting the few things that his rescuers had managed to
bring to him from the wreck. The worst loss was the sheaf of

papers about the *Spelljammer* that Cirathorn had given him. The scroll tube must have come loose during the crash, meaning that it was undoubtedly resting on the bottom of Lake Crashsplash this very moment. He gritted his teeth at the thought, but there was no help for it. Maybe this slug, One Six Nine or whatever it was, would know more.

Teldin slung his small bag of personal belongings over his shoulder, then looked the room over before he left. Seeing that it was fairly clean, he closed the door behind him and set off down the hall in search of real food.

At least, he reflected as he started down the stairs, he would be traveling with people he knew he could trust.

Chapter Nine

● ● ●

"It should be right in this next berth . . . no, wrong one, just ignore the mess. There! Here it is! This one right here, this beautiful ship, this is the *Perilous Halibut*, my labor of love for many years. Glorious, isn't she?" Dressed in a brown tweed suit with a lime-green shirt and a yellow tie that could blind onlookers within ten feet of it, Dyffed stood before the long black ship he had named and beamed up at its bow. His face was wreathed in beatific happiness. "I feel ninety years old all over again," he sighed.

There was a long silence as Teldin, Aelfred, and Sylvie stared at the ship with thoughtful expressions.

"It's very"—Teldin struggled for a word, glancing at Aelfred for help but finding none—"interesting," he finished. It looks like a black banana with fins, he thought.

"I absolutely agree," said Dyffed, reaching up to pat the bottom of the ship's metal-plated hull. "The *Perilous Halibut* was called such because, first, it is sort of like a fish, and the Office of Yachting Names, Designations, Codes, and Other Completely Nonmilitary Appellations had run out of all the other fish-type names, and all the paperwork with our previous suggestions had already been filed and lost. Secondly, it is perilous because it's a dangerous ship—I mean, dangerous to our enemies, of course. We built it, so it can't be dangerous to us. We were originally going to paint it blue to go with Vice Rear Admiral Blekinmangrars's new uniform, but we had already run out of that particular shade and Midnight Ebony was all the supply office had left, which was a very fortunate error for all concerned, because now the ship is perfectly camouflaged against the blackness of space, though we might someday have to paint stars on it here and there to make the camouflage more authen—ouch!"

The gnome hastily stuck a finger in his mouth. "Dratted riveting," he muttered, popping his finger out for a second to speak, then putting it back in.

Teldin stepped around to the side to gauge the ship's size. The *Perilous Halibut* rested on a massive and complex framework of wooden supports inside the gigantic hangar on Port Walkaway. The ship appeared to be about the same length as the *Probe*, two hundred feet or so, and was about twenty-five feet thick and prism-shaped, octagonal in cross section. A rectangular black tower stuck out from the upper deck of the ship, almost like a shark's fin, and smaller fins stuck out from several places along its sides. The ship's tail retained the fishlike imagery, with the lower end of the tail falling well below the bottom of the ship itself. The ship would lose its tail if it landed on solid ground, but Teldin guessed it had been meant to land on water.

Teldin's eyes scanned the upper deck of the *Perilous Halibut*, noting a simple gold railing running around the edge. The railing was, of course, at the height of a typical gnome's waist—in other words, just about the height of a human's knees. It wouldn't do to get close to it and trip over the side of the ship.

"I can't believe we're lucky enough to have this whole ship to ourselves," Aelfred said. Teldin and Sylvie turned to stare at him in amazement. Aelfred glanced aside at them, putting a finger momentarily to his lips.

"Ah, nothing lucky about it at all," said Dyffed, pleased. He dismissed the idea with a wave of his hand. "Nothing at all. Experimental ships are sent out all the time from here, and most have come back. Or some of them have, at least. I last heard the return figure was closer to twelve point eight percent, including all ships bearing the expected casualties but not counting fragmental returns if they couldn't tell which ship the fragments belonged to. But that's neither here nor there, of course, for though this is its first flight test, the *Perilous Halibut* is of a proven theoretical model, the first of its kind to be built, and we have nothing whatsoever to fear, nothing at all, unless the tail falls off." Dyffed chuckled, glancing at the tall threesome behind him. "An old gnomish joke, you understand."

No one else so much as smiled.

Dyffed coughed and went back to admiring the *Perilous Halibut*. "Yes, this lovely ship will be ready to fly at any time, right after a few last adjustments are made. Then she'll be fit for space."

"Ah, adjustments," said Aelfred with interest, "by which you mean . . ." He waited and looked at the gnome.

"Oh, the usual things, of course," said the gnome. "Check a few fittings, tighten a few bolts, install the lavatories, order the weapons, unpack the helm and install that, then run the usual experiments to find out if it can float. It should float, or at least it does on paper. By that, I mean that the ship doesn't float on paper, but rather it floats on water, as the expression—"

"Do you mean the ship has no weapons or helm right now?" Teldin asked, barely beating Aelfred to the question.

Dyffed cleared his throat and managed to look everywhere but directly at Teldin. "Well, deck weapons were accidentally left off the design prints at first—careless of me—but we did manage to find places to put one, a ballista, right there on the front—the bow, as I believe it's called. Perhaps someday we'll have our, um, ah, birthday party mounted there instead."

"Birthday party?" Sylvie asked, an eyebrow raised. "Are you serious?"

Dyffed quickly eyed Teldin, then grinned and waved his arms elaborately. "Yes, oh, yes, we're going to have a birthday party—right, Teldin?—to celebrate her first birthday. I mean, to celebrate the admiral's birthday. We should have the helm installed within the hour, give or take a bit, if we can get the paperwork filled out. All we can do in the meanwhile is sit back with our fingers in our ears and hope everything works properly. Ah, which reminds me, I need to bring out a piece of old equipment and run some tests on it before we leave for One Six Nine. It's a locating device, something One Six Nine called a 'thingfinder,' which he made for us. We, of course, have improved upon it—just a tiny bit, mind you—and if it hasn't decayed or been sat upon, it should lead us right to old Thirteen Squared's address without fail. Remarkable device—operates completely on thought power. Not as efficient as hydrodynamics, I know, but—ah, I see someone signaling me, so I shall have to leave you here to marvel at the marvel, as it were. Don't touch the riveting or the tail." Dyffed was off at once, striding purposefully toward a group of other gnomes standing near a maze of scaffolding at the ship's stern.

Teldin watched Dyffed go, shaking his head slightly as he did. He turned away and kept his arms crossed in front of him as he looked the outside of the ship over, occasionally chewing on a thumbnail.

"Do you know," said Aelfred, who had adopted a similar posture, "that in the last three and a half years, I have never once taken a long voyage on a spelljammer other than the *Probe*? And not once, never, did I ever ride on a gnomish ship." He nodded thoughtfully.

"I don't like this," Sylvie said, her hands jammed into her pockets. "Our chances of getting killed look awfully good."

The three stood in silence after that, looking at the ship and listening to the gnomes argue and hammer things in the distance.

Teldin sighed, rubbing his face with his hands. "I'm not crazy about this, either, but I sailed on a gnomish ship once, when I left Krynn, and I'm still alive. Of course, I wasn't on it very long. Let's find out when this thing takes off. We may as well enjoy ourselves before we have to go."

"What's this 'birthday party' he was talking about?" asked Sylvie, looking at Teldin. "He thought you knew about it."

"It's some sort of secret weapon that they're taking with us on the ship," Teldin said. "Dyffed won't say anything about it that I can understand."

"Secret weapon," said Aelfred noncommittally. All three stared at the black ship a little while longer.

Aelfred finally uncrossed his arms and sighed heavily. "Teldin, did the gnomes recover any of those sagecoarse casks from the *Probe*?" he asked.

Teldin thought. "Just one. It's at the lake docks, Pier

Twelve, with the rest of what they could salvage."

Aelfred nodded solemnly. He took a last look at the *Perilous Halibut*, then turned without a word and walked off at a casual pace toward the hangar doors and the docks beyond. Sylvie followed with only a slight hesitation.

Teldin watched them go, then looked back at the black ship and sighed.

*   *   *   *   *

There had been no sign of Gaye at the infirmary in the morning. Inquiries to the gnomes who were carrying the personal belongings of Teldin and his companions to the *Perilous Halibut* brought a variety of long responses, all of which could be boiled down to a simple "I don't know." Gomja said he would take a walk around the base and find out what she was up to, then he disappeared, too.

Teldin wandered aimlessly around the base for several hours, inspecting the variety of bizarre gnomish ships. He was mildly fascinated by the heavily armed, shiplike deathglories and the tiny clockwork spellfighters, watching as they took off on their deep-space patrols. In time, he found himself standing inside a hangar, feeling his cloak flap against his legs. The cloak had become a dark rich emerald hue, almost black, just within the last hour.

Did that color mean anything? he wondered. Why does this cloak do anything at all? What's the point of it? The frustration was neverending.

He looked around, frowned, and spotted Dyffed speaking with two other gnomes across the hangar, perhaps two hundred feet away. They were bunched together and appeared very secretive, but their arms were waving and gesturing wildly in some intense discussion.

Teldin was suddenly seized with a perverse urge to know what they were talking about. He couldn't walk over to them and ask. That is, he couldn't—unless he were a gnome. He pushed the thought away, but it came back unbidden. What would he learn if he were suddenly a gnome? What would they tell him?

He'd never tried to use his cloak's powers to change his

shape into a gnome. He'd had good success with human-sized male and female forms, but this was different. His old inhibitions against assuming other forms had eroded steadily in recent weeks under the twin pressures of curiosity and frustration. Things had been out of his control for too long.

Teldin looked around and spotted some gnomish work clothing hanging from a peg. On impulse, he casually walked over to pick it up. The gnomes paid no attention to him. Teldin walked on until he had stepped behind a large stack of wooden crates shrouded in darkness. After a brief, final moral struggle, he carefully looked around, ·then removed his own clothing. He felt intensely foolish, worrying that someone would see him at any moment. Why am I doing this? he asked himself, struggling out of his pants. Because I want to know what's going on, he answered himself. I want to know what this secret big-named device is that Dyffed's so fired up about. I'm tired of being left in the dark.

When he was undressed, he hesitated and strained to hear any sounds of someone approaching. Satisfied, he closed his eyes and stood perfectly still.

Miggins. He remembered the friendly little gnome who once had traveled with him on the *Probe* and was now left far behind on Toril; then he pictured his own features and body slowly melting down to Miggins's size. He felt a tingle of power surge through his shoulders as the cloak released its energies, and he avoided opening his eyes to look around. The floor grew larger, making his feet scuff the floor as they pulled apart. In his mind, his face took on Miggins's features, down to the gnome's excited grin.

When Teldin felt the power stop flowing, he opened his eyes again. The floor was much closer to his face now, and the hangar seemed bigger. He raised his arms, noted how short and brown they were, how stubby his fingers looked. His hand came up to his face and touched it, and he knew without doubt that those whiskers and that outrageously big nose were his. Teldin tugged on a chin hair and winced. It had worked. He was now a gnome. He was so astounded that he could hardly speak.

He reached for the gnome clothing, marveling at how different everything seemed from his new height and how far he had to reach to get anything. It was like being a child again. He noticed then that he was still wearing the cloak in its full-length version, and he quickly shrank it down to necklace size. Moments later, he had tugged on the work clothing—Gods, he wondered to himself, do these gnomes ever take baths?— and carefully hid his own clothing. With a deep breath, he walked with short, quick paces out from behind the crates and headed as nonchalantly as he could toward the three gnomes across the hangar.

It took a lot longer to get to the gnomes than he had expected, being as unused to his short legs as he was. Nonetheless, he was within hearing distance before his legs felt as if they would give out from the rapid pace.

Dyffed was examining a red box held by one of the other gnomes, a shaggy-haired character with spectacle lenses as thick as the bottoms of ale steins. The wild-haired gnome was dressed in a filthy gray smock, and he constantly mumbled short phrases like "Careful!" and "No! There!" The third gnome looked like a bored bureaucrat type, wearing a loud striped suit that Teldin was coming to associate with the government officials on this particular world. The three spoke in Gnomish, which Teldin understood, thanks to his cloak. Teldin was becoming accustomed to having the cloak translate foreign languages for him, and it appeared to be more proficient at it now than it once had been. Translated or not, however, Teldin could barely understand anything the gnomes were saying at the moment.

"I don't see where the meridional field radiation is being bottled," said Dyffed. "See, you've got this—"

"No, not there," mumbled the wild-haired gnome. He tried to point something out to Dyffed, but the other gnome paid no attention and tried to pull the red box from the wild-haired gnome's hands.

"See, it's all reversed here in the paraboloid process," Dyffed said, rattling the object and poking a finger into it. "The bottle should be flow separated here, by the little blue widget—"

"Careful!" said the wild-haired gnome, stepping back and sheltering the box in his arms, a fierce look on his bearded face. "Don't touch that!"

"Oh, for the love of Reorx's maiden aunt, I wasn't going to touch the little blue widget." Dyffed grabbed for the box and poked around inside it again. "Oops," he suddenly announced, an expression of surprise as he jerked back his finger.

Remembering that "Oops!" was a universal word of danger among the tinker gnomes of Krynn, Teldin slowed and came to a stop only a dozen feet from the threesome. He could see that the red box had a dark, glassy plate at one end. The back of the box was open and filled with gears, wires, and glowing things.

"Aaagh!" cried the wild-haired gnome, tugging the red box away from Dyffed's fingers and peering into it with an agonized expression. " 'S all ruint!"

"There, there," Dyffed soothed, snatching the box away from the other gnome. "Let's simply give it a field test and see if it's really ruined." Dyffed looked around briefly, spied Teldin's gnomish shape and ignored him, then scanned the hangar. "I know! We'll look for Teldin Moore!"

For a second, Teldin feared he had been found out, even though he hadn't the faintest idea of how that was possible. The gnomes watched as Dyffed held the red box up to his face so that he peered into the dark glass plate.

"All I should have to do is concentrate, of course, and this should . . . do the trick . . ." Dyffed's voice faded as he slowly rotated in a counterclockwise direction. Teldin noted that the other two gnomes carefully ducked when the box was aimed in their direction, and he would have done the same except that Dyffed gave a peculiar little cry and aimed the box directly at him.

"Why . . ." Dyffed raised the box, looked hard at Teldin's gnomish form, then looked into the box again, pointing it at Teldin's head. "Obviously a defect," he muttered. "Cheap foreign parts."

"Locate *him*," said the wild-haired gnome in a worried voice, nudging Dyffed and pointing at Teldin.

"What? Oh!" Dyffed lowered the box and looked excitedly at Teldin. "Your name is . . . ?"

Teldin's mind went blank for a second before he answered, "Muggins." It sounded like Miggins, whose form he was copying, so it would probably do.

"Ah, Muggins, excellent," said Dyffed, pleased. "You must have lived around humans a lot to have such a short name. We'll search for Muggins, then, and hope that proximity of the target to the universal locator apparatus doesn't result in a feedback loop and the subsequent breakdown of matter on an elemental level, as it did on that unfortunate spelljammer that the Salvage Committee was telling me about yesterday. Quite a shame. Not much salvage value in sawdust." With that, Dyffed poked a finger inside the open end of the box to make some hurried adjustments. The wild-haired gnome looked on with the expression of a mother finding an infant playing with a box full of her finest crystal glassware. The bureaucrat gnome yawned broadly.

It took five seconds for the gnome's words to sink into Teldin's consciousness and make sense. He didn't catch it all, but he caught enough. "Ahhhh. . . ." he began, backing away and looking around for an excuse to leave.

"Won't take but a second!" Dyffed said, raising the box to his face and aiming the open end at Teldin. "Do cover your face in case the field unbottles itself. Very messy, but that's science for you. Can't make an omelet without killing a few chickens first."

"Wait! Don't do it!" Teldin cried, remembering only at the last moment that his voice had not been changed along with his physical form. He put up his hands to shield his face, not knowing what would happen next.

To his infinite relief, nothing happened at all. "Oh, gullion splat," muttered Dyffed. "This isn't working. I'm not getting anything at all now." He handed the box to the wild-haired gnome, who held it up to his face and peered into it in Teldin's direction. The latter gnome grunted and turned the box upside down, then sideways, then backward.

"'S broke," mumbled the wild-haired gnome sadly, lowering the box and looking down at it like a child at a smashed toy.

The bureaucrat gnome yawned again, looked around, and scratched himself. "Well," he said in a rumbling bass voice, "it's about time for my budget and appropriations meeting, so if you don't mind, I'll take the development of this new invention into consideration for the next fiscal year's budget and let this year's—"

"But we need the funding!" Dyffed cried in a stricken voice. "I'm absolutely totally, completely, positively, and error-free certain that we will have the locator up and running within no more than . . . no more than . . ." He stopped as all three gnomes turned toward the hangar door in puzzlement. "I say," he finished, "what is that most bizarre sound?"

Teldin turned to look and listen, too, but he heard nothing at all. Could the gnomes naturally hear things he could not, even in his new form?

"It's the emergency siren from the ranch," said the bureaucrat gnome in mild surprise. "Now, what could possibly—"

"Uh-oh," said the wild-haired gnome.

Teldin and the other two gnomes immediately turned to look at the speaker.

The wild-haired gnome started to back away from the hangar entrance. "Hamsters," he said, with not a little concern in his voice.

"Oh, my," said the bureaucrat gnome, looking about the hangar. "Oh, my, then I suppose we'd best—"

"Yes, immediately, I would think," said Dyffed, his eyes suddenly as large and round as saucers. The gnome looked at Teldin, then hurried over to him.

"Here!" Dyffed said, thrusting the box into Teldin's small hands. "Take this to Teldin Moore immediately! I'll bring the instructions later. Don't get caught!" With that, the three gnomes ran off into the depths of the hangar, looking anxiously over their shoulders and pushing each other along as they made their escape. The last that Teldin heard of them was Dyffed's cry, "Hurry before they get here!" A distant door slammed, and silence fell.

Hamsters? The cloak had translated the gnomish word but had provided no explanation for what the word meant. Teldin had to assume a hamster was some sort of animal, and to be caught by one was obviously regarded as a terrible thing.

"Then what am I doing here?" he suddenly asked himself aloud. Clutching the box, he turned to run back for his hidden clothing. He would have to change back into his normal size and get his sword. With his cloak's powers, he could better deal with the situation.

He would have done this, except that, when he turned around, he found his way blocked. He jumped back in fright, yelled, and dropped the red box as a golden-brown, grizzly-bear-sized animal, with an impossibly big pink mouth, smelly, hot breath, and ivory incisors the size of axe blades, lunged—

And ate him.

* * * * *

"I'm sorry," said Gaye, leaning against the infirmary door. She heard the sound of water splashing, but no reply.

"Teldin, I said I was sorry," she repeated. "I talked the gnomes out of keeping you here overnight for observation and testing, so you can say 'thank you' if you want, but if you're mad at me and you don't, I understand, because it was my fault the hamsters got loose and ate you and spit you out in the laundry pool. I didn't think they had mouths that big."

There was a pause on the other side of the door, then the sound of more water splashing. He was certainly going to be difficult about this one, she thought.

"Teldin, why don't you speak to me?" she called. "I know you're angry about being stuffed into a cheek pouch and covered with hamster spit and then thrown in the laundry pool and losing your old clothes, but you know, I don't understand how you lost your clothes to begin with. I mean, you weren't running around wearing old gnome clothes for fun, were you? That's kind of weird, you know? I didn't know you did that sort of thing, but I guess I can understand it if you said you'd been robbed at sword point and forced to change clothes with a gnome, but you haven't said that, so I have to assume—"

"Gaye!" roared Teldin. "Just shut up!"

Startled, the kender backed away from the door. "That's a fine way to talk," she mumbled. She surveyed the door for a moment. "Do you really mean that?" she called.

A few splashing sounds came from behind the door, then silence. Gaye listened carefully, thinking she could hear someone moving around in the room. "Teldin, are you okay?" she asked. There was no reply.

Maybe he slipped on some water while getting out of the tub, she thought. Maybe he's just drying off—but if he needs help, he could need it now. Do I wait or not? If I wait and he's hurt, I'll never forgive myself. He was pretty angry, and angry people don't think clearly. She eyed the door handle, then decided to risk it. She found the door unlocked (like all the infirmary doors), and threw it open.

"What?" Teldin spun around, clutching the towel with which he had been drying off. "Gaye! Gaye, get out of here!" he yelled.

Startled, the kender did exactly that. She reappeared two seconds later to close the door.

"*Gaaaaye!*"

She ran off again, finding a position safely down the hallway while Teldin slammed the bath door shut with a bang. She heard something dragging across the floor—probably the wash stand—and heard the object being set against the bath door. Then footsteps stomped away from the door, and there was silence again.

"Rats," she said, alone in the dimly lit hall. Well, it's my own fault, she decided. The gnomes told me about the giant space hamsters they use to power their ships, and they told me they raised the giant hamsters here, and I just had to see what a hamster was, and they looked so awfully cute in the barn that I went and let one out, and they all got out, and now the gnomes hate me and the humans hate me and even Teldin hates me. She decided she could live with everything except the last.

She was getting to like Teldin a lot; he was really mysterious. What was his big secret, anyway? It had to do with his magical cloak, but no one would tell her about it. Now he never would.

Gaye turned and walked away down the hall toward the dark, narrow staircase. She avoided a stack of short wooden curtain rods leaning against one door, though she was tempted to kick it. The gnomes had all left a while ago for some reason, so there was no one else to talk to. It was going to be a bad day.

At the top of the stairs, Gaye heard the echo of a door slamming downstairs somewhere, then heavy footsteps coming rapidly up the steps toward her. It sounded like the giff general. She hoped he wasn't angry with her, too.

She was halfway down the upper flight, feeling rotten about

everything, when the other stair-climber reached the landing. She barely looked up as she came down.

"If you're looking for Teldin," she mumbled, "he's not in a good mood."

The dark figure stopped short with a quick grunt. An odd and unpleasant body odor reached Gaye's nose. It was like old sweat and filth and fresh blood. She looked up. It was hard to see except for the faint light from a hall window, upstairs behind her. She could barely see the huge figure lift his right hand as he came at her. The figure was holding a long blade, and he was twice her height. He wasn't a giff.

Gaye dodged to her left as the sword slashed down and smashed into the wooden step where she had been standing, splintering the step into kindling. She instantly fled, her legs pumping as she ran back up the steps toward the dim light. Boots crashed hard and fast on the stairs behind her. She heard the attacker panting hard as he came after her. His armor scraped against the walls right behind her.

She reached the top of the steps and dived right, just as a sudden, sharp pain stabbed her left heel. Something thumped into the hall floor behind her at the same time. She lost her balance and fell, crashing into the curtain rods and knocking them down with a clatter, then got up again. Her heel hurt badly, but the pain was muted as yet. She ran down the dark hall for the room where Teldin had been taking his bath and jerked on the door handle as hard as she could.

The door wouldn't budge. She realized that Teldin had probably stuck the wash stand under the door handle on the other side, jamming it shut.

"*Teldin!*" she screamed, rattling the door handle. She looked back. The attacker was upon her, his head scraping the hall ceiling. The sword went up for a downward cut.

She gave up thinking. She dived forward at the giant's right side as the sword sliced down with a snap of air. Her small hands caught the hilt of the sword between the giant's huge fists and pulled it down and to the side farther than the giant had meant it to go. The giant staggered forward, off balance. The sword slammed into the floor as the assailant fell heavily on his side, the sword almost but not quite pulled out of his grasp. Gaye ran back down the hall, past him, and snatched up a wooden curtain rod before she ran back. Her heel screamed pain with every step.

"*Teldin!*" Gaye screamed again, gasping. The giant was already getting to his feet outside Teldin's door, the sword firmly clutched in one massive hand. With the light behind her now, Gaye could see that her attacker had a dull yellow-orange face with short tusks sticking up over its upper lip, and wore black, spike-studded armor, well oiled. His eyes were all wrong, with white pupils floating in round jet-black seas. An ogre, she thought, as the attacker's lips parted and she saw his sharklike teeth. He raised his sword again, uttering no sound, reaching her with two swift strides.

Gaye stepped aside at the last second, feeling the awful pain in her heel, and thrust the curtain rod up at the ogre's forearm as the sword came down. The ogre's blow was deflected off the stick, but the strike was still powerful enough to stagger her. Without waiting, she pushed the upper end of the rod into the path of the ogre's descending face, and it struck him in the right eye, punching in hard.

As the ogre let go of his sword, his hands clawed at his face and his mouth soundlessly opened. Gaye danced back out of the way, taking the stick with her and raising it to block the next attack. The ogre dropped to his knees and felt for the sword with one hand, the other clamped over his right eye. When he heard a door open, he lifted his sword and got to his feet to hunt for his tormentor with one good, squinting eye.

Instead, what he saw coming was a human who moved with a blur of speed, wearing ill-fitting trousers and a dark red cape. A short sword flashed in the human's right hand. The human ran up before the ogre knew it and drove the short blade straight into the ogre's chest, completely through his leather armor, right up to the weapon's hilt.

A fantastic jolt of pain cut through the ogre's next breath. He dropped his own sword again and tried to grasp the short sword's hilt with both hands, releasing his injured eye at the same time, but the world began to spin and grow black around the edges. The walls tilted, and he felt himself fall—then the world was gone.

A bright light flashed in the window at the end of the hall, followed almost at once by an ear-shattering boom of thunder.

Teldin stepped back from the dead ogre and looked at
Gaye. She took a hesitant step toward him.

"I hope you're not mad at me," she said. Then her eyes
rolled up, and she fell forward on her face.

.   *   *   *   *   *

Outside, Teldin saw a huge fire burning out of control along
the lake docks. A strange vessel, like a giant blue scorpion, lay
tilted to one side, half of it crashed into a storage shed by the
lake. Flames licked around the vessel's jointed legs and up its
arched tail. Scorpion ship, Teldin thought dully, holding the
kender's limp body close in his arms. The orcs found us. How?
How could they, with a whole world to search? How have any
of them ever found me? It was driving him mad.

A fast shadow shot by over his head. Teldin instinctively
ducked and started to run, crouching over Gaye to shield her.
He heard the distant shouts of gnomes in hand-to-hand combat, wild cries and curses from nonhuman throats. Another
shadow passed by overhead, and something dropped from it
to strike the roof of a large warehouse to his left. A wide ball of
orange fire splashed upward from the oily impact, the muffled
whoomp of the blast stinging him with its heat.

Sirens were going off everywhere. The air was filled with
echoing cracks and thumps as the air-defense engines fired. A
chorus of screams sounded above and behind him, followed
by a tremendous crash and the shattering of wood as a
spelljammer fell and pancaked upside-down into the pavement near the infirmary.

"Teldin Moore!" came a loud, nasal shout. Teldin looked
around and saw Dyffed waving at him from the low, wide door
of a gnomish troop barracks. He instantly ran for the gnome,
Gaye held tight against his chest. Dyffed's neat brown suit was
ripped and burned, and he clutched a pair of pistols. As
Teldin came up, the gnome stepped out of the doorway to let
him by, then raised both pistols and fired them simultane-
ously into the air. A hideous cry rang out, and Teldin turned in
time to see a body fall from a snakelike spelljammer passing
overhead. Dyffed stepped back into the barracks as the body
smacked the stones a short distance away.

"Damned inconvenient time for an air raid," Dyffed said conversationally, picking up two more loaded pistols from a table that appeared to be covered with them. Teldin noticed then that two other gnomes were in the room, loading pistols from chests full of smokepowder, shot, and weapons as quickly as their short fingers could move. The hazy air stank of burned powder.

"I was just going over for supper," Dyffed went on, squinting into the sky from the doorway again. "The cooks, Reorx bless them, had promised me a hot bowl of their best seven-weed soup. Never got as far as the third armory. I heard the alert siren and was told to set up an ambush point here, and then there were ships all about me, falling right out of the sky through the clouds like hail. How's the kender?"

"Her ankle's cut badly," Teldin said, laying the kender down on a gnome's child-sized bunk bed. He banged his head on the bottom of the upper bunk as he tried to straighten up, swore, then carefully stood and rubbed his head. "I've wrapped the wound, but she needs a spell or potion to heal it. I couldn't find anyone in the infirmary, not even the patients."

"That's because they're all at their antispelljammer stations. Didn't you hear the warning siren?" Dyffed looked at Teldin, then looked back outside. "Ah, I forgot. You're a human, of course, silly of me. Haven't got the same range of hearing as we do—a shame, too, if you ask me. We do have sirens that humans can hear—and elves and goblins and everyone else can hear them, too, for that matter—but we always sound the high-pitched gnome sirens first, as it gives us a leg up, you might—oops!" Dyffed instantly raised both pistols and fired, aiming them straight out the door. The loud reports stung Teldin's ears, but he still heard the clatter and thump of a body falling on the pavement outside. "As you might say, I was saying," Dyffed finished, tossing the pistols on the floor and grabbing two more from the table. "It makes the enemy think we didn't know they were coming. I could use a hand here, if you don't mind."

Teldin grabbed for two pistols himself, torn between watching Gaye and fighting. Dyffed didn't look up as Teldin joined him. The gnome merely raised his pistols and fired out the door. Teldin raised his weapons and found himself staring right at a wounded humanoid warrior in studded black armor, looking vaguely like a pig-nosed man, not ten feet away. It staggered toward the door with a curved sword clenched in his gloved fist. Teldin's fingers tightened on the triggers, guns aimed at the humanoid's head. The sharp double crack snapped off his hearing, filling his head with a painful whine, and acrid smoke instantly obscured his vision and stabbed his nostrils. Dyffed shoved Teldin in the legs, pushing him out of the doorway and back into the room as the black-armored humanoid collapsed across the doorway, sword clattering into the room. Bloody droplets splashed across the floor at Teldin's feet.

"The gods made us all," said Dyffed, grabbing two more pistols, "but smokepowder made us all equal. Old gnome saying, you understand. Seemed appropriate."

Teldin grabbed two more pistols himself from the huge stack of them now on the table. The two gnomes loading them worked madly. A figure suddenly appeared in the doorway. Teldin snapped his pistols up—and froze just before he could squeeze both shots off.

It was Sylvie, her clothing splattered with blood, clutching a messy, long dagger in her hands. He lowered the pistols at once. "Teldin!" Sylvie called, out of breath. "Teldin, we've got . . . we've got to get to the *Halibut*! The gnomes are taking off! The base . . ."

Dyffed shoved at Sylvie's legs and forced her into the barracks room, then fired twice out the door again. Teldin tried to get to the door and listen to Sylvie at the same time, but she stopped him with her free hand.

"There are . . ." she finally said, after swallowing hard. "There are humanoid ships, apparently orcish, landing all over the place. We have to get out of here. Aelfred's been looking for you, and Gomja. Gomja had brought us back to the hangar just before the orcs came. We're going to get into wildspace, where they can't catch us, before it's too late." A low, muffled boom echoed across the port.

Teldin nodded back at the silent form on the bunk bed. "Can you carry her?" he shouted, too excited to think that Sylvie was right in front of him. The half-elf navigator saw

Gaye and gasped, hurrying over to the kender's side and sheathing her dagger without wiping it off. In a moment, she had Gaye cradled in her arms.

"I'll never get my seven-weed soup tonight," Dyffed said sadly, stuffing four pistols into his wide belt and carrying two more. "First the hamsters, then this. Not my day at all. Shall we be off?"

Teldin nodded, taking a deep breath. Sylvie came up behind him. "Teldin, she's still bleeding," she whispered.

Teldin glanced at Gaye's pale face, then looked outside, across the broad, clear pavement, to the far-away hangar where the *Perilous Halibut* waited. Fires leaped into the sky everywhere, and black clouds rolled and drifted across the whole base. Few figures were visible in the open, most dodging from building to distant building. The sky was clear of spelljammers. They've all crashed or landed, Teldin decided. The orcs must be down and waiting for us, too.

"Let's go," he said, then dashed out of the building, pistols up, running for the distant hangar. "Come on!" he shouted back, waving Dyffed and Sylvie on as they followed him.

Behind them, oblivious to everything, the two gnomes loaded pistols until there was no place left to put them.

*   *   *   *   *

Twenty minutes later, the *Perilous Halibut*, its helm having been installed by accident two days earlier, burst through the thin wooden roof of the hangar. Cracked lumber and splinters sprayed through the air behind it. Sylvie was at the helm, there being no one else with the spell power to fly the ship as fast as she. The *Halibut* roared along beneath the cloud cover for many miles, leaving the naval base and a mass of pinned-down and burning humanoid ships far behind it. Borrowing an idea from Dyffed, Sylvie had the cloud-concealed ship simply fly off the edge of Ironpiece, where enemy ships were not likely to look for it. Luck was with them. The sky was overcast right to the edge, and they saw no sign of any humanoid ships when they sped away into the void. The ship's dark, nonreflective color proved to be a marvelous asset in hiding it against the black backdrop of wildspace.

Teldin looked out of the open jettison platform at the *Halibut*'s stern as they left Ironpiece. Seen edge-on, the world was now just a rapidly receding band of light against the distant constellations. Once they were safely away, he knew, Sylvie would take the time to draw out the course through the phlogiston to get to Herdspace. Sylvie, alone out of everyone else, had remembered to ask the gnomes for the navigational charts to Herdspace. This she'd done shortly after she had been taken to the infirmary, and she'd stored the charts with her belongings. We don't deserve to have someone that smart with us, he mused.

Not that Gomja was a slouch, either. He had taken charge of the evacuation, pointing out that the humanoids obviously knew where Teldin and company were, and waiting at the base for the humanoids to go away was a losing game. It was better to get off-planet into wildspace again and try to outdistance the enemy fleet before it caught on. Funny, thought Teldin, how we thought landing on Ironpiece would solve our troubles. Instead, our troubles just followed us right down to the ground.

A heavy hand dropped on Teldin's shoulder, startling him. "Someone wants to see you, old son," Aelfred said with a crooked smile. "We managed to scrape a healing potion together from somewhere for our kender."

Wordlessly, Teldin followed his friend down the too-narrow corridor to the equally cramped room that was now serving as Gaye's room. He had barely begun to figure out where anything was aboard this flying black coffin. Already he was starting to hate it.

Aelfred opened the door. Teldin had to stoop slightly because of the low ceiling and barely fit through the doorway. Gaye was in bed, looking at him with a pale, anxious face.

"You mad?" she asked in a soft voice.

Teldin half smiled. "No. You okay?"

Gaye's face cleared with relief, and she settled back in her small bed. It had been sized for a gnome, and she just barely fit it. "I'm okay."

Teldin managed to sit on the edge of her bed without crowding her too much. "I saw you poke the ogre in the face with that stick. That was a lucky shot, but you should have just run and let me handle it."

"Oh," she said. She was about to say more but didn't, simply shrugging instead. "Thanks."

Teldin rubbed his face, thinking. "We're heading for that sphere that Cirathorn called Herdspace, though I don't know how we're going to find the fal once we get there. Dyffed was going to give us a device, a locator of some kind, that we could use when we got to Herdspace. I got it, then lost it when the, uh, hamster swallowed me. We'll have to hope for a lucky break when we get there."

Gaye looked down at her lap. "What did the locator look like?" she asked.

"Little red box," he said. "He called it a thingfinder. The humanoids might have gotten it, but its more likely that one of the gnomes on the base has it now. We can't go back for it. The scro are all over the place." He patted Gaye's feet under the blanket, then stood up to leave. "I've got to find out what's going on aboard our new ship. I'll come back to check on you in a little while."

Gaye didn't look up as Teldin headed for the door. He heard her call his name once, and he turned before he left.

Gaye was still looking down. Her arm was out, handing something to him. It was a red box with an open back and a dark glass window on it.

"I found this when I was out earlier," she said. "Is this it?" She dared to look up.

*　*　*　*　*

Ironpiece was a bright spot of light against a stupendous backdrop of stars as the pair of doors at the stern of the *Perilous Halibut* came open. The figure there looked out but was oblivious to the splendor of wildspace. Instead, the figure stepped around the rear jettison, from which shrapnel could be launched at trailing foes, then carefully scanned the void.

Despite its apparently mechanical trappings, the gnomish covered lantern the figure bore was powered by a simple magical spell that provided continual light. The gnomes had merely added assorted gears and sparking devices that made the lantern weigh three times what it normally would, yet none of the devices worked and all had frozen in place with rust. Still, the light inside was as bright as ever.

After a few moments, the figure spotted a faint, blinking light trailing the ship. It was the signal. Carefully, the figure raised the lantern and, recalling the code that had been so painfully learned, began to open and shut the lantern's cover, sending the first of many messages that its master awaited. Only the stars saw the figure's face and noted its grief.

Chapter Ten

• • •

The scro who broke the news did not sweeten its bitter taste, simply gave the facts.

"Sir, five ships out of Captain Sharak's force of twelve have reported back from Ironpiece. The rest were disabled by ground fire. Our casualties are estimated at one hundred and fifteen troops. The gnomes were somehow able to detect Sharak's approach even after our fleet had distracted or disabled their orbital scouts, as the gnomes were quite ready for us on the ground. Neither Teldin Moore nor his companions could be found. He may have escaped us."

The eight naval and marine commanders crowded into General Vorr's office said nothing in their humiliation. Vorr looked calmly at the tall, black-armored scro, who stared back without apparent qualms. "Captain Geraz, do you have any idea of where Teldin might be?"

"Sir, I've heard several reports of gnomish ships fleeing during the fighting," Geraz said, slurring his words a bit. "One ship crashed through the rooftop of a hangar and fled into the sky, another took off normally, and a third crashed into the lake. Our troops were able to capture enough papers to indicate that one of the ships that got away was of an experimental design, a long-range craft, but Intelligence is having trouble translating the gnomes' notes.

"We followed the lich's directions for finding Teldin in the infirmary. One of our ogres, your bodyguard Gargon, found

him in the infirmary, but Gargon was slain. We recovered the
body for questioning by the war priests and learned that the
ogre was killed by a human in a cloak—Teldin, we believe.
Two scro reported seeing a man in a cloak with a female half-
elf and a gnome enter a hangar just before a black spelljammer
craft smashed through the roof and fled."

So, Teldin had killed Gargon. Lost in thought, Vorr drew in
his breath. This human would spend hours in torture before
he died. It would be an interesting show for the troops.

"Exactly what damage was the force able to inflict on the
gnomes?" said a slow, venomous voice. All heads turned to
the speaker, propped up in a heavy chair. Admiral Halker's
face was pale and his expression haggard, but an unnatural
light burned deep in his eyes.

Captain Geraz's lifeless eyes looked into the admiral's. "Sir,
we destroyed five small craft in orbit, and two small and two
large craft on the ground. At least four buildings, two of them
hangars or storehouses, were set ablaze with class-two aerial
bombs. Of the gnomes' casualties, we estimate that they suffered forty dead and wounded at the very least."

"So, the ground mission was a failure," finished the admiral, an edge to his voice. He leaned forward in his seat.

Captain Geraz stared back without blinking. "Yes, sir. We
were apparently anticipated, as I mentioned earlier."

Silence drew out in the cramped command room aboard the
Tarantula's Trident. "How could that be possible, Captain?"
asked the admiral in a voice like a serpent's hiss. "Why are you
so sure that the gnomes knew in advance of the attack?"

"Sir, for all their cleverness, gnomes are still gnomes, and
they almost never fight efficiently without strong, decisive
leadership. A surprise attack is only rarely repulsed by them.
Yet ground fire began immediately after our ships broke cloud
cover, and it remained heavy throughout the attack. The entire base was effectively on alert status when Captain Sharak's
force arrived. Gnome units had already sealed most of the crit-
ical base buildings, and ground fighting was reportedly severe
and without quarter. I cannot believe that the gnomes were
capable of this without foreknowledge of the assault, though I
am at a loss to say how they possibly could have learned of it."

Halker sucked in his cheeks as he looked at the captain.

"You sound regretfully close to saying we have a spy among us, Captain."

The thought hung in the air for a few moments before Vorr broke in. "Or the gnomes have spell-casters or mechanical devices that can do their spying for them."

"Or our most venerable foes have decided to send their own intelligence on to the gnomes," added an aged voice. Everyone turned to look at the withered Oriental man in flowerprint robes of silk. Usso casually gestured at the ceiling, as if to the stars. "The elves have cloaking helms, have they not? They could have seen Captain Sharak's ships depart from our fleet while one of their man-o-wars was barely more than hailing distance away. With but a spell or two, they could have sent warning to the gnomes, despite their earlier differences in the battle. Remember, the elves stood to lose nothing by telling the gnomes of our plans, and they stood to gain much: the restoration of some of the gnomes' goodwill, the destruction of our ships and soldiers, and the safety of Teldin Moore and his cloak. I must consider this the most likely alternative, as I have detected no sign of weakness or treason among our own fleet. I must dismiss General Vorr's concerns, as I have armored the command offices of our fleet with lead mesh to prevent outside agencies from scrying upon us, and the reports filed by the survivors of the expedition gave no sign that the gnomes made use of any wizardry, whether their own or hired. I believe the elves have again made fools of us."

Admiral Halker broke the brief silence that followed. "Of all the alternatives," he said softly, "I find that one to be the most disturbing. A traitor can be rooted out. A wizard's spells can be blocked. But to think that the elves have outfoxed us, that they can become invisible at will . . ." Halker's fingers dug into the arms of his chair. "The elves whipped our ancestors like mongrels, broke their fleets, drove them from the rich worlds, shut them out of the light of a hundred suns, gave them dust to drink and rock to eat and filth with which to clothe themselves, and laughed at the thought that we, the children of Dukagsh, would ever repay the blood debt owed them. That we must swallow this elven vomit for our meals, that we must endure the laughter that must surely ring in their ships—Almighty Dukagsh must long to put out his own eyes to spare him our shame." The admiral's grip tightened on the chair arms until his hands were corded knots.

One of the admiral's hands suddenly arose, a narrow finger sweeping the room. "But I say now, 'no more.' I charge you to find a way, a dozen ways, a thousand ways to counter this threat. I want to find those elves with all the effort we are putting into finding this Teldin Moore, and find a thousand ways to destroy them. I want to see their lifeblood spill into space. I want their heads to hang from our ships and their bodies to grace our tables as dessert. I want them to fear us. I want to avenge our lost brothers and ancestors, to avenge the lives and spirits that were crushed under the golden heel of the elves! Find those ways, and avenge us!"

"Sir," said Captain Geraz, his face still expressionless, "our strategies appear to have been laughably weak of late. When we cannot outsmart gnomes, we should look elsewhere for military advice. The lich might have a better idea of what to do than we have had. Perhaps we should consult him."

General Vorr flushed with shock and rage. No scro had ever spoken so to a superior officer, much less a room full of them. The other scro captains and commanders stirred with equal rage, teeth bared and murmuring curses.

"Captain Geraz—ex-Captain, I should say—you are out of line." Admiral Halker's eyes burned into the young captain. "This is a matter for scro and the living, not for the mad and the dead. Moreover, you are disrespectful, and you will pay for that." The admiral's words dropped in volume but redoubled in intensity. "It is likely that you will pay with your life." He dropped a hand to the golden ceremonial dagger on his belt.

General Vorr, at the same moment, reached down for his sword hilt. He could see almost every other scro captain do the same thing. Scro justice was nothing if not fast.

"You cannot collect from that which has no currency," said the scro captain, making no move to draw his own weapons. He raised his hands and pulled away his helmet.

The admiral's eyes grew large, and his mouth fell open, revealing hardened gums. Two of the scro ship captains sitting near Geraz leaped to their feet with shouted oaths.

The top of Captain Geraz's head was gone, the skullcap cut away. The vile odor of rotting flesh spilled into the room. A red-brown crust of blood matted Geraz's short, bristly hair. The wound obviously had been cleaned sufficiently to be hidden by the helmet. Those closest to Geraz saw that his brain was gone, his skull left empty, and they withdrew from the animated corpse as if it were poisoned.

"I am beyond the world of the living now," said the scro captain dully. "I was killed by catapult shot from an elven ship during the attack by the elves. My body was recovered from the *Cursed Shadow* and enspelled to serve you on Ironpiece and bear a message from your ally Skarkesh."

Vorr stared in disbelief at the undead scro. The false lich did this? He dared do this to a scro and show off the results? Something caught fire in his blood and spread to the core of his soul. That someone would do such a thing was unthinkable, a violation that had but one punishment.

Admiral Halker, for all his rage, had the presence of mind to respond. "Your message from Skarkesh is?" he asked hoarsely, fingers still clutching his golden dagger.

"Skarkesh has located Teldin Moore in wildspace, aboard a gnomish ship. He is on course for one of this crystal sphere's portals. Here is his heading." The undead scro pulled a flattened, rolled parchment from his belt, offering it to the admiral. General Vorr intercepted it, knowing that his touch would nullify any cursed item designed to harm a living being, but he didn't look at the paper.

"And here," the scro said, untying a belt pouch and pulling a second sheet of parchment from it, "are a few ways to counter the cloaking helms of the elves. Skarkesh, in his wisdom, has seen fit to present these to you as gifts, to better enable you to do your jobs." General Vorr took that, too.

"Have you any further requests?" asked the undead scro.

"Only one," said Admiral Halker, breaking a short, tense silence. The admiral half stood from his seat and raised his right hand, bearing the steel symbol of the eyes of Dukagsh from a necklace he wore. "By the powers invested in me as a war priest of the Chosen of Dukagsh, I command you, undead, to be destroyed and return to dust."

Geraz's body rocked on its feet, then collapsed on the floor. The other scro edged back in case there was another trick, but nothing further occurred.

General Vorr carefully reached down and checked the body. Captain Geraz had definitely been dead for some time; his skin was cold to the touch. The spell cast over him had overcome the corpse's natural rigidity, which was even now taking effect. Vorr took his fingers from the scro's neck and sat back on his heels. Captain Geraz had been a good warrior. It was a mortal insult to have abused him like this.

Vorr looked back at the admiral, then stood up. "Sir," he said, "this would be a good time to adjourn and have Captain Geraz's body cared for."

The old scro nodded, his expression unreadable. "I agree," he said quietly, letting his holy symbol fall. "Everyone but General Vorr is to leave and await further orders. Take Captain Geraz with you and see to his proper burial in space."

The other officers immediately stood and saluted, their voices shouting the Elvish curse in unison. They filed out, some carrying Geraz's remains, to talk among themselves on the squid ship's main deck. Usso left with a thoughtful look on his aged man's face. Admiral Halker seemed lost in a reverie, staring at the far wall from his chair.

When the door had closed, the admiral turned to Vorr. "Whatever else we do on our little jaunt through the spheres," he said, "I want to see something done about the lich. He has made a fool of me before my officers. I want him to burn for this—not now, but one day, and soon. We've got the ships and the soldiers he needs to recover that cloak, but we'll have precious little of our command and respect if we let that filth pile get away with this. Start making plans for an assault on his pyramid ship, to be carried out at a future date."

"Yes, sir," said Vorr crisply. He had been toying with this very idea since he had first met Skarkesh.

The admiral craned his head at the papers Vorr held. "You may as well see if there's anything useful there. I don't want to lose Teldin's course, so you should get that first message to the helm. When you've done that, let's look at the second message and see what our . . . partner recommends as prudent courses to foil the elves. I'll meet you back here in one hour." The admiral slowly got to his feet.

Vorr headed for the door and saluted on his way out. Behind him, he heard the admiral call, "Remember that first order first, General."

I will, Vorr promised himself. I will.

*   *   *   *   *

The humanoid fleet took up a new, tighter formation as it set out in pursuit of the lone gnomish ship. Invisible now because of the thousands of miles between them and the humanoids, the four surviving elven warships tracked their foes. Before long, two of the man-o-war spelljammers moved in to reconnoiter the humanoid ships.

One ship came back.

"They found us, my admiral," said Captain Melwan, who just two days ago had been the second officer of the *Free Wind's Fury*. "We sustained considerable damage to the forward areas of both the main and battle decks in the orcs' initial volley. The *Leaping Hart* lost its helm at once and was set aflame. We could not render aid. Captain Sirithea was wounded on the bridge, and First Officer Eal Dornal was killed by a shot outside the spelljammer's cabin. Three others were killed, sixteen wounded. I took command and ordered a retreat, using a false movement pattern to avoid giving away the location of our fleet. I had to assume after the attack that the orcs were able to track us as they wished, and we made all speed back once we were certain we were not being followed."

Admiral Cirathorn raised a finger from his command throne. "How do you know," he said tonelessly, "that you were not followed?"

Melwan, a tall elf with dull gray hair and eyes, hesitated. "Sir, our battlewizard's spells assured us that—"

"Are you certain?" Cirathorn's voice was quiet and ruthless. "Are you certain? You were, after all, detected while your ship was cloaked. If the orcs could do that, how can you be sure they did not track you all the way back here?"

The captains and battlewizards in the *Empress Dorianne*'s conference room looked at one another. The idea that a cloaking helm could be defeated was unthinkable. Cloaking helms were distributed by the Imperial Fleet to only a handful of ships, and these had never been known to suffer casualties while cloaked. If the cloak was dropped early, the ship could be attacked at will.

"Sir," said the tall elf, his face nearly white, "I did not order the *Free Wind's Fury* to uncloak. Our closest approach to the orcish fleet was five hundred feet from the trailing vessel, an ancient vipership. We suddenly encountered a minor nebula, and the enemy fleet opened fire upon us moments afterward. I took command—"

"Ahh." Cirathorn leaned back in his chair, his expression thoughtful. "I see now. The orcs detected the image of your ship as you passed through the nebula. It is the same principle a groundling adventurer would use against an invisible foe—hurling a sack of flour in the air to detect the opponent's body after the flour coats it—only your ship blundered into a natural trap." Cirathorn leaned forward in his chair. "Why did Captain Sirithea allow the *Fury* to enter the nebula? Was she not aware that this would happen?"

"I . . . haven't any idea, sir," said Melwan. "She's in a coma and is being tended by—"

"I'm aware of her condition," said Cirathorn. His hands were clasped together in front of him, elbows resting on the arms of his throne. "I want your opinion."

The tall elf was silent for a few moments. "None of us saw the nebula, sir, before we entered it. It appeared suddenly as the orcish fleet was passing through it."

The admiral stared down at the new captain. "Could it be that the orcs have suddenly become rather clever and have merely found a way to detect our ships by, say, firing flour, dust, or other particulate debris from their jettisons and catapults, in essence creating their own temporary nebulae?"

Melwan's eyes widened as he considered this. "Sir, after the incident, I did notice that our ship was covered with a fine white powder, which I assumed to have been from the nebula. We are still cleaning up the ship as well as repairing it, but I can have the material checked for its composition."

"Do so immediately," said the brown-haired admiral, his eyes sharp. "Report back before this watch is out."

Melwan snapped off a salute and left with his battlewizard within five seconds. When the door shut behind him, Cirathorn turned to the other elves in the spacious room beneath the crystal chandelier. Paintings of landscapes hung on the walls, softly lit by the chandelier's many candles.

"The orcs have become much brighter since we last met them on the field of battle," the admiral said tiredly. He looked up without seeming to see anyone present. "Perhaps they are far smarter than we would like to believe. Perhaps they are far stronger and far better fighters, too. The loss of the *Unicorn's Wing* gave me pause, but this disaster while under cloaking has instilled me with dread. I have the gravest concerns for our safety, and for the safety of our entire Imperial Fleet and people. I believe a second Unhuman War is upon us, and we might not live to see it through."

The other elves stared at Cirathorn in shock and disbelief. "Sir," started one, an amber-haired male with a white mask painted on his face, "I don't believe the orcs could possibly have the intellect to plan such undertakings as you have described. We are speaking of orcs, and they are incapable of any form of foresight and planning beyond a day's time."

Cirathorn smiled grimly. "Then how have they done so well so far?" he asked. "In the old days, we would have consumed their fleet by now with but the forces we have here. Yet we harry them from hiding like guerillas, not like the lords of wildspace we imagine ourselves to be. We dare not approach them again in direct battle without an invincible edge, one that will allow us to crush them quickly and decisively. As of yet, we lack that edge. Even the firepower of this armada is not sufficient. We need something more."

None of the other elves spoke. Several looked away—whether in shame or thought, Cirathorn could not tell. It was obvious that no one had any new ideas.

Cirathorn let out his breath and leaned back in his throne. "We are less than a fortnight from this crystal sphere's portal. Teldin Moore and his ship will not likely be caught before then if he is able to use the powers of his cloak to take his ship out of harm's way. Once beyond the portal, it is twenty-nine days, with an error of three days, to Herdspace and the falmadaraatha. We must prepare ourselves as best we can for our next meeting with these orcs, or whatever they are calling themselves these days. We shall reconvene this evening for a discussion of tactics in such an event. You will each come prepared with at least two workable tactics, one fleet tactic and one ship tactic, given the caustic knowledge in which we have bathed ourselves this day."

The other elves slowly came to their feet and made their way out of the room to their own chambers on a lower level of the armada. Cirathorn rubbed his eyes, feeling an ache in his head flow and ebb with each beat of his heart.

"Are you well, my admiral?" came a silk-soft voice.

"No." He dropped his hands and looked at his battle-wizard. "No, I am not well. Our people are not well, and our future is ill—but we have a chance, one pathway to salvation. You have been our best guide, and your direction has served us well. I must trust to the gods that it will be enough."

The pale battlewizard nodded but said nothing.

"Have you heard any more from the lookouts about the signal light emitted from the gnomes' ship?" Cirathorn asked. "Has anyone been able to translate the code?"

Mirandel mumbled a response to the negative.

"We will need to warn our ally with Teldin, then." Cirathorn's gaze ran up and down the female elf's thin frame. "You still grieve for your sister," he said. "Why?"

"She and I were very close," said the battlewizard, her voice failing. Her shoulders slumped. "Since the battle, I . . . I feel lost. She was my only friend when we were children. I . . ." Her voice trailed off as she looked at the floor, unable to speak further. She appeared to be ready to cry.

Cirathorn frowned, sitting up. "I need you, Mirandel. Don't leave me now to fall inside yourself. I lost six generations of my family when Aerlofalyn was taken. We are in the crucible. For all that we have lost, we will lose far more if we give in to weakness now. Be strong, my Mirandel. We will avenge your sister Yolantha and all who died with her."

The battlewizard nodded her head slightly, barely enough to detect. "Yes," she whispered. "I am sorry to be so weak, my admiral, but it is hard. I miss her."

The admiral got up from his throne, his robes rustling, and stepped down to put a hand on the battlewizard's warm cheek. With a careful stroke, he brushed her long white hair with his fingertips. She never looked up.

"You are my strength," he said softly. "You devised the plan by which we can keep a closer watch over Teldin Moore, and we were able to use that plan to warn the accursed gnomes of the orcs' invasion. I need your brilliance in this darkness. Help me find a way to fight the orcs. Save us."

The battlewizard nodded after a pause. "Yes, my admiral." Her voice was so weak that he could barely hear her.

Cirathorn smiled. He would wear the Cloak of the First Pilot before long, of that he was certain. He would then have the *Spelljammer*, and the orcs across all space would feel the flaming spear of elven rage. Mirandel would come through with something clever. She would not fail him now.

He pressed his lips to Mirandel's smooth forehead as his arms encircled her and her thin body leaned into his for comfort. She was the best of all battlewizards, the best of all spouses, the truest of lovers. It was a shame he did not love her back, but surely she knew that and accepted it. There was no time for love now in these days of blood and war. There was time now for only vengeance.

* * * * *

"Well," said Dyffed heartily, as he sat down to breakfast, "I have some good news and some bad news."

As one, Teldin, Aelfred, Sylvie, Gaye, and Gomja paused, exchanging glances. They then put down their wooden spoons and looked in the gnome's direction. The group was packed so closely together in the ship's narrow dining area that Teldin feared he would go mad from claustrophobia if the diet of creamed soaked grains did not kill him first. Gomja sat on the floor beside the table, unable to squeeze into one of the absurdly confining wooden seats, each mounted to the wall. Whoever was at the far end of the table was trapped there by everyone else who took a seat afterward. On this day, the eighth one out from Ironpiece, Teldin was the one who got to be trapped. The air was overly warm and stale, reinforcing his sense of confinement. His stomach was queasy and tense.

Dressed in the same clothes he'd worn since landing on Ironpiece, Dyffed spooned large dollops of sludgy gray creamed soaked grains into his bowl, taking them from the steaming pot resting at the near end of the table. He took a deep sniff of its flavorless aroma, sighed with contentment, and took a seat next to Aelfred, who looked at Sylvie with a why-me expression and shrugged. Sylvie fought back a smile.

"What's the news?" said Teldin, unable to wait any longer. "Your good and bad news."

"Hmm?" said Dyffed absently, about to take his first bite. "Oh! Yes, of course. I have some good news and some bad news. The good news is that we're about to run out of food." With that, he began to consume huge spoonfuls of creamed soaked grains, each bite accompanied by much lip smacking and "Mmmmmm!" sounds.

Teldin felt an irrational urge to jump on his chair, run across the tabletop, and strangle the unkempt gnome. He closed his eyes and counted to ten instead. It didn't help.

"I suppose that can be considered good news," remarked Aelfred dryly. His bowl was half finished, consumed only to avoid starvation. "So, what's the bad news?"

Dyffed took a moment to swallow. "Ah!" he said, spitting out a few bits of cereal, "the bad news is that we won't be able to steer or take showers." He chuckled to himself. "That's quite the funniest thing, really." The gnome shoveled another spoonful of creamed soaked grains into his mouth.

There was a fragile silence. Gomja used the break to carefully heave his enormous bulk up from the floor and help himself to his sixth bowl of gray mash this morning. Unlike everyone else but the gnomes, Gomja, a vegetarian from birth, loved creamed soaked grains ("Gnomes know how to cook!" he once had confided to Teldin).

"Dyffed," said Teldin, his patience virtually gone, "what are you talking about?" He was aware that everyone but the gnome was staring at him, and he tried with little success to stem his rising anger. He had spent the last eight days stumbling over gnomes in hallways, finding them repairing springs in the middle of the night under his bed, and wedging himself into impossibly small spaces that obviously had been built for gnomes and no one else. Aelfred ran things aboard the ship, directing the gnomes in their duties, but he couldn't be everywhere at once. The gnomes were restless and ill at ease these days, and they were always in the way.

Gaye put a hand on Teldin's arm and squeezed to distract him. Teldin tried to relax, contenting himself with imagining how terrible it would be if he were to give in to his baser urges and begin throwing gnomes off the ship.

"Well," said Dyffed, wiping his mouth on his once-white shirt front, "once we run out of the creamed soaked grains, we shall have nothing left to feed the two giant hamsters in the hydrodynamic pumping station, and we shall be forced to eat them instead, and once we butcher them, we shall, of course, have nothing to make the water pumps operate, so our showers will stop, and we will also be unable to connect the steering gyroscope's drive shaft to the pumping station, since our hamsters are being baked, unless we gnomes run inside the giant wheels in place of the hamsters. It's quite simple."

Gomja stopped eating his cereal and wrinkled his nose in disgust at the mention of eating the giant hamsters. Gaye looked positively stricken, her mouth falling open in shock.

"What happens when we run out of hamster meat?" asked Sylvie, clearly not looking forward to the answer.

"Oo, wuh fine sunthun en thuh galley," mumbled Dyffed, his mouth full again. "Don worra aboud id."

"Can't we find something else to eat besides hamsters?" asked Gaye, her voice breaking. She turned to Teldin and pulled on his sleeve. "Teldin, please talk to them! I know how to cook! Don't let them do that! Do something!"

Breakfast disintegrated shortly thereafter. Teldin retired to his room, having extracted a promise from the gnomes that they would "check the galley carefully first" before serving up hamster meat. He found out a few minutes later that Gaye had gone rearward and managed to lock herself in the hydrodynamic pumping station with Ruff and Widget, the giant hamsters, and was refusing to let any gnome near them. He wished he had a strong drink.

"Do you have a moment, sir?" came Gomja's deep voice from the hallway.

"Sure." Teldin got to his feet from the cramped bed, his back aching, and stretched out. He opened the door and let the massive giff inside, moving to the far side of the narrow room to give Gomja a chance to sit on the edge of the bed. It was the only furniture in the room strong enough to hold the giff's weight. Nonetheless, the bed groaned and cracked as Gomja settled his weight on it.

"I was talking with one of the gnomes, named Loomfinger, sir," said Gomja. "He's turned out to be a novice mage who says he took up illusions as a hobby. I made him an assistant helmsman to Sylvie, and he's also helping her with navigational duties. He says the trip to Herdspace will take about thirty days after we enter the phlogiston. I think we should use the time to drill the gnomes and set up a chain of command. I would be the logical choice to lead them in a fight, but I would not like to command the ship. Aelfred would be the best one for that. Having no one in charge is troublesome, and it could hurt us if the orcs catch up to us."

Teldin nodded briefly. "I have no problem with that. I've been thinking the same thing. But this is the gnomes' ship. Maybe they'd want a say in who ran things here."

"Yes, sir, but I suspect they'll go along with whomever we designate as leader. None of the gnomes on this ship have any military experience. They're just technicians that I rounded up as soon as I heard the initial alert sirens. They're used to being given orders, not to giving them. It's worse than the situation at Mount Nevermind."

Teldin sighed and ran a hand through his hair. "If they and everyone else agree to it, it sounds fine to me. I only wish this ship was bigger. It helps to go out on deck, but then I hate to come back inside."

Gomja nodded sympathetically. Teldin knew his big friend was forced to sleep on the ship's upper deck, as there was no place to put him without blocking hall traffic; the giff fit no bed aboard. Gomja also snored like a lion roaring.

"It's uncomfortable, I know," said Gomja, "but we were lucky just to have gotten this far, sir. Once Aelfred and I get the gnomes organized and teach them some basic tactics and drills, we should have a chance in case the orcs attack us again and try to grapple and board us."

"It's your fate to command gnomes all the rest of your life," Teldin said, managing a grin. "I hardly envy you that."

Gomja smiled, too, his little ears perking up. "There are worse troops, sir," he said. "I would be afraid to command a force of kender, for instance."

Teldin nodded in agreement. "Speaking of which, I've just heard that she's gone and—"

"She's still there, sir," Gomja finished. "I was going to ask if you can talk her out. This ship has plenty of supplies hidden in the galley. I found them not five minutes ago. Even with the creamed soaked grains gone, we have lots of food left before we'd ever have to eat a hamster." The giff made a sour face. "I'm afraid I'm in agreement with Gaye on that, sir."

Teldin frowned. "That's odd. Dyffed told us earlier that no one had gotten around to loading up the ship with food supplies, much less putting in the helm and weaponry."

Gomja looked at him blankly. "I hadn't heard that, sir. I suppose that Dyffed wasn't aware whether things had been loaded on or not. Perhaps they supplied the ship and forgot about it." He shrugged his gigantic shoulders. "Who knows?"

The giff got to his feet, stooping to avoid striking the ceiling. "Carry on, sir," he said, giving a quick salute. "We've nothing left to do until we get to Herdspace. I'm looking forward to finding out why it's called that. None of the gnomes know but Dyffed, and he laughs when I mention it. Oh, and don't forget about Gaye, sir."

"I'll tell her," Teldin said, returning the salute with feeling. "I'll see you later."

When the giff was gone, Teldin considered lying down again for a few moments more, but decided not to bother. His back was killing him, and he couldn't rest with Gaye all stirred up. He straightened his clothes and prepared to leave for the besieged kender.

It wasn't until he was going to see Gaye that Teldin though about Gomja's comment about the alert on Ironpiece. Hadn't the first siren been one that only the gnomes could hear? Yet Gomja had said he'd begun rounding up gnomes at that time. The giff had never displayed any ability to hear the high-pitched sounds gnomes could detect, but maybe he could anyway. Maybe the gnomes had heard the first siren and had told him about it. It was only a mildly interesting thought, and Teldin decided he would ask Gomja about it the following day. He promptly forgot all about it.

Thirty-four days passed. Gaye cooked. The gnomes trained. Everyone waited.

And the scro caught up with them.

Chapter Eleven

· · ·

"The portal! It's opening!" Gaye shouted, clutching the bow railing on the top deck of the *Perilous Halibut*. Ahead of her, impossibly far away but drawing nearer, was a dark gray wall that stretched from one end of the universe to the other. In the center of the wall was a burning yellow whirlpool of light whose arms rotated with agonizing slowness. At the hub of the yellow whirlpool was a sky-blue dot that grew steadily larger as the arms turned.

Gaye thought of the pupil and iris of an unspeakably mighty god, and she shivered with excitement even as she puzzled over the color beyond the portal. She was looking into the crystal sphere of Herdspace, of course—but wasn't it always black beyond a portal, in the wildspace beyond?

"Prepare to fire!" thundered Gomja's voice from aft. Gaye turned and saw the giff, wearing a freshly cleaned white uniform and clutching a crossbow as long as a man's arm. Gomja had demanded the chance to fight the enemy, and Aelfred had finally agreed to stay below and handle shipboard activities there in case of boarding. The gnomes were already filling the ship with boobytraps.

With his free hand, Gomja was directing the array of crossbow-bearing gnomes who knelt along the ship's railing or crewed the newly installed deck ballista. The gnomes wore a chaotic assortment of armor manufactured from cooking utensils, metal scraps, and ship's supplies. The giff stood by the trailing edge of the ship's huge vertical fin, lit all around by the infinite depths of the rainbow-hued phlogiston. The "flow" was a sky painted by a mad deity with every color a god's palette could hold. The colors ran and blurred together in evershifting swirls larger than worlds.

Gaye never got tired of looking at the flow, even if it now held the shape of a trailing enemy ship. It was only about a mile behind now, a greenish scorpion ship with its great claws extended and open as it came on for the *Perilous Halibut's* tail.

A tiny, dark shape detached itself from the upraised tail of the scorpion ship, gaining rapidly on the gnomes' ship. "Incoming fire!" Gomja roared. "Flatten and hold fast!"

The two dozen gnomes on deck threw themselves flat as they watched the catapult shot close in—and take an increasingly obvious path to their right. As the yard-wide rock flew by at a distance of only a few hundred feet, Gaye sighed with relief, only now remembering that she hadn't ducked, too. She heard a ragged cheer erupt from the gnomes. Several sent their crossbow bolts chasing after the stone, and a few others fired at the scorpion.

"Company, hold your fire until I give the command!" Gomja ordered. "Those dogs will get a taste of our bolts yet, but we're going to make each shot count!"

Gaye looked ahead again. The flaming yellow whirlpool was much closer, but she couldn't begin to estimate its distance or size even now. It was vast and painfully beautiful. The blue pupil continued to grow. No stars were visible beyond. How bizarre, she thought. Dyffed had said that Herdspace was different from other crystal spheres, and he'd tried to explain how, but she'd never caught on to the specifics of his unbearably detailed lecture. Herdspace was a sphere with no planets—she had caught that part, and Dyffed's reference to everything living on the inside of a gigantic bubble, but the concept hadn't quite jelled yet in her mind as to what he had meant by that. The gnome also kept talking about a something-something "mega-fawn" on which the fal, One Six Nine, was said to live. Gaye pushed it out of her mind as she watched the yellow whirlpool's blue center open. She'd have to see it to understand it.

"Begin the climb!" the giff shouted. Gaye looked back even though she knew he wasn't yelling for her. He was calling through the voice tube to the helm, where Sylvie had been sitting for the last two days since the orcs in the lone scorpion had begun to gain on them. In moments, the *Perilous Halibut*'s long black bow rose, lifting up and away from the vast portal ahead. The gnomes, looking sternward, took aim at the scorpion with their light crossbows over the heads of their fellows—exactly the result Gomja had wanted, to allow all the gnomes to fire at once.

"Sir!" came the shrill cry of a gnome somewhere aft. "Potentially hostile spelljamming vessel apparently crewed by unidentified humanoids is now trailing at fifteen hundred yards, with an estimated error of one hun—"

"Fire!" Gomja bawled, drowning out the gnome.

"Immediately activate the mechanism according to the preset trajectory!" Gaye heard a gnome shout rapidly. The command was interrupted after the first word by the heavy thump of a ballista and the crack of two dozen crossbow bolts being released. Then came the creaking sounds of the ballista mechanism being cranked back for a second shot. A small cloud of bolts could be seen for a second, flashing toward the scorpion. The gnomes immediately reloaded their crossbows, snatching bolts from the huge pile of ammunition carefully stacked along the deck.

"Roll her over and climb!" Gomja shouted, leaning back. The backdrop around the *Perilous Halibut* began to rotate, starting to send the lone trailing ship below the deck's horizon. Quickly, though, the spelljammer changed course and climbed again in the opposite direction that it had originally taken, like a fish unable to decide which way was up. By the time the gnomes had reloaded their crossbows, the scorpion was again in view—now upside down, but with its main deck—and the crew on it—clearly visible.

"Prepare to fire! Hold it, hold it—Fire!" Gomja shouted. Gaye heard the crossbows and ballista snap in unison. It was incredible to think that, only a month ago, those same gnomes could barely be made to breathe at the same time, much less function as a military unit. Gomja's constant drilling had taken care of that, even if the constant stream of shouted orders kept everyone else awake some nights.

Gaye had turned back to look at the opening portal when she heard someone climb the ladder from the deck below. She saw with relief that it was Teldin Moore, a short sword belted on under his dull maroon cloak. Everyone had given up trying to explain the cloak's seemingly random color changes.

"What's the—oh," Teldin said, turning around to see the gnomes still firing at the scorpion ship. He looked back at Gaye, who was wearing a remarkably low-cut red dress with a skirt made of cloth strips. Teldin knew better than to ask where she'd gotten it; she produced clothing out of thin air, but never admitted how she did it. "Where's your shield?" he asked in astonishment. "Didn't you pick up a shield?"

"It was too much of a bother to carry around," Gaye replied with a smile. "If my thread's going to get cut, it'll get cut, and a shield isn't going to help. Besides, I get a much better view without it. Isn't it grand?" She punctuated her last comment by waving a hand at the oncoming portal, visible but dropping below the bow as the ship maneuvered.

Lips parted, Teldin stared at the yellow whirlpool and its blue eye. The sight literally took his breath away. "We're going to go through it in only a few more minutes," he finally mumbled. "I was just talking with Sylvie."

"How's she looking? She's been on the helm for—"

"She's exhausted," Teldin said, tearing his gaze away from the yellow maelstrom. "We can't replace her as long as the orcs are coming up on us like this. I'm here to bring you back inside. That scorpion's crew might board us soon, and you've got to get out of here before it does. Now, move."

Gaye got a surprised and indignant look on her elfin face. "Teldin Moore, what right do you have to—"

"Incoming! Shields up!" Gomja roared from the stern. Both Gaye and Teldin looked rearward. Gnomes snatched up the wooden shields beside them. Recognizing the danger, Teldin instantly threw himself over Gaye, knocking her down with a thud and flattening her against the black, metal-plated deck. The kender gasped, the wind knocked from her lungs.

There came a brief clattering sound across the length of the ship, not unlike hail on a metal roof. A gnome gave a brief cry of fear. Teldin felt something punch him hard against his cloak under his left shoulder blade, and he grunted and clenched his teeth against the stab.

"Teldin," came Gaye's muffled voice as she struggled beneath him, "I like you, too, but I can't breathe. Let me up."

Teldin risked a look around, wincing with pain. All the gnomes seemed to be okay, aiming their shields in the direction of the scorpion ship. Gomja held an enormous tower shield made from the ship's galley door. "Lower shields!" he shouted, suddenly setting his shield aside and hefting his huge crossbow. "Reload and prepare to fire! Ballista with us!"

"Teldin!" Gaye wheezed, trying to shove him off her chest. "Darn you!"

"Get below, now!" Teldin ordered the kender, getting up. His left shoulder blade hurt abominably; an arrow clattered to the deck as he moved. No doubt the magical cloak had kept it from punching through his ribs. He kept his cloak positioned above Gaye as she rolled over on her side, still trying to get her breath. With a dirty look up at Teldin, Gaye crept to the deck hatchway, stopping only as she was ready to descend.

"I want to stay up and watch," she said petulantly.

"Not a chance," Teldin said, and he pushed her head down into the ship. He flipped the hatch shut, jammed the locking bar in place, then got to his feet. Only a gnome ship would have locks on both sides of its hatchways, he noted.

"Roll her over and climb!" Gomja called as the gnomes raised their crossbows again. "Prepare to fire!"

Teldin could see that the scorpion ship was much closer now than before, only minutes from catching up. The orcs must have put their best spell-caster on the helm, he thought grimly. The last month had been so peaceful that he'd thought they had escaped. For the hundredth time, Teldin considered asking the gnomes about their "birthday party" weapon, but discarded the notion. Any gnome-made secret weapon would be deadlier to its users than to its target. Teldin never even brought up the topic, for fear of getting Dyffed interested in testing the device, wherever it was.

"Fire!" Crossbow and ballista bolts leaped out at the scorpion ship. Teldin cursed himself when he realized he didn't have a missile weapon. He had come up to the deck after he'd heard Gaye was here in the thick of the trouble, and now that she was safe he didn't feel he could abandon Gomja and the gnomes. He hurried aft to see if a spare crossbow was available for him.

The gnomes steadily continued their loading and firing and paid no attention to Teldin as he ran up. Gomja reloaded his bow and shouted for the ship to roll over and climb again, always keeping the scorpion in view. The giff saw Teldin approach from the corner of one eye and looked around. "You shouldn't be here, sir!" Gomja said in astonishment. "You don't have a shield, and there's no place to take cover!"

Teldin saw several spare light crossbows on the deck. He grabbed one and cranked it back. "My cloak's good enough," he said, quickly setting the bowstring and reaching for a bolt, "and I'm getting claustrophobia anyway."

Gomja stared at him, then nodded and raised his crossbow once more at the scorpion. "As you wish, sir," he said, sighting in with a proud grin. "My sire always said, 'A brave heart seeks the heart of the action.' Prepare to fire!"

Teldin raised his crossbow, stepping back to get out of the giff's way. Gomja would have preferred to use the musket strapped to the inside of his shield, or the pistols stuck in his belt, but the phlogiston's flammable nature precluded use of any firearms.

"Fire!" Gomja shouted. Teldin concentrated, but his cloak did nothing to improve his aim or sharpen his senses. He hastily squeezed off a shot.

As he hastily reloaded, Teldin couldn't help thinking that it was nothing short of a miracle that the supply rooms aboard the ship had turned out to be well stocked with personal weapons and ammunition, even the deck ballista, just as the galley had been overstocked with food—this despite the fact that none of the thirty-one gnomes aboard the ship remembered having stocked anything before the ship took off. All had been busy examining the ship's hull for scratches on its paint job and talking about the "birthday party" Dyffed was fond of referring to. They were confounded when Gomja confronted them with the spare materials, which he had uncovered while making a detailed inspection of the ship just before they had entered the phlogiston.

As a result of the discovery, Ruff and Widget, the giant

hamsters, had been saved from the dinner table. Gaye promised never to lock herself in a room again, and there was enough ammunition for the giff to have the gnomes practice with their crossbows for several days without threatening the whole supply. Gomja had shaken his broad head when he had told Teldin, Aelfred, and the others of the situation, putting it down to the gnomes' ability to have their left hands not know what their right hands were doing at any given time.

"One last volley, lads!" Gomja ordered, cranking his enormous bow's string back. A few firearms, too, had been among the supplies in storage, and Gomja had taken all of them from the moment he'd laid eyes on them. "The scorpion's too close for us to stay in the open. We're going to spin the ship to put the scorpion beneath us and hope we can drop something on it from the jettison before they get aboard! It's going to be blood and fire, but they'll not try to take us without dying for it! Are you with me?"

The gnomes, who had been peaceful maintenance workers only a month before, gave out a mighty cheer and waved their shields and crossbows in the air. Gomja gave them a wide, savage grin, his huge blue face flushed with anticipation of the coming battle. He gave a quick look at Teldin. "Last chance to get below, sir!"

"Not a chance," Teldin answered. He thought of the days when he had been a mule skinner in the War of the Lance, a naive soldier who hunted for glory and found only death and sorrow. There was no glory even now—but there was the chance to save his friends, and he meant to pay back a part of the debt owed him by the forces that had hunted him.

Gomja nodded with satisfaction. "Prepare to fire!" he said, raising his crossbow once again.

Teldin aimed and thought he saw something coming at him from the scorpion. The object flashed by—and a moment later cracked as it broke against the deck. A half-dozen or more other missiles also slammed into the ship. A gnome to Teldin's left gave an agonized cry and fell over the railing, gone. The other gnomes gasped in horror.

"Steady!" Gomja said in a commanding voice. "Now, fire!"

Teldin looked down the sights of his crossbow—and felt a

peculiar clarity of thought. Time slowed down. It's about time the cloak started working again! Teldin thought jubilantly.

Teldin's senses were now sharpened to nearly unbearable levels. Suddenly he saw the scorpion ship as if it were only twenty yards away instead of hundreds. He heard odd noises, the tiny sounds of the joints in his body moving and the rush of blood in his ears. He smelled his own sweat, the unwashed bodies of the gnomes, the heavy scent of the giff, even the aroma of the wood of his crossbow. He was drowning in a torrent of sensations.

He held the crossbow steady, quickly selecting a target: an ogre crewing a ballista on the scorpion's main deck, below the ship's upraised tail. Teldin fixed the ogre's face in the sights, then squeezed the trigger. The crossbow released its bolt with a lazy thump.

Time returned to normal. The flood of sensations died. Teldin lowered the crossbow and tried to see what he'd done, but the scorpion ship was too far away.

Teldin turned to say something to Gomja, but a bright light from the bow of the ship distracted him. The titanic whirlpool on the crystal sphere was right on them. The ship was flying through the center of it, into a pure blue sky.

Teldin gaped. The giff and several of the gnomes saw the sight, too, and stopped moving.

Directly ahead of the *Perilous Halibut*, in the midst of the blue sea, was a huge, bright yellowish-white star. Teldin could look at it directly for only a second before shielding his eyes. It appeared to be twice as large as other suns he had seen. At the same moment, Teldin had a peculiar feeling that everything was slowing down. He realized the ship had dropped to tactical speed. What was going on? he wondered. The ship behind them wasn't within range to do that!

"Oh, wow!" came Gaye's voice, directly behind Teldin. "Oh, wow, it's beautiful!"

Teldin looked back, startled to hear her voice—and a blast of wind hit him from the bow, building rapidly in strength. Teldin staggered and crouched low, then grabbed the railing, as did almost everyone else. Bolts and weapons stacked on the deck swiftly blew away, falling behind the ship in a shower. A few crossbows and shields were lost as well, but fortunately none of the gnomes. Three gnomes clung to the deck ballista. Gomja merely stood firm, hunched down a bit as the white lapels and flaps on his uniform snapped in the wind.

Teldin could hardly believe it—they'd entered an atmosphere upon entering the crystal sphere! No wonder they were at tactical speed. The ship's speed continued to drop, allowing a degree of movement on the deck, though Teldin hardly trusted himself to stand. He looked aft again—and saw the inside of the crystal sphere they had just entered.

The scene behind them could have come straight from his homeland on Krynn. He looked down on an endless green countryside, lined with roads and checked with cultivated fields and clusters of small houses. Forests stretched away to all sides, with a few round lakes dotting the landscape.

There was no sign of the portal, however. No phlogiston. No scorpion ship. Just grassy hills and a dirt road.

Teldin gaped, unable to imagine what had happened.

People lived on the inside of the sphere itself.

"I've never seen anything like this." Gaye sighed, her eyes as big as cartwheels as she clung to the low railing. She stared aft again, then gasped. "It's a gate! Here they come!"

Teldin looked back and saw, for the briefest moment, a huge, circular opening into the phlogiston around the scorpion ship. Then the gateway vanished, and the scorpion ship was driving up from the ground to catch them in the air.

Not only did people live on the inside of this crystal sphere, Teldin realized, but they would never be disturbed by entering vessels. The ships must have been gated past the crystal sphere and directly inside it. But then how did anyone ever get out of this sphere?

"Shields up, if you've got them!" Gomja bellowed. "Helm, turn us over!"

Teldin thrust all other questions aside. "Get back below!" he said, suddenly realizing Gaye's danger. "How'd you get up here, anyway?" He reached out to grab her and force her back below, noticing an open hatchway in the vertical "shark's fin" of the ship. So that was it.

Gaye squirmed out of his reach and ran against the wind toward the bow. Teldin started to give chase, then gave up. If she wanted to stay outside and get shot, it wasn't his problem.

He looked back just as the black ship began rotating.
Suddenly he saw the tail catapult on the scorpion fire again.
The rock it hurled was right on target.

"Flatten!" Gomja cried, ignoring his own advice. "Hang
on to the railing!"

The *Perilous Halibut* continued to rotate. Teldin threw
himself flat again, eyes fixed on the rock as it came at him—
and flew by to the left by a matter of twenty feet at most.
Teldin felt his stomach churn with terror.

"Jettison!" Gomja shouted. "Jettison away!"

There was a deep thumping sound that ran throughout the
ship, and a spray of metallic shards and debris was launched
from the rear port of the ship, spreading out in a glittering
cloud as it flew toward the scorpion. Teldin noticed no major
change to the orcish ship itself as the jettison struck home; the
scorpion was now close enough that he could see the shrapnel
bounce off its hull. He saw no casualties being taken by the
shot, however. Then the scorpion vanished below the deck's
"horizon," hidden by the *Perilous Halibut*'s own mass in case
the orcs fired again.

"Stand by to repel boarders!" Gomja was now reloading his
huge crossbow. A few of the gnomes managed to load their
crossbows while clinging to the railing at the same time. "On
my command, when we rotate the ship again, fire at the
enemy crew, then draw your weapons and fight as we come
alongside! Cut all ropes launched over to us! Use your size
against your foe! Take no prisoners!"

Teldin tried to ready his own crossbow, but he had no bolts
left near him; they'd all been blown away. He waited in a half
crouch with his long cloak flapping around him. The twenty or
so gnomes were obviously nervous and afraid, but they
clutched their weapons and stole glances at the resolute figure
of the giff as he towered over them, crossbow at the ready in
one hand and long sword drawn in the other.

"Helm!" Gomja cried. "Rotate and pull alongside the scorpion before our gravity fields match up!"

There was silence then, except for the roaring wind. The few
gnomes who had managed to hold on to their crossbows rested
them against the railing and aimed them in different directions, unsure of which direction the ship would rotate. Teldin

had the presence of mind to look for Gaye, and he saw her on the bow, clutching the railing there. He saw, too, that she held a short pole in one hand. The stick was as long as she was tall. Now, where did she get *that*? She hadn't even been able to say how she'd hidden the thingfinder on her person weeks ago, on Ironpiece. That was a kender for you.

The ship rotated counterclockwise. The scorpion would come up on Teldin's side. He dropped the useless crossbow and freed one hand from the railing. His cloak once had enabled him to cast a curtain of energy before him that protected him during a fight. He had an inspiration, and now wanted to see if the cloak could turn that energy into a weapon. Could he fire magical missiles or bolts from his fingertips? No other weapon was left to him. If the cloak couldn't obey his commands, he'd be dead very soon. He concentrated on the image of a magical bolt of energy, keeping his fingers extended.

The scorpion ship came up into view. Its deck was full of black-armored figures with long poles in their hands. Some had ropes. Some had crossbows themselves, but the high wind made it difficult to aim them. Draped over the side railing was the body of an ogre, an arrow protruding from its forehead. I did that, thought Teldin.

"Fire!" Gomja roared, his crossbow snapping loudly.

One of the orcs dropped when Gomja fired. Another fell with a gnome's bolt in him. The orcs fired back, and two gnomes were hit; one fell from the ship and vanished. Teldin concentrated as hard as he could, putting his whole mind in his fingertips. Just like hitting the ogre, he thought.

Power bloomed inside him. He felt he would burst with it. It burned as it ran through his veins, filling him like a cup under a waterfall, spilling over. Radiant energy poured out from his fingers, flashing straight into the orcs on the scorpion ship. The orcs fell as if they had been scythed down. Only three out of a dozen were left standing when it was over a moment later. The power was gone from Teldin as quickly as it had appeared, and he went limp with exhaustion.

"By the Great Captain!" Gomja gasped behind him. "We've got them good now!" He then bellowed out to the world. "Pull alongside the scorpion! Company, prepare to fire again!"

Even as Gomja spoke and the *Perilous Halibut* slid close to the scorpion, more orcs appeared on the deck of the enemy ship, apparently coming up from one or more ladders below. Regaining his energy, Teldin cautiously got to his feet and noticed that both ships were traveling parallel to the ground, miles below them. Wispy clouds, like white horses' tails, were scattered above and below.

With wild whoops, the orcs on the scorpion suddenly hurled ropes and grappling hooks across at the gnomes' ship. A few of the hooks caught, enough for the black-armored orcs to start reeling the ships together. A few of the gnomes drew knives and meat cleavers to hack at the ropes.

Gomja was more direct. He seized a grapple and jerked on it with all his might. The orc holding the opposite end of the rope flipped headfirst off his ship, to fall screaming between the ships until no one could hear him.

Teldin drew his short sword as the ships closed, side by side in the roaring wind. Suddenly the orcs gave out wild cries and leaped over their railing onto the deck of the *Perilous Halibut*, swords held high. Some slipped and fell down the slick sides of the latter ship, but a dozen made it aboard, and the fight was joined.

As a particularly huge orc came at him with its scimitar aloft, it struck Teldin that these orcs were somewhat larger than the ones Gomja and Aelfred had described while crossing the phlogiston. Teldin dodged the downward blow the orc aimed at his head, slashing the orc across his black-armored chest. His wild blow hardly penetrated the orc's thick leather armor, bouncing off the metal studs across its front.

Teldin tried to back up, realizing in an instant that he'd made a mistake. The orc advanced quickly, lunging forward and almost skewering Teldin with the scimitar. Teldin tried to cut at the orc, but his blow went wild again. I'm screwing this up! he thought, almost in panic. I can't get this right! He almost fell against the orc as the wind shifted suddenly, and the huge warrior drew its sword arm back for another lunge, one that Teldin could see he wasn't going to avoid.

A small, feminine figure with long, wind-blown black hair appeared and jammed a wooden pole between the orc's elbow and its back, shoving the pole back as if it were a lever. The orc spun around, surprise on its face, and fell back on its side. Teldin lunged forward himself, avoiding the scimitar, and plunged his short sword into the orc's stomach. The orc died with a choking cry.

Gaye glanced at Teldin long enough to see that he was unhurt, then turned away to meet a second attacker. Teldin turned just in time to avoid being struck from behind by an orc that had circled around the fight, parrying the blow by sheer luck. Back to back, Teldin and Gaye fought their opponents as the fight raged around them. Even as he beat back the orc's attacks, Teldin heard Gomja's bombastic curses and the garbled cries of gnomes shouting detailed directions to each other.

The *Perilous Halibut* shifted its heading away from the orcish ship for a moment, then drifted back, slamming into the side of the latter ship. Teldin staggered at the unexpected blow, almost losing his balance. It went for nothing, as the orc could not recover its footing and collapsed against Teldin, knocking them both to the deck. Teldin blocked a badly aimed chop from the orc, then dived on his foe to wrestle in grim silence, weapons still clutched in their hands. Gathering all his strength, Teldin managed to turn his weapon and shove it into the orc's neck, only moments before the orc would have driven his own sword through Teldin's ribs. The orc choked, dropping his scimitar and giving a gurgling scream as he died. Teldin pulled his sword free and started to get up, splattered with gore.

The two ships suddenly struck again, and the *Perilous Halibut* shook with the collision. Teldin fell on his back, away from the dead orc. The orcish ship again came out second best, its entire forward side smashed inward. Abruptly, the port claw of the scorpion, which had been jammed against the *Perilous Halibut*'s bow, snapped and fell away. The two ships skittered apart, then slammed together once more. Unable to regain his footing, Teldin heard a shrieking sound like thick metal being crushed; for an awful moment, he feared that the gnomes' ship was the source. The scorpion ship then rose, nose up, its entire bow caved in on the near side. Its long metal legs scraped the starboard side of the *Perilous Halibut* as the orcish ship flipped over in the air, fell behind the gnomes' ship, and began a long, twisting dive toward the ground.

Teldin saw two more orcs on the top deck fighting gnomes, their backs to him. He dove at them without thinking, killing each with a single blow through the lower back. When the last had fallen, he turned to see the rest of the battle.

The fight was almost over. The black deck of the gnomes' ship was slippery with smeared streaks and pools of blood, the bodies of orcs and gnomes thrown together across it. Only a dozen gnomes were left standing, several clutching the railing. Some of the gnomes were shoving the bodies of slain orcs over the side of the ship.

Gomja was hammering a battered orc lying flat on the deck with his huge, ham-sized fists. Seeing that his opponent was no longer fighting back, he grabbed the orc by its black-armored shoulders, lifted it from the deck, and casually hurled it off the side of the ship into empty space. "Now you know the hazards of inviting yourselves onto other people's ships without asking first!" he roared, clapping his two thick hands together to dust them off.

Gomja looked back and surveyed the ship. Teldin, Gaye, and the gnomes were sweating heavily, their clothing askew and splattered with red. The gnomes had taken the worst of the fighting, having had so little experience with it before; half of their numbers on deck were dead, and the rest were exhausted and wounded. The wind whipped at the survivors as they stood on the deck beneath the huge sun, miles above the ground.

"Well, lads," said Gomja softly. "We've won." He took a last look around, then walked over to catch a gnome who was on the verge of letting go of the railing and falling overboard. "Gather your gear! All hands below!" he shouted. "We've won! Let's tell the rest!"

The weary gnomes staggered against the wind, toward the nearest hatch, some still clutching their weapons. Gaye wandered over to Teldin and fell against him, wrapping her arms around his waist and burying her face in his stained shirt. He held her to him, thinking of the mounting toll of dead, all for the sake of his cloak, which snapped in the wind behind him like a flag.

* * * * *

"We need to put down right away," Aelfred said when he met Teldin in a narrow corridor near the helm. Teldin had just been on his way to check on Sylvie. "I've got to get her off the helm before she falls asleep. She's almost too tired to think straight. No—don't go see her. The gnomes haven't found all their boobytraps yet, and I've got that gnome mage, Loomfinger, in there with her to keep her awake until she can set us down. I wish this ship had a second helm so I could just have Loomfinger take over for her."

Teldin looked down the corridor to the helm room. "If there's anything I can do . . ." he said.

Aelfred clamped a hand on Teldin's shoulder. "Old son, you've done more than your share already. Sylvie said you took out almost the whole upper deck of the scorpion with some spell you threw at them. She could see it from her helm. It really picked her up for a while." Aelfred's twisted grin came back. "She said your sword fighting needed work, though. Looks like we have to start getting together again on that."

Word came a few minutes later from Loomfinger that Sylvie had spotted a place to land, and Aelfred went to the helm room to be with her. Avoiding several undismantled boobytraps in the corridors, Teldin went to his cabin to peer out the porthole over his too-short bed, not willing to risk being on the top deck when the ship came down.

Fortunately, the ship was circling its prospective landing site in such a way that his cabin was facing the site itself. It was along the coast of a large sea with a very smooth, regular coastline that curved off into the distance. The ship dropped toward the water at a comfortable speed, though Teldin found himself worrying about the impact when the ship hit the water. Sylvie was a much better pilot than he had been when he had brought the *Probe* down, he knew, but the knowledge did not take the edge off his worries.

"Can I see?"

Teldin jumped when he heard Gaye's voice behind him, striking his head against a shelf mounted right over the porthole. He felt his head, detecting no serious harm, and forced himself to relax. He got up from his bed.

"Don't you ever knock?" he said irritably.

Gaye climbed on the bed and peered out the window. She was wearing what looked like a silk bathrobe, tied around the waist with one of Teldin's belts—a belt he did not recall having ever loaned to anyone, least of all her. Her hair was wet and hung down over her face and shoulders in thick strands. Water dripped in the bed from her hair, and her feet left huge wet spots on the sheets wherever she stood.

"My cabin's on the wrong side," she said by way of apology, her face pressed to the portal. "This should be fun, huh? Dyffed says this ship was made to travel underwater if we want it to. Maybe we could go exploring and see what lives under the lake, then take off and see the fal."

"You not only don't knock," Teldin remarked, "but you also don't dress properly, and you're making a mess of things. Did you just get out of the shower?"

Gaye looked back with a frown. "Boy, you're in a bad mood. Yes, I just got out of the shower. I couldn't stand to run around a moment longer without cleaning up. You could use a shower yourself, Mister Cloak Man. Why are you so grumpy, huh? The fight was pretty awful, but at least we're alive. Or is it me? You pick at me a lot lately. Why?"

Teldin started to reply, then stopped. He didn't really know why. He stared at her, wrapped in her bathrobe and still dripping bath water on his bed, and it finally dawned on him why she bothered him. It wasn't because she was a kender; he'd known a kender or two during the War of the Lance, and though they were irritating at times, they could be quite likable, too. Gaye was very likable, in fact—and that was the problem.

He dropped his gaze and rubbed his face with both hands. "I'm sorry," he said. "Everything has me on edge lately." He sat down uncomfortably on the gnome-sized chair behind him, feeling his back ache a little as he did so, and reflected on how much of the problem he wanted to discuss with her. He heard Gaye move away from the window and sit down on the edge of his bed.

"Gaye," he began, "ever since I put on this cloak, I've watched everyone I've ever known be killed or injured because of it. My neighbors, my friends, my enemies, everyone. I can't take it. I can't even count the number of people who have died because someone wanted to get this cloak at every cost. I can't lead anything remotely like a normal life with half the universe out to kill or capture me. The neogi caught me once and tried to cut me up and break all my joints just for fun." He hesitated, seeing one grim memory in particular, then went on. "I even knew a woman once, someone I loved, who betrayed me to the neogi so she could get my cloak. She and I . . . I thought we were very close, but it meant nothing at all to her. She just wanted the cloak. Aelfred and I . . . we had to kill her when she tried to kill me."

Teldin covered his eyes with his fingers. "I know you want to be my friend. You're like Aelfred in a way. Nothing gets to him for long. He always comes back, ready to fight and move on. I like people like that, but . . . I don't want people to get too close to me these days. I can't take the thought of being responsible for their being killed."

The kender thought this over. "Or maybe for them betraying you," she said quietly.

Teldin thought that one over. "Yes, maybe that, too. It just seems easier not to get . . . involved."

Gaye sighed as she regarded Teldin. "You know, if there was ever a time when you needed people, this is the time. My father tried to handle everything in our family business after my mother died, and it made me crazy to see him wear himself out. He had people who were willing to help, but he turned them away. For what? The work just made him ill, until . . . well." Gaye shrugged slightly, looking down for a moment. "Anyway, you can't afford to do that same thing, and you have no end of help. Gomja said he quit his job with the gnomes because you're his best friend and he wanted to help you out. Aelfred told me he and Sylvie decided they would stick it out with you, no matter what, because they both really like you and they don't want any bad guys to get your cloak. Dyffed's here because he's . . . well, because he's a gnome, but he likes you, too."

Gaye pushed herself up from the bed and padded over to Teldin on her bare feet. Before he could react, she leaned close, her eyes looking deep into his own. She had used some sort of fragrant soap when she had showered, and the scent surprised him. She reached out and took his head in her warm hands.

"And I'm here," she said in a low voice, "because—"

There was a sudden thundering sound outside, all across the hull of the ship. Just as suddenly, everything on the ship was hurled forward toward the bow, which dived downward. The light from the porthole went out. Teldin felt Gaye slam into him with a muffled cry as the room tilted up almost vertically. Loose items around the room crashed into the wall near him. Then the ship struck something more solid than water, and Teldin's head snapped back and slammed the wall behind him. He saw an amazing assortment of stars explode in his vision, then saw nothing at all.

Chapter Twelve

•••

Teldin felt the top deck of the *Perilous Halibut* slowly roll with the waves, and, despite his headache, he steadied himself easily as it did. The ship kept a surprisingly even keel for a gnome-built craft, he thought—particularly a craft that had just been through a nearly disastrous landing. As the throbbing in his head came and went, Teldin watched a group of six gnomes paddle for the shoreline in their small raft, cobbled together from doors and wooden beams knocked from the interior of the ship. He mulled for a moment over Sylvie's bad news, which he'd received shortly after the splash-landing, then sourly pushed it from his mind. Things were looking worse all the time.

Looking down, Teldin checked the railing where a thick rope had been tied off. Once the gnomes got ashore, they would take the other end of the rope and tie it to one of the trees there; then the crew of the *Perilous Halibut* would pull the ship in. The screws and paddles the gnomes had originally designed for powering the ship no longer functioned. The screws were made to be turned by the giant hamsters, both of which had been knocked unconscious in the crash and were still "woozy," Gaye had reported. The paddles were nearly all broken, having been badly stored, and the mechanisms for the screws had also taken some damage in the crash; they could not be fixed without two days of work. It was easier to simply haul the ship in by force.

Someone walked heavily from the stern of the ship to stand behind Teldin. He heard the being stretch and yawn, then casually straighten his uniform.

"Lovely day, if you don't mind my saying so, sir," said Gomja, carefully shading his small eyes with a thick blue-gray hand as he watched the gnomes' progress. "Unless, of course, we're attacked by the local militia or those scro find us, but we can handle that, I'll wager. By the Great Captain's blunderbuss, a good fight would get the blood stirring. We gave better than we got up there."

"Scro?" Teldin asked, half turning to look at the huge giff. The giff's pleased remembrance of the battle was starting to annoy him. "What are scro?"

"Scro are space orcs, sir," said Gomja, still watching the gnomes. "I didn't realize it at first when we were fighting them, but it came to me afterward. My sire told me a few tales about them. Scro are orcish survivors of the Unhuman War, hundreds of years ago, when the elves and humanoids fought for control of all the spheres. The survivors spelled the name 'orcs' backward when they cut their ties with their ancestors. They've been just an occasional nuisance until now. Scro are much more dangerous than common orcs, and even ogres will leave them alone. They're supposed to be partially resistant to magical spells, and all are well trained for combat. They fought well, I must admit. I wish I had saved one of their suits of armor as a trophy."

Teldin looked back at the shore. The gnomes were climbing out of their boat at the beach, a hundred yards away. Two gnomes fell into the water and disappeared as he watched. "But the scro, or whatever you call them, are dead, and we aren't," he said, summing up all he cared to recall about the battle. "I wouldn't like to see them get another chance at us."

Gomja grunted. The gnomes had managed to upset their entire raft, and it appeared to have come apart. There was nothing that could be done about it.

"The scro should have an easy time with us now that we're stuck here," Teldin said grimly. He turned to look back at the dozen or so gnomes on the top deck, each holding a loaded crossbow and nervously watching the sky for other spelljammers. Teldin lowered his voice in hopes that the gnomes couldn't hear him. "With the helm gone, we don't have much of a chance to escape them."

Gomja looked down sharply. "Where did you hear that, sir? The helm's quite functional. Its magic was merely nullified by the antimagical properties of this lake water."

"What?" Teldin frowned at Gomja. "Sylvie said that the helm wouldn't work, no matter what magic or effort she used on it. That was why we lost control and went underwater, hitting the lake bottom. The helm is simply dead."

"I am sure she would say now that she spoke too soon, sir," Gomja said promptly. "Before I came on deck, I asked her about the ship, and she explained what she had discovered about the antimagical properties of the water in this lake. It's quite remarkable, sir. The water doesn't remove a magical item's powers, but the water will keep the item from functioning. All we have to do is pull the ship onto the shore, out of the water, and we'll be off."

Teldin snorted softly, crossing his arms in front of him. "I wonder if the water would shut off the powers in my cloak long enough to let me take it off."

"That is possible, sir, but not likely." Gomja looked over the side of the ship briefly. "You could try it, but the ladder came off in the landing, and you'd have no way to get up the side of the ship and on deck again unless you used a rope."

Teldin made up his mind to try it anyway—closer to shore. "If we run into one more minor setback like antimagical water that interrupts spelljamming," he muttered, "the scro, the neogi, the elves, and everyone else can fight over the cloak and my smashed body at their leisure." He felt the dull throbbing of his headache behind his eyes. He'd have to try the cold compresses that Gaye had applied to him when he'd recovered in his cabin, surrounded by his scattered belongings. He couldn't for the life of him recall anything that had gone on for a few minutes before the crash; he remembered only that he was trying to get to his cabin to lie down. He'd asked Gaye, since she'd been in the cabin with him, but she'd shrugged and said only that she'd discuss it later.

In the distance, the gnomes made it to the shore and managed to pull part of their raft onto the beach. After some confusion, the gnomes worked their way up the bank to the closest of the many trees there, the rope trailing behind them into the water. It took them about twenty minutes to tie the rope down. When they finished, the huge giff braced himself on the deck and began pulling on the rope, hand over hand. The ship creaked and groaned, changing its heading to face the shore, and slowly moved toward land.

"Antimagical water," Teldin said, half to himself. "What else does this place have in store for us?"

He turned away to look out over the lake. Thus, Gomja, not Teldin, was the first to see the horse-sized, green-and-gray insect that broke through the tree branches behind the tired gnomes. One of the centaurlike creature's clawed hands grasped the rope that the gnomes had just finished tying off. With a curved saber in its other hand, the creature chopped through the rope with a single cut.

An instant later, dozens of the multilegged horrors crashed out of the woods, rushing down the slope at the startled gnomes with long bows drawn and curved swords raised.

*   *   *   *   *

Bony hands seized the gilded frame of the mirror, lifting it swiftly out of its cradle.

"Accursed you will be!" shrieked an inhuman voice. "Accursed by all the powers of darkness forever you will be!" The bony hands raised the heavy mirror over the lich's skull and shook it, then—carefully—placed it back on its stand.

General Vorr drew in a breath of foul air, held it for a moment, then released it while inspecting a clawed fingernail. He had been listening to the lich rave for the last ten minutes, its odor of decay growing ever worse, and he was getting bored. The lich's initial news about the fate of the scorpion and its crew was bad enough; he couldn't afford to lose another ship without good cause. The possibility that Usso had been killed in the crash bothered him only in that it would be difficult at this date to replace her with someone equally capable as a spell-caster, even if she was a traitorous slut. Her information-gathering talents—among others—would be missed if she hadn't teleported out in time.

Vorr ignored the lich's ranting as he glanced around the

small stone chamber again and stood near the open archway
where he'd entered. The room was not large but was mildly
impressive, if one liked ancient tombs. General Vorr didn't
care for tombs, himself—unless they were for his enemies.

"Teldin Moore where is? Answer! Answer your master now,
or to the burning planes of the Abyss and rotting shall you
go!" The lich uttered another string of curses in a foreign language, then waved its arms in impotent fury.

Vorr swallowed a yawn.

The lich regarded the looking glass for a few moments, then
turned away, muttering. "Gone he is! A power of the cloak
this might be? An act by live meat this might be?" It shook its
head, thinking furiously. "Not possible it is. Weak and simple
his mind is, this live meat Teldin, and not for the tinkering
with artifacts was it made." The lich paused as it turned, considering the objects that lay upon its rickety workbench. It
looked up then and seemed to see the general for the first
time.

"I take it you can't find Teldin Moore as you once said you
could," Vorr said dryly.

The animated skeleton waved a bony hand in Vorr's direction as if dismissing him. "The gnomes' ship vanished it has,
gone," it said. "Cloaked the cloak is—but what this could do?
Wildspace this could not do. Metals thick as a lordserv—as an
umber hulk this could not do. A crystal sphere this could not
do." It pondered, staring at the faded paintings on a nearby
wall with empty eye sockets.

The answer came easily for the general, but he resisted saying it aloud as even his answer didn't explain everything.
Since Vorr knew he was himself completely antimagical at
birth, a sort of antimagical field suggested itself as the cause of
Teldin's disappearance. Could some antimagical device or
creature have affected the gnomish ship? It would have to be a
remarkable effect, given the size of the ship. The only other
alternative was to assume that the gnomes' ship had disintegrated on impact, and Teldin was dead. This was reasonable
enough, but the general knew enough not to jump to conclu-
sions. What was the truth?

Vorr stared at the preoccupied lich and once again hated the
thought that he needed to keep this reeking abomination

alive—well, unharmed was a better word—for the time being. It was still of some value in leading them all to Teldin Moore—and the *Spelljammer*'s cloak.

It dawned on the general that if the lich was no longer able to find Teldin, there was no reason to keep it . . . unharmed. The corners of his mouth crept upward. He would give it a little more time to find Teldin—but only a little. He was interested in finding out what sort of being it really was before he broke it into vase-sized pieces.

"I later with you will speak," said the lich, turning away toward a dusty shelf of scrolls and papers. It began sorting through the papers and paid no further attention to Vorr.

The general nodded solemnly, as if the lich could still see him. His almost-smile was gone. "We will await your word," he said smoothly. Then he left, walking through the stone archway and down the broad corridor toward the ship docks. He passed rows of skeletal soldiers, his face registering his disgust as he looked down their crooked lines. The skeletons were nothing more than bones made mobile with a necromancer's spell, as mindless as the true dead could be. A force of scro could make short work of the pyramid's entire force, with the exception of the lich itself—but the general could dispose of that problem. The umber hulks would be tough to crack, too, but not impossible.

This thought kept him happy as he swiftly descended several ladders and stairs, eventually coming to the flying pyramid's cargo deck, an open area of ancient stonework with faded pictograms adorning the cracked walls. A spell on one far wall cast dim yellow light across the bay, illuminating a pile of stones, scraps of old wood, and a few scattered bones.

Vorr's squid ship was drifting in space only a few feet from one open cargo-bay door. A boarding rope tied around a thick pillar led out to the ship, and Vorr walked up to it and caught the rope without breaking stride. He swung hand over hand out through the cargo-bay doors, out across the abyss of space. If he fell, it was of no consequence, as he would only hit the pyramid ship's gravity plane and bounce. For a few moments, though, he imagined that if he let go, he'd fall forever toward the stars, never reaching them. It was a pleasant sensation.

"General aboard!" shouted an armored scro as Vorr approached. Every scro on the deck snapped to attention and saluted, black-gloved fists up, the tarantula emblem facing out. Vorr swung over the squid ship's railing and dropped onto the forecastle deck with a heavy thump. It was pleasant to smell clean air again. "Ship away!" another scro called, casting off the boarding rope, and the stars turned around the squid ship as it pulled away from the flying pyramid.

Vorr trotted down the stairs to the main deck, then turned and went through the door to the galley and his own offices beyond. Scro eating their meals in the galley leaped to their feet as he entered, but he bypassed them, opening his office door and closing it behind him after he entered.

"You missed a rotten fight," came a familiar but subdued voice from the floor mat where Vorr slept.

"A pity," Vorr said. He glanced at Usso, who sat in the corner with her legs drawn up to her chin, then he took a seat at a heavy wooden desk and picked up a feathered pen. "Was this the fight in which you lost control of your ship when it was battered by a gnomish one, and you teleported away but left the crew behind to die?"

"That was the one," she said. Her voice lacked its usual liveliness, an indicator that she was depressed or upset. "How did you know? Could the lich see it all?"

"If Skarkesh can track Teldin Moore by his cloak, I imagine he can track more than that if he wants to," Vorr replied. He scribbled a few notes to himself on a sheet of paper. "He informed me of the ship and crew's fate, then tried to contact Teldin again, just to prove to me he could do it, but he couldn't find Teldin." Notes finished, Vorr turned on his stool to face the beautiful Oriental woman in the corner. "It was as if Teldin Moore's ship had vanished, he said. I thought of an antimagic field. Would that block our bone man's ability to spy on Teldin?"

The woman's face twisted with hurt and anger. "Kobas, you bastard, I almost died! The port wall of the helm room was broken through, and I was almost caught in the helm when the whole damned wall fell on it. All you can talk about is that filthy cloak! You don't give a rotting damn about me!"

Vorr looked steadily at Usso. "You're alive. My scro are not. This expedition is costing us more with each passing minute.

Do you want to waste my time, or help me get Teldin Moore's cloak before we are reduced to one battered ship and a crew of corpses commanded by a monster?"

"Take a jump right to the bottom of the Abyss, you fat, dung-eating, bootlick—no! No!" Usso broke off her retort as Vorr launched himself across the room, seizing one of her arms. Usso covered her face with her other arm, pulling her legs in against her stomach. "Don't kick me!" she cried. "Don't do it! I'll stop—ow! No! Owwww!"

Vorr held her delicate wrist in one massive hand and slowly rotated her wrist and forearm in a direction they were not meant to go. Usso writhed, trying to pull free. "Kobas! Kobas, stop it, stop it!" She screamed incoherently, her face pressed down against the bed mat.

Vorr eased the pressure off, leaving just enough to make Usso acutely aware the pain would return in an instant. The usual dining noises from the galley outside his door had ceased; if the scro were smart, they had gone elsewhere to eat.

"Your mouth will be your tombstone," he said, his voice as soft as a silken glove. "I found you, I made you strong, and I gave you power. I can take it away like this." He did something with Usso's arm, and she screamed again until he eased off once more. "Let's be reasonable before I lose all interest in reason. Teldin's cloak is the goal. We shall endure. Our enemies will decay on forgotten battlefields, but we shall endure—if you cooperate with me." He stopped and waited.

"Yes," Usso panted, her face hidden by her mass of long black hair, which lay spilled across the mat. "I'll help. Don't hurt me, Kobas. Please don't hurt me. I'll be good. I'll help you. Don't hurt me anymore."

He eased more of the pressure off, but not enough so that she could get up. "Could an antimagical field block the lich's attempts to spy on Teldin Moore?" he asked.

"It might. It can do that. It won't hurt the cloak, but it can stop magic coming from it. I'll be good, Kobas."

He reflected on the news. "What would happen," he said, "if I were to touch the cloak? Could Teldin be traced? Could he use any of the cloak's magical powers?"

Usso was panting hard, trying to get her breath back. "I think you would negate the cloak's powers, but only as long as

you were holding it or touching it. It would work if you let it
go. I believe it's very powerful. You couldn't destroy it, but
you could stop it. He can probably spelljam with it. I told you
that weeks ago. He must have used it when he escaped from us
the first time. I saw him throw spells from it, magical missiles,
just before we crashed. He killed a lot of scro before they
boarded his ship.''

Vorr listened to the woman's panting, then looked down
her back. Clearly visible under her long white gown, her fox-
like tail lay flat on the mat between her legs. Usso could lie,
but her tail never could. She was like all of her kind: clever,
arrogant, strong in the face of the weak, and weak in the face
of the strong. All she cared about was herself.

It was a mistake to let her live, and Vorr knew it. Usso would
sell out the gods themselves for more power. She no doubt had
her own designs on the cloak Teldin wore; Vorr didn't mind
that, because it would be easier to deal with her treachery than
it would be to deal with the lich. If she could just keep her
mouth shut more often and rein in her emotions, she could
have a much cozier and more comfortable life—but she could
never manage that, no matter how many warnings she got.

That was fine, too, Vorr thought. He sometimes enjoyed administering a loving warning or two to the fox-woman. If she
pushed things hard enough at the wrong time, he'd administer a final warning one of these days, and he'd take his time at
it. The thought was a pleasant one.

Vorr got to his feet again. He kept one broad, iron-muscled
hand on Usso's wrist, forcing her to stay down until he was
completely up. He gave her arm a final sharp twist and released her as she yelped and crawled away, sobbing.

It was all show, he knew. Usso, like all *hu hsien*, could heal
her wounds and eliminate pain quickly. She was just hurt in
the heart, or whatever she had that passed for one, because he
didn't want to listen to her.

Vorr walked back to his desk and picked up his pen again.
He imagined Teldin, wearing his cloak, attacking him with a
sword. How could he get a grip on that cloak? What could he
do with it when he got it in his hands? Could he use the cloak
against Teldin in a face-to-face fight?

Images began to move in the general's mind as he listened

to the *hu hsien* weep worthless tears. When he met Teldin at last, Vorr sincerely hoped the man would give his very best shot at trying to kill his opponent. Vorr wanted it that way. He wanted it to be a fight to always remember.

*   *   *   *   *

The shoreline grew nearer, foot by foot, as Teldin clumsily paddled the raft toward the shoreline. His legs were already awash in water up to his hips, but it mattered little as he had fallen into the lake once already and was completely soaked. His raft was barely more than a few more doors from the ship roped together, and his oar was a broken one from the ship's hold, but it worked. Nothing else was available.

Far behind him, Gomja and Aelfred watched anxiously from the ship's deck. They carried an assortment of wheel-lock pistols and muskets, primed and loaded, with more on the deck within reach. Lining the ship's railings and facing the shore was the ship's remaining crew, crossbows cocked and aimed, bolts piled behind them. Only Sylvie and Gaye remained inside the ship, and Teldin was positive that Gaye would not stay there long.

Teldin's cloak had pulled up into its necklace form when he'd hit the water earlier. For just a moment he wondered if he should use the cloak's powers to shapechange into one of the centaurlike insectoid creatures that lined the bank. Perhaps he could then use the cloak's translating abilities to convince these creatures that they were friendly. However, they had already seen him, and they would suspect the worst of any sudden transformation now. If he were them, he certainly would. The translating power would have to serve alone—that, and whatever he had in the way of oratory.

The insectoid creatures that awaited him on shore had hardly moved an inch since they seized the six gnomes and cut the rope. Teldin counted about three dozen of them, many armed with long bows. Each creature was striped and spotted in a peculiar pattern of gray and green, which Teldin realized made them hard to spot against forested backgrounds. Crossing the chest of each eight-legged being were various straps and bandoliers, including a long quiver of arrows and numerous long-handled daggers. Only a few of the creatures held hand weapons, long scimitars and pole axes, and these troops were clustered around the group of wet, frightened gnomes they had captured.

When he was only twenty feet from the shore, Teldin remembered that the lake water was supposed to be antimagical. That meant his cloak . . . he stopped paddling, almost paralyzed with fear at his next thought. Would his cloak's powers even work? It was too late now. He didn't even want to try to take the necklace off, for fear it would fall into the lake and be lost. Slowly, he resumed his progress toward shore, his heart sinking inside him. When he was close enough, he carefully slid off the raft and stood in the algae-thick water up to his knees, pulling the raft behind him until he could lay one end of it on the sand and rock bank. That done, he rose and faced the creatures, standing erect with his hands open at his sides. Cold water dripped from his soaked trousers and spilled out of his boots.

One of the insect-beings flipped its saber behind it, neatly dropping it into a broad sheath. It moved through the ranks of its fellow soldiers until it stood about ten feet before Teldin, looking him over with many-faceted black eyes as broad as the span of a man's hand. The head of the insect-centaur resembled that of an ant, with two huge antennae that twisted to and fro on its head, and a pair of dark mandibles larger than any animal's claws. It made a come-hither motion, and Teldin carefully stepped closer, away from the shoreline.

"Ship you sail sky?" the creature asked. Its voice was not unpleasant, almost like a chirping song. It gestured with one long, clawed hand toward the *Perilous Halibut*.

Teldin couldn't be sure if the creature was really speaking the Common tongue, as it seemed to be, or if the cloak was translating its words. "Yes," he said simply. "We came down and landed in the lake. We wish to rest." He canceled the idea of telling the insect folk that the ship wouldn't fly yet.

The creature regarded the *Perilous Halibut* without expression. "You no sail sky now? Ship you no sail lake? Home you here find?"

Teldin hesitated, not sure what the creature meant. "Ship fly . . . Our ship flies, yes. We just want to rest here, then leave. We will not bother you." He looked in the direction of the gnomes. "Please release our crew. They meant no harm."

In answer, the creature called out in an incomprehensible singsong language over its shoulder. There was some motion near the gnomes, then another insect-centaur appeared from the rest, holding a gnome aloft under the armpits. The gnome, his face as white as his beard, appeared frozen with terror, but the insect-centaur merely deposited him on the ground in the long, flat grass near Teldin. With a push from behind, the creature sent the gnome in Teldin's direction.

Teldin felt the urge to reach down and snatch up the gnome as he would a returned child, but he resisted it. He did crouch and force a smile as the gnome walked nervously to him, looking over his shoulders every few seconds at the insect people. "Are you hurt?" Teldin asked.

The gnome shook his head, rubbing his chest where the insect being's claws had held him. "Fine," the gnome said—the shortest phrase Teldin recalled ever hearing from a gnome. He recalled this particular gnome was named Druushi.

Teldin clasped a hand on the gnome's shoulder with false bravado, then stood again. "Thank you for returning him," he said, feeling only slightly more confident. "We want the rest of our crew, too. I give you our word we will not bother you. We wish only to rest, then leave and, um, sail the sky."

"Trade," said the insect being. "You trade talk. We trade crew. You trade true talk. Ship you no sail sky. Lake no sail. Home here you find?"

"No, we are not making our home here," Teldin said. He judged that these beings knew the lake water was antimagical, and he further had the impression that they were not evil. It was only a hunch, but he had nothing else, so he plunged ahead. "We didn't know the lake would stop our ship from flying—sailing the sky, I mean. We had to land, and we will leave again as soon as we get our ship out of the lake."

The insect-centaur turned and repeated its earlier gesture. Another insect warrior left the group surrounding the remaining gnomes, another frightened gnome clutched in its clawed hands. This gnome, too, was sent on his way toward Teldin, and Druushi welcomed him briefly, if anxiously.

That leaves four gnomes left, Teldin thought. Was he going

to have to talk all the rest of them out of captivity? "I don't know what else I can tell you," Teldin said finally. "Will you allow us to come to shore?"

The insect being considered this. Within moments, Teldin felt a change in the atmosphere. Several of the insect beings close to the speaker lowered their bows. Moments later, large numbers of them followed suit, appearing to relax as they stood. Several even put their bows away, shoving them back into leathery sheaths strapped to their long tail sections. Teldin felt his nose twitch. He was going to sneeze.

He fought the impulse as long as he could. "If you want to trade talk," he said, "we can tell you some of our stories. True stories. You seem to know we can fly—sail, whatever. We can tell you where we've been. We can tell you about the . . ." He sneezed then, violently, four times in a row. Eyes watering, he forced himself to stop and looked up, then waved a hand to encompass the entire sky. "We can tell you about the universe, the worlds beyond the sky, if you let our crew go."

Huge black eyes gleamed as they looked Teldin over again. "You say true?" it chirped-sang.

"On my word of honor," Teldin answered, his nose starting to run. What in the Abyss was happening? Was he allergic to something in the air? "I say true."

For a moment, nothing happened. Then, to Teldin's astonishment, all of the insect folk put away their weapons and relaxed their postures. They moved away from the gnomes, who hesitantly began side-stepping toward Teldin and their two compatriots. When it was obvious the insect beings did not care, the gnomes broke into a run and collided, arms out, into drawn-out hugs with their friends. "What's that odd smell?" he heard one of the gnomes ask another.

Teldin felt his knees grow weak with relief. He started to say "Thank you" to the insect being when he was seized with an uncontrollable urge to sneeze. He could barely do anything else, and the sneezing went on and on.

"You say ship crew, all good," said the insect being, out of Teldin's sight. "We and you pull ship. Trade talk and talk. You and crew rest." The creature hesitated, then looked curiously at Teldin, who was also being regarded with some concern by the gnomes.

"I . . . I can't . . . stop!" Teldin gasped, then sneezed again twice. "I . . . can't . . . *stop!*"

* * * * *

"Of course, I did tell you that medical matters were not in my central curriculum when I was at the university of Lirak's Cube," said Dyffed, examining Teldin's red, swollen face. "I was in engineering—none of this tinkering with the insides of dead things or trying to make trees grow watermelons or cross-breeding dragons with giant hamsters. No, I had the clean feel of the slide rule, the virgin expanses of fresh paper, the thrill of multiple equations, the afterglow of a correct sum. I was young then, only fifty, young and foolish, eager to yield my-self to the temptations of differential mathematics and spell-jamming theory. Some fools called it infatuation, but they wouldn't have known verifiable ardor even if it chose to affix its incisors on their ischial tuberosities." He sighed and looked off into space. "Ah, it was an exciting time to be alive."

"What's wrong with Teldin?" Gaye asked, unable to wait any longer.

"What? Oh." Dyffed cleared his throat. "He's got a runny nose and he's sneezing a lot."

"Yes, we know that!" Gaye exclaimed. "But why?"

"Beats me," said the gnome with a shrug. "Maybe it's something in the air."

"It's the rastipedes," said Aelfred with a smile. "I dealt with one a few years ago in Greyspace. They communicate with each other by smell. Most of us can barely detect it, but I'll bet a year's pay that our man Teldin is allergic to the odor. A buddy of mine had the same thing. There's nothing you can do about it except avoid rastipedes whenever possible. Sorry about that, old son."

"Teldin's allergic to those bugs?" Gaye asked. "Thank Paladine it wasn't kender."

I almost wish it had been kender, Teldin thought miserably. His sinuses were swollen far beyond normal limits, and he could barely breathe. He had never had an allergy before in his life, and he hoped he'd never get another.

"It will pass," Aelfred added, raising a mug of ale to his

lips. "Give it a couple of days, and you'll be fine. In the meantime, the rastipedes and our crew are building a wagon for the ship. We should have it out of the water by this evening." He drank deeply and smacked his lips.

"Any other news?" Teldin managed to ask, his voice now outrageously nasal. He heard Gaye giggle.

"They're giving us a map of the area," said Aelfred. "It should give us a start on finding what we came here for."

The fal, Teldin thought, rubbing his face. He tried to picture a giant black slug that could talk, but it wasn't possible. He'd almost forgotten about the fal in the last few days since the—what were they again?—since the scro's ship began trailing them.

"Here he comes," said Gaye, "and he's got a map!"

Teldin's eyes watered again as the rastipede jogged up on its eight legs, moving more rapidly than seemed possible for its size. The creature did indeed have a large rolled-up sheet of paper in its claws, which it presented to Aelfred and Gaye.

"Teldin sick?" asked the insect being.

"I'm afraid so," said Aelfred, unrolling the map. "Where are we now on this?"

The rastipede turned its attention to the map, trotting over to stand behind the big, blond warrior. A clawed green finger reached down and pointed to a spot on the map that Teldin could not see from where he sat. "We here."

"There?" asked Aelfred, surprise in his voice. "What's this in the center, then?"

"Lake," said the rastipede, looking up from the map to point toward the shore where the other insect folk and the gnomes were laboring.

Gaye gasped, and Teldin could see her eyes widen as she peered at the sheet of paper. "Isn't that weird? Dyffed, look at this! Isn't that bizarre?"

Teldin could stand it no longer. He got up from the rock and tried to get into the crowd, even as his nose stopped up completely as he approached the insect being. "What's going on?" he wheezed, hating the sound of his voice.

Aelfred managed to lower the top end of the map. Teldin looked down. A large blue footprint appeared to take up most of the center of the map. Teldin blinked, his teary vision clear-

ing for a moment, and he saw the rastipede's claw pointing
steadily to a forested spot on the leading edge of one of the
footprint's four thick toes.

Aelfred looked up at the lake, then down at the map. He
snorted and smiled. "Mother Nature having one of its jokes,"
he said. "Looks like something stepped there, doesn't it?"

"Something did step there," said Dyffed, peering at the
map through his gold-rimmed spectacles. "Quadrupedal
megafauna. One of the bigger ones, I'd say."

There was a short silence.

"Dyffed," said Aelfred conversationally, "that lake is about
a hundred and twenty miles long."

The gnome merely nodded. "I'd say a hundred and thirty,
myself, a third the size of Ironpiece. Just a rough guess, of
course. We can make more accurate measurements when we're
airborne again."

The silence returned. Aelfred lowered the map and looked
off into the distance, in the direction the leading edge of the
footprint indicated. "Then how big . . . ?" he started to say,
but his voice trailed away. Teldin and Gaye followed his gaze,
looking over the treetops and into the infinite blue beyond.

"We'll know soon enough," Dyffed said cheerfully, still
looking at the map. "One Six Nine lives on top of one."

Chapter Thirteen

• • •

Within a few hours, Teldin's allergy had begun to clear up. His head felt less likely to burst, and he could go for almost twenty minutes before sneezing. The frustration of it was still torture, but he felt he could command at least a shred of dignity when he walked about, as long as he kept upwind of the rastipedes.

He also learned from Sylvie and the now-friendly rastipedes that the antimagical effects of the lake water apparently extended for a few feet around the lake itself. The leader of the armed rastipedes, he recalled, had been careful to motion Teldin away from the water when he came ashore, no doubt so that its own spell for translating languages would function.

By the time Teldin thought to see if his cloak's powers had been negated by the lake water, the necklace part had dried off and was working normally. Given the presence of the rastipedes, Teldin put off any further test of lake-water effects on the cloak until later.

"We've just about got the ship in position," Aelfred said, sitting down beside Teldin on a fallen tree near the edge of the forest. The big warrior held a wooden cup full of ale, fresh from the ship's stores. "Those rastipedes are damn good engineers. Between them and the gnomes, they had some weird crane-and-pulley system set up and going in about three hours. They hauled the ship right out of the water like it was a toy. Amazing what you can do without magic." He took a swallow from his cup, then offered it to Teldin.

"No, thanks," Teldin said. "I've had more than my share already." He sniffed and rubbed his stuffed-up nose. "Medicinal purposes, of course."

Aelfred gave his friend a lopsided grin. "You've saved our lives several times running now, and the gods reward you with this. There's no justice." He turned around, hearing footsteps from behind them. "Come on over," he called. Teldin turned just as Sylvie walked up and casually sat on the log beside Aelfred.

"You get some rest?" Aelfred asked, nudging the half-elf gently in the side. "You've stayed up too long already."

Sylvie elbowed Aelfred back, though more sharply. "I can't get to sleep now," she said glumly. "Sunset and night can't be possible in this sphere because the land area is exposed to overhead sunlight all the time. I can't find a place that's dark enough to sleep. Someone did a bad design job when this sphere was being made." She poked at the leaves on the ground with the toes of her soft shoes. "I'm in a bad mood. Just ignore me."

Aelfred laughed, but Teldin stared at Sylvie in astonishment at her revelation that night wasn't possible here. He'd been wondering for some time now when the huge sun was going to drop toward the horizon; he now felt intensely foolish for not having realized that "sunset" was out of the question. How did the natives get along without night? This was the strangest world he had seen since entering wildspace.

"Lady, you can be as mean as you want, and I promise not to pay any attention to you at all," said Aelfred, grinning from ear to ear. He began to stroke Sylvie's back with his right hand. After a moment, she closed her eyes and visibly relaxed. "Besides, some people do manage to get to sleep here. The rastipedes live underground, for instance. They sleep in shifts, so two-thirds of their colony is always awake. I was talking with their leader a while ago—he has no name, as we know it, since their language is based in part on smell—and he told me about their life here. They're descended from a spelljammer crew. Their ship landed in the lake just like ours did, but their ship broke up on landing, so they just stayed on. They run the forest and most of the land on this side of the lake. One of them could give an ogre a fit. Teldin did us a real favor in talking things out with them, even if our buddy the giff wanted to charge them." Aelfred reached over and gave Teldin another punch to the shoulder.

"You know," said Sylvie slowly, "I was thinking earlier that there was something odd about the horizon, where the view was clear through the trees. The earth and sky fade together in a blur, with the land reaching slightly up into the sky. Then it hit me that I was seeing the curvature of the inside of the crystal sphere."

Sylvie suddenly turned around to face both Aelfred and Teldin. "Did either of you think about how big this place is?" she asked. "Seriously, I mean. Do you know how huge this place really is?"

"Looked damn big to me," Aelfred said, "but Dyffed told me a few weeks ago in the phlogiston that Herdspace wasn't the biggest crystal sphere there was."

"That doesn't matter," Sylvie said, brushing her long silver hair back over her pointed ears. "This crystal sphere could be half the size of any major one, but it would still have more living space inside it than a million planets. Think about it: We're living on the inside of a crystal sphere, which is maybe a million times bigger than a world. Do you see what I'm saying?"

Teldin thought about it and shivered slightly. The idea was almost too crazy to believe. He realized that he could not picture how truly big a single world was, much less imagine the size of the inside of a crystal sphere. "Then what's beyond the atmosphere?" he said, pointing up at the sky.

Sylvie looked up for a moment, shading her eyes and squinting against the glare. "There could be some planets orbiting the sun, but I don't see any of them. Dyffed said there weren't any there, anyway. Maybe the air envelope on the inside of this sphere extends all the way up to the sun, though—blue sky everywhere you go, and clouds a thousand miles high. I don't know."

Teldin saw Sylvie frown as she stared straight up. "That's odd," she whispered. "Is the sun getting darker?"

Teldin and Aelfred immediately leaned back and looked up. Teldin thought he had noticed a slight dimming in the light, but he had put it down as a visual quirk.

"Damn," said Aelfred. "It is getting darker. I can tell now. Gods of Toril, what's going on here?"

Teldin heard a sudden increase in the volume of the gnomes' distant conversation. Several were calling to each other about the sun going out. They sounded quite panicked. He hardly blamed them.

"Maybe we'd better get back to the ship," said Aelfred, rising to his feet, his cup forgotten on the ground. "We can ask our multilegged friends if this is natural and harmless, or if we're supposed to scream now."

"Aelfred," said Sylvie. "If the sun is—"

"You no fear," said a chirping, singsong voice behind them. They turned in surprise to see a tall rastipede approaching, its eight legs thumping softly through the undergrowth. Teldin couldn't tell if it was the leader he had spoken with earlier. They all looked so much alike.

"Sun is healthy," said the insect-centaur. "Sun have not much light now. World is dark soon. World you have no night? You fear dark?"

"You mean the sun is going out?" Teldin asked in amazement. His nose twitched, but he fought the urge to sneeze. "We are not afraid of the night, but we thought there was no night here because the sun couldn't set."

"I not listen you true," said the rastipede, twisting its head slightly. "You say 'set'? What is 'set'?"

Teldin started to explain what a sunset was, but the urge to sneeze overcame him too rapidly. He backed away, trying not to fall over, as he sneezed violently two dozen times in a row. Sylvie abruptly took over for him, quickly explaining to the rastipede the rudiments of day and night on spherical worlds. The rastipede appeared to be even more confused as she spoke, asking a stream of strange questions, until Sylvie finally gave up.

"It's no use," she said. "They've lived here for so many generations that they don't remember what it's like to live on a regular planet. They've never seen their sun set. The sun just goes out, and it gets dark. The sun goes back on again eventually, and that's dawn here." She looked up at the rapidly darkening star. Teldin looked up, too, and found that he could now see the sun's broad, reddened disk clearly. It was feature-less and smooth, seemingly perfect.

Aelfred dropped his gaze. "I'm in serious need of a drink. If there's anything left of that little keg of ale we pulled off the ship, let's drain it a nd get some sleep. This place has been very entertaining, but I've almost lost all sense of time. And you," he said, nudging Sylvie again, "you need your beauty rest. You've worked too hard. I'm your captain, and I'm or-dering you to turn yourself in for a nap."

"Will you tuck me in?" Sylvie asked straight-faced, then glanced at Teldin and colored, biting her lip.

Aelfred saw her expression and laughed, putting his arm around her. "Sure, I'll tuck you in," he said. "Excuse us, Teldin. I've got some official duties to perform."

Sylvie mumbled something in embarrassment as Aelfred led her away to the ship. Teldin managed to smile in spite of himself, then sneezed and sneezed until he felt he would never stop. When he finally finished, exhausted, he looked up and noticed that the rastipede was gone, too.

Grandfather, he thought to himself as the red sun went out overhead, the things you've missed. If I die from this wretched allergy and find you by Paladine's side, I'm going to tell you some tales that will lay you out all over again.

*   *   *   *   *

Nightfall could not have come soon enough for the ship's tired crew. Dyffed and the other gnomes, once they had got-ten used to the phenomenon, watched the sun go out until the gnomes were nearly incapacitated from stiff necks. During the sun's fade-out, the gnomes built a bonfire and talked with the rastipedes until exhaustion overcame the former and they fell asleep across the lakeshore in every possible spot. The in-sect folk stayed up, moving to and fro among the sleeping travelers and keeping guard over them.

Teldin watched it all, unable to sleep because of his allergy. The rastipedes were changing their guard in shifts, he noticed; a few would leave together just as other rastipedes would ap-proach the informal encampment. He decided the new crea-tures were fresh from the underground home that Aelfred had spoken of. It was impossible to tell, really, but as a theory it wasn't a bad one. If they were communicating by smell, as Aelfred had suggested earlier, then they were "talking" up a storm.

Teldin found Gaye asleep under a tree, wrapped in a light blanket that Teldin recognized in the firelight as having come from his cabin aboard the ship. The night air was warm enough that he didn't think she really needed it, but he wasn't in the mood to bother her about it. After making sure she was in good shape, he got up and continued his slow walk around the lakeshore, sniffing and sneezing and wishing, just a little bit, that he could cut off his nose.

His feet finally brought him to the numerous poles and ropes strung from the lakeshore to a hastily built framework about a hundred feet inland, on which the *Perilous Halibut* rested about a man's height off the ground. The ship's tail fin had been straightened, the oars and propeller drive had been repaired with the rastipedes' astounding carpentry skills, and the two large mounds of active fur tied on long rope tethers to a nearby tree attested to the complete recovery of the giant hamsters. Teldin listened to the hamsters' rumbling *reeep! reeep!* sounds, then turned away, shaking his head and smiling despite his sinus agony.

It was then that Teldin heard a faint, deep voice from the other side of the ship. He stopped and listened, trying to make out the words, but the noise from the obviously nocturnal giant hamsters drowned it out. He hesitated for a moment, then walked toward the source of the talking as quietly as he could.

"We should leave in the morning, shortly after the sun lights up," he heard the voice say. It sounded like Gomja. He must be talking with a rastipede leader, one that could cast a language-translating spell. He knew from talking with Sylvie and other wizards that such a spell was fairly minor, but the idea that insects could cast spells at all still surprised him, even when he felt nothing could surprise him anymore.

Still moving in silence, Teldin rounded the side of the ship. It was impossible to see anything clearly in the darkness. The bonfire was far on the other side of the ship, and Teldin had noticed earlier that the sky had no stars; it was pitch black above him, though he imagined he could see faint, distant lights near the horizon.

"No, they've been very friendly so far," Gomja's voice said. "Our situation is quite good. We shouldn't need any assistance unless . . . oh." Teldin heard a rustling in the darkness. "Sir? Is that you?"

"Who are you talking to?" Teldin asked. He wished his eyes would stop tearing up. He could barely see as it was. He walked forward slowly, one hand out to keep from walking into the wooden struts holding up the *Perilous Halibut*. "I thought I heard you talking with someone."

"Oh," said Gomja. Teldin heard something big move right in front of him, and he stopped. He could hear the giff breathing hoarsely and rapidly, perhaps only ten feet away. "I, um, was talking with myself, sir. Forgive me for that. I don't do it very often."

"I don't mind," said Teldin, puzzled. He looked around, seeing and hearing no other being. "I just thought that . . . well, forget it. You should get some sleep, First Colonel-Commander. We could have a busy day tomorrow."

"Yes, sir!" said Gomja, heartily and quickly. "I'll turn in in a short while, not long at all. I was having trouble getting used to things here, I'm afraid. You must admit, sir, that this is a very queer place." Teldin heard the giff yawn. It was still too dark to see more than Gomja's outline.

Teldin nodded, then turned to go. "Well, good night to you. Let's hope we get off the ground without any trouble. We have a giant four-legged beast to find, Dyffed says. I don't want you to blink and miss it."

"Oh, very good, sir!" Gomja said, laughing briefly. "Good night to you, too!"

Teldin made his way back around the ship to the vicinity of the campfire. He wiped his face with his hands, feeling his thick moustache and realizing how long it had been since he'd shaved. He'd have to take care of that first thing in the morning. Was this antimagical lake water good to shave with? He'd know soon enough.

He found a spot at random and lay down, settling himself near a tree, and forced himself to relax and ignore his sinuses. It was difficult, but he managed to drift off after a long period and enter a realm full of strange and bothersome dreams.

He was in his room aboard the *Perilous Halibut* with Gaye. It was night, and she was leaning close to him. "Teldin," she said softly. He could smell her perfume as she started to reach for him. He knew they were doing wrong, and they were about to crash. The ship was falling straight down toward the other side of the darkened sphere, falling like a rock from an infinite tower. He tried to hold on to something and tried to protect Gaye, but he couldn't find a way to do it. They were falling toward the sea on the far side of the black sphere. In the sea were monstrous shapes greater than whales, their blackness darker than the night-lit waters in which they swam. "*Teldin*," Gaye said, holding his face. A titanic shark leaped out of the sea, its white-fanged mouth wider than a world. It wasn't going to miss them.

"Teldin, wake up!" Gaye said, shaking his arm. He blinked, then involuntarily shielded his face against the brilliant sky. Gaye looked down at him, her black tangled hair littered with small sticks and bits of leaves and grass. "Time to get up. The sun's on again! Boy, you slept like a rock!"

* * * * *

After two hours of traveling straight up, Teldin could see that the footprint shape of the lake was much clearer. His sinuses clearing up at last, he stared out of his cabin porthole, feeling a curious sense of *deja vu*. Hadn't he done this before? He had the feeling that someone was about to enter his cabin, but he shrugged off the feeling and concentrated on the view. He guessed that they were about seventy miles up.

Loomfinger was on the helm for now. Sylvie had slept badly the night before, and she was so exhausted that she could not be awakened. Aelfred had made the helm substitution so the ship could get on its way as soon as possible. With enough altitude, Aelfred hoped the ship's speed would increase regardless of who ran it. Then, too, if they had to find a beast like the one that had made those unbelievable footprints, they would need all the altitude they could get.

Someone knocked on Teldin's door. Gaye, he thought, not quite sure why he believed it was her. He heaved a sigh and left the bed, walking over to his door. He crouched as he

THE MAELSTROM'S EYE 209

opened it, to avoid banging his head on the door frame.

"Ah, Teldin!" cried Dyffed. "Just the man I wanted to see, and here I am, seeing you!" The gnome gave a hearty chuckle. Dyffed had not changed his clothes in the last month; his brown tweed suit was fraying apart at the elbows, his lime-green shirt was a lifeless green-brown, and his bright yellow tie was decorated with hundreds of food stains.

Maybe seeing Gaye wouldn't have been such a bad idea, Teldin thought. "What do you want?" he asked tiredly.

"Miss Gaeadrelle Goldring informs me that you have the thingfinder!" Seeing Teldin's blank expression, the gnome hurried on. "The thingfinder! Smallish crimson box, about so big, which I thought I had lost when the hamsters got loose but which Miss Gaeadrelle Goldring says she found and took with her when we left Ironpiece, then—"

"I've got it," Teldin said, leaving the door open to walk back to his bed. He reached down and opened a drawer in a bedside dresser, then pulled out the red box. He gave it to Dyffed. "I forgot all about it. Forgive me for that."

The bald gnome inspected the box, then gave Teldin a glowing smile. "Marvelous—it's in perfect shape! You've taken excellent care of it, not what I would have expected from someone not born to the rigors and demands of science and technology, the exacting care that they—oops." He gingerly withdrew and pocketed a broken gear fragment from the open back of the box. "Do hope that wasn't important," he muttered. He looked up at Teldin again, the incident forgotten. "As I was saying, let's be off!"

"Off where?" Teldin asked cautiously.

"Why, off to find the fal, of course!" announced the gnome, as if the goal had been perfectly obvious from the start. "We'll go topside and swing our little thingfinder around and see what thing we find!"

Teldin looked down at the red box as if it were a live serpent. He remembered the way the gnomes with Dyffed had ducked when it was pointed in their direction, back in the hangar on Ironpiece. "Is that thing dangerous to use?"

"Dangerous? You mean dangerous?" The gnome appeared astonished. "Why, not at all. It's perfectly safe. There's not a thing it could do to harm either of us. At least, not that I know of. I mean, my colleagues on Ironpiece had made only this one model, and they hadn't had time to properly test it, but they gave me their utmost assurances that nothing could go wrong, nothing that they could possibly imagine. It's as safe as the Bank of Ironpiece, Reorx bless it." The gnome chewed his lower lip. "But I guess I shouldn't say that now, should I. How fast they go. The bank had experienced some difficulties, but no one had thought . . ."

Five minutes later, the two were on the top deck. The wind wasn't particularly troublesome because the gnome at the helm couldn't give the spelljammer the speed that the more-experienced wizard Sylvie could, but Teldin still kept his cloak reduced to necklace length to keep it from flapping against him. He suddenly felt queazy about approaching the low railing around the top deck while the ship was in flight. The suddenness with which the ship had entered Herdspace and the excitement of the earlier air battle had negated all his nervousness before; now the situation was very different. He kept low, reaching the railing and sitting down next to it with one leg against a railing post for additional support.

There were few clouds around. Teldin remembered how clear the sky had been that morning, and he wondered if the weather was merely going through a pleasant period or if this was the natural state of things. With luck, they wouldn't be in this crystal sphere long enough to find out.

Dyffed had no qualms about being on the top deck, and he peered over the side of the ship to the ground, now many miles below them. Teldin almost closed his eyes, not wanting to see the gnome fall over by accident. "Lovely view, just lovely," murmured the gnome, then stood back with the red thingfinder in his hands. "Now, let's see what we shall see."

Teldin's teeth gritted together as the gnome made a few adjustments inside the box, then raised it to his face. "We're looking for our friend the falmadaraatha, One Six Nine, or old 'Thirteen Squared,' as we used to call him. That's an inside joke, you see, because the value of thirteen squared is—"

"You've already told me about that," said Teldin wearily. "Just let me know if you see anything."

The gnome began scanning ahead of the ship, the wind whipping his filthy tie around his neck. "You see, this device works on a certain amount of latent psionic energy present in the mind of the operator. You need not be a fully accredited psionicist to use it, since we all possess a certain degree of—"

"Dyffed," interrupted Teldin. "I haven't the faintest idea of what you are talking about. Pretend that I'm stupid, then explain it to me."

"Oh," said the gnome. "Well, um, what you do . . . you think of something, then you look for it through here"—he indicated the dark glass window on the box with a finger—"and then the box front, here, lets you see the object. I tried to locate you once with this, before we left Ironpiece, and got the most curious reaction when this perfectly imbecilic moron got in the way. Would you believe that this silly box said that this obviously low-grade-but-still-gnomish gnome was actually you? I was quite annoyed, really. Thought I was going to have my funding cut off for it, but then the hamsters escaped, and you know, I can't see a single thing through this." The gnome lowered the red box and turned it over. "Ah. Forgot to turn it on." He made a final adjustment, then looked through it again. "Ah, much better. One Six Nine, One Six Nine, One Six Nine . . . really quite a nice chap, I must say. Makes an excellent carrot dip. I remember once when I came here with—"

"Can you find the *Spelljammer* with that?" Teldin asked abruptly, amazed he hadn't thought to ask before now.

"Why, certainly," said Dyffed, "if it's in this sphere, then we should . . ." The gnome swung the thingfinder in several wide arcs, eventually covering the range of the sky and ship. "Well, so much for that. Must be in another crystal sphere. Back to One Six Nine. Fine chap, as I was saying—"

"Dyffed," interrupted Teldin again. "If you've been to this sphere before, and you've visited One Six Nine's home, then why don't you know the way to get there? Why didn't you say anything about what we should expect when we got to this sphere, like these 'megafauna' you talk about?"

"What?" The gnome lowered the thingfinder and looked at Teldin in surprise. "Oh, well, I . . . I . . ." He looked confused, staring at the view wi th a vaguely troubled look. "I forgot about it, I'm afraid. Because this sphere pops ships inside it, so they never go through it, it's almost impossible to come in where you want to be. You just can't tell from the outside, you know. I also meant to tell you about the megafauna, I really did. I was going to say something about the antimagical water, too, since I've read some papers about that—quite fascinating, really. The megafauna's tracks destroy all magical power beneath them, simply crush it out, voiding the dweomer. We are speaking of pressures greater than three point one four one five nine two six five three five nine times ten to the thirty-seventh power scruples per square acre, of course, far beyond any known magical tolerance levels, once the megafauna puts down its foot—a process which takes centuries, as you can imagine. There are local legends in Herdspace to the effect that eventually all of the megafauna will crush out all magical power, and magic will cease to exist in this sphere. That's the 'Quiet Whimper' theory, you see, and the other view is the 'Unsteady State' theory, in which the footsteps taken by megafauna *after* the magic is crushed out will then bring magic *back*. A fascinating idea, the latter, but, as yet, there's no real—"

"Wait," Teldin interrupted. "One more question: How do we get out of this sphere?"

"Ah!" Dyffed's face lit up. "Ah, I did see that. You simply dive back toward the place you came in! Marvelous system. The gateways open up at regular intervals, the same time each day for an hour or so, and—assuming that you've been able to time your exit using a properly built timekeeping device, such as gnomes are known for making—you leave!"

"Good," said Teldin in relief. "Now, look for the fal."

"The fal, yes," said the gnome, raising the red box to his face again. He rotated, scanning the sky in all directions at eye level, then looked higher. "Perhaps this cursed device really is just a tad out of adjustme—oh! By Reorx!" The excited gnome started to point to a place forward, up, and to the starboard side of the ship, then did a very unexpected thing. He dropped the red box.

Stunned, Teldin lunged for the box, which bounced on the deck toward the side of the ship. His fingers missed a clean grab, instead knocking the box back on the deck and away from him. Dyffed lunged for the box again and missed, stumbling over his own feet to fall facedown on the deck. Teldin lunged for the thingfinder, slapping a hand over it and pinning it to the deck.

Heaving a sigh, Teldin pulled the thingfinder to him and picked it up. As Dyffed mumbled apologies, Teldin held up the box as he had seen Dyffed do, placing the glass plate in front of his face. He tried to face it in the same direction as the gnome had aimed it, thinking all the while about a giant, talking black slug—as best as he could visualize one.

Almost at once, he felt a sort of tickling sensation inside his head. It was difficult to describe it as anything else. The image of a giant slug sharpened in his mind until he thought he could see it: a creature perhaps a third the length of the old *Probe*, gleaming black and very thick. From the near end of the beast sprouted a handful of whiplike tentacles, two of them especially thick and having bulbous ends. Between the tentacle roots was a huge, circular mouth rimmed with a double row of long yellow-gray fangs. Curiously, above the great central mouth was a large human-type mouth.

With a shock, Teldin realized that he *was* looking at such a creature. It was clearly visible before him. He knew that the image was not displayed on the glass plate of the thingfinder; instead, the view of the fal replaced his normal vision, blocking out everything else as if it were the only object in sight. The being appeared to be resting, stretched out full length on invisible ground somewhere.

Abruptly, the bulbous antennae writhed and moved, sweeping slowly around as if searching for something nearby. A sense of dread grew in the back of Teldin's mind, and he was certain that somehow the creature knew it was being watched, but he fought the urge to tear his gaze away from it. This is impossible, he thought; what I'm seeing is merely some sort of magical image the thingfinder is creating. Even if this was the fal, it could not possibly know that—

The creature lifted the front third of its great bulk into the air with an unhurried motion. The head—if he could call it that—tilted and moved until it was aimed directly at Teldin, the two thickest antennae pointing at him from their widely separated directions. The upper humanlike mouth moved.

You are greeted. The sensation of the beast's words in Teldin's mind was nothing at all like that when he had once conversed with the mind flayer Estriss, slain months ago in a battle with a neogi over Toril. The fal's words were thick and cool, poured into his mind in slow, precise shapes.

You wish to speak with me, came the thoughts. *You are Teldin Moore. You are in great danger because of your cloak, I see. You have far to go. You must run. You must look behind as well as ahead of you, Teldin Moore.*

Teldin fought to break the contact. It was like struggling to awaken from a nightmare in which he was paralyzed and helpless, unable to twitch or blink, doomed to remain imprisoned in his body in a black dreamland. Chills spilled down his spine and through his body.

You must look behind you, Teldin Moore.

The image of the slug monster came closer and looked more real with each passing second. He had to look away. He had to look away right *now*.

You must look behind you, Teldin Moore.

With an inhuman scream, Teldin tore the box away from his face. It slammed into his lap, gripped in his white hands and shaking unstoppably. For several seconds, he was unable to get control of himself. If anyone had touched him, he feared he would have gone uncontrollably mad.

The panic attack passed. His chest hurt as if a thick rope were tied around it; he recognized the symptoms of breathing too fast and too shallowly, and he forced himself to relax.

Dyffed cleared his throat. Teldin glanced over at him, then carefully handed over the red box. His hand still shook a bit.

"Sorry," Teldin said as the gnome took the thingfinder. "Caught me off guard. I'll be fine."

The gnome nodded, looking the box over carefully. "Couldn't hurt to do a little adjusting," he mumbled softly. "The gain may be turned up too high. It makes the images a little too real to the cerebral sensory interfaces and causes a few minor problems, paranoia, delusional insanity, that sort of thing. We should have it licked with the next prototype." Dyffed looked up. "Did you see One Six Nine? Wonderful old fellow."

Teldin blew out a long breath. "He . . . used telepathy with me, speaking in my mind. He looked like some kind of a . . ." He thought better of what he was about to say and substituted quickly. "He looked fine."

The gnome smiled and looked off into the infinite blue sky. "Did he say anything in particular? He's quite a talkative chap for a falmadaraatha. Very much into literature, high-brow stuff. A wheeler-dealer—for a fal, that is."

Teldin thought, then remembered. "He kept saying that I should look behind me." He turned at that moment and did just that, but saw nothing behind the *Perilous Halibut* but blue sky, miles above the ground.

And a faint cloud of specks on the horizon.

"Dyffed," Teldin said, pointing back. "What in the Abyss are those?"

Dyffed held the box up to his face as he looked back. The wind whipped his clothing.

"Oh, hamster pellets," the gnome said. "Those are—"

The hatchway groaned and was flung open. A huge blue hippopotamus face appeared, blinking in the light wind.

"*Battle stations!*" Gomja roared.

Chapter Fourteen

• • •

"Are those the scro?" Teldin asked, pointing aft at the swarm of distant objects on the horizon. He felt like a fool to ask, but he wanted to be sure.

"That they are, sir!" Gomja shouted, unnecessarily loudly. "We're clearing the decks for helm changeover, so you'll have to come inside! You, too, Mister Jammermaker!"

Teldin quickly got to his feet and headed for the open hatch, still not entirely comfortable to be walking around on the open deck so far from the ground. "We found the fal!" he called. "It's off that way, ahead but up and to the right, to starboard!" He looked down at Dyffed, but the gnome was busy watching the approaching fleet through his thingfinder. Teldin grabbed the gnome by the shoulders and propelled him toward the hatch.

One minute later, Teldin pulled the hatch shut behind him and bolted it tight, then descended the last few rungs on the ladder to the deck. He fought down a brief surge of claustrophobia, telling himself that one day he wouldn't have to face being cooped up in a gnomish ship ever again—at least, not if the gods were kind.

"We've been going too slowly for too long, sir," Gomja said, checking Teldin's bolting of the hatch. He climbed down the ladder, looking grim. "Aelfred wants to pull Loomfinger off the helm and put Sylvie back on. You should go to your cabin during changeover. I believe we'll have some trouble there, but it shouldn't last long. I'll handle everything else around here."

"I can give a hand, I'm sure," Teldin started to say.

The huge giff shook his head vigorously. "That won't be necessary. We're not going to go above to shoot back at the scro this time. We lack the troops, and the wind will be too great when Sylvie takes over. Just—"

The door into the room banged open unexpectedly. An overweight, sweating gnome hurried into the room, panting as if he'd run a long distance, and bounced off Gomja's massive left leg before coming to a stop. "Telbin Mayor," he announced, red faced and out of breath. "Captain Albert Silverhand requests—no, wait. Captain Albert Silverhorn requests your—Captain Aelfred Hornsilver requests—oh, bother! The captain would like to see you in the helm room right away if you have a moment for an emergency now, unless it's a bother."

Gomja appeared stunned for a moment at the message but quickly recovered himself. "Calm yourself and get your message straight, Private," Gomja ordered the gnome. The gnome immediately sat down and tried to catch his breath, repeating his message softly to himself to straighten it out. Gomja turned back to Teldin with a concerned look on his face. "I wouldn't worry about it, sir. I think Gurfley here has his message twisted around. I'll get it straightened out and tell you later in your cabin. Get some rest."

"I think I got the basic idea of what the message was," Teldin said. "I'll find out what's going on with Aelfred."

"But sir!" Gomja called anxiously. "Changeover could be dangerous. I don't think it would be wise to go there yet. Wait until it's over, at least."

Teldin hesitated. Gomja might have a point. He waved to the giff and said, "Whatever you say," then left the room, closing the door behind him. On impulse, he set off for the helm room anyway. Aelfred wouldn't ask for him unless it was at least remotely important.

Teldin made the trip through the low, narrow corridors of the ship with better than usual speed, stumbling over gnomes only twice. When he arrived in the helm room, he found Loomfinger on the elaborately decorated helm, perched nervously on the edge of the thronelike seat. Aelfred and Sylvie were there, as was Gaye, standing almost in a corner of the room. Gaye immediately smiled and waved at Teldin when he entered. Aelfred glanced at him, then turned his attention back to Sylvie.

"You sure you're up to this?" Aelfred asked with concern. He stood by Sylvie, who was seated on a stool just in front of the helm and rubbing her face vigorously.

"Damn it, I'm fine," the half-elf muttered. "I got a little sleep, anyway. If we make it quick, we won't drop more than a few hundred feet, a thousand at most. How high are we? Are we above the clouds? No—I mean, are we above—are we high enough to make that drop okay? You know what I mean, Aelfred. Just tell me."

Aelfred looked up at Teldin and gave a quick shake of his head, his lips pressed into a line.

Teldin then caught on to what was happening. "Aelfred, do you want me to take the helm?" he asked. "I don't know anything about how to make this thing work, and the last time I tried running the helm, it didn't work."

"You did pretty damn well when we flew out of the reach of those scro at Ironpiece," Aelfred said flatly. "We don't have time to quibble. We've got to get up and out of this atmosphere, or we'll never get anywhere. We don't know how high the air goes, but it will be faster sailing for us all the farther we get from the ground and the scro. No offense, Loomfinger, but we need the best person in that helm right now. Sylvie's too tired to do it, and I want you to try, Teldin." Aelfred looked back at the gnome on the helm. "What's the situation out there?"

The gnome swallowed. "The fleet is still behind us, sir," he said, his speech growing more rapid with each second. "We are at two and a half miles altitude and I count twenty ships to aft so far, and they are gaining on us and should be upon us in ten minutes or so unless we change helmsmen, but I can still run the helm in an emergency if you need me anytime. Just call me and I can run the helm in a jiffy and never—"

"Forget it! Just forget it, Loomfinger," Sylvie interrupted, standing suddenly and swaying. She caught Teldin's arm in a tight grip but did not relax it. "I can do it. Bring me some water so I can wash my face off, and I can get on the helm. Hurry it up."

Aelfred stared at Sylvie, who was still swaying, then looked at Teldin with desperation. "You up to this, old son?" he asked. "Can you make that cloak of yours run a ship again?"

"Aelfred, I said I would try it!" Sylvie yelled suddenly. She angrily whirled around, looking at everyone. "Would you all just get out of here? You're driving me crazy!"

"Sylvie, calm down!" Aelfred said, reaching out to put a hand on her shoulder. "You haven't had any sleep, and— Teldin!"

Without a word, Teldin acted on impulse. He reached out, caught Loomfinger under the arms, and lifted the surprised gnome off the helm to set him on the floor. At that same moment, Teldin had a curious feeling, as if he had stepped off a high cliff and was starting to fall. He lunged for the helm in panic, not having expected the change so soon. His cape flowed out behind him as if he were underwater. Everyone in the room fought to keep from falling over as the gravity left. Sylvie shrieked, flailing with her arms.

"Gods, Teldin!" roared Aelfred, his face turning white. His feet had left the floor. "You idiot!"

Teldin's right hand grasped the back of the helm, and he heaved himself clumsily into the helm's seat, holding himself down by grasping the arms of the chair.

Nothing happened.

Now weightless, with the screams of everyone in the room ringing in his ears, Teldin felt a terror that he'd never dreamed he could feel. He had just murdered everyone aboard the ship. They were going to die because of his stupidity. And dying was going to take a long, long time at this altitude.

Wildly, he clutched at the arms of the chair, concentrating on making the ship rise with every bit of willpower he had.

Nothing happened.

"*Noooooo!*" he roared. There was a cracking sound, and one of the arms of the helm broke loose in his grip.

Time slowed down.

Warmth flooded through his body again, as it had on the *Probe*. This time the warmth and surge of power felt even stronger and clearer than before. In a daze, he pulled himself down to the helm. As he did, he felt his spirit pull loose from his body and flow out through the ship and into every part of it. He felt himself fully become the *Perilous Halibut*.

With the ship's internal gravity restored, Teldin felt himself slowly thump down onto the helm's seat, his cloak glowing with bright pinkish light. He was vaguely aware that everyone else was flailing about in slow motion, but all were falling toward the floor now. Luckily, they didn't have far to fall.

Spelljamming the *Halibut* was a strange sensation, somewhat different than it had been on the *Probe*. He could see everyone in the helm room with him, and he could also see all around the outside of the long, black ship. He saw both the floor of the room and the ground miles below the ship. It took only a few seconds to look back, without turning his head, and see the nearing fleet of scro ships above the horizon. They were hovering almost motionless, but he knew that they were just slowed by his perceptions. The *Perilous Halibut* had fallen quite a distance in the last few seconds.

Strangest of all, Teldin felt as if he *was* the ship. The ship's hull became like a second skin, though he could feel no heat or pressure from it. It was simply there, a part of him now. He wondered if he was gaining more awareness of things as he acquired experience with spelljamming.

Business first, he thought. Aelfred had wanted to gain altitude in hopes the ship could move more quickly. Teldin focused all of his energies into going up. He felt no different sitting on the helm. His view outside, however, revealed at once that the *Perilous Halibut* was climbing rapidly.

Time returned to normal again.

For a few seconds, the room was filled with cries and struggling bodies on the floor.

"Teldin!" Aelfred thrust his face right into Teldin's own, the pink light from Teldin's cloak reflecting on them both. "Teldin Moore, you son of a bitch, what in the Nine Hells possessed you to do that?" Aelfred shouted at the top of his lungs, his face pale with fear and rage. "Damn you for screwing around with the helm! We all could have been killed! Don't you ever think first?"

Teldin looked at Aelfred and felt an onrush of shame. He knew he had acted too quickly and had endangered everyone, but he felt his anger spill out instead. "It was either act or stand there and listen to everyone argue," he retorted. "I apologize for the shock, but we're gaining altitude from the scro fleet. They won't catch us now. It worked!"

Aelfred continued to stare into Teldin's face at eye level. "Wonderful, but don't ever do it again," he said. "You scared the crap out of me. The gods damn you for that."

Teldin nodded, his face deep red. He switched to looking outside the ship. The sky above the ship was getting darker, bit by bit. How high did the air envelope extend, all the way to the sun? They'd know soon enough.

Sylvie looked at Teldin, blinking rapidly. "You've torn the arm off the helm, but you're flying the ship."

Teldin looked down and nodded. "The cloak must work only if there's no functioning helm on a ship," he said slowly. "That's why it wouldn't fly for me before now, and why I could fly the *Probe* with both helms down."

Sylvie stared at him. "I see." She tried to rub her face, but her hands were shaking too much. Swaying from foot to foot, she turned and left the room without another word.

Aelfred followed her to the door. "I want to talk with Teldin for a while, so go ahead. I won't wake you up again. Gaye and Loomfinger, you two can leave, too."

"I wanted to talk with Teldin, too," said Gaye, as Loomfinger picked himself up and scuttled for the door.

"Out," said Aelfred, jerking a thumb at the entrance. Gaye rolled her eyes and mumbled, "Darn," as she left.

When the door closed behind everyone, Aelfred stepped back from Teldin and took a deep breath. "You've saved us again, but this time I can't think of a good excuse for it," he said in a calm but hard voice. "You took a chance and blew it, then you broke the helm and, by an incredibly stupid piece of luck, you saved us. But if anything had gone wrong—the ship rolling over, you missing the helm, whatever—we'd be at the bottom of a crater about now. For all your powers, Teldin, you still don't know dirt about spelljamming, and you'd better leave decisions on it to people who do know dirt about it. Think before you act! Do you want to kill us?"

Teldin couldn't meet his friend's gaze. He nodded, face-down.

Aelfred shook his head and looked away. "I almost soiled myself when you pulled Loomfinger off his seat." He shivered for a moment. "It's different in wildspace. You don't fall anywhere there if someone gets off the helm to go to the head. The ship keeps on flying. You can't do that in a gravity field." He glanced back at Teldin. "As long as you're up there, are there any signs of our followers?"

Teldin looked, using his helm's-eye view of the outside of the ship. "None that I can see. We're not leaving the atmosphere yet. The air envelope here must be very thick. Where should we go next? The fal?"

Aelfred nodded. "Of course. If I'm going to put my life on the line for you every few days, I want to know some of the reasons why. That slug had better have some good answers, too. I heard Dyffed knew how to get there, using some little magical box of his. Any truth to that?"

Teldin had almost forgotten about the gnome. "He has a device that picked out the fal's location just a few moments before Gomja came up and warned us about the scro fleet. It works on mental energy in some way. I don't pretend to understand it. He may be able to set a course for us using it. He said we had to use it outside the ship on the deck, or at least I had that impression."

Aelfred looked at Teldin with an odd expression. "Messing with the helm has addled your brain. I think you meant that Gomja found out about the scro fleet from you when he came up on deck, don't you?"

"No," said Teldin. "He told us."

Aelfred looked at Teldin blankly. "Now, how could that be? Gomja's been inside the ship this whole time. I assumed he'd gone up to see you and you'd warned him then, or else you'd come in yourself to tell him."

"Wait, let me think about this," said Teldin, becoming confused. "Couldn't he have found out from Loomfinger? When he was on the helm, didn't Loomfinger see the fleet behind him and warn everyone?"

"I wasn't here, but Loomfinger wouldn't know a fleet from a flock of gullions," Aelfred said. "He's not much more than a minor illusionist with a handful of spells, and he can barely pay enough attention to the real world to keep from getting killed on a daily basis. I guess it's possible that he could have warned Gomja. I never asked the giff how he found out about the scro. He practically dragged me out of my hammock to tell me about them. I ran to get Sylvie right after that, and Gaye showed up wondering what everyone was doing in the helm room, then you showed up, and there you are. I should ask Loomfinger, just out of curiosity, I suppose, but I don't know if it matters now. Maybe I should give him a medal."

"We should find Dyffed first and get that thingfinder from him." Teldin tried a weak smile. "Not that I'm telling you what to do, mind you."

Aelfred didn't smile back, but he relaxed slightly. "I'll arm wrestle you for control of the ship, if you like," he said, "then you can try to command a crew of gnomes."

Teldin shook his head. "I'm afraid I threw my arm out when I was rowing over to the shore to meet those rastipedes," he said sorrowfully. "As soon as it's better, I'll let you know."

Aelfred laughed. "That's what I like," he said, "job security. I'll go find Dyffed."

When Aelfred had left, Teldin's smile faded. He knew that he had done a nearly disastrous thing in pulling the gnome from the helm. Now that it was all over, he couldn't believe he had done it. What if things hadn't turned out, as Aelfred had said? What had made him do it? He remembered thinking, for just a moment as he grabbed for Loomfinger, that he could do anything he wanted to with the cloak, and it would work if he tried hard enough. Had he been getting cocky, then, with his new powers? He knew he would have to use his intelligence from now on, not his ego.

For a few minutes, Teldin concentrated on the *Perilous Halibut*'s climb away from the ground, and toward . . . what? He wasn't sure. Was there a wildspace-type vacuum in the middle of this sphere? Or was there air all the way through it? He had visited several crystal spheres in the months since he'd left Krynn, and no two of them were much alike at all. This one took the prize so far, though he recalled some tales that Aelfred told of a sphere in which a gigantic tree grew, with planets nestled in its branches. He shook his head. Less than a year ago, he would have laughed. Now he believed every word of it.

Suddenly, he thought to look down, using his helm-given view of the ship's outside. He'd been looking up and across for some time, seeing little other than blue sky, wispy clouds of every possible shape, and the huge sun overhead. The sky was still fairly clear. The view should be interesting.

So he looked down.

"Paladine," he breathed. "Oh, great Paladine."

Teldin had seen worlds from space before. He'd never forgotten his first view of Krynn from orbit: the beautiful blue seas, green and brown lands, white clouds. It was one world among a multitude, but it was his world. In his mind, it had become precious beyond the value of any treasure, and he loved it for all of its flaws and heartaches. It was just one little world, but he had felt a strange emotion upon seeing it as a whole for the first time.

But Teldin had never dreamed of seeing a world that had no end, a world that got bigger the farther one traveled from it. As he looked down, Teldin could see the outlines of four mighty rivers, two mountain ranges, and two vast blue seas that rivaled the largest lakes that Krynn could offer. The view went on and on. As he looked down, he became aware that he must be hundreds of miles up now. The view extended off to his left and right to a considerable distance, though it faded into blue sky, hidden by the thickness of the atmosphere.

He had to admit that the lake below him did, indeed, resemble a gigantic beast's footprint. He looked at the other lake he had seen—and saw that it, too, resembled a footprint. In fact, so did the next huge lake he saw, lying in the opposite direction on roughly a straight line with the previous two lakes. It must be true, Teldin thought, that these are footprints. Even as he thought it, part of his mind would not accept it. What in the name of all the gods in the universe could possibly be so huge as to carve out a sea with each step? He had thought he'd accepted the idea of Dyffed's "megafauna" before, but . . .

Teldin's outside vision became blurred for a moment. The ship passed through a mild sort of turbulence. He look wildly around the outside of the ship. The blue sky was gone, and in its place was a patchwork sky of blues, browns, greens, and white—the full view of Herdspace.

He slowly realized he must have left the atmosphere's upper boundary, which was fairly distinct here instead of being a gradual shift from air to vacuum as on a normal world. Why this place was different, he hadn't a clue. With the thick air gone except for the ships' own air envelope, he could now see perfectly in all directions. He could make out very few distinct features beyond a certain distance, as they were too far away, but he could see the outlines of continents that were larger than planets, and oceans that could swallow a dozen Krynns. Gone was the blackness of wildspace and the glorious constellations. Now, all he could see was sand-colored land and blue water, until it faded into the reaches of infinity.

The *Perilous Halibut* was moving much faster now, he noticed, at full wildspace speed. A thousand miles flashed by with each second of travel in wildspace, he recalled Sylvie saying, and with each second, his view of the land below subtly shifted, revealing new vistas that tugged at his already overstretched imagination. Now he could see a line of footprint lakes and valleys, an unmistakable path of stupendous craters that reached off into the distance toward . . . toward . . .

"Great gods of Krynn," Teldin breathed.

*   *   *   *   *

Aelfred was busy elsewhere on the ship now, so Gaye decided it was safe to visit Teldin in the helm room. Sylvie wouldn't talk to her when the half-elf was on the helm, and Loomfinger didn't know how to explain things very well, but Teldin could tell her what it was like to be on the helm. She was dying to find out. What did it feel like? How could you see outside the ship, as she'd always heard could be done, and still see the inside of the ship? She'd had a million questions all bottled up inside her for years, and now she had someone who could tell her the answers at last.

Gaye padded softly to the helm room door. Get a grip on yourself, she thought. Don't get too close to him too soon; men never liked that. Just take your time and get him to talk, like he was just before the splashdown in the lake. He's got so much on his mind, but maybe there's room for a little more. She thought again of his blue eyes, so much like her father's, and she shivered. It wasn't cold in the corridor.

No one else was around the door, and she could hear nothing inside the room, so Teldin must be alone. She took a deep breath and knocked.

No answer came. She waited, knocked again, then tried the door handle. It was unlocked, so she peeked inside.

Teldin sat in the helm, facing the door. Maps hung on the walls around him in the small room, and low tables held stacks of papers and books. A magical ceiling light spread soft radiance across the room, blending with the shining pink from Teldin's spelljamming cloak.

She smiled and opened her mouth to say hi, but she saw the expression on Teldin's face and stopped. He seemed to be stunned at something he was staring at over the door. Gaye carefully looked up but saw nothing except the door frame and another map on the wall.

She slid into the room and shut the door behind her. "Teldin?" she asked. "Are you okay?"

His jaw worked slightly. "Yes," he said in a whisper. He never looked at her.

"You just look strange," she said. "Is it because you're spelljamming? Is the helm comfortable? You just have the funniest look on your face."

Teldin tried to swallow with a dry mouth. Still he gazed into the distance at some invisible scene. "It's . . . you can't see it from in here. You could if you were on deck." He tried to smile. "I found one of Dyffed's megafauna. Great gods of Krynn, you can't believe this thing."

"What? What's it look like? How big is it?" Gaye was instantly torn between rushing to the upper deck and staying with Teldin. She thought she would go nuts with indecision. "Talk to me!" she said.

"I can't be sure how big it is," Teldin said slowly. "It has a huge blue-and-red-striped body, with a long neck and a tail. I think only its legs are in the atmosphere; the rest of it rises out far beyond it. Maybe it's ten thousand miles high, I don't know. Wait—the hatches are opening on the main deck. Gnomes, some gnomes and Aelfred are coming out. Maybe they saw it through the portholes. There's Gomja, too. They're just looking at the creature. I've adjusted our course so that we can fly around it, and I've dropped our altitude a few thousand miles so that we can be on its level." His voice faded off, his vision still riveted on the sight.

"Keep talking," said Gaye.

Teldin licked his lips. He was aware of a pleasant scent in the air. Gaye, probably. She was wearing some kind of perfume again. "We're coming closer to the creature. It has a tremendous multicolored shadow on the ground, fuzzy. I can see a vague sort of haze around its neck and head, maybe gas or clouds. It might have its own air envelope around it, maybe its own gravity field. It would have to, wouldn't it, since it's so big. The head is very strange, like a lizard with fanlike ears. There might be gills on the side of its head, ahead of the neck. It has only one eye, very big and dark green. Some of the gnomes are waving at it, but I don't think it sees us. No one seems to be saying much. It's so big that it looks like it could walk over a planet."

Gaye was silent, picturing the scene herself. She glanced down, lost in her reverie, and saw Teldin's left hand lying limp on the arm of the helm. After a moment, she reached out slowly and put her right hand on top of his and squeezed. His skin was very warm, almost hot. Something happened inside her when she felt his heat. He didn't pull his hand away, but he didn't return the squeeze.

"It's beautiful," Teldin said, unaware of her. "I never dreamed it would ever be like this."

Gaye felt her cheeks flush with a heat of her own. She couldn't look up at him. After a moment, she came to and looked around, then pulled her hand away.

"I'll go up on deck," she said softly. "Look for me up there."

"I will," Teldin said, still looking into space.

Gaye closed the door and walked through the ship for the nearest ladder to the upper deck. Her heart pounded in her ears every step of the way.

This is stupid, she thought. I can't believe I'm doing this. I've never had this happen to me. I'm falling for him. He's a human, but so was my father. He and Mom worked out pretty well. But why this guy? Why am I breathing so fast? This is the dumbest thing I've ever done. Where is the ladder? I missed it—I have to go back two doors now. What is the matter with me? Will he see me if I'm on deck? Where will I have to stand for him to see me? Will I be able to see him, or what?

She found the ladder and climbed through the already open hatchway. Light poured down from the great, perfect sun at the zenith. A vault of dim color arced overhead, swirls of blue and white and dark green and tan everywhere. She stood up, looked in the direction everyone else was looking, and immediately forgot about Teldin.

But only for a little while.

*　*　*　*　*

"We should be there in less than an hour," said Aelfred in the helm room. "Dyffed got a good fix with the thingfinder on our buddy, the slug, and he just went topside to take one last look at it. I wish Sylvie was up, but the longer she sleeps now, the better off she and the rest of us will be. She should be able to use the helm now that it's fixed. We'll just take the arm off when you want to use it."

"Speaking of Dyffed," said Teldin, "I can see him on the top deck now. Doesn't he ever change clothes?"

Aelfred laughed. He was slowly becoming the old Aelfred Teldin knew, one less stressed than he'd been since arriving at this bizarre sphere. "I could ask Gomja to catch him and hold him down while we scrub him off, but neither of us would like to get that close to him. I'll see what I can do to suggest a change. He is getting a bit stale."

Teldin was silent for a moment, obviously using his helm vision. "I'm trying to see what Dyffed is looking at with that thingfinder," he said. "I don't see another world-beast yet, but I probably will, soon. Did Dyffed say what the one we want looks like, or do they all look the same?"

"I had the impression from Dyffed that these monsters were unique. Half the time, though, he talks too far over my head to catch what he's saying. If he'd talk normally instead of using twelve-syllable words, maybe I'd—what's wrong?"

Teldin's body went rigid, his fingers digging into the arms of the helm. "Aelfred, get someone on the top deck!" he said. "Dyffed's thingfinder blew up on him!"

* * * * *

"Kobas," said a soft voice in the darkness of the room.

General Vorr was instantly awake. His right hand strayed down to his side and tugged free his sword, oiled so that it made no sound.

"Kobas, wake up." Her voice came from the room's far side. Vorr listened carefully but heard nothing out of the ordinary.

"What do you want?" he asked. It had to be an emergency. Usso had been warned too many times to never disturb his sleep for any other reason. He reached for the wall beside his floor mat and pressed his hand against it. The magical lights in the ceiling came on as he did.

Usso flinched at the lights, then steadied herself. She sat in a respectful posture by the doorway, hands folded in her lap, fox tail curled around her side.

"Let's hear it," he said, sliding his sword back into its sheath and sitting up. He wore only his kilt.

"Something weird just happened," Usso said. Her face was tight with tension. "I was on deck, invisible, when I noticed one of the scro, Sergeant Dlavish, at the signaling lamp. I thought he was working on it, but I recalled that the lamp had been in perfect shape earlier, so I investigated. Dlavish was aiming the lamp at the pyramid ship, two miles trailing, and was preparing to send a message. I read his mind with a spell, then confirmed my findings with other spells. He was acting as a spy for the false lich, Skarkesh. I checked him magically using a few devices of my own and found that he had been placed under a spell of charming recently. He was about to send a message that indicated our current crew, weapons, and supply status."

Vorr grunted and rubbed at his face. He'd been expecting news like this for some time. "Go on," he said.

"I didn't want to alert Dlavish or the lich that I had caught on to the situation, so I cast a ventriloquism spell to make him think someone was approaching. He shut down the lamp and went on about his normal duties. Once he came below decks, I was able get the assistance of several officers to have him arrested and held in his cabin under guard, where he is now. I do not believe I alerted Skarkesh by my actions."

"Had Sergeant Dlavish ever been in contact with Skarkesh?" Vorr asked hoarsely.

"Not at all. To my knowledge, there is no way a charm-type spell could have been cast on him. The range was always too great. My belief is that either Skarkesh used a new charm spell with a very long range, that he managed to get Dlavish to touch some object that had the spell imbued in it, or that Skarkesh cast the spell through the medium of a magical device with scrying abilities, like a crystal ball or magical mirror, perhaps one that produces an image of the caster through which other spells can be cast. If the latter is true, then Skarkesh can spy upon us as well as cast spells on our troops, and we are in terrible danger."

Vorr thought of the magical mirror he had seen Skarkesh try to use the previous day, without success. "What's our tactical situation?"

"We should reach the edge of the atmosphere in one hour. Skarkesh's last message indicated that Teldin Moore and his ship had set off for a specific point on the inside of this sphere, about ninety thousand miles from here. Teldin must be using his cloak to spelljam the gnomish ship, because of its extraordinary speed. At best, we should be about two or three hours behind him, unless he is delayed. It appears that he will be meeting with a creature of some kind, something called a fal. All ships are in full readiness and are in standard flight formation with us. I should add that we've neither heard from nor seen the elves at any time since we entered this sphere."

Vorr looked down in deep thought, then got to his feet. He reached for a fresh uniform in a wardrobe and began to get dressed. "I want you to check the rest of the crew aboard this ship and find out if any of them have been charmed. Do it as quickly as you can. After you check Admiral Halker and Captain Azofin, have them meet me here immediately. Under no circumstances is any word of this to be released to the troops. I don't even want other ships notified yet. We've got to find a way to check everyone on the other ships. I think the war priests have spells that would help. Just get the admiral and captain and start checking everyone."

Usso nodded quickly and got to her feet.

"Usso," said Vorr.

The fox-woman turned, then jumped. Vorr had moved across the room to her in two swift strides. He caught her by the arm, his grip like a gentle vice. "If you had been charmed," he said in an even voice, "the charm would be negated now by contact with me. Are you lying to me, Usso?"

"No," she said in a shaking voice, shrinking back from him. "Kobas, please don't hurt me. I'm not lying. I'm not charmed. I'm telling the truth. Please don't."

Vorr stared down at her, then let go. "If we pull out of this, Usso, I'll owe you a special reward—but don't fail me."

"No," she said, rubbing her arm. She moved closer to the door, her eyes still on the general, then pressed an amulet against the door's wood. She then walked through the door as if it were not there, and was gone.

"Skarkesh," said General Vorr with clenched teeth, "You're going to wish you had just stayed dead."

Chapter Fifteen

• • •

The cheerless giff wore his spotless red-and-gold uniform when he reported to Teldin in the helm room. "Hello, sir," Gomja said, giving a halfhearted salute with a thick blue hand. "I thought I would bring you up to date on Dyffed's condition."

"It looked like his hands were injured when the box exploded," said Teldin, shifting positions in the helm seat. The helm wasn't the most comfortable chair, and Teldin's lower back ached. The room wasn't ventilated, either, and his clothes were already stained with sweat.

"I'm afraid that I have some bad news on that," the giff said heavily, his shoulders drooping. "We've run out of all healing potions and magical curatives, and none of the crew aboard has any clerical spell power. Gaye was able to bandage Dyffed's hands after cleaning the wounds, but he lost two fingers from each hand in the explosion. Without magic, the damage cannot be repaired."

Teldin groaned softly at the news and looked away. He had somehow imagined that nothing bad would happen to the little guy. Gomja sighed and continued. "He has some burns on his face, as well as both arms and hands, but these aren't life-threatening. There were worse injuries with four of the gnomes who took part in the fight on the deck when we entered this sphere, and they're pulling through well, though we had the last of our healing potions for them."

Gomja held up a blackened box in his thick right hand, flecks of red paint still showing around the box's edges. "I'm afraid this is all that's left of Dyffed's thingfinder, sir. We're on our own as far as finding the fal's megafauna."

"Maybe that won't be so difficult after all," said Teldin, his eyes unfocused. "I don't know if it's the right one, but there's some kind of giant animal ahead of us now. I have no idea how far away it is. We should arrive there in a few minutes. Can Dyffed still see?"

"Oh, certainly he can," the giff hastened to add. "Only his nose and beard were harmed in the explosion, sir. Gaye was forced to give his beard a fairly close trim."

Teldin sighed with relief. "Fine. See if he can identify the megafauna we're approaching. I haven't any idea if I'm supposed to land on this monster's back or head or what in order for us to get to the fal. He should know."

Gomja nodded, then had a thought and held up the ruined thingfinder. "Did you want this saved, sir?"

Teldin shook his head with a look of disgust. "No. It might still be dangerous. Dispose of it in the safest way possible before someone else gets hurt with it."

Gomja nodded agreement. "I'll send it out the back of the ship on the jettison, sir, and I'll then see if Dyffed is up to one more trip to the top deck." He opened the door, but he hesitated before leaving. "Any sign of the scro outside the ship, sir?"

Teldin took a long look aft, below, and around the ship. "Nothing so far. We seem to have left them behind for now, maybe for good."

The giff appeared pleased with the news. "I'll take care of things, sir," he said, and closed the door.

Gomja had been gone only a minute before there was another knock at the door, this one from the lower part of the door itself. Dyffed? Teldin wondered. "Come in, it's open," he called, wishing he could see everywhere inside the ship as well as he could see everywhere outside. On second thought, perhaps it was just as well that he couldn't.

Someone fumbled at the door. It then opened to reveal a gnome with wide brown eyes and a curly beard—Loomfinger. He peered in hesitantly, looking all around before entering.

"Um, Mister Aelfred Silverhand said you wanted to see me about something that I did, but I didn't mean to do anything wrong, honest. I was just following orders, and everything was going along fine, and I had nothing to do with anything."

"What?" Teldin said in confusion. Maybe the gnome thought he'd done something wrong while he was on the helm. "Oh, don't worry about that," said Teldin, feeling foolish now. "I don't want to reprimand you. I'm just trying to sort out something. I'm not sure it was very important, but I wanted to check anyway."

The pale gnome nodded, then pushed the door closed behind him without completely shutting it. He looked up at Teldin with sweat beading up on his forehead, wringing his hands in front of him. "Anything you say, no problem." He swallowed. "You aren't going to grab me and throw me around, are you?"

Teldin had the good grace to be embarrassed. "No, and I do feel badly about that. I was curious about something. When did you find out about the scro fleet chasing us, after we took off from the rastipedes' forest?"

The gnome stared at Teldin, then visibly relaxed. "Oh, that!" he said. "Oh, that's what you wanted! Oh, that's simple, of course, because I was just sitting there in the helm and everything was quiet, and then First Colonel-Commander Gomja came in and we were talking and I saw the scro fleet right there behind us. I didn't know what you were talking about, and here I've been all worried and everything, and I won't let anything bad happen, I promise."

"So you did see the fleet," said Teldin. He felt doubly foolish now. He hadn't the faintest idea of why he had suspected something was funny earlier.

"That's right," said the gnome, almost gaily. "I looked right where First Colonel-Commander Gomja said to look, and there the scro were, and I told him, and he said 'Excellent,' and he left."

There was a short silence as Teldin stared down at the beaming gnome. "You looked where Gomja said to look," Teldin repeated, not believing he was hearing this. "Gomja told you where the scro were?"

"Yes, sir!" said Loomfinger. "Boy, this was a relief, I can tell you, because I had all sorts of things going through my mind about what you wanted to ask about, and gosh if it wasn't something unimportant and routine and not something I could be thrown off the ship for, like . . . um, nevermind. I feel so much better now, just loads."

The shock of the gnome's news was passing. In its place was a strange feeling of anger and fear, still tempered by disbelief. "I want you to find Aelfred and have him see me at once," he said. "And hurry." His helm vision was revealing more of the distant megafauna; at this distance, it resembled an earless elephant with a rhino horn.

"Get Aelfred?" exclaimed the gnome with mounting panic. "Why? Do you think I did something after all? It wasn't me, really. Please don't do it. Please don't get Aelfred, because I didn't do it!" He hid his face in his hands.

"What in the Abyss are you talking about?" Teldin demanded. "I just want to see Aelfred!"

Loomfinger peeked out from his fingers, then hastily grabbed for the doorknob. "No problem then! I'll be right back with Aelfred!" In a second, the gnome was gone.

*　*　*　*　*

"Thas id!" said Dyffed through puffy lips. He pointed with one cloth-wrapped arm. "Thas the begafauna on wigde One Six Nine lives. Id sdill has ids leff foreleg ub afder all this dibe. Of course, id will dake another five hundred and sixdy years for id to—"

"Dyffed," said Teldin. "Don't talk."

"Okay," said Dyffed reluctantly, and subsided.

"Wow," said Gaye, leaning on the ship's railing. "An elephant unicorn. He needs a mustache like you, Teldin."

"Idz nod a unicorn or an elephand, because idz—"

"Dyffed," Teldin warned.

"Okay," said the gnome with a frustrated sigh.

Teldin grimaced and looked away from the gnome's red, blistered face. He hoped this giant slug had some healing spells on hand, not only for Dyffed but for the other injured gnomes aboard who hadn't completely recovered from their earlier battle and from the crash into the footprint lake.

As he looked again at the approaching megafauna, Teldin wondered if he was becoming jaded after having seen the first one. Aelfred had placed Loomfinger on the now-repaired helm while the ship was still coasting through airless wildspace to allow Teldin the chance to see the creature directly from the deck; Sylvie was still asleep. This one was still a shocker: a diamond-patterned creature of black, red, and yellow that Dyffed had said stood twelve hundred miles high. It was vaguely elephantine with a rhinolike face, tiny ears, and a huge horn projecting from where a unicorn's horn would grow. A reptilian-type tail half as long as its body hung from the rear, sweeping hundreds of miles above the ground at its lowest point.

Traveling at a much reduced speed but still covering a thousand miles of space every few minutes, the *Perilous Halibut* slowly circled the creature. The gnomes who had come up on deck to see the beast were much more talkative now than before with the first monster, and Teldin guessed that they, too, were becoming used to such marvels. We're going to be spoiled rotten by the time this trip is over, Teldin decided. A dragon? Ho-hum. A flying castle? Booooring.

"Where's the best place to land so we can get to the fal's place?" Aelfred asked the half-mummified gnome.

"Idz . . ." Dyffed stopped and looked up at Teldin questioningly. When Teldin nodded, he continued. "Idz ride on dop of the horn there," he said, pointing again. "Bud we can'd land on the horn. We have do land on idz head and walk up do the horn. We can go up frob there."

Aelfred nodded and headed for the ship's huge vertical fin. "I'll call directions down to Loomfinger," he told Teldin.

"We should bake sure thad . . . bake sure thad . . ." Dyffed stopped, looking puzzled.

Teldin looked down. "Make sure that what?"

The gnome rubbed the side of his head with a bandaged hand. "I forgod. Id was ride there on by bind and id fell off or sobething."

Teldin shrugged and looked back at the megafauna. The ship's course adjusted after Aelfred called the instructions down, and the ship made its way toward the hundred-mile-wide top of the creature's head.

Something thumped heavily up the ladder toward the top deck. Teldin glanced at Aelfred, who nodded and looked away, busying himself with a set of mooring ropes. As Gomja's broad hippopotamus face appeared in the hatchway, Teldin forced a smile.

Are you a traitor? he wanted to ask. What's going on with you? I was a fool not to have seen it before.

"How do you like the view?" Teldin asked instead, waving a hand at the megafauna in the distance.

You certainly changed your mind suddenly enough, back at the hospital on the morning we were leaving, Teldin thought. I told you I trusted you. I don't understand what happened.

"Certainly a big fellow, isn't it, sir?" Gomja said, carefully adjusting his uniform.

Teldin's gaze flicked briefly down to the two pistols at Gomja's belt. He felt the revelations coming faster and faster in his mind. You, not the gnomes, must have stocked the *Perilous Halibut*. You made sure you had a big supply of pistols and powder, and that there was enough provisions for all of us on our trip. You made sure the gnomes were there at the ship when the attack came. You made sure that almost everyone in our tight little group from the *Probe* was at the *Perilous Halibut* then, too; but you couldn't find Gaye and me before the attack came, so you had the gnomes track us down. You just got lucky there.

"Are we heading for the beast's head?" Gomja asked. When Teldin nodded, the huge giff looked curiously at the proposed destination. "How are we going to land, sir? We have a tail fin that drops below the ship's bottom. Is there water there?"

"We'll hover first, with Loomfinger on the helm," Aelfred said, stepping up. He was the model of a ship's captain, casually watching the beast's head draw nearer. They were perhaps a thousand miles away, their velocity slowing as they drew closer to the top. Teldin could see immense valleys and cracks in the beast's folded hide, and in some places he thought he could see brief gleams of light that might be reflections from the sun on standing water. Maybe there would be a place to land after all, if they could be sure there would not be a repeat performance of the footprint-lake landing.

Gomja sniffed, his broad nostrils flaring. "It is not exactly proper, landing on someone's head, but . . ." He grinned. "Perhaps we could build a landing platform for the ship as we did when we were with the rastipedes, sir."

I'd almost forgotten about the night you were talking to yourself behind the ship, Teldin thought, looking at the giff. *Aelfred thinks you were actually talking to someone with a scrying spell, someone who could hear and see you—and probably me as well, once I got close enough. All this time, I never thought about it at all.*

The giff looked at Teldin and blinked. "Sir?"

"What?" said Teldin. He was suddenly aware that he was staring hard at the giff. "Sorry?"

"Is something wrong, sir?"

"No, nothing." Teldin waved the question away and looked back at the beast's head, his arms folded across his chest. The top of the creature's horn reached at least fifty miles above them, a great whorled spike of ivory and red tilted forward in the direction of the megafauna's line of travel.

Several times as they approached, Teldin had to blink, shake his head, or wipe at his eyes, trying to adjust to the immensity of the beast and the bizarre perspectives it presented. He felt more and more like a dust mote, or even one of the unbreakable and minute particles that some sages claimed made up all matter. The world-beast was everything. He was nothing. With but a few steps, this beast could span Ansalon, the continent where Teldin had been raised. It could ford the deepest seas and never know it had gotten wet.

It became apparent as they drew closer that some of the creature's diamond-pattern decoration was due to patterns of forestation on its hide. Conversation faded away on the top deck as the crew looked at tracts of woodland wilderness hundreds of miles across, spread over the world-beast's neck and head. Broad lakes appeared, as Teldin had suspected, and thin clouds and areas of low-lying fog or mist became evident.

"Id has idz own gravidy field," said Dyffed, forgetting his earlier promises. "See how the drees grow oud frob idz neck? And thad lake, on idz cheek—there, you see id. Idz nod spilling off indo space. Gravidy!"

Teldin felt overwhelmed. "Does this thing have a name?"

"Oh, of course id does. The fal knows id. I think id goes like . . . like this." The gnome hummed to himself, then started to sing a scalelike melody entirely out of tune.

"Dyffed," said Teldin.

"You asked!"

Teldin looked back at the megafauna, ending the conversation. "I suppose we should get as close to the horn as we can, as long as we don't have to walk farther than a few miles. How about that lake, over there?" He looked questioningly at Aelfred, who nodded agreement and walked back for the speaking tube.

"It wouldn't hurt to find something farther from those trees, sir," Gomja offered. "We haven't any idea if this creature is inhabited."

Teldin wrestled with the idea, not knowing if Gomja had something unpleasant in mind. "I think I'd rather keep out of sight, in case the scro are following us," he finally said. "The closer to those trees we can set this down, the better the cover we'll have from aerial fly-bys."

Gomja looked uncomfortable. "Yes, sir, but I think we're in less danger from the scro than the native wildlife. The last forest we found had those rastipedes, and—"

"Damn it!" Teldin bit off the rest of his response, forcing himself to relax. "Gomja," he finally said, "thanks, but no. We'll put it down there, by those big redwoods."

Gomja looked thunderstruck at Teldin's outburst. His broad mouth slowly fell open. "Well . . ." he said uncertainly.

"I'm with Teldin," Aelfred said. He raised a muscular arm and pointed. "There are a few places where trees have fallen into the lake, and if we set down next to those trunks, the scro will have a hell of a time trying to separate the ship from the rotting trunks. I doubt that anything big enough to worry about will have made it this far up into the sky. Twelve hundred miles is a long way up."

Teldin found his hands had balled up into fists. He forced himself to relax. He looked around and caught Gomja staring down at the lake, fingering some of the medals on his chest. Teldin fought the urge to ask Gomja where he'd purchased them. It would serve nothing to cause trouble now. They had some distance to go yet, and Gomja might prove to be dangerous.

Long minutes passed as the *Perilous Halibut* drifted down in silence toward the forest. The megafauna's head, seen from so close, had now become simply a mountaintop. It could even be mistaken for a small asteroid, thought Teldin, recalling the Rock of Bral. In any event, he had to admire Loomfinger's skill on the helm. For a gnome, he was doing a masterful job.

"This water isn't antimagical, is it?" asked Aelfred suddenly, peering over the railing. Teldin froze, having forgotten to ask and fearing that he had doomed the ship from his inattention.

"Oh, no, idz perfedly safe," the gnome said cheerily. "My ships always landed nearer the horn, bud this is fine. We should have a nice walk frob here."

Teldin questioned the nice walk. It was becoming obvious that the redwoods were far larger than he'd first guessed. Some appeared to reach many hundreds of feet up, and they were crowded together so closely as to produce considerable darkness within them. Teldin stepped back from the railing, prepared to help Aelfred with the mooring lines.

Gomja drew his pistol so quickly that Teldin had no time to prepare himself for it. He flung himself back, raising his hands to shield his face as the grim-faced giff aimed and fired.

In the next instant in which he could think rationally, Teldin saw that the giff was aiming away from him, at something below, near the tree line. He looked, hearing the gnomes cry out in fear at the same moment, and saw a huge oil-black bird sail out of the woods, then dip a wing and sail around and back into the darkness. As it went, Teldin distinctly heard a drawn-out, warbling screech issue from the creature and echo in the forest before it vanished.

"Skullbird," said Aelfred. "Gomja, give me a pistol."

The giff was already pulling another pistol from his belt. "I have more experience with these, I believe. I've fought skullbirds before, too, and I know where they are vulnerable. Let me handle this."

Aelfred swore and looked around. "Give me that crossbow," he ordered a nearby gnome. He took the proffered weapon, cocked it back with one jerk of his arm, and loaded it with a razor-headed bolt. Teldin suddenly realized he would need a crossbow himself, but he saw no others available.

"All hands!" Gomja bawled at the shocked gnomes. "Arm yourselves immediately! I want a full-time guard on deck, eight troops, with stockpiled missiles! Move!" The gnomes scattered in haste, several climbing down hatchways and shouting to other gnomes below them. Within a minute, supplies of crossbows, armor, and weapons began pouring out in bucket-brigade fashion from the interior of the ship, until the top deck was awash in stacks of bolts, throwing axes, daggers, and other items.

The ship, now only fifty feet above the water's surface, slowly turned so that it was parallel with a particularly huge fallen redwood in the water. Slowly, then, it sank toward the water's surface.

"We could stand to get a little closer to shore," Aelfred muttered. "That tree isn't a dock, and it's probably slick. It will make for bad shooting if tha t skullbird comes back. I hope it wasn't gathering friends."

"What will it do?" Teldin asked in a low voice. He had finished cocking and loading his own crossbow.

Aelfred grinned. "Whatever it damn well wants. Those things are purest evil. Did you ever hear any tales about them?" Teldin shook his head, no. "Good," said Aelfred, his voice barely audible. "We're actually in luck that these gnomes aren't experienced sailors. The rumors about skullbirds are all bad ones, and morale always takes a blow when one appears. They're harbingers of bad luck. If they roost on your ship, it means your vessel will be destroyed. Besides, they're not particular about what they eat, and they can pick a man off the deck as easily as anything, then carry him off and eat him in midair. I hate the bastards. At least scavvers don't know good from evil. Skullbirds know they're evil, and they love it."

The water below them was twenty feet away, then ten, then five. The ship splashed gently down, huge ripples rolling away through the algae-choked water. Odd, thought Teldin, how the lake had looked much more inviting from far above.

"Shore party!" shouted Gomja. "I want ten volunteers! The rest stay with the ship!" He looked hesitantly at Teldin, his pistols lowering until they pointed down at the steel deck. "We are about five miles from the base of the horn, sir. May I accompany you to meet the fal?"

Teldin glanced at Aelfred.

"You'd better come with us," said Aelfred easily. "You can keep an eye out for flying friends while we see the fal. I don't trust the wildlife here."

The look of satisfaction and joy on Gomja's face would have been heartwarming if Teldin had trusted him at all. "I've been looking forward to a little action," commented the giff, easing his grip on his pistols, "but I'm still not convinced that this is the best place for us to land."

"Yeah, well, we're here," said Aelfred. "We should be able to handle things. Dyffed will be going with us, of course. Gaye and Sylvie should stay back here. I'd better go below and tell them what's up. Gaye won't like it, I know."

Teldin nodded. Gaye had something on her mind lately. She was acting strangely around him, and he couldn't figure out what the problem was. He pushed the image of the raven-haired kender out of his mind. Her problems weren't his concern right now.

The shore party took ten minutes to form. Aelfred and Gomja led the way from the ship onto the huge redwood trunk, using grapples and planks. The trunk wasn't as slippery as they had feared. Walking in close order behind the front two came Dyffed and most of the other gnomes, each holding a crossbow and outfitted in armor and assorted weapons. Dyffed had put his armor on over his old clothes, making him appear in Teldin's eyes to be an overstuffed doll. Teldin and a group of three gnomes formed a tight cluster that brought up the rear.

Teldin looked up into the mighty redwoods on the shore and felt a deep sense of unease. He glanced back at the ship and saw Gaye and a few gnomes watching them from the top deck. The ship's cheery banners drooped in the still, warm air. He raised a hand and waved good-bye. Everyone but Gaye returned the wave; Gaye stared silently back, her expression unreadable. Maybe she was pouting because she had to stay behind. See if I care, thought Teldin, and dropped his gaze to the bulk of the ship. He wondered whether Sylvie or Loomfinger was on the helm, watching them leave. Sylvie had gotten a little more sleep and was looking much better now. Aelfred had given her the news on their current location, and she'd hardly believed a word of it.

The walk across the fallen tree was uneventful, though getting down from the thirty-foot-high trunk once the shore was reached proved difficult. Gomja managed to find a huge tangle of rotting roots and vines that served as a rope ladder, and everyone was sent down before the giff tried his luck. The vines held, but only barely.

"Thad way," said Dyffed, pointing with a bandaged right hand. Teldin winced at the sight of the injuries the bursting of the thingfinder had caused; the gnome's index and middle fingers were missing, and the white cloth wrapping his hand was already slightly stained with red.

Gomja took a breath and readied his two pistols. "In formation, road step," he said in his normal, sea-deep voice. "Forward!" Everyone fell in behind him as he set off with confident strides into the dark and pathless wood.

It wasn't long before the stench of rotting algae and wood was replaced by the smell of redwoods and earth. The ancient trees reached over their heads like the pillars of a tremendous cathedral. Shrieking birdlike cries echoed through the forest, many originating from far overhead among the distant branches. Teldin once thought he heard the skullbird again, but he saw no sign of it.

They marched for at least ten minutes before Teldin saw a gnome in the middle of the formation turn his head to the left, as if he was listening to something. The gnome poked another one beside him, whispered, and both looked to the left with wide and curious eyes. Teldin looked, too, but saw and heard nothing. Nonetheless . . .

Teldin clapped his hands together once, giving the signal Aelfred had arranged for stopping the column. All the gnomes halted at once, with Gomja and Aelfred doing so a moment later and looking back in confusion. The gnomes quickly looked to the left and listened with grave concentration.

"Interesting arrangement of rhythmic low-frequency noise, remarkably similar to slow bipedal ambulatory movements," said Dyffed, cupping both hands around his big ears. "Must be a big one."

"Then let's keep moving," said Aelfred, hoisting his crossbow and starting ahead again. Gomja nodded and waved the column on. For a moment, Teldin was almost glad the big giff was with them. He thought he'd understood Dyffed to say that the noises the gnomes could hear were like footsteps— big ones. If so, he wanted to keep moving as well. Gnomes heard things humans and others never would.

They proceeded on for perhaps another five minutes before one of the gnomes looked to the left, gave a wild gasp, and accidentally fired his crossbow into the air. Everyone stopped and looked.

An immense, ragged figure was now visible among the most distant of the mighty trees. It was making its way with long, slow footsteps that cracked saplings and crushed fallen logs with each step. The creature was vaguely manlike, but grotesquely thick bodied, with short, twisted legs and a flat, misshapen head. It was of astounding size, as tall and as broad across the shoulders as the main mast of the *Probe*. The cyclopes Teldin remembered from the Rock of Bral would not have reached past this creature's wide belly.

A skullbird's high-pitched screech rang through the forest, as if offering encouragement and directions. Within moments, the titanic creature caught sight of the party. It started to smile. It took a house-spanning step forward.

"Run for it!" shouted Aelfred.

"Prepare to fire!" roared Gomja, raising his pistols.

"The hell we'll fight!" Aelfred shouted back. "That thing could break our ship in half!"

The gnomes were paralyzed with anxiety and fear, unsure of which commander to obey. The oncoming monster made the choice for them by stopping to seize a young redwood in its hands. The tree was every inch of one hundred feet high, but the giant merely wrapped his gargantuan hands around it and tugged once on the trunk. With an awful groaning and snapping, the tree tore free of the earth, trailing its broken roots. With a crooked-toothed leer, the colossus shook the tree briefly, snapping off its upper branches, then slowly advanced on the party again. It clutched the tree like a spear.

"Perhaps we should find more defensible ground," said Gomja thoughtfully, lowering his pistols. "Then we can—"

"Run for the horn!" Aelfred shouted. The gnomes took this as their signal, and they instantly broke formation, running pell-mell through the redwoods as fast as their short legs could carry them. Aelfred took the lead, Gomja stayed in the middle, and Teldin brought up the rear.

Teldin fought the urge to run at full speed, knowing that the gnomes could not possibly catch up to him if he did. He forced himself into a jog, but the cold hand of panic urged him on as the rumbling thunder of the humanoid colossus came on behind him. Some of the gnomes dropped or threw away their weapons to speed their flight, but Teldin held his as tightly as he could. Aelfred and Gomja did the same.

The long, regular thunder behind them grew steadily louder, mixed with the cracking of branches and the calls of frightened animals. Teldin risked a glance behind him as he ran, seeing that the human mountain was slowed by the narrow spacing of the redwoods. The giant's tree-sized spear snagged and caught other trees, tearing out house-sized chunks of bark. Teldin guessed the creature was only a fifth of a mile behind them and gaining.

Ahead, Teldin saw what appeared to be a break in the forest leading to open air. He took another look behind and saw that none of the gnomes had fallen down—a miracle if there ever was one. The giant was now closer still, each stride sweeping over the forest floor with ponderous ease.

Teldin looked ahead again. Aelfred and two unusually quick gnomes had broken out of the tree line into the open space. Moments later, the rest of the gnomes and Gomja poured out of the forest behind them, with Teldin at the rear. The titanic humanoid was only five hundred feet back and still gaining with each earth-shaking step.

For some reason, Teldin noticed, the huge giff was slowing down now and looking up into the sky, as if searching for something. Teldin had no time to find out what it was. He knew the whole group had but seconds left before the monstrous creature was upon them. Far ahead, across a long stretch of bumpy ground, Teldin noticed a vast, whorled spire, which he recognized as the megafauna's horn. Somewhere at the top of the horn was the fal, but the horn itself was still several miles away. There was no way to get to it in time to escape the colossus.

Teldin slowed down and shouted out at the top of his lungs. "Split up and run for the horn! It can't catch us all!"

The gnomes paid no attention to him, as they were already running off in different directions in their awful panic. Teldin turned around, facing back toward the forest. As he did, the colossus broke through the tree line and strode out into the open with broad, slow steps that shook the ground at Teldin's feet. The behemoth's monstrous spear was clutched tightly in its wagon-sized fists. It was perhaps three hundred feet away.

"Teldin!" The roaring voice was Gomja's. He turned and saw the giff motioning for Teldin to run to him. The giff was off to one side, maybe two hundred feet away.

Something moved in the sky behind the giff. To Teldin's astonishment, the object appeared to be a large green butterfly, swooping down toward the tall grass of the field. He recognized it as a small spelljamming ship of some kind. Something about it looked familiar.

"Run, sir!" Gomja roared out, pointing to the green butterfly behind him as it approached and slowed down to hover in the air, a man's height above the ground. "Run for that ship!"

Teldin stared in amazement, then looked behind him and saw the humanoid giant was moving again—toward him. It was raising its tree-trunk spear. The giant's two huge, dark eyes squinted beneath beetled brows, sizing Teldin up and appearing to mark him as a worthy target.

Teldin backpedaled, forgetting about Gomja and the green ship. Maybe if I move fast to one side just as he's thrusting down, he thought, I can get out of the way. He looks too slow to do any harm. I can't outrun him, but I can sure dance around him.

Fate apparently decided to test that theory. The giant thrust with the log, seemingly in slow motion. Teldin bolted, not waiting to see if the giant's aim was true. There was a rush of wind, then an earth-shaking crash as the spear slammed into the ground to Teldin's left. The tree trunk sank more than twenty feet into the earth, flinging a fountain of soil and stone into the air. Teldin threw his hands in front of his face and dropped the crossbow, almost stumbling over it as he ran.

A long shadow passed over him. He heard the sudden whistling of wind from a large, fast-moving object, and he dived to the ground to roll and escape it. Could the giant have thrown something else at him, too? He didn't want to wait and find out.

"Sir!" Gomja bawled again. "This way!"

Teldin scrambled to his feet and looked back. The giff ran toward him, his huge girth swaying. Gomja waved a pistol in one hand, heedless of the colossus's presence. "Go to the ship!" he bellowed urgently. "They want to help you! Go to the ship!" The green butterfly came on behind him, trailing by a dozen yards.

The colossus roared, its booming voice almost deafening Teldin as it washed out all other sounds. A long shadow passed over the ground near him again—this time heading for the giant. Teldin began running from the giant again, but had enough time to look back once over his shoulder.

The *Perilous Halibut* had arrived. In his momentary glimpse of it, Teldin saw that the ship was flying straight for the titan's head.

Something caught Teldin's foot and he stumbled and fell forward into the grass, knocking the wind out of him. He got to his feet, his lungs full of knives, and at that moment he heard the colossus scream. The sound was an awful, roaring cry that went on and on. When he heard it, Teldin felt a sudden pity for the creature. It sounded almost like a huge human child who had been badly hurt.

Teldin looked back as he continued to run. The giant had clapped both hands over the right side of its face and stood in place. Huge, jagged teeth showed in its loose-lipped mouth. Circling around from behind the behemoth came the *Perilous Halibut*. It looked different now. After a moment, Teldin realized that the ship was missing its long, drooping tail fin.

"Sir! Sir! Stop!" Still clutching his pistol, Gomja was lumbering along behind Teldin. The giff was obviously winded and near collapse. The green butterfly, revealing a wingspan of fifty feet, continued to drift on behind him.

Teldin saw that the giant wasn't about to attack while it was holding its injured face. He slowed just enough to shout back. "Who's in that thing? What's going on?"

"Let . . . them . . . explain!" Gomja shouted, gasping for breath. "Let . . . them . . ."

Without warning, the green butterfly sped up, rocketing toward the running giff. With a simple twist as it flew, a movement Teldin knew could not have been accidental, the ship turned so that the lower edge of one wing swept the giff's feet out from beneath him. Gomja fell, arms flailing. The ship shot over him and came directly at Teldin.

Instinctively, Teldin threw himself to the ground. The green butterfly flew over him a moment later, the lower edges of its wings scything through the tall grass. When Teldin got to his knees, he saw that the ship had come to an abrupt halt only twenty feet in front of him. Uncertain of which way to run, Teldin got up in a crouch.

A door in the green ship opened as it hovered, revealing a small, cramped cargo bay. Two silver-armored figures stood within it, each clutching a short stick of wood in one hand that was kept pointed at Teldin.

"You can get aboard of your own will, or with our assistance," said one of the silver-armored beings with an Elvish accent. "The former would be less troublesome."

"Who are you?" Teldin shouted, still backing up. "What in the name of the gods are you doing?"

"The colossus is moving!" yelled someone farther back in the ship, in Elvish. "Take him now!"

The two silver warriors raised their wands and chanted a phrase in unison.

Teldin felt a mad rush of panic, raising his hands to shield his face.

Suddenly, time slowed down.

The cloak! he thought, then leaped to his right as fast as possible. As he moved, he had a momentary glimpse of two long gray beams of light flicker out from the wands through the spot where he'd once stood.

How in the Abyss did the elves find me? he wondered. The answer was obvious: Gomja. But how did they set *that* up? *How?* He ran through the tall grass, which was now stiffer and more resistant to his passing. He saw the colossus to one side, in the act of taking a huge step toward him; it moved with infinite slowness now. Teldin saw Aelfred running slowly toward him in the distance, a crossbow in one hand and his red face registering his effort.

Teldin tried to think as he ran. Too much was happening all at once. He had to keep away from the giant and avoid the elves' butterfly ship at the same time. He needed a weapon, but he had nothing that would make any difference.

Gomja! Gomja had been holding a pistol, and it had not gone off when the ship had knocked him down.

Teldin ran in a wide circle, marveling that his exhaustion had been dispelled by the cloak's time-slowing effects. He raced back to where he thought the giff had fallen, the grass whipping his clothing as he went. It almost felt like running through water, though he felt he was making good headway.

The green ship, he saw, had lifted away from the ground and was trying to move toward him, but he was now moving so fast that it could only track where he had last been. Teldin saw a flash of red in the grass ahead of him and tried to come to a stop, skidding clumsily through the weeds and nearly losing his balance. He had passed the prone giff.

Teldin ran back, finding Gomja sprawled in the dirt and grass in a heap, his pristine red uniform now stained with soil and sweat. Damn you, Teldin thought, you were my best friend once, you lying son of a bitch. Seeing Gomja down still brought a stab of pain to Teldin's heart, but he thrust all emotion aside. The pistol was not in sight.

A low sound of thunder vibrated in the earth. The colossus had taken another step. One more step, and it would be right where Teldin stood.

Teldin glanced up and saw that the green butterfly was now getting a fix on his location. It was beginning to rotate its stern toward him again. He could see that the rear door on the ship was still open, and the two silver-armored elves were still there. He looked down, sweeping the grass away with his hands as fast as he could. Then he thought to trace Gomja's footprints back to see if the pistol might be there, closer to where the green butterfly had struck the giff.

Almost immediately, he found the pistol, lying in a clump of grass.

Teldin reached down and snatched the pistol up in a blur. He raised it in the direction of the rotating green butterfly.

Without warning, time sped up again.

Teldin almost cried out in exhaustion and pain, his aim on the butterfly waving wildly as his hands shook. The cloak had cut off its power! What was wrong with it? Gods, what was wrong with the damned thing?

Someone was shouting a garbled command inside the green butterfly from between the two rearward elves. The two armored elves aimed their wands at Teldin, again chanting in unison. Teldin gripped the pistol with both hands and squeezed the trigger, just as the wands flashed together in gray light. The pistol's explosion wiped out all other sound and filled Teldin's head with a screaming whine that rang endlessly through his ears.

The gray light struck Teldin and surrounded him. In an instant, he felt his entire body stiffen, clutched in total paralysis. The wands' magic had been dead on target—and he saw that neither of the two elves in the rear of the green butterfly were injured by the pistol's bullet. Helpless, Teldin saw the two elves shout in triumph.

The green butterfly abruptly tilted forward, going into a slow roll in the air. The two elves suddenly clutched at separate sides of the door to avoid falling out. As Teldin watched in shock, his body rigid in the grip of the elves' magic, the front of the green butterfly appeared from below, upside-down, as the ship continued to roll over. The limp body of the butterfly's helmsman was visible in the center of the forward window, dangling from straps that held him into his helm chair. A splash of crimson stained the upper part of the helmsman's white shirt. His eyes were wide with surprise. The window in front of him was shattered where the pistol ball had smashed through it after passing through the elf.

The ship then made a quick turn to the right, drifting away from Teldin, before one of its wings caught the ground. The entire ship tumbled wildly as it rolled, its ceramiclike wings breaking and shattering in huge shards. The body of a silver-armored elf flew into the air.

A foot the size of a large cottage came down and slammed into the remains of the ship, crushing them flat. Teldin rolled his eyes up and saw the colossus soaring above him like a thunderhead. The giant held one huge hand to the right side of its face, from which ran rivers of pinkish fluid. Its scraggly teeth set in a grimace, the giant reached down for Teldin with its left hand.

The shadow of the *Perilous Halibut* passed over Teldin as the ship shot by overhead, just missing the giant's head. Teldin saw a cloud of debris fall from the ship's stern and strike the titan in its grotesquely muscled chest.

A flash of sparkling light enveloped the giant on the instant, hiding it entirely from view. A moment later, soundlessly, the giant vanished.

*   *   *   *   *

Later, when the paralysis spell had worn off Teldin, everyone tried to sort it out as they gathered in the grass outside the *Perilous Halibut*. Now missing its tail fin, the ship was easily able to land on the grassy plain, though it was tilted a bit on the rough ground. Ropes had to be used to climb down from the upper deck to the ground. The loss of the tail had changed the ship's gravity plane slightly, but the ship was still airworthy, despite Dyffed's jests to the contrary long ago.

"Sylvie sent me to the jettison when we heard the giant in the woods, and we took off after you in a flash," Gaye recalled, unconsciously winding a lock of her hair around a finger as she spoke. "When the gnomes yelled to fire, I just pulled the lever, and *thunk!* the jettison threw everything out. Then I looked out the back and said, 'Wow! Where'd the giant go?' and that's all I know. Do you think the gods got mad at him? That happened on Krynn once, you know. The gods got mad, and *boosh!* They dropped a whole flaming mountain on this one really mean country, just flattening it! It was really wild! You know about that, Teldin, right? Could the gods blow up the giant just like that? Could the gods have made the jettison flatten him? What do you think, Teldin?"

"Oh, no, id wasn'd the gods, nod ad all," interrupted Dyffed, waving a bandaged hand in dismissal. "I exabined the area and found no elebendal drace of the bonsder ad all. Id was cobplede disindegration of badder on an adobic level, exacdly the kind of thing I did by thesis on ad Lirak's Cube the year thad the dweoberfusion alchebical laboradory dook off and landed in Inediblegreensludge Bay. Thad was also the sabe year by advisor bisdook his giand habsder for his wife when he cabe hobe frob class, and the poor fellow was—"

"The thingfinder," Teldin interrupted. "Gomja threw the thingfinder in the jettison. Could that have done it?"

"The thingfinder?" Dyffed said, blinking. "Whad a sdrange idea. I forgod all aboud id. Id was durned on when I had by accidend, and there always was sobe concern aboud the resulds of a promixidy-induced feedback loop through the liddle blue widged, although I personally said the plasba flow was sdable enough do allow—"

"Was it possible that the thingfinder did it?" Teldin said, his patience gone and his voice just shy of a shout.

Dyffed appeared taken aback at Teldin's vehemence. "Well, now thad you bention id, I suppose so, bud I sdill feel—"

"Teldin!" Aelfred called. All heads turned to see the brawny blond warrior waving a hand from the ship's stern. "Gomja's coming around. You'd better get back here."

Teldin nodded and waved back once. "This isn't getting us anywhere," he said to the group. "Let's just drop it. The giant's gone, we're alive, and I've got to see a giff about a little problem and hope he's going to enlighten me. Then I'm probably going to be tempted to throw him off this damned giant animal and let him think about things for a thousand miles or so on his way down."

Teldin felt a gentle hand on his arm. He pulled away from it. "General Gomja wouldn't betray us," Gaye said softly, looking up at him with wide dark eyes. "I can't believe it. He really cares about you, Teldin. He—"

"He was feeding the elves information on us!" Teldin shouted back in a red rage. "Only the gods know how he was doing it, but he kept the elves right behind us, every step of the way, just so that they could try to kidnap me! That big son of a bitch was working for *them*! He's another Rianna Wyvernsbane, eager for some cash and ready to sell a friend out! I was a blind, gods-damned fool not to have seen it! Damn you, Gaye, what do you know, anyway?"

Gaye looked up at him as all the color drained from her face. Her mouth was barely open, but no words came out. She suddenly looked down and let go of her curl, her hands falling limp at her sides.

"Teldin!" Aelfred called again.

Teldin knew he had gone too far, but he was too angry to take it back or think about it. With a last look at the silent kender, he left the group and walked off through the grass. "Coming," he called to Aelfred, his voice cracking. He felt very tired. What was the point to all this? Who cared about the cloak at all? If he could have given his cloak away at that moment to just anyone, he would have done so, and gladly. He was sick of this whole quest and everyone in it. He just wanted to leave.

But first, he promised himself, he would have some answers.

Chapter Sixteen

● ● ●

"Ease it in," said General Vorr. His face was solid, eyes focused on the flying pyramid only five hundred feet away. Only three other scro were out, two of them on the forecastle deck with the general. The general slowly drummed his thick fingers on the railing, stifling a sudden yawn. He looked away from the pyramid ship just ahead and glanced at the distant shape of the one-horned world-monster where Teldin and the gnomes had gone. He shrugged. It was an hour away, but it could wait. An interesting sphere, this was, and worthy of a closer look after the elves were crushed.

He turned to the scro to his left, the first mate of the *Tarantula's Trident*. The pale-skinned scro appeared almost fat, his girth straining against his spiked black armor. The general knew that all of that "fat" was muscle. The first mate glanced back, his huge boar's tusks shining dully in the bright sunlight overhead, and he winked. Vorr gave a curt nod. The first mate looked back at the pyramid, seemingly relaxed, his hands open and hovering near the hilt of the broadsword and the handle of the axe that hung from his thick belt.

Almost there, thought the general. Almost there. The false lich didn't seem to suspect a thing about the request for a short conference before making the close assault on Teldin and his allies. Usso had done her work well with only hours to spare; she'd get a nice reward out of this one, even if she was a bitch otherwise. The *Trident* coasted toward its unknowing prey, only seconds away from the gravity plane of the deceptively small stone pyramid. The ziggurat had twice the mass of the much-larger squid ship, and a miscalculated move would smash the two ships together, leaving the squid ship sitting in front of several batteries of catapults and ballistae at dead-zero range, its ram jammed into stone.

But there would be no error. Vorr slowly took a breath through his nose, held it for a few moments, then slowly let it out through his lips. No error at all. It was good to be back at war again.

The *Trident* jerked and shifted. They'd hit the pyramid's gravity plane dead on.

Vorr grasped the railing with one hand and turned to the speaking tube that led to the helm. "Roll over!" he shouted. Then he threw his head back, drew a swift breath, and roared at the top of his lungs at all the universe. He felt his power go out as he screamed, unstoppable, born into fire and death.

Dozens of muffled screams answered his own, and pounding feet thundered three steps at a time up from the ship's cargo deck, where Usso had hidden the scro and ogre warriors after teleporting them in from the other ships. Howling soldiers in full battle gear, black leather gleaming, poured out from their hiding places. Weapons clanged against spiked armor; eyes glowed green with rage.

The view of the universe around the *Tarantula's Trident* immediately spun in a tight circle as the ship shot forward, crossing the pyramid's gravity plane and approaching from below. The ship lifted slightly to clear the edge of the bottom of the pyramid, then slid to a full stop as its hull scraped across the rough stone of the base. If there were any hatches or bay doors on the pyramid's bottom, they were jammed shut now. Screaming battle cries and curses, the scro and ogres on the main deck snatched up ropes hidden by the railings, then hurled themselves over the sides of the ship, rappelling to the stones below.

Vorr was the first one over the side, ignoring the ropes for the twenty-five-foot fall. He tumbled when he hit but was up at once, and he began waving on the horde. Tight units of ogres and scro, led by war priests, thundered on metal-shod boots for the sides of the pyramid.

"Move it! Move it!" Vorr shouted, now heading for the edge himself amid the screaming mob. "Send the bastards back to the Hells! Almighty Dukagsh watches you!"

Vorr knew they were already luckier than they deserved. Usso said she had found at least one scro aboard each ship who been charmed into the lich's service. The fox-woman had used up nearly all of her precious scrolls and spell books in undoing the charms and freeing the scro from the lich's domination. It had been easy thereafter to piece together the lich's plot to spy on his scro allies and set up saboteurs in their midst, traitors who would slay the helmsmen of their own ships and send their fleet into a thousand-mile dive to the ground below. The once-charmed scro were now the most frenzied of those leading the attack, berserk in their desire for vengeance. Not even skeletons would be spared; the war priests would destroy them, rather than command them into service with their powers. Skarkesh had gone too far. Dukagsh, wherever he was, would look down and be proud this day.

Vorr gripped the stones at the edge of the pyramid's base and climbed down. Moments later, he felt a rush of nausea come and go as he crossed the pyramid's gravity plane, now greatly altered with the landing of the squid ship. He turned around on the stone wall and began climbing up the stonework of the pyramid's face, surrounded on all sides by his troops on hands and knees.

Luck was still with him: He was on a face leading to the pyramid's cargo doors. The massive, ancient bronze gates were sealed, as were the weapons' bay doors farther up the pyramid's slope. There was no point in trying to force the latter open; it would only waste time.

"Satchel!" a war priest shouted. Moments later, a scro scrambled up the slope to the bronze doors and tore off his thick backpack. The war priest began a short chant, then finished by slapping his bare right hand against the base of the doors at their separation. The war priest then seized the backpack and jammed it against the doors. The scro in the area moved away from the doors as fast as they could go, then hunkered down, shielding their faces with their armored arms. No one stayed below the doors.

The spell, a minor fire-lighting magic, went off. A burst of flame erupted around the backpack for a moment before the smokepowder in the backpack ignited. The white-hot blast blew a fountain of rock and twisted metal into the air, with shrapnel screaming over the scro backs. With a wrenching metallic sound, one of the two cargo bay doors fell forward and clanged down the side of the pyramid, falling free to bounce through the ship's gravity plane like a flat yo-yo.

Vorr was on his hands and feet on the instant, crossing the stone face for the opening. He had claimed the right of first entry into the lich's pyramid. He had reasons other than sheer glory for wanting this particular honor. When he got to the entryway, he grabbed a bag from his side and emptied its brightly shining contents into his hand, then flung them into the space beyond. The two-dozen pebbles each had permanent light spells on them. Without further delay, Vorr pulled his huge sword free, gripped it with both hands, and jumped down into the space where the left cargo bay door had once stood. He looked into the pyramid.

The dead were waiting for him inside.

Another maddened war cry erupted from his lips, and Vorr leaped into the thick of the sword-wielding skeletons before him. His sword whipped out and around, shearing through skulls, spines, and rib cages. The filthy stench of decay and rot assailed his nostrils and filled his lungs. The dead surged forward, fearless, mindless, reaching at him with bone fingers and thrusting with dulled sabers and long swords. In a parody of the living, the animated nightmares came on by the dozens, perhaps by the hundreds. The lich had packed the cargo bay with them.

Wild screams sounded behind the general as scro and ogres poured into the room and joined battle with the undead. Ear-splitting shots rang out in the bay as starwheel pistols and heavy arquebuses were fired at point-blank range into the skeletal army. Bone fragments ricocheted from the walls and floor, scattering across the room.

Vorr's sword swept tirelessly through the dead, severing hands and arms, chopping through their old weapons like a razor through flesh. He spun as he advanced, hewing at every side, eschewing any tactic except slaughter. I'm killing the dead, he thought, and laughed even as the white dead continued to come at him in droves.

A bright tongue of flame flashed into being to Vorr's right. It was the war priests again, he knew, and fought on. The hoard of spell scrolls captured from the elven world of Spiral had been unexpectedly rich. Flame-strike spells burst up from the rear of the room, enveloping the skeletons packed there and incinerating them at once. Waves of searing heat washed through the room and across Vorr's exposed face, but he hardly noticed them.

The ranks of the dead thinned out. Scro and ogres had already found the many ladders leading to levels above and below the cargo deck, and they swarmed up and down, their swords and axes ready. Vorr made a roundhouse swing through two skeletons charging him, shattering them like glass, then made for one of the ladders leading up. He clutched the hilt of his sword with one hand as he climbed, not daring to sheath it again. Several of his troops immediately followed him.

Vorr remembered the pyramid in the Glowrings Sphere, and how its lich had placed two helms within it, one at the pyramid's apex and the other atop a small building in an open space in the middle of the pyramid. The fastest way to either locale was straight up. The middle helm could be reached by leaping across a balcony that ringed the open space; the apex would take many ladder climbings to reach. The false lich would have nowhere to run. Vorr could hardly wait.

Vorr reached the next level up. Nothing waited for him there except for other scro, pouring up the other ladders. Seeing no sign of combat, Vorr continued up the ladder to the next level. It was then, in the dim light from above, that he thought he saw something moving over the open hatchway. He hurried his climb, taking the steps four at a time in hopes of catching whoever was there off guard. He tensed, preparing for rocks or worse to be dropped through the hatch onto him.

As his head and shoulders hurtled up through the hatchway to the next level, something huge with thick claws swiped at his head. Vorr tried to duck but succeeded only in negating part of the blow. Iron claws tore away his steel helmet and slashed his left cheek open to the bone.

Vorr let go of the ladder. He found his grip on his sword, then thrust it with all his might into the umber hulk standing right beside the ladder. His blade struck the 'hulk's leather belly and tore through it, driving into its vitals, all the way to its back and out. With a deafening inhuman squeal, the 'hulk lurched back, almost dragging the sword from Vorr's fingers. A moment later, it lunged again, its four alien eyes aglow. A death scream sounded from across the room, where a scro doubtless had worse luck with another of the monsters.

There being no room to swing his blade, Vorr again thrust his sword into the creature, aiming for its head. The monster's claws slashed down into his armored shoulders as the sword's tip plunged into the 'hulk's open mouth, between its mandibles, and broke through the back of its skull. With all the strength he could muster, Vorr swung his sword aside at the same time, so the 'hulk's momentum carried it past the general and flung it away into a siege machine nearby. The sword cut its mouth open to twice its normal width. The giant beetlelike monster crashed through wooden supports and ballista bolts, rolling over and over in a tangled heap of shattered wood and rope.

Vorr jumped from the ladder and charged the umber hulk. The creature was getting to its feet again when the sword came down and split its head apart.

For a moment, Vorr had time to take in his surroundings. Dim red light spilled down from overhead glass fixtures, relics of a forgotten age. This floor was barely forty feet square, with a twenty-foot-wide square opening in the middle of the room surrounded by a low stone wall. Ballistae and catapults were positioned here, crewless but in good condition. He was on a weapons deck. He heard another scream and spotted movement across the room.

A second umber hulk looked up from the ladder hatch it had been defending, having been half-hidden by the low wall ringing the center pit. The 'hulk started upon seeing Vorr, then charged around the pit for the general. Its eyes sparkled with magical light, attempting to drive the general insane as it had doubtless just done to some scro who had subsequently fallen from the ladder to the depths below.

Vorr noted that the ballista to his left had been loaded, no doubt by the skeletons serving the false lich. He dropped his sword and grabbed the ballista's wooden frame, dragging it around and toward him so that it faced the oncoming 'hulk. Before the monster could understand what was happening, Vorr found the trigger and pulled it. The ballista fired its bolt with a loud bang as its taut rope slammed into the bowlike crosspiece.

The 'hulk stumbled as the bolt hit it and passed through it, shattering against the stone wall beyond. The beast got up with a gurgling squeal, appearing unusually slow and uncoordinated. Vorr snatched up his sword and dived around the ballista. He hewed at the umber hulk until its ichor splattered the floor and walls, and the monstrosity fell back with a curiously childlike shriek. The sword rose and fell ceaselessly, one stroke with every heartbeat, until the heat of battle rage left Vorr for a moment and he saw that the fight was long over.

An explosion boomed through the pyramid's corridors and halls. His chest heaving, Vorr suddenly looked around and saw a half-dozen troops cheering him, their numbers still pouring up from the two ladders leading to this level. One raised a long, leather-wrapped device in both hands as his comrades screamed approval, and he held it out to the general.

Vorr blinked, then he stepped forward suddenly and grasped the bulky object with a free hand. He threw down his sword and tore the leather covering free of the device.

Black steel glistened in the red lights above. Twin bolts of polished metal, wicked notches cut in their barbed heads, projected from the double-barrelled end. His troops had brought his harpoon-bombard, loaded and ready.

Vorr looked up at his troops, who stamped the stone floor, raised their black-gloved fists, waved jagged swords and axes, and called his name. Their screams and stamping grew ever louder and louder, until it became like a physical thing, like a wall of power.

Slowly, like the opening of a door into an old, familiar torture chamber, a smile came to the general's lips.

Vorr whirled, the harpoon-bombard clenched in his hands, and he leaned over the low wall to look down into the next level. Below him was the primary helm, resting atop a stone block perhaps fifteen feet across. The ancient throne there was smashed and empty. There was only one place left for the lich to hide. He looked up to the next balconylike level, and he remembered the way the Glowrings Sphere lich had raised its rotting hands in front of its face to ward off the last blows Vorr had rained down upon it.

Vorr looked around and spotted the one ladder left in the room that led upward. He ran for it, holding the bombard in one hand as he nearly leaped up the rungs. He reached the next level, which was laid out much like the last, though with no weaponry. In fact, this level contained nothing at all— except one last ladder, positioned adjacent to the walled opening in the center of the room. The general climbed away from the ladder from the weapons deck and reached the last ladder up in two strides. His free hand caught the rusted wrought iron.

"How is a blonde not like a hammership?"

The voice was an inhuman scream. It was deafening and mad. Vorr looked straight up.

A thing let go of the ladder fifteen feet over his head and leaped down at him. It had not been there a moment ago.

Vorr had just enough time to swing the harpoon-bombard up and squeeze both triggers. The weapon went off next to his right ear and eye; the explosions maimed hearing and sight with concussions and powder burns. The massive thing landed right on him anyway, its clawed hands larger than anvils and its goat-skull jaws open wide in insane laughter.

Vorr's grip was torn from the ladder by the impact, and he was knocked sprawling to the floor. For a wild second he thought the huge creature was an undead chimera or lion, but it had only one skeletal head within its great, ragged mane. Brass scales covered its hide. Demonic bat wings whipped into the air on either side of the beast. Vorr kicked up into the beast's chest and abdomen, feeling thick ribs snap and flesh tear as his metal-plated boots ground in. He couldn't bring the harpoon-bombard up to strike, as the creature held his arm pinned down with both of its own great forearms, each fully half again as large as Vorr's own. Vorr's other arm was trapped beneath the creature's mass, crushed against his chest. The monster's strength was relentless.

"How is a blonde not like a hammership?" the beast screamed again, bright purple flames dancing in its eye sockets. Vorr now saw the butt ends of the two barbed harpoons

protruding from the monster's maned shoulders on opposite sides of its head. The spears had gone straight into the beast, but it had barely noticed them. Purple-black blood spurted from the wounds and spilled down its scraggly mane, dripping on Vorr's face and armored chest.

Suddenly, the monster belched a cloud of white gas from its mouth, the opaque mist blinding Vorr but doing no other harm. Twisting beneath his attacker's weight, Vorr found the leverage to free his left hand. His fingers came up beneath the monster's jaw and found its scaled throat. Vorr's fingers clenched the loose skin tightly, then he quickly raised his legs from beneath the beast and wrapped them around the beast's back, locking his heels together across its spine, just behind its great black wings. He squeezed with his legs, using every ounce of strength to crush the monster's windpipe shut at the same time.

The skull-headed beast jerked its head back and bucked, trying to leap away from the leg-lock, but could not get its footing. The goat-skull face came down abruptly, snapping at Vorr's face but missing by only a foot, held back by Vorr's left arm; it then tried to breath gas on him, but only wisps of white vapor came out. Vorr saw the creature's eyes turn from violet flames into golden ones.

The creature released its grip on Vorr's right arm with both hands, attempting to drag his other arm away from its throat. The bombard instantly came up, propelled by Vorr's right arm, and he jammed its barrel straight into the monster's nearest eye socket and pushed.

A flash of white lightning burned the air for a fraction of a second, spilling from the creature's eye and playing along the bombard barrel into the air in a dozen directions. Nearly blinded, Vorr felt nothing and realized the bolt was magical, so it could not harm him. He pushed on the bombard until something in the monster's skull broke, and the barrel was suddenly thrust out the other eye socket.

"*That's not the answer!*" the beast shrieked. Without warning, the monster exploded. A huge circle of interlocking bolts of lightning took its place, snaking across Vorr's limbs and chest in a wild dance—and the lightning vanished, leaving no trace of the beast.

Vorr fell back on the floor, his feet thumping into the stone. He half sat up, still exerting himself against the monster's now-vanished throat. After a second to look around, he quickly got to his feet. Nothing was left.

All was quiet again, except for a horrible ringing noise in his ears. He looked up the ladder again and saw that the hatchway was open at the top. If the false lich was anywhere, it was up there.

Slowly and deliberately, the general drew a long dagger from a thick sheath at his belt. He reached for the ladder again, placing the dagger in his teeth, and started up.

"Worked my last defense, hidden no more, has not," said a familiar voice from the top room. "My astrosphinx much trouble to collect was. Immune to spells, I see, the treacherous general is, and I on the helm sit, spells of my own gone for this ship to feed. Bad my condition looks."

Vorr continued climbing. He was halfway up.

"To bargain for my existence I should like," said the voice. "Material items you will take. Knowledge from my head you will not. Perhaps this knowledge valuable is?"

Vorr reached the top of the ladder. Cautiously, he peered into the room beyond. As expected, the room was very small, roughly cubical and barely fifteen feet along each side. No decorations graced the walls, as far as he could see. He crouched slightly, then charged up the last few steps and leaped free of the ladder and into the room, turning to see if enemies stood behind him.

The room was almost empty. An undistinguished helm sat against the far wall. In it sat the false lich, motionless. Next to the helm chair was a rickety table of rough-hewn wood, on which sat a few small items, including a jade bowl, a small cloth sack, and a mirror on a stand. Vorr recognized the mirror at once as the one Skarkesh had relied upon for scrying on Teldin Moore. He supposed the lich's medallion was in the sack. Four torches burned against the walls at eye level, their flames giving off warmth and odor but no smoke.

"Not good enough was our bargain?" asked the robed skeleton. "Not good enough for the scro general to keep his word to an old one? More does the general want—perhaps the *Spelljammer* as well as the treasure within it?"

"You betrayed us, Skarkesh," said Vorr softly, turning his full attention to the skeleton. The huge knife turned in his hand. "You set our own soldiers against us. You meant to sabotage our fleet once you got the cloak from Teldin Moore." Vorr took a slow, quiet step forward.

"Lie you do, lie to justify treason," hissed the skeleton, "and unwise it would be to carve on these old bones. Immune to magic maybe you are, but to ignorance not. The *Spelljammer* find I can. The cloak find I can. Of more I know, much more, but not for telling when this body . . . dead is."

Vorr came closer. He was six steps away. The knife blade's tip rose. "I weep for you," he said.

"These treasures yours are," said the skeleton, making a brief gesture toward the table. "The seeing disk of the *Spelljammer*, yes, and a magical mirror, for spying upon Teldin Moore—"

"—and scro allies," Vorr finished, five steps away.

"*Not* scro allies, fool!" snapped the skeleton. "But good it is for the projecting of my image, to allow the casting of spells to charm or compel action, to plant a traitor among the friends of Teldin Moore and reveal all their plans upon the making! A traitor among them now is, and Teldin's secrets to me it has been sending all along!"

Vorr glanced at the mirror. Four steps. "Who?"

Skarkesh made a tiny gesture with one finger. "Who? One word, then, am I worth, then with galley slop to be put out on a jettison when it I speak? Done it is." A skeletal hand reached out toward the table and made a gesture at the mirror's surface. Immediately, the silvered glass turned black.

"Watch you must, and learn," whispered the false lich, never turning its luminescent eye sockets from the general. "If bargain for existence I must, all clever secrets shared with the general alone will be."

Vorr kept his attention focused on the skeleton, then gave a fast look at the mirror when he saw an image forming on it out of the corner of his eye. He did not recognize the person there, but he memorized the face and clothing. The person would not be difficult to locate among Teldin's followers.

"Of great value that one is, beyond worth to me as a spy. Alive must that one be taken when all others are cut down.

Sufficient that is to keep your interest?" Skarkesh stared impassively at the general. "Satisfied you are that these bones must together stay? Willing you are to work with this old one to gain the *Spelljammer?*"

Vorr glanced once more at the mirror, but the image was fading, to be replaced by the normal mirror's image of the torchlit room. He looked back at the false lich. A thick thumb slid against the edge of the knife blade, feeling its sharpness. A bead of red appeared where blade and skin met.

"No," said Vorr.

He lunged forward. The lich snatched the jade bowl at its side, flinging it and its contents at the general.

Vorr instinctively turned his body and raised his arm to block the blow, trying to prevent any liquid from splashing in his face. He had almost reached the helm when the gloppy substance in the bowl struck his chest armor, spattering pieces of green goo everywhere. Vorr grabbed for the skeleton with his free hand.

The false lich simply vanished in his grasp. A new monster took shape on the helm, a smaller one that easily evaded his grasp and hurtled past him, under his outstretched arm. It looked for all the world like a withered bright-red spider with a serpent's head and pale, glowing eyes.

A neogi. An undead neogi wizard.

A tremendous heat began to burn through Vorr's chest armor. With the first real fear he had felt in decades, General Vorr cut at his armor with his knife, scraping a huge chunk of the glop away and flinging it against a stone wall, where the slime hung, green and glistening.

A dozen pinpricks of white-hot pain stabbed into his face where the green slime had struck him. It was the deadliest living substance in all the known spheres. He had only a dozen or two heartbeats left until the rapidly growing slime devoured his entire body, with all of his weapons and armor, turning him into a vile pool of ooze on the ancient stones of this ship. With a flick of his wrist, he stabbed through the straps holding his plate armor together, hurriedly flinging the chest plate away from him with the vast majority of the slime attached to it. The rest of the upper half of his armor followed only moments later, the sizzling sound becoming more pronounced as the slime dissolved the steel and leather like the most powerful acid.

The clicking of the neogi's claws sounded behind Vorr's back. He spun and saw the little creature as it reached the hatchway down to the next level. He remembered that he still held his slime-encrusted knife, and he threw it.

The blade struck the little spider-being in its neck, knocking it off balance and against the stone wall beyond it. The neogi staggered, then emitted a peculiar warbling shriek.

"Eating at me! Eating at me!" it screamed, and began a mad circular dance around its end of the room.

Vorr felt as if his face had been splashed with acid. He could barely see through the haze of agony. Desperately, he grasped one of the torches from the wall and broke it free of its sconce. The torch flickered as he grabbed it, almost going out. It must have been kept fueled by magic, he knew; now that he held it, the fire consumed the wooden torchstick normally. Eyes and lips squeezed shut, he held his face in the bright searing flames and thought of life.

* * * * *

The war priests came up later and destroyed the rest of the slime, including the little spider-shaped pool near the hatch. The magical trinkets by the helm were saved, as was the helm itself. A new suit of armor was brought up for the general.

"The pyramid's ours," said Usso. She avoided looking at Vorr's face directly. The war priests had done all they could for him, but it had not been enough. "We took only light casualties: nine dead, twenty-three wounded, roughly equal between scro and ogres. Most of the trouble came with the umber hulks, especially the ones on the lowest level, but we got them all. The mirror's a high-quality scrying device that let our little friend cast spells through it, just as he said he could. It will take time for me to learn to use it. We found a few other trinkets, but nothing else of interest."

The huge figure sat on a stone ledge and looked down at his hands. Grotesque scars, gouges, and burned patches were chiseled deeply into his gray face and forehead, the damage arrested and healed indirectly by minor spells. Usso swallowed, fighting down the urge to vomit. She had always hated and feared ugly things.

Carefully, the general held up his hands and fingerspelled a few words for Usso to see. His mouth was seared shut.

"The *Trident* lost part of its hull bottom when we landed," she replied. "It's been moved, but it will sink if it lands on water again. Should we keep it or . . ." The figure made a cutting gesture with his hands, and Usso nodded quickly. "We'll strip it, then, and use it as a ram if need be."

The general fingerspelled a few more words. Dark eyes looked out from the hideous patchwork of his face.

Usso nodded again. "Certainly. The pyramid is sturdy enough to hold a great many troops. We can—" She stopped as the general began to spell out a long message. Minutes passed as she watched and read and thought.

Finally, the general's hands stopped moving and dropped to his sides. He stared at the fox-woman with dark eyes.

"I can do that," she said. "I have some scrolls that could take care of it. But what if the elves—"

Vorr snorted and waved a hand in dismissal. Usso bit back a retort and considered the general's idea. It was clever enough, and there was no reason it should fail. The pyramid was strong enough. If they pulled it off quickly enough, they could get away with it.

She reflected a few seconds more. This shouldn't interrupt her plans, really. It might even help her in the long run. Vorr would be distracted enough to miss all the clues. She was good at staying on top of things. If she could keep it up just a while longer, she would be on top of the universe.

Her tail wagged.

Vorr saw her do it and nodded thoughtfully. She couldn't read his mind and for that he was glad. Once in a while, though, he wished he could read hers. He'd tell her about the traitor in Teldin's group later. In the meantime, he was glad he'd pocketed the lich's medallion before she'd come up. She would have been impossible otherwise.

Chapter Seventeen

•••

"What happened?" Gomja's rumbling voice was barely above a whisper, but Teldin and Aelfred did not have to strain to hear him. Teldin stood, his cloak flapping lightly in the breeze. Aelfred sat cross-legged on the ground, apparently relaxed and comfortable. Sylvie sat to the side on a stool from the ship, leaning forward with her elbows on her knees and her hands covering her mouth as she watched. Teldin noticed she held a copper coin in her fingers.

Gomja, still blinking into wakefulness, was tied up so thoroughly that Teldin thought it was a wonder he could still breathe. The barrel-chested giff sat on the ground, propped upright against an old tree stump. His once-pristine uniform was stained by mud, sweat, and crushed grass; rips showed in several places. Some of his medals and gold braid were missing as well.

"What happened?" Gomja repeated, then noticed his condition. "What—what's this? Why am I . . . what—"

"Your elven friends apparently thought you were in the way, so they moved you," Aelfred said easily. "You'd already served their purposes. Maybe they wanted to shut you up for good to cover their trail when they tried to kidnap Teldin, but they muffed their plan." He looked at Gomja thoughtfully. "I was glad to meet you after all that Teldin had said about you, but I never figured you for a traitor."

Gomja lifted his head and stared angrily at the blond warrior, then drew himself up. "You would not spout such lies if I were able to make you account for them, Mister Silverhorn. You have a brave mouth, but you lack any sort of real honor such as we giff know."

"Is that the same code of honor that lets you sell us out to the elves?" Aelfred asked suddenly, his eyes narrowed.

Gomja quickly turned bright blue with rage. His arms and chest swelled against the ropes and stretched them uncomfortably far. "Untie me, mongrel," he said, "and I promise to give you a personal demonstration of our code of honor, one that you will never forget. You are a vomit-eating dog and a—"

"You were working for the elves," said Teldin angrily, breaking in. "You were helping them to kidnap me so they could get my cloak. I want to know why."

Gomja looked at Teldin, and his manner changed at once. To Teldin's astonishment, the giff's rage was gone in an instant. "That's just not true, sir!" he said in a wounded voice. "I was helping the elves protect you! The very least you can do is to ask the elves themselves. They should tell you all about . . ." He looked away, his dark eyes searching the vicinity. "Unless, of course, the giant . . ."

Aelfred grinned without humor. "The giant's dead, and so are your Imperial Fleet buddies. They dropped the spear on this one. We know you set Teldin up to be grabbed. Before we figure out what to do with you, we just want the truth, if we can get anything close to it from you."

"I do not lie!" Gomja roared suddenly, struggling at his bonds. Teldin stepped back at the violence in the giff's voice. "Wildspace scum, I do not lie! If there is a liar among us, it is certainly you!"

"Gomja," Teldin said. The giff looked at him again, anger fading once more from his small black eyes. "I want to know the whole story about the elves, and I want it now."

The giff hesitated, glancing around once more in search of something.

"Talk," said Teldin. "The elves are dead. I want to know how you got mixed up with them, before we decide to leave you here or do something worse."

Gomja slowly relaxed in his bonds as he looked back up at Teldin. "Very well," he said softly, "but it's not what you think, sir. I'm not a traitor. The elves contacted me when we were on Ironpiece. They remembered me from the times I tried to get work from the Imperial Fleet, and they used a spell or device to talk to me. At first I though it was psionics—those are mental powers, something like spells, I think—but they told me it was just magic. We giff know little of real magic, so—at any rate, sir, they—"

"Stop calling me 'sir,' " said Teldin softly. "I think we're long past that point now."

Gomja looked at Teldin in disbelief, his mouth open. Somehow he grew smaller as his face lost all expression. "Yes, sir," said the giff, his voice barely audible. He grimaced as he caught himself. "I mean, yes, I understand." The giff cleared his throat with a rumble, his eyes glistening, then continued. "Well, the first thing the elves did was to warn me of the scro assault. That was on the first night after I pulled you from the water when the *Probe* crashed into the lake. The elves . . ." Gomja's voice drifted off as he looked from Teldin to Aelfred and Sylvie, staring for a moment at Sylvie in particular. He swallowed, then looked back at Teldin. "Can we talk privately, sir?" He bit his lower lip. "Sorry."

"Whatever you have to say, you can say it in front of these two," Teldin responded curtly. "I trust *them*." The emphasis he put on the last word was lost on no one.

Gomja looked anxiously at the others, then went on. "The elves warned me not to tell you they were communicating with me, because . . . there was a spy among your group," he said faintly, looking at Teldin. "Someone was signaling our plans to the scro behind us, and the elves, who were behind the scro, saw the signal lights. The elves didn't know who it was, but they were very much afraid for your safety. They asked me to find a way to go with you and protect you from any"—he looked again at Aelfred and Sylvie—"internal dangers, while the elves would try to fend off the scro fleet with their own ships."

"Old son," said Aelfred with an easy smile, "you're imply-ing that either myself or this lady might be that spy."

Gomja looked Aelfred in the face as he spoke. "The possi-bility has crossed my mind on a few occasions. I've seen noth-ing so far that would imply that there was any truth to it, and it is obvious to me that Teldin trusts you greatly, but my first loyalty is still to Teldin's safety. When stake s are high, one should tread carefully and carry a big firearm."

"If you were so concerned about my safety," Teldin said abruptly, "then why did you lead that ship to me so that it could try to snatch me like some kind of war booty? What did they offer you? Gold? A ship? Smokepowder?"

Gomja turned pale blue, but he looked Teldin steadily in the eye. "I can't believe they would have done anything as crude as that, but in any event they offered me nothing, nothing at all. They merely said that if I cared for you, then I would have to help them protect you. They gave me accurate reports on the wildspace battle near Ironpiece. They apologized for firing on some gnomish ships in the confusion. They warned me of the attack on Port Walkaway, and I was able to prepare for it with the help of my troops. They continued to give me warnings about the scro when we were in the phlogiston and when we entered this crystal sphere, and they told me about the scro fleet's presence behind us when we left the rastipedes. They did help us, s—Teldin."

No one spoke. "The elves said that at some point they wanted to talk to you personally," Gomja continued. "They wanted to convince you to go with them to find the *Spelljammer*. They'd had a change of heart in not becoming involved in your quest, so they followed you. They said it was a good thing they did, too. All they wanted was a chance to talk and help."

"Are you at all aware of what they did when they found me?" Teldin asked heatedly. "They knocked you down on purpose, they tried to kidnap me, and they finally managed to paralyze me with their wands before their ship went out of control and was smashed by that giant. Talk to me? Hell, they wanted this"—Teldin grabbed an edge of his cloak in one hand and held it up—"and you almost helped them get it. Didn't you even have a clue about this?"

Gomja's ears drooped and he appeared to get even paler. His tiny eyes were wide and rimmed with white. "That can't be true, sir!" he cried, forgetting himself. "They promised me that all they wanted to do was to talk to you and help you find the *Spelljammer*! Maybe they were just trying to get you out of the area, away from the giant. They didn't hurt you, did they?"

"If they weren't after me, then why did they turn their wands at me, and not at the giant?" Teldin shouted suddenly. "Why did they treat me like a criminal? Why?"

Gomja looked stricken. He started to say something, but no words came out of his mouth.

"Why?" Teldin said more quietly, stepping forward and leaning down to the giff's wide face. "I'll tell you why. Because they wanted my cloak. If I hadn't shot their helmsman, they would have had it, too." Teldin stabbed a finger into the distance. "You want to talk to the elves? They're over there, smeared over the ground in the wreckage of their ship! If you really were trying to help me, then damn you for not telling me about all this! Damn you for keeping it a secret and nearly getting me killed! Damn you for making me have to *kill them!*"

No one spoke. Teldin drew back, his face hard with rage. "The only difference between the Imperial Fleet and those scro is that the elves won't cut my throat right away to get the cloak. It must offend their sensibilities, but I have a feeling that they might change their mind on this before long. They can't resist the lure. I was betrayed by an old war comrade on Krynn for this cloak. Damn you, Gomja, I was betrayed by a woman I trusted completely. She tried to kill me, and I had to help kill her! But *you!* You, of all the—"

"I didn't betray you!" Gomja howled, drowning out Teldin's words. Teldin saw tears forming under the giff's eyes, and they slid down his heavy jowls. "I didn't betray you, sir! I have been trying to protect you ever since you landed on Ironpiece! By all the smokepowder in wildspace, I truly thought the elves wanted to protect you, too! You're my friend!"

For a long moment, Teldin and Gomja stared at one another. Gomja's eyes were now puffy and blue around the edges; he was almost panting.

Teldin felt as if his mind were locked inside a maze with no exit. Had the elves strung the gullible Gomja along? Was he lying through his thick teeth? Or was he just—

"He's telling the truth," said Sylvie quietly, "and he's not charmed. You can untie him and let him go."

Teldin and Aelfred turned to stare at her, as if the half-elf had just turned blue herself, like the giff. "What in the Nine Hells are you talking about?" asked Aelfred.

"I'm reading his mind," said Sylvie, lowering her hands from her mouth. The copper piece was gone from her fingers. "I cast the spell a little while ago. Gomja's telling the truth. I think Admiral Cirathorn found out about him somehow, learned about his past connection with Teldin, and gambled that he could get to Teldin through Gomja. Cirathorn probably would have abandoned the rest of us if he could have gotten the cloak. Teldin's right, too. Cirathorn's not going to stop, if he's really behind this."

"What?" said Gomja stupidly, scarcely daring to breathe. "You're reading my *mind*?"

Sylvie smiled at the giff. "Not all of it, but just enough to know the truth," she said. "Whatever you think of, I can sense it." Sylvie got to her feet and brushed off her clothes. "Let him go," she said. "We've got to see the fal before someone else dive-bombs us."

Teldin looked from Sylvie to Gomja and felt his rage slowly melt away, leaving behind a sea of emptiness and confusion. At a shrug from Aelfred, Teldin rubbed at his face, looked at the others, then walked over to untie the dirt-encrusted giff.

"Why couldn't you have done this before?" Aelfred mumbled to Sylvie as he moved to help Teldin.

"I couldn't find a copper for the spell, so I borrowed one from Gaye. If you ever need anything, ask a kender."

No one laughed, but it lightened the atmosphere anyway. Gomja sniffed, obviously relieved, and straightened his posture to build his shattered dignity.

"Next time," said Teldin, finishing with one of the giff's arms, "just tell the truth from the start. By the gods, I hope the fal didn't see us acting like this."

There was a pause of exactly two heartbeats.

I did, said a voice in Teldin's head.

Everyone jumped. Aelfred shot to his feet, tugging his sword free. Teldin and Sylvie spun around on their knees, crouching, while Gomja got one arm out of the ropes and hastily felt for a weapon that he no longer had.

The gnomes near the ship cried out, and Teldin heard Gaye

shriek, "There it is!" He got up, his own sword in hand, and saw a huge black shape forming only twenty feet from the *Perilous Halibut*. Although smaller than the gnomish ship, it shared a similarly long and cylindrical form and was equally dark—but the surface of the new form slowly rippled and undulated. The nearer end rose from the ground to the height of a tall man and leisurely looked over the assembled crew.

"Splendid!" cried Dyffed, spreading his arms. "Thirdeen Squared, you look barvelous, simply barvelous! You haven'd changed a bid in sixdy years!"

I am indebted to you, my youthful friend, said the voice in Teldin's head. The now-solid monstrosity by the ship, fully the size and length of a horse barn, was exactly as Teldin had seen it through the thingfinder. Bile rose in Teldin's throat. The sight of the pulpy black monster made him queasy, but he forced himself to be calm. It turned the upper part of its sluglike body toward the gnome, its rubbery tentacles writhing in a seemingly random fashion. *You honor me with your presence and that of your companions. You have suffered physical harm in coming here. I grieve to see you so. I ask to repair your damage and see you whole.*

"Oh, this?" Dyffed looked down at his mutilated hands, then hid them behind his back as if embarrassed. "Oh, thad's quide all ride, they're hardly a bother now, but I'b afraid sobe of us did ged a drifle knocked around on the way here, and if you could do sobething aboud thad, then we—"

I will do that, said the voice. Teldin suddenly heard distinct gasps from some of the gnomes, and a few whooped as they looked down at their now-healed injuries. Dyffed appeared surprised, then carefully unwound the bandages over his hands using his teeth. Teldin saw the gnome thoughtfully examine his hands—still missing certain fingers, but otherwise fully healed. Dyffed looked up abruptly as if someone that Teldin could not hear had just spoken to him.

"Oh, that's quite all right," he said hurriedly. "The pain is gone, and that itself is marvelous." He put a hand to his mouth, running fingers over his lips. "Just wonderful, simply wonderful. One Six Nine, you are the dearest old fellow."

You have suffered the threat of physical extinction in searching for me, said One Six Nine, the large humanlike mouth moving in rhythm to its thoughts. *I watched your arrival from my tcha, where my true body lies now, at the peak of the megafauna's horn. You see but my image, created by my powers. I was impressed with your removal of the humanoid colossus by using your damaged quasi-psionic locater device as an aerial missile. You have earned my admiration. You have, however, only limited opportunity for discussion. I acknowledge the imminent arrival of antagonistic forces. You wish to acquire knowledge concerning the cloak Teldin Moore wears?*

"Yes," Teldin broke in. "I was told that I had to find the *Spelljammer*, but I haven't any idea how to find it or even if that's what I'm supposed to do. I haven't been able to talk with anyone I can really trust on this." He colored as he said the last part, hoping that no one present took offense.

You must come closer, said the fal. Its front tentacles twisted and waved gently in his direction as its fore-part—Teldin couldn't bring himself to call it a head—faced him.

Teldin took a deep breath and approached the fal, coming to a stop a dozen paces from its open, man-sized maw. He found himself staring at the dozens of razor-sharp teeth set in multiple rows inside its circular mouth, like the teeth on a shark's jaw Teldin once had seen on Krynn.

I am not carnivorous, said One Six Nine. The two largest tentacles, on opposite sides of its central mouth, examined Teldin from two widely separate points, looking him over with uncomfortable thoroughness for perhaps a minute.

I am satisfied, said the mental voice at last. *You are wearing an authentic ultimate helm. You possess potential of an open-ended nature. You are the Cloakmaster, Teldin Moore, the future captain of the* Spelljammer. *You need only find your ship to claim it.*

Teldin felt as if he had been physically struck. The blood ran from his face. It was difficult to think straight. "I'm what?" he said faintly.

You wear an ultimate helm, a device imbued with the power to command the Spelljammer, *the largest and most powerful ship in all known spheres. You must find the Spelljammer in order to take command of it. You have open-ended potential—infinite, unlimited, of import to the gods themselves, given time.*

"Of import to . . ." Teldin's mouth was completely dry. He felt light-headed. "But why me?"

You were randomly selected, said the fal. *You were in the right place at the right time, as your kind is fond of saying. I know of no preconceived reason for it. You have taken a path from which you cannot turn back.*

It once had seemed to Teldin that he had a thousand questions to ask the fal, but now he could not think of where to start. He took a deep breath, but the fal's telepathic messages flowed into his mind before he could begin.

You need to know much from me, Teldin Moore, said One Six Nine. *I fear I may not have much to tell you that you need to know. I have studied the legends of the* Spelljammer *for an age of time. I have examined trinkets said to bear clues to its origin and whereabouts. I have even seen the* Spelljammer *as it passed through this sphere six thousand seven hundred twelve days ago, local time, on its endless journey through the spheres. I have deduced from all my research only that nearly all of what people know of the* Spelljammer *is wrong. There is little that is right.*

There was a pause, and Teldin had a mental image of someone smiling wryly at a private joke. He looked around and noticed that everyone standing around him—Aelfred, Sylvie, the gnomes, Gaye, even Gomja, still half-tied on the ground—appeared to be listening to their own internal voices.

You should not be concerned that they can hear what I am to reveal you, said One Six Nine, inclining its head in Teldin's direction. *I have been able to project my thoughts into others from the time of my generation as an individual, unlike others of my kind, though I can read only your surface thoughts in return. I am able to carry on two such conversations at once— again, a unique ability. I am giving your comrades a speech welcoming them to my abode. I find this an easy speech to give, and I am not troubled by its habit. I wish to speak with you alone now. You fear that you can trust no one. I will strike a bargain with you, Teldin Moore. I will tell you what is true about the* Spelljammer *if, when you find it, you will return and tell me all that you find to be true about it.*

Teldin blinked and dropped his gaze, considering. It was an easy enough thing to promise. The fal obviously was powerful and had no real reason to lie. He had the distinct feeling that it wasn't interested in his cloak in the slightest; only pure knowledge would satisfy it. As far as he was concerned, that was a fair enough price to pay for more practical knowledge. If the fal's advice was true enough, he'd owe the creature a thousand favors.

He made his decision and looked up. "It's a deal," he said simply. "I'll do what I can for you if I make it to the *Spelljammer.*"

I am pleased, said One Six Nine. *I trust you and have faith in your ability. You must listen carefully to my next words.*

I must tell you first that you must be prepared to meet dangers that will make all you have seen until now appear tame. You will face uncounted enemies on your quest, their ranks growing with each passing day. You must have courage beyond measure to go on to the end, for even if you retreat from hunting for that ship, your enemies will do their utmost to slay you for your cloak as you sleep. You were, are now, and will be hunted, no matter what you do. You cannot escape this fate.

I must tell you second that your cloak is not unique. You have one of many devices with the potential to control the mighty Spelljammer. *You are one of many other beings from across the known spheres and beyond who seek the prize of command of that ship. You must move with all speed to your destination if you wish to have a chance at capturing it for yourself, to whatever ends.*

"Wait, wait," Teldin mumbled, dazed. He had expected the grim, first revelation, but not the second. "There are others? But how could there be? I don't—"

I have little time left, Teldin Moore, said One Six Nine almost sadly. *I sense the arrival of your enemies is at hand. I must tell you third that the goal you seek is itself dangerous to you. I have met others before you who sought the* Spelljammer, *and they have vanished, their ultimate fates unknown to all but themselves. I have heard reliable stories of whole crews who went aboard that ship but were swallowed up by their goal. You must be wary of all dangers when you set foot on its decks, and you must watch for destruction such as no being has ever faced before, for no one has yet successfully prepared for it or escaped it.*

I must tell you fourth that I alone know a clue to the mystery of the Spelljammer, one that was revealed to me when last the Spelljammer passed through this sphere. I reached out to the ship with my mind, across the millions of miles of open space beneath our sun, in an effort to communicate with those powers aboard it. I discovered in doing so that which I had not expected. I know that the Spelljammer is alive.

"Alive?" Teldin said faintly. "The ship's alive? How?"

I do not know how. I caught only the briefest look into what consciousness it has, and I looked into alien depths I could barely fathom. I captured but one image out of that foreign abyss of thought and dream, one bit of real knowledge. I offer you the knowledge that to find the truth about the Spelljammer, you must seek its birthplace: a broken sphere. I know no more, Teldin Moore.

One Six Nine shifted, raising its forward bulk off the ground so that it towered over the assembly beside the *Perilous Halibut*. Its tentacles twisted in great agitation.

I sense that your enemies have arrived, the fal said to all. *I can do nothing to protect you but to give you warning. You must fight or flee. I am glad to have seen you, Dyffed, my young friend. I send you my best wishes and the hope that we will again meet in peace.*

Without warning, the vast black image of the fal vanished.

Teldin stared stupidly at where the fal's head had been, then roused himself and turned to look at Aelfred, Sylvie, and Gomja. With horror, he realized that Gomja was still entangled in rope, and he hastily dropped to his knees to untie his friend as fast as possible.

"You heard him!" Aelfred roared at the top of his lungs. "Arm yourselves! Get to the ship!" The gnomes nearly fell over themselves to comply with his command, squabbling over who would be first to ascend the rope ladder to the ship.

Gomja struggled to untie a complex knot on his feet, then hesitated, his hands frozen in the act of fumbling with the ropes. Teldin glanced up at the giff's broad face. Gomja was looking over Teldin's head at something in the sky behind him.

"By the arm of the Great Captain," the giff muttered, then bent to finish untying his legs. Teldin risked a fast look behind him, knowing that whatever he saw would be something he wouldn't like.

He was surprised to find that the immense orange butterfly hovering in the sky behind him was actually quite beautiful. The wingspan of the ship had to be three times the length of the *Perilous Halibut*'s hull, maybe five hundred feet or more across. The delicate panes of its purple-veined wings were lit like stained glass by the vast sun overhead. It could not have been more than a few hundred yards above them, silent and magnificent. Teldin could not imagine how it had gotten there so suddenly.

A bit of movement attracted his eye. On the tips of the butterfly's wings were tiny figures wearing the silver armor of the Imperial Fleet.

It was only a moment later that the giant orange butterfly opened fire. Teldin saw something coming right for him, perhaps a ballista bolt. It was too late to dodge it. A moment later, the bolt zipped over his head—and someone behind Teldin gasped and fell.

Chapter Eighteen

• • •

"*No!*" Aelfred's voice rang out as Teldin turned. Teldin had a momentary glimpse of Aelfred's curly blond hair, the big warrior's face blank with shock as he looked at the ground near Teldin's feet. Then Aelfred rushed forward and bent down over someone lying on the ground only two steps behind Teldin. Teldin looked down and saw silver hair spilled over the long, flattened grass.

The figure on the ground was Sylvie.

Sylvie's sky-blue blouse was glistening purple in an ever-expanding patch around the yard-long shaft of dark wood that projected from her chest. As Teldin looked on, her thin white fingers slipped down the bolt's shaft and fell to her sides. Her head eased back into Aelfred's big hands, her eyes now open but unseeing. Aelfred whispered her name, cradling her head. There was no response.

Someone spoke Teldin's name. He looked away and saw the gnomes still boarding the *Perilous Halibut*, the cold orange butterfly hovering in the air beyond. Gomja was on his feet now at Teldin's side, his broad hippopotamus face almost white as he looked down at Sylvie and Aelfred. The giff swallowed, then he looked at Teldin and motioned to the ship. "You have to go, sir," he said, his voice hollow. "The elves are still firing at us. Get to the ship."

Gomja gave Teldin a slight push, then turned to Aelfred and Sylvie, blocking Teldin's view, and knelt down. Teldin broke his gaze away and numbly started back for the ship. His blue cloak flapped against his legs as he walked. He felt nothing. How curious, he thought; she's dead, and I feel nothing at all. He looked up at the ship and saw Gaye's golden face, framed by her black hair and rainbow dress. She was looking over Teldin's head at the scene behind him. Then she buried her face in her hands and wailed.

*   *   *   *   *

"Cease fire," said Cirathorn. "Signal the *Free Wind's Fury* and *Emerald Hornet* to drop their cloaks. If the gnome ship lifts off, resume firing until it is brought down, then cease firing again. Go and do."

"Yes, Admiral," Mirandel whispered. The battlewizard left quietly to relay Cirathorn's orders, leaving him alone on the forward bridge at the right oval window. He gazed down through the tinted glass at the scene on the ground, hundreds of feet below. The initial volley of ballista bolts appeared to have struck down at least one of the gnomish ship's crewmen, judging from the little cluster of beings near the black vessel. Death was regrettable, if unavoidable in getting the point across. In the larger scheme, it mattered not. Such events were insignificant from this height. He was the one who was looking down, not they. He was the one who spun the plans, not someone who was caught within them. Only the grand scheme mattered in the universe. No one cared for the fate of one lone creature.

Cirathorn frowned slightly. The spider imagery that had come to mind was unappealing, one fit more for the drow, the true elves' twisted cousins who lived in underground realms, forsaking the light. Better, he reflected, to use the image of the caterpillar and its cocoon, the transformation to a higher state of consciousness. He was the caterpillar, the one who would restructure his world—indeed, all the known spheres— with his boldness and daring. His seizing of the cloak of Teldin Moore would deliver the ultimate vehicle of change into his hands, the *Spelljammer*, and with that he would transform the faces of all worlds at once. It would be a new age, a time of glory, in which all elvenkind would be forever free to sail the spheres, the masters evermore of wildspace and the flow, and of all the—

"My admiral," interrupted a soft voice behind him.

"Yes, battlewizard," said Cirathorn frostily after a pause. She had spoiled his thoughts. He swung around, his eyes like the bottom of a frozen pond.

Mirandel's voice was empty of emotion. "The *Free Wind's Fury* has sighted an unidentified man-o-war, approaching from the sun. It is being pursued by elements of the orcish fleet, and it will reach us in five minutes."

The coldness went out of his eyes. "A man-o-war? What pattern?"

"Bright yellow, my admiral, without markings." Mirandel licked her lips uncertainly. "I believe it would be a modified or lost ship, as there is no mention of any ship of this type in our records."

"Of course." There had been a yellow-and-red pattern grown two centuries ago, but it had not been an especially aesthetic design and had been discontinued. Perhaps this was a renegade ship, now seeking assistance against the orcs. Its captain and crew could be dealt with later for their transgressions, which would perhaps include capital theft and mutiny, but there might be extenuating circumstances. One never knew with elves, he thought, and smiled tightly. "Did the *Fury* and the *Hornet* drop their cloaks?" Cirathorn asked. "And how many orcish ships are pursuing the newcomer?"

"The *Hornet* did, but the *Fury* retained its cloak once it saw the approaching ships. We have heard that only four ships are pursuing."

Two big ships alone would be enough to scare the gnomes into surrender. "Excellent," he said. "Have the *Fury* immediately investigate the oncoming man-o-war and send recognition and greetings. Permit no boarding, and have the *Fury* avoid combat. We must gain the cloak from Teldin Moore. Then we can be free to deal with the orcs, which should take only a few minutes' work."

Mirandel nodded. "Yes, my admiral," she said, and turned to leave. She staggered, off balance, as she did so, catching hold of the door frame to keep from falling. Mumbling an apology, she left the bridge.

Cirathorn chewed the inside of his cheek. Mirandel had barely eaten since her sister's death. This foolishness would have to stop, or she would be replaced and sent to her cabin under arrest, wife or not. She had no right to act in this manner. The admiral had lost almost his whole family line during the Unhuman War, but he had never stopped for rest in his mission of vengeance. Mirandel showed disturbing signs of weakness, and weaklings were a liability in these times of fire and blood.

He turned around again to look out the right window. The *Emerald Hornet* now rode the sky to starboard, the second point in an aerial triangle above the black gnomish ship. The third point, soon to be unoccupied, would be the invisible *Free Wind's Fury.* Two ships would be enough to get what he wanted. He would have to send down another flitter and hope for better success than the now-smashed first one had found. The admiral made a mental note to have commendations sent to the families of the elves who had died in the crash while trying to capture Teldin Moore. There was no need now to be polite about it. Teldin Moore, tragically, would have to be killed.

And it would be best if the admiral did it himself, he thought, fitting and proper in the grand scheme.

Far below him, specks crowded around the black ship.

* * * * *

"We cannot retreat," said Gomja, matter-of-factly. He checked the firing mechanism on his fourth pistol, then jammed it into his belt beside his other weapons. Like Teldin, Gaye, and a handful of gnomes, including Dyffed, he crouched on the grass beneath the bulk of the *Halibut*, his back pressed against the cool black metal of the hull. "I do not normally favor escape, sir, but I've learned prudence. We would be shot down at once if we tried to flee."

Teldin exhaled slowly and looked across the trampled grass to Aelfred's hunched figure. From this position, Teldin could not see Sylvie's body, and for that he was glad. "So you're saying we should surrender."

Gomja snorted and gave Teldin a disgusted stare. "No. We

should make the elves regret their unprovoked attack."

"Make them regret it?" Teldin asked in disbelief. "How in the name of all the gods can you just say something like that? You have got to be the craziest person I've ever met in my life. When I first met you, you gave me this incredible speech about how you were going to kill me, then your pistol blew up. You lead an attack on a neogi deathspider with a few dozen gnomes, and you crash the whole ship into a lake. You were helping out the elves—" Teldin broke off, sensing he had said too much.

The giff looked down, carefully pulling his uniform's front together and buttoning it where it had come loose. "I freely admit that the elves used me, sir, but they have killed our navigator and chief helmsman. We must make them regret it by being prepared to take advantage of their every mistake from this moment forward. They have two ships above us, but neither ship can land. We are at an impasse unless the elves have more of their small flitters to come after you personally. Even if the elves win, their casualties will cause them to mourn their victory."

Teldin said nothing at all to this. He looked down at the grass on which he sat, with his cloak bunched up beneath him. After a moment, he turned to his right, where Dyffed and Gaye sat, almost within arm's reach.

Gaye's tear-streaked face was almost hidden in her black tresses. She still watched Aelfred but made no sound at all. Occasionally she would sniff and wipe her nose on her sleeve. Dyffed sat with his knees drawn up to his chest, idly picking at a thumbnail. He sensed that Teldin was watching him, and he looked up blankly and shrugged, carefully avoiding any glance in Aelfred's direction.

Something clicked in Teldin's mind but wouldn't quite surface. Something about Dyffed and the *Halibut*. Something with an unpronounceable name.

"Your secret weapon," said Teldin. "Dyffed, where's your secret weapon? The birthday party?"

The gnome peered through his thick spectacles and blinked rapidly. "The what?"

"The birthday party, damn you! You told me that you had a secret weapon aboard the ship, something you and One Six

Nine had been working on. Where's your weapon?"

Dyffed's blank look vanished. "Yes, it's . . ." The gnome hesitated and looked around, but no one else had the slightest interest in either him or what he was saying. "It's here with me, all finished. Why? What did you want with it?"

I must be dreaming, Teldin thought. "What did I want with it? I want you to use it! Use it on the elves! Can you use it to blow up their ships?"

Dyffed's eyes glazed over as he became absorbed in the idea. "What a thought," he finally mumbled. "It could certainly do that. I have no idea if there's any limit to what it can do. We should set up some tests, then arrange for a field demonstration, then—"

"You idiot!" Teldin yelled. Everyone but Aelfred turned to look at him. "We have no time for testing it! We have no time left for anything! Pull out that secret weapon and show us the damned thing!"

Again, Dyffed looked around. Seeing all eyes upon him, he made a decision and sighed heavily. "This goes against all my better judgment and scientific ethics," he said, "not to mention the members' code of Ironpiece Dweomerfusion Industries, Ordnance, and Technology, but perhaps you have a point." He reached into his dirty vest and carefully extracted a slip of folded paper. This he handed, after a moment's hesitation, to Teldin. "Here it is."

Teldin took the paper in disbelief. After staring at the gnome, he looked down and slowly unfolded the paper. He read it without comment. "This is it?" he finally said.

The gnome looked down and nodded somberly. "Took me decades just to get it right," he said with a trace of satisfaction. "One Six Nine was a joll y help, just perfect. Fine old boy."

"Is this a spell?" Teldin asked.

"Oh, no, no, not at all. That's just the theory. We'll have to get the raw materials and some equipment, assemble a device or two, develop a delivery system, conduct at least a few tests, then we'll be ready to put it into production."

Teldin said nothing. After a few moments, the slip of paper dropped from his fingers. His head sagged forward until it dropped into his upraised hands, his palms and fingers covering his face.

Dyffed grabbed for the paper, but Gaye caught it first and held it up to her wide, dark eyes. All that was written on the scrap was a simple notation:

$$E = mc^2$$

"Eee mik two," she said, just before Dyffed snatched the paper away. "I don't get it."

"It's actually rather simple," Dyffed said irritably, folding the paper up again and putting it safely away in his inside vest pocket. "It's the relationship between mass and magical potential in all the spheres, throughout the cosmos. The equation shows clearly that—"

"The armada's sending down a flitter, sir," said Gomja in a flat, deep voice. He was looking up into the sky. His large, blunt fingers closed on the butts of two of the pistols at his belt. "You and the others had better get inside the ship. I can stall the flitter crewmen if they still think I'm helping them. I might be able to force my way inside and take the crew hostage, using them to get our freedom." The giff shoved himself unsteadily to his feet. He looked down and saw that no one else had moved. "Sir, you and the others had better get inside now," he repeated.

Teldin's face turned to look into Gomja's own. The giff shifted uncomfortably. There was something new in Teldin's face that the giff did not recall ever having seen before. It was so intense that Gomja swallowed, almost turning away.

"I'm going with you," Teldin said, and abruptly got to his feet. His cloak was at full length, so blue that it seemed almost purple. He waved at the gnomes and Gaye. "Get the hell inside the ship, right now. Move."

With only the slightest pause and without even the slightest comment, the kender and the gnomes did exactly as they were told, though Gaye stopped before him long enough to look into his face. Her hand came out as if to touch him, but it then pulled back, and she followed the others to the rope ladder to climb inside.

Teldin and Gomja glanced up at the tiny green-and-white striped flitter that slowly descended from the orange butterfly ship in the sky. Teldin looked over for a moment at Aelfred.

The big warrior was stroking Sylvie's face with his fingertips, still cradling her head with his other hand. His face was hidden. Teldin looked away and began walking in the flitter's general direction. After a moment, Gomja straightened his posture, lifted his chin, and followed.

* * * * *

Mirandel watched the flitter fall toward the ground. It was impossible to tell at this close distance that what lay beneath them was the surface of the head of a creature larger than many worlds, whose footsteps could span continents. The *Empress Dorianne* hovered over what seemed like a high hill, with a patchwork sky of green, blue, and brown overhead. With her husband gone to meet Teldin Moore, she felt a faint stirring of interest in things, no longer having to face his frigid, uncompromising expression and hide her feelings. It was still best to keep busy, however; the ghosts within her mind would gain control the moment she gave them a foothold. It was impossible to think straight.

A noise caught her attention. The battlewizard, now acting captain for the armada, stepped away from the window when she heard footsteps and rattling armor hurrying toward the open bridge door. An officer burst into the room, his face flushed and obviously out of breath.

"Captain!" he gasped, staggering to a stop. "Captain, the *Fury* has sent a message that it has been found and is under attack. The whole orcish fleet is behind the four pursuing craft, each ship protected by fog clouds and illusions. The sun blocked our view!"

Mirandel started toward the speaking crystal that would transmit her voice to the helm room, then stopped. She had thought to order the *Empress* to move in to support the *Fury*, but she remembered then that Cirathorn was below on the unarmed flitter—an unavoidable target for any orcish ship that came near enough to see it.

"Order the *Hornet* to support the *Fury*!" she shouted at the officer. "Have Second Battlewizard Ervar contact the flitter and request its immediate return! We must stay long enough to get the admiral back before we can join battle with the orcs.

All weapons crews are to fire on any enemy ship that threatens either the *Empress* or the flitter. Abandon all ground targets. Go and do!"

* * * * *

"The *Trident* has rammed!" Usso's squeal rang throughout the tiny helm room. She gripped the arms of the ill-made helm chair with trembling fingers, her face alive with the vision of the battle outside. "It drove through the back of the man-o-war. There's considerable debris falling." She pulled back from the scene, blinking with surprise. Her eyes registered nothing in the room where she sat. "The man-o-war lost its port wing. It's begun to fall apart. The *Trident* is going down with the hull and starboard wing. It cannot pull free— it's falling now. The man-o-war must have lost its helm. They're both falling. The *Trident* is losing deck gear. A deck hand has fallen free . . ." Usso stopped. For several seconds, she pursed her lips together. "Both ships are falling out of control," she continued. "They're . . . they've both crashed." She exhaled slowly, then looked up at the armored giant who stood before her. "A search for survivors is not advised."

Vorr nodded curtly, making a brief fingerspelling gesture with his left hand. He then stuck out his other hand and made a cutting gesture across his wrist with the blade of the left hand. His expression could not be read through the many scars and burns across his face.

Usso nodded at Vorr's last command, her long black hair swaying gently. "Within the next two minutes, General. The last man-o-war has engaged the fleet but is now trying to break off and escape. We are almost in position for the final blow."

And so I am, she thought. So am I.

* * * * *

The flitter glided down in complete silence. Only the wind in the tall grass sounded around Teldin and Gomja as they stood to greet the ship.

"Forgive me, sir," muttered Gomja from behind. "It's better this way." Teldin heard the hammer being drawn back on a flintlock pistol, then felt something like a thick finger poke him in the back of the head.

Teldin felt that he couldn't be surprised any longer. "So you're still working for the elves," he said evenly, looking up at the striped flitter.

The giff drew in his breath as if to make a reply, then let out his breath, saying nothing. The flitter dropped until it was only a dozen feet above the ground, thirty feet away. Gradually it drifted down and closer, its four spindly legs soon making contact with the ground and settling down under the weight of the ship. It was barely twenty feet away and facing them. A lone elven pilot was visible through the darkened forward window, his face impassive and calm.

A door opened in the back of the flitter. Teldin heard boots thump into the grass, then saw a figure slowly walk around the starboard wing of the flitter. It was an autumn-haired elf in silver armor, his helmet in the crook of his left arm. The elf smiled slightly as he stopped a dozen feet short of Teldin and Gomja, eyeing both the human and the thick-bodied giff. He wore no obvious weapons but appeared relaxed and sure.

"Teldin Moore," said Admiral Cirathorn. "I have come a long way to find you."

Teldin stared at the elf in undisguised hatred. "Go to hell."

"I might for what I'm about to do," the admiral said. "I need your cloak, Teldin Moore. The elven people need it. We are at war, and your cloak is the key to victory. I must take that cloak from you in any way I can. If First Colonel-Commander Herphan Gomja will oblige me, I will perform the deed myself." With that, Cirathorn raised his right hand, appearing to pull a leafy decoration from the top of his helmet. He raised his hand, now clenched around a silvery pistol-like device, which he aimed directly between Teldin's eyes. "Your cloak is likely to block magic or weapons aimed at your body, but not a lead bullet aimed at your head," he said. "Cloaks, even magical ones, are not the best of armor."

"I wish to perform the deed," Gomja rumbled suddenly. The object sticking in the back of Teldin's head poked him slightly, though Teldin did not move. "I have been waiting for this moment for some time, sir."

Cirathorn grinned. "Then wait no more."

A huge hand grabbed Teldin by the left shoulder and shoved him out of the way. As Teldin fell back, he caught a momentary glimpse of Gomja hurling himself forward and bringing his pistol directly into the admiral's face. Then Teldin struck the grass and rolled.

Two shots tore the air, coming so close together that Teldin could barely tell them apart. He sprang to his feet, giving a wild look at the combatants by the flitter. A thick haze of smoke almost obscured the both of them.

"Stupid giff," said Cirathorn with scorn. His hand and pistol were still extended. There was not a mark on him.

Gomja stepped forward one more pace, then went down on his knees. The pistol fell from his fingers. His broad hippopotamus face looked down at his dirty red uniform front in disbelief. Teldin saw the giff put a thick blue hand to his great chest. The hand came away as brightly colored as the crimson uniform once had been.

"Not even lead bullets can penetrate a spell that is proof against nonmagical missiles," said Cirathorn. "It's a fairly basic spell in the Imperial Fleet, but I recall that you giff have little faith in magical things. A pity."

Gomja looked up at the elf, who was on eye level with him. His thick lips and jowls moved.

"Before you die," the giff said, pronouncing each word with care, "know that your slayer is Herphan Gomja, commander of ship's . . . marines, assigned to the . . . *Perilous Halib*—"

The giff fell forward into the grass.

"Gomja!" Teldin shouted. His eyes burned with tears. "Gomja, you son of a bitch, get up!"

"Not likely," said Cirathorn. He reached down to drop his silver pistol and pull a new one from Gomja's belt. "He was a very poor actor, anyway. We never charmed him or magically compelled any behavior from him. He was much easier to manipulate directly. If he believed he was doing you good, Teldin Moore, he would do anything. He was faithful and loyal to the end. Not very bright, but faithful, certainly. Giff overplay their parts, and pretending to betray you by turning you over to me was only to be expected. But he tried. He gave it his last full measure." Cirathorn looked up at Teldin and raised his new pistol, steadying his aim once again on Teldin's face.

"And you gave your last full measure and more, Teldin Moore, but the Cloak of the First Pilot does not recognize that. It responds only to who is the more clever and powerful and dangerous. That would be me, I believe."

On impulse, Teldin raised his hand and pointed a finger at Cirathorn. "Die," he said, not knowing how the cloak would respond. "Die and rot in the Abyss."

Cirathorn did not move for several moments, his face frozen in surprise. Nothing happened. Then he smiled broadly. "Interesting," he said. "I feel fine. And now, it's your—"

There was a movement behind him. A thick blue hand stained with gleaming red came up swiftly and caught the admiral by the leg. Cirathorn started involuntarily and half turned, the pistol swinging around at his assailant.

A second blue fist the size of a baked ham swung up and slammed into the elf's midsection. Metallic armor crumpled under the force of the blow. The admiral gasped and choked, the wind knocked out of him. Swiftly, Gomja came to his feet, one hand still locked on the admiral's leg and causing the elf to fall halfway to the ground.

The wide-eyed pilot of the flitter, who had not moved a muscle until this moment, suddenly grabbed for the arms of his helm chair in obvious panic. Gomja spun on his feet at the same moment, whirling the admiral in a tight orbit once around his body, pulling the elf close to avoid striking Teldin or the flitter. On the second pass, as the flitter was beginning to lift away from the ground, Gomja gave a mighty heave and flung the armored elf at the nose of the small ship.

The port window was smashed instantly as the admiral struck it. The flitter rolled backward suddenly, its wings digging into the ground and pivoting the craft onto its back. With a sound like shattering glass, the two wings on the ship broke apart, the shards flying through the air. The ship's fuselage leaped up, free of all but its wing stubs, and flung the admiral's body out of the port window. It then flipped again onto the ground. This time, it lay still.

"Gomja!" Teldin cried out, rushing forward to the giff. Gomja stepped back clumsily from looking at the flitter's wreckage and turned to see Teldin. The front of his crimson jacket was splashed with a darker red that spread down over his barrel chest toward his waist. The giff tried to swallow.

"I hope he heard my name," Gomja said. Then he sagged and fell backward to the ground just as Teldin reached him, the giff's thick arms spread-eagle on the grass and weeds.

"Damn you, you are not going to die on me!" Teldin roared, kneeling and tearing at Gomja's uniform coat. He had the idea that by shouting, Gomja would hear him and would know enough to stay alive. "You're going to live, you stinking giff! You're going to live, and I'm going to beat the hell out of you for scaring me like that! Damn you, live! Live, you ugly blue monster, live!"

"There's . . . no need to be profane," came a husky, gasping whisper from the giff's thick lips. "I'm . . . hardly deaf either. I'm just . . . a litt le tired, sir." The giff's small black eyes blinked open and stared up at the sky. "Giff are notoriously . . . hard to stop."

Teldin found the bullet wound: a round hole nearly in the center of the giff's chest, bleeding profusely. He quickly tore the giff's coat at the entry hole for the bullet and wadded one red strip into a thick bandage, which he pressed to the wound. "Hold this!" he ordered. It had been years since he had done this, during the War of the Lance, when he had cared for several victims of arrow attacks in his unit on Krynn. He was amazed he remembered anything at all about first aid.

"You should get to . . . the ship, sir," Gomja wheezed, slowly raising a thick blue hand to press on the bandage. "Leave me here, and I'll—"

"Just shut up!" Teldin yelled. "We're both going to the ship and we're getting our butts off this monster for wildspace! Knock off this noble crap, and just shut up and move! Keep that bandage on tightly, as tight as you can!"

Gomja did not reply right away, but after a moment he did make an effort to get up on one elbow, his other hand pressing the bandage to his chest. "I'm not deaf," he repeated petulantly, in a barely audible voice.

Gomja had almost made it to his feet when he froze, his wide-eyed face turned up toward the sky. Merciful Paladine, not again, Teldin thought in despair. What now?

"Look out, sir!" Gomja began. "That—"

The explosion overhead drowned out the rest.

* * * * *

The yellow man-o-war was too close, Mirandel noticed. It didn't matter. She looked down again at the wreckage of the flitter and the sprawled silver body that lay among the green litter. She knew, without using a spell or device of any sort, that her husband's family line had now ended—except for her.

There was some sort of alarm going off, a howling collision alert. She looked up at the window and saw the yellow man-o-war coming straight for the *Empress Dorianne*—straight for her window, in fact.

It didn't matter. Her lips moved. She would see her sister soon, her beloved sister, and all would be well.

She had started to say her sister's name when the yellow man-o-war hit the bridge.

* * * * *

Only Gomja and a handful of other onlookers saw the transformation as the yellow man-o-war collided with the armada's bridge. The man-o-war had looped in as if seeking refuge from its pursuers, then had dived dead-on at its prey. As the two made contact, the yellow-winged ship vanished in a glittering shower of magical lightning and fire that burst across the gigantic armada as its bridge was destroyed. The craft that was the man-o-war exited the blast and was now revealed to be a tan stone pyramid much smaller than the armada but obviously far more compact. One point on the pyramid's base had pierced the bridge, like a chisel point through the head of an insect.

The debris from the falling armada rained down across an area a thousand feet wide, and the giff and the human were right in the middle of it.

Chapter Nineteen

• • •

Fire fell from the sky. Teldin looked up and said, "No."

Power surged through his body. Time slowed down. The flaming debris fell lazily now. Teldin grabbed for Gomja's free arm and heaved. The giff seemed to be unusually light, and Teldin was able to drag the blue-skinned, red-suited goliath at a respectable speed. As he did, Gomja's face slowly turned to face Teldin with a look of astonishment, one hand still pressing the bloodied bandage to his chest.

A shadow drifted over the grass around Teldin. He looked up and saw a gigantic orange wing tumbling directly at him, magical sparks and flames pouring in rivers across its surface from where it had been torn free of the armada's hull. The wing was two hundred feet across. It fell quickly, even in slow time, and it was too big to avoid. He tried to speed up his pace, but he was still too slow. The orange wing covered the sky, seconds from striking him.

You will fear not, said a voice in Teldin's mind. Teldin slammed into something incredibly hard that he had not seen before him just a moment earlier. Stars exploded in his vision.

He came to on the grass, Gomja gasping for breath at his side. He thought his head was split open, judging from the pain he felt, but he had only smashed his nose. He couldn't remember how he'd gotten here. And what was Gomja doing here? What was going on? Flames roared all around.

I owe you my apologies, said a strangely familiar voice in his head. *I want you to sleep very deeply for now, both of you. You will feel no more pain. You soon will awaken and be refreshed.*

Teldin clawed at the earth to get to his knees. Darkness overtook him before he could manage to get halfway up. He never felt the ground when he hit it.

*   *   *   *   *

The wreckage of the armada was stupendous. Vorr allowed himself to be impressed as the pyramid ship settled down toward the earth, casually passing over the smoldering, smoking pyre of the elven warship. There was no sign of the last man-o-war, which had broken free of combat after the armada was destroyed and had fled. Several ships were chasing it, but the man-o-war had the edge in speed. Vorr could accept its loss, given the magnitude of the victory over the other elven forces.

"My general," called a scro from inside the cargo deck. Vorr turned from the doorless opening where his forces had entered the deck. He shifted his grip on the newly loaded harpoon bombard as the scro continued his message. "Usso reports that he has located the body of Teldin Moore. We will be there in a moment."

Vorr nodded and looked out of the cargo doorway again. The pyramid ship was only a hundred feet off the ground. Thick smoke drifted past him, causing him to wrinkle his nose in disgust. He would take a long vacation after this, away from everything but clean air and pure water. Anyone who disturbed him would be ground up and eaten.

"How are you doing, General?" Vorr stepped back from the entrance momentarily and gave a brief salute to Admiral Halker, who was walking up behind him. The toothless old scro was looking especially cheerful. "The scars giving you any trouble?" he asked.

Vorr shrugged and gestured at his ruined face, turning to look back out of the cargo bay, the bombard held loosely in his fingers.

"I've heard that Usso has located Teldin Moore, who is conveniently dead." The admiral positively beamed. "We should be able to gain the cloak in one more minute. Do you wish the honors?"

Vorr stared down into the burning chunks of ceramiclike material that once had been one of the mightiest ships in the known spheres. He nodded, his eyes searching.

He then caught sight of a flash of royal blue among the shattered remains of a vast orange wing, spread out across the green ground. Vorr slapped his hands together to get Halker's attention, then pointed. The old scro came forward instantly to see, standing fearlessly on the edge of the cargo doorway only a few feet from where Vorr stood. Vorr reached out to steady the admiral, but the scro saw the gesture and recoiled, stepping out of reach. "I can manage!" he snapped. "I'm not a cripple yet!"

Vorr withdrew his hand, giving Halker a curious look before he turned his attention again to the ground. The patch of blue was definitely Teldin Moore and his cloak, sprawled on the smoking ground. Beside him lay a giff in a red military uniform. They were both badly wounded, if not already dead, judging from the amount of blood visible even from this height. Both obviously had been caught in the rain of falling debris from the armada.

The pyramid drifted closer and closer, now only man-height off the ground. Vorr stepped up on the edge of the cargo doorway, preparing to jump down. The pyramid came to a stop a moment later. Vorr dropped over the side of the pyramid, landing crouched on his feet with the bombard held outstretched in one arm. He then straightened slowly and walked over to the pair on the ground.

It took only a glance to see that both of them were dead. A falling armada packed a hell of a punch. The cloak on Teldin's back appeared undamaged, however. Not a scrap of dust was on it. Nice magic, Vorr thought, and he reached down for the clasp on Teldin's neck. It popped open at his touch.

With a single motion, General Vorr pulled the blue cloak free and raised it in the gentle wind and smoke. It didn't feel any different than a regular cloak would feel. Magical things were all the same to him. A shame, really, that he couldn't just wear it himself. It would have been interesting to have commanded the *Spelljammer*, but it would do just as well to have Admiral Halker do it. It made for a guaranteed job for years to come, a far safer position than if the undead neogi Skarkesh had been in charge—or Usso, for that matter.

Vorr looked up and saw Halker on the periphery of the cargo doorway. The old scro's face was alive with naked desire, and his arms were stretched out to Vorr as if Vorr held the scro's very existence in his hands. Vorr suddenly gave a broad grin, wadded the cloak up with one hand, and tossed it to Halker like a ball. He'd give the old coot Skarkesh's medallion when he got aboard, and cement his future.

Halker snatched the cloak out of the air, clutching it to his chest in ecstacy. As Vorr stepped forward toward the low stone base of the floating pyramid and tossed his bombard into the cargo bay doorway, Halker made a single thumb's-up gesture into the air outside the pyramid.

The pyramid lifted rapidly away from the ground.

Vorr slowed his pace for a moment, stunned—then bolted for the pyramid. He leaped at the last moment, mighty hands spread out to catch any part of the stonework and pull himself aboard. Halker! he thought. Halker, what in the—

He missed and fell, tumbling into a pile of wreckage. As he struggled to his feet, he heard a peal of feminine laughter.

Vorr saw Halker throw his harpoon-bombard somewhere into the wreckage, then continued to watch as the pyramid rose and became a small black square against the patchwork sky, then a square dot, then a mote that faded away as it dropped toward the horizon. For perhaps five minutes, he did nothing else. Then he uttered a word, one that could not have been understood by any listener, through his tortured lips, fused together by slime and torch flame.

"Usso."

He turned and looked back at the bodies of Teldin Moore and his giff companion.

They weren't there.

*   *   *   *   *

Admiral Halker announced to the crew that General Vorr had wished to explore the wreckage for suitably glorious souvenirs; he would be picked up later by another ship. The scro and ogre warriors smiled and nodded, as they knew the general was just like that. No one but the helmsman noticed that there was one additional passenger aboard the pyramid as it took off, a passenger who had climbed on at the moment Vorr had jumped off, but no one was going up to ask the helmsman anything.

Just before the wizard's last meeting with Admiral Halker, before the armada was destroyed, Usso had announced his intention to run the helm himself, freeing the war priests for other duties. Only one warrior, an ogre, happened to hear the feminine laughter coming from the direction of Admiral Halker at the cargo bay doors, but he knew that couldn't have happened. He did think it was curious that Halker appeared to be pantomiming the act of putting on a cloak when he had nothing at all in his hands. But he knew that couldn't have happened, either. He snorted and went on about his duties.

* * * * *

It had been child's play to convince Vorr of Skarkesh's evil intent toward the Tarantula Fleet, requiring only charm spells on Sergeant Dlavish and a few other scro, who had never known what had hit them. Vorr hated undead of any kind, especially liches, and he had been more than willing to believe that Skarkesh would have sold out the scro after Skarkesh's heavy-handed use of Captain Geraz. Usso had no doubt that Skarkesh was not fond of scro, but she suspected that the rotting neogi gladly would have kept the scro around as its servants. Neogi were neogi, dead or alive, and they craved power over anyone that they could find. Scro were as useful as slaves as anyone else.

It had been tricky, she admitted, and she had almost lost control of things once or twice, but she had pulled it off. The victory left her weak in the knees, but she felt an exhilaration that she couldn't believe was possible. She had the cloak to the *Spelljammer*. General Vorr was far behind on the top of a thousand-mile-high beast's head. Admiral Halker was under her control, charmed by her powers of fascination into crewing the working helm at the pyramid's apex, but eventually he would be dropped over the side or discarded in some other manner, once a nicer ship could be found.

Usso looked out of the broad doorway of the pyramid's cargo bay and watched the landscape rise up to meet her with increasing speed. The pyramid was falling through wildspace toward the ground, where they would rest before leaving this sphere. Usso had ordered the rest of the crewmen to their quarters aboard the pyramid. She still wore her magical disguise as Halker; maintaining it was as effortless as it had been to appear to be an old Oriental man or any other humanlike person she chose. It was one of her innate powers as a *hu hsien*. A marvelous power it was, too.

The rest of the Tarantula Fleet had been given orders by "Halker" to stay behind for a day, hunting for the last man-o-war and any other local elven ships, then to rendezvous back at Spiral. With luck, it would be months before they figured out that something had gone wrong. The scro weren't impossibly stupid, but their obedience to orders made them the perfect victims of deceptions such as this.

Usso noticed that it would be only seconds before the air envelope around the inside of the Herdspace sphere would be contacted. The ship would slow to tactical speed, but the cargo bay would still be almost unlivable without the protective doors. Damn the scro for being efficient. She turned away from the door and wandered through the empty cargo area for one of the ladders upstairs to the helm room, then began to climb.

* * * * *

Teldin hesitated as he stepped over a scorched chunk of debris. Something was moving in the smoke ahead.

"Gomja," he whispered. "There's—"

"I see it, sir," the giff rumbled. "It looks too big to be an elf." Teldin heard the giff fumble with his pistol, then a muttered curse as Gomja threw the weapon to the ground. "Flint's gone," he said. "Useless."

"You've got that sword you found, right?" Teldin asked. He reached up and scratched at his nose as Gomja grunted in the affirmative. When he had awakened only minutes ago, he'd found his freshly broken nose had completely healed. The fal must have set up some sort of protective magical wall around Gomja and himself to prevent the wing of the armada from striking him. The wall had been crude, but it had worked. Perhaps he should be grateful.

"Sir," said Gomja, stopping short behind him.

In the thick smoke ahead stood a huge black-armored figure. It obviously had heard them coming through the debris, and it was waiting for them to approach.

Teldin recognized the black plate-metal armor and its steel studs at once. "Scro," he whispered, drawing his short sword.

The scro became clearer. It was gray-skinned and nearly of ogre size, as thick across its chest as a tree trunk. Its arms and legs were similarly muscled, surpassing even Gomja's bulk.

What stopped Teldin short was the scro's face. Hideously scarred by either fire or acid, it was barely recognizable as even remotely humanoid, except for its squashed nose and two large black eyes. It regarded Teldin and Gomja without comment. With a start, Teldin realized that the scro's mouth was blistered and burned so badly that the lips were shut.

The scro made a muffled sound, then breathed heavily for a moment. With a slow, steady motion, it raised its left arm, revealing a large, three-tined fork of black metal. This the scro brought to its mouth and made a quick slashing motion. Blood and pus ran down the scro's jaw to drip from its chin.

"Teldin Moore," the scro croaked hoarsely in the Common tongue. "I certainly hope that is really you. I've looked forward to meeting you."

"Sir!" Gomja's hammy hand clamped down on Teldin's shoulder. "Get back. You don't have the experience or the strength to deal with an opponent like this one."

"We can take it together," said Teldin. He knew Gomja was right, but he knew of no way to get out of this now. "You go right. I'll go left."

"You're being foolish, sir," Gomja muttered back, taking a step past Teldin toward the scro. "This is the sort of fight I've been hoping to have for months. A worthy opponent is—"

The scro moved rapidly at Gomja before either Teldin or the giff were fully prepared for it. Gomja jerked his sword up and struck down. At the same moment, the scro whirled on one foot, catching the sword in the black fork and coming to stand side by side with the giff, pulling Gomja's sword arm around in an arc. Reversing the arc, the scro flung the entrapped sword back up over Gomja's head, tearing it out of the surprised giff's grasp. The scro's right knee came up at the same moment and smashed into Gomja's midsection with a loud thump. The giff gasped aloud, staggering back to get his balance. The scro whirled, reversing its grip on its black fork, and brought the butt end down on Gomja's broad, thick forehead with an audible crack.

Gomja dropped like a lead weight and did not get up.

The scro gazed down at its foe, then turned and looked down at Teldin. Its mouth bled freely, splattering droplets of blood across the front of its black steel armor.

"I seem to have been the victim of some magical hoax," said the scro, spitting blood carelessly as it spoke. "I thought I had found you dead and taken your cloak. I see that I was wrong, but I can fix that. It's your turn now. Give me a real fight."

Teldin backed up. Gomja was breathing, but he was out cold. Teldin's foot caught on a piece of metal and he stumbled, catching himself at the last moment. He swallowed and looked around. Only smoke and wreckage were visible.

"A fight," said the scro. "Use your cloak."

The cloak! Teldin stopped and concentrated, raising his left hand and pointing his index finger at the scro's head. Power suddenly rushed through his body, setting the hairs on his neck and arms on end.

"Here's a fight for you!" Teldin shouted.

A brilliant stream of magical bolts flew from his fingers and struck the scro in the face. The burst lasted for several seconds, sending dozens of fiery projectiles at his foe. The energy stream ended abruptly.

The scro appeared completely unaffected.

"Try again," said the scro.

Teldin caught a hint of something in the scro's voice, and he realized it was useless. The scro must be resistant to magic in some manner, probably because of a magical item it wore. Using the cloak was not the answer.

But if it wasn't the answer, what was?

The scro took another step toward Teldin. "You killed Gargon, my bodyguard, on Ironpiece," it said. "He was a good soldier. He is going to be hell to replace."

Teldin had no idea what the scro was talking about. Did he mean the ogre who had tried to kill Gaye? Teldin glanced behind him and continued backing up, avoiding the debris.

"I'm disappointed," said the scro. "I had expected better. Word of your abilities has long preceded you. I was counting on a fight with an opponent equal to me."

Equal to you, Teldin thought. Equal to you.

Teldin came to a stop. He adjusted his grip on his sword. He had one trick left. It was all he could think of.

"If you wanted your equal," said Teldin, "then why didn't you say so?"

He concentrated on the scro, taking in his opponent's size and musculature. Once he had it fixed in his mind, he focused on his cloak and opened himself to its powers.

For a moment he noticed no change, then felt a rushing of energy through his body that dwarfed everything he had previously felt when using the cloak. He felt his clothing grow tight across his chest and thighs, binding and pulling over his neck and upper arms. He seemed to be getting taller. Fabric ripped and split down his left and right sides. His belt tightened until he thought he would be crushed, then snapped apart and fell away. The sword in his hand seemed to shrink until it was merely of dagger size.

The scro had frozen in place as the transformation started, watching Teldin with wide, dark eyes. Blood continued to fall from its mouth as it stared.

"Impressive," the scro said as the transformation ended. "You are me. Two General Vorrs. You have become my equal—perhaps."

Teldin said nothing. He took a deep breath and stepped forward, sword raised. "Soon you will be my lesser," he replied. He felt none of the bravado he put into his voice, feeling instead that he had been pushed beyond all rational limits. He had nothing left to do but fight.

General Vorr charged him. Teldin saw the gray warrior make a peculiar feint with his black fork-weapon as he came on. Not knowing what to expect, Teldin merely slashed out at Vorr's face, then impulsively turned completely around and slashed out again. He felt his wild strike bite into the flesh at Vorr's neck—and felt the impact of the butt of Vorr's weapon strike him dead center in his chest. Ribs broke, and blinding spikes of white-hot pain shot through Teldin's lungs. He staggered back, trying to breathe, and felt that he had been stabbed by a half-dozen spears.

Vorr came at him again. Teldin lunged forward, shielding his face with one hand and trying to impale Vorr with his sword in the other. The general sidestepped Teldin and hit him in the back with his fist, unable to bring his black fork to bear. Teldin kicked out in reflex, striking Vorr in the leg and knocking him off balance, then fell on his face and rolled to get up. He wanted to scream in agony from the pain in his chest and back. He knew he was going to die, but first he wanted to take this scro with him as payment for everything the scro, the neogi, and everyone else had done to him.

A round piece of ceramic material lay at Teldin's feet as he got up. He bent down, seized it, and flung it at Vorr, then grabbed a long steel pipe as well and whipped it at the monstrous scro. The ceramic disk burst when it slammed into Vorr's chest, scattering bright shards everywhere. The general had recovered his balance again when the pipe slammed into his legs and knocked him back down.

Teldin felt a new surge of power flow through him. He wanted to kill this Vorr. Nothing else mattered. With a wild scream that tore his lungs as if they were set aflame, Teldin rushed at the fallen scro and leaped, his cloak and the rags of his clothing flapping in the air. Vorr came up, hands out and empty, and grabbed him by the arms, flinging him over his head and into the grassy earth beyond.

The impact jarred Teldin to the bone. He couldn't see straight; the world was spinning crazily. With an effort, he rolled back to his hands and knees, just in time to see Vorr come at him, take a short leap, and lash out with his foot for Teldin's head. Teldin never felt the blow.

*   *   *   *   *

Vorr fell to his knees and rested there, panting, for several minutes. It had not been the most challenging fight he had ever had—the fight with the zwarth on Spiral still had that honor—but it had been exciting nonetheless. Teldin had put up a surprisingly good, if brief, fight, mostly because he obviously had so little formal combat training that he could do things to catch a better opponent off guard. Not the best fight, but a worthy one. Vorr was satisfied.

A glance at Teldin's fallen body brought a brief surprise: Teldin had now assumed his original shape. The cloak must not work when its owner was knocked out or dead, Vorr thought. I should be jealous that I can't use something like that, Vorr thought with a smile, but then, I don't need it.

A moment later, Vorr had reached Teldin's side. The human was unconscious. The boot to the head had almost killed him, but his neck had not broken; taking Vorr's own shape had saved Teldin at the last moment. The scro general sighed, then reached down for Teldin's cloak. He touched the material. It felt real. Carefully rolling the human over, Vorr touched the lion-headed clasp of the silver necklace, then tried to undo it.

It came open in his hands.

Vorr pulled the cloak free and stood up. Now he had the real cloak, and Usso had nothing at all. Or did she? What exactly had happened earlier? He looked down at Teldin, then dropped the cloak by Teldin's side. He should finish the job with Teldin and the giff, then move on and find some food. Perhaps he could signal someone from the fleet later, if he could avoid the pyramid ship.

He had just started to reach down for the black fork when he saw a tiny female figure only thirty feet away. Vorr blinked. It appeared to be a young human or elf girl dressed in dirty, smeared clothing that once had been bright and colorful. Her thick black hair was mussed and wild. She was carrying some sort of stick.

Vorr rubbed his eyes briefly, then looked again.

"My sensei is going to hate me for this," said the little, black-haired female. "*Sayonara.*"

Bracing herself, Gaye pulled both triggers of the harpoon-bombard at the same time.

*   *   *   *   *

Usso was halfway up the ladder out of the cargo bay when everything changed. A blast of wind suddenly stirred the air in the cargo deck, then arose to an ear-splitting roar. At the same moment, the pyramid tilted, as if its internal gravity had shifted slightly—then the gravity was gone.

Suddenly weightless, Usso clutched the ladder's iron rungs in numbing-cold terror. If there was no gravity when the pyramid reached the gravity field of the Herdspace sphere, that meant the helm was abandoned—or destroyed.

The cloak! She suddenly recalled that she could use the powers of the cloak to control the pyramid. She reached back with one hand to grasp the soft fabric as she prepared to concentrate and activate the cloak's powers.

Her hand closed on nothing. The cloak was gone. Her hand flew to her throat but found no silver chain and clasp. It was as if the cloak had never existed. That wasn't possible. She knew it. The cloak must have fallen off. There was no time to retrieve it now. She had to get to the helm.

Usso reached the top of the ladder leading into the helm room barely three minutes later, having had to polymorph herself into a spider at one point to cross a ceiling to the next ladder. The pyramid was apparently rotating slowly in free fall, heading for the ground of Herdspace at hundreds of miles an hour. Against the roaring from the cargo deck Usso could hear the screams and curses of the scro and ogres below as they left their quarters on the lower floors of the pyramid to tumble about helplessly in the stony rooms and corridors.

The door to the helm room had been broken open by someone with reasonably great strength. Usso froze when she saw it. Vorr? Was Vorr alive and here in the pyramid? Impossible! It took all her willpower to keep from fleeing down the ladder. How could he have gotten aboard?

Trickles of blood ran down the sides of the hatchway from the floor above. Usso readied a spell, one hand gripping the ladder rung until the metal dug into her hands. Forgetting all caution in her panic, she stood up on the ladder and looked into the room.

The bloodied face of Admiral Halker looked back at her from the floor by the hatch, one sleeve of his armor snagged by a metal staple in the floor. Someone had cut his throat. Blood trailed across the floor around him in long streams.

She raised her shocked gaze. Beyond Halker's pale green

face was the helm—what was left of it. Someone had hacked at it with an edged weapon, either a sword or axe, and it was in ruins. Both arms were missing from the chair, and the back was split in two. Splinters rattled across the walls and floor.

Without a helm, the pyramid was going to hit the ground so hard that nothing larger than gravel would be left, scattered across the bottom of a crater hundreds of feet deep and wide. Usso knew she had to flee the pyramid at once. She might still have the time to polymorph into a bird before—

Someone grabbed her by her long black hair and pulled her off the ladder with a single jerk. She screamed from the sudden pain and felt a powerful arm clutch her to a muscular chest. Whirling, she looked into the face of her assailant. Vorr, it must be Vorr.

But it wasn't Vorr.

Her assailant was a human male of indeterminate age, tall and broad, with short, curly blond hair. His face was contorted with the effort of holding Usso with one hand while clutching a metal hook on the wall behind him with the other.

"Now it's your turn to lose a ship," he said as the room slowly spun through the air.

*   *   *   *   *

Things hadn't made any sense to Aelfred Silverhorn since that first night on Ironpiece. He had already planned to go with Teldin Moore to avenge the loss of his ship, the *Probe* (and maybe to see Teldin become the captain of the *Spelljammer*, too—you never knew how things would go), but there was that awful dream that he couldn't talk about, coming on the morning the group had left Ironpiece on the *Perilous Halibut* during the scro attack. Someone had been in the dream, making him into a slave of some kind, and he woke up still feeling he was a slave. It had made no sense.

Worse, he had done things he could not understand. He found himself compelled to set up a signal light in the rear of the ship, next to the jettison, and send messages to the scro chasing them. He would forget about it while he was awake, but his dreams were thick with terror, and before awakening every morning he knew he had been up and about in his sleep, carrying out his tasks. No one had known what he was doing. Everyone had trusted him completely.

Over time, he pieced together an image of his taskmaster. It was an undead thing, he knew, but he knew little more. He suspected it was part of the scro fleet. He had some mental image of a pyramid-shaped ship, probably the one he'd seen off Ironpiece. He knew it was hopeless to fight his compulsion to betray his friends—so he stopped worrying about it. Instead, he planned his revenge.

It was Sylvie's death that had freed him. As he knelt in the grass beside her body, he had felt the chains of the compulsion melt from his soul like ice in the sun. It must have been the stress, he thought. He was overcome with guilt that his unwilling behavior had brought on her death. She had been his best friend, his anchor to his new life in space. He could not put all the blood back into her body. He could only leave her behind and find someone on whom to vent his fury.

Aelfred had watched as the elves who had killed Sylvie died themselves. The elves' killers, however, had come down to earth right afterward—in a giant pyramid ship.

It had been easy to rush forward through the burning wreckage—easy, perhaps, given that he had ignored the burns and injuries he had suffered on his run. He had made it aboard the pyramid just before it left for good, climbing on as it rested above the ground for a moment. It had taken a long while to find an upper hatch and climb inside. No one was home, as far as he could tell, so he had gone looking for the helm. He'd heard the helms on pyramids were on top.

It was a scro ship, he had found. He knew he was on the right ship, the one from which he had been possessed, but he didn't know who or what had done it. It didn't matter. It took only a moment to chop the old scro on the helm into bloody meat and hack the helm into splinters. The last descent began immediately after that.

Getting back to the hatch was troublesome but necessary. Someone might come up to see what was the problem, and he wanted to stop any attempt to fix the helm. He was holding onto a hook in the wall behind the hatch when an Oriental woman came up the ladder, and he grabbed her. He wasn't sure at first if she was a friend or foe. When she turned into a python, he decided she was a foe, and he held on as she changed shape over and over in her panic to escape him. It was when she had turned into a wolf and had almost gotten away from him that the pyramid struck the ground at a speed many times faster than a hawk could dive. There was an instant of chaos and impact, then nothing at all.

*   *   *   *   *

Teldin awoke, feeling something cool wash across his face. He blinked and looked up into a too-bright sky, the sun directly overhead as always. He shut his eyes again, half raising his hands to shield his face.

"Relax," came a young girl's voice. It sounded familiar but he couldn't place it. "Everything's fine." A wet cloth began to wipe his face again, spreading its coolness across his brow.

It felt like heaven. Teldin sighed and rolled his head to one side. A wadded blue cloak supported his head. His cheek rested against something cool and metallic.

Thin fingers reached under his cheek and removed the large bronze disk and chain that lay on the ground there. After a brief look at it, Gaye tucked the medallion down the front of her blouse and into the magical bag that was carefully strapped across her chest. The bag opened into another dimension and would hold almost anything—poles, coins, extra clothing, food, even lost thingfinders. She'd give the medallion to Teldin later when he recovered. It had belonged to the gray ogre, having been tucked into his chest armor, and had come partially free when he had fallen to the ground, but picking it up had been difficult, given that she couldn't bare to look at what the two harpoons had done to the ogre's face. Her body still ached from the bombard's recoil.

The effects the medallion had on her when she first touched it had been shocking. What deep-space vista was that? What otherworldly view was she seeing? It had been tempting to keep the medallion for herself, but Gaye knew that Teldin might make better use of it wherever he was going on his search for the *Spelljammer*—and she knew he would be going without her. He'd make sure of it now, with all the deaths and horror he had faced.

And she would be left far behind, she who loved him.

"You never knew, did you?" she said softly as she picked up the cloth and wiped Teldin's face again. "You never did figure it out." Her free hand came up to stroke Teldin's cheek as he faded into sleep. Hearing the change in his breathing, Gaye slowly released the cloth and leaned over Teldin's still form. Her black hair fell across his chest and covered his face like a tent. Eyes closed, she pressed her lips to his. His mustache tickled her nose. "You never will know," she whispered, then bent down again and with delicate fingers, reconnected the silver clasp at Teldin's neck.

He was once again the Cloakmaster.

* * * * *

"I'd like some answers, if you have them," said Teldin.

You may ask, said the spelljammer-sized slug. Its pulpy body shook and rippled like black jelly as it rose up to turn its head in Teldin's direction.

Teldin swallowed. He would never get used to the fal's foul appearance. After returning to heal Teldin and Gomja, the fal—or its image, Teldin wasn't sure which—had reported that the surviving elven and scro ships were leaving and probably were on their way out of the sphere. Once Gaye had given Teldin the bronze medallion, the fal then informed Teldin of the medallion's purpose—it having been mentioned in a few old epics about the *Spelljammer*—and had devised a set of instructions on how to use the ancient item to track the mighty ship. One Six Nine also had brought the news of Aelfred's fate, much to everyone's distress.

"Why couldn't you have done something to help Aelfred?" Teldin asked. He knew the fal would have a good answer, but he had to know. "You have so many powers, but . . . why?"

I greatly regret that I was unaware of his actions, but I was maintaining a set of mental illusions in my attempt to draw away the scro fleet. I dropped the illusions only to divine his fate too late to intervene, as he apparently had completed his sabotage and was beyond my reach.

Teldin snorted softly. It was useless to beat the issue. He rubbed his eyes. It was so hard to believe both Aelfred and

Sylvie were gone. "I don't understand what you mean when
you talk about psionics, for another thing," Teldin said, dropping his hand and changing the topic. "I have enough trouble
understanding magic. You said something about mental illusions just now. Were you talking about psionics?"

You are correct. The enormous bulk of the fal gave an oily
ripple in the sunlight. *I am implanting in your mind my own
image, to which you are speaking. You could touch my image
but would discover that I feel quite real to you, though I am
not truly in your vicinity. I am able to so control your perceptions that I am, for all purposes, real to you. I can do this only
with a limited number of beings, however. I do not enjoy du-
plicity, except when it serves to protect my person or my allies.*

*You may have guessed that General Vorr, whom you fought,
fell victim earlier to one of my mental decoys. I wished for the
scro to depart without further bloodshed, and my plan was
almost entirely successful. You were thought by the general to
be dead, based on a mental illusion he and an ally of his had
observed earlier. I did not intend for the general to be left
behind by his cohorts, for which I offer my apologies, just as I
had not meant for Aelfred to die aboard the pyramid ship that
he apparently sabotaged.*

"No one's plans work perfectly," said Teldin with a bitter
smile, "least of all mine. I'm still confused, though, because
the general claimed he was immune to magic. How could psionics have affected him?"

*You must understand that psionics is like magic, but it is
not magic. I would like to explain the subtle differences between them, but it would serve no purpose. You need know
only that the two do not affect one another, so Vorr's immu-
nity to magic helped him not against any psionic attack I cared
to make against him. I created what I wished him to see and
feel, and that he did.*

What if I was seeing only what you wished me to see right
now? thought Teldin uncomfortably. Not just your image, but
everything, even this whole megafauna-being we're on. What
if everything I saw and felt was unreal?

He shook himself, quickly abandoning the thought. "I'll
let it go," he muttered. "It's beyond me. Anyway, we should
get underway and start looking for the *Spelljammer* before

some other fleet comes looking for us. We still have to bury Sylvie with Aelfred on our way out, too, if we can find out where he . . . you know." Teldin waved his hand vaguely.

I will guide you there, Teldin. I assume that you also will need funds, as well as guidance, to fulfil our bargain for you to find the Spelljammer. You will find at your feet a pouch containing several dozen small gems, which you may convert into currency at your next destination. You may wish to purchase a new ship if you must eventually part from the giff and gnomes.

Teldin moved his left foot forward without looking down. His foot tapped something soft, like a small bag. Sighing, he leaned down and retrieved the pouch. He didn't want to know how the fal had done it; it didn't matter. "I want to leave everyone behind as soon as possible. Everyone's in too much danger with me around now. Your gems are appreciated, but if I knew where the broken sphere that you mentioned was, I'd be better able to fulfil our bargain. It could be on any world in all the crystal spheres." Teldin hesitated. "The sphere you were talking about, by the way. Did you mean a sphere like a planet or an asteroid, or—"

I meant a broken crystal sphere, Teldin. The black image of the fal's head lowered in his direction. *The Spelljammer was born in a broken crystal sphere.*

For a moment, the thought didn't fully register. As it did, he let out his breath. "Broken? How could a crystal sphere be broken? I don't . . . oh, forget it." Teldin stuffed the pouch of gems into the pocket of his pants. "We should go," he finished, looking around.

Gaye was waiting by the ship, wearing a deep purple dress that reached the ground. Her dark eyes were rimmed with red, and she kept her arms folded across her chest as Teldin coughed and then approached.

Best to keep it brief, Teldin thought. He nodded at the small kender. "We'll miss you. I'm still not sure why you want to stay around here, but maybe it's for the best. Things aren't going to be safe for me or for anyone—"

"I know," said Gaye abruptly. She blinked up at him. "It's for the best."

Teldin looked away from her wildspace eyes. Something

hurt down in his heart. He knew that he had been starting to fall for Gaye, and that would never have worked out. The idea of loving a kender was one problem, but seeing her slain as a result of the attacks that inevitably would be made against him—he couldn't face that. She was just another face in a long line of faces that he was leaving behind. He wondered if it would ever stop. He had so little faith that it would.

"Well, good-bye, then," Teldin said, and turned away. Gaye watched as he walked over to the *Perilous Halibut* and grabbed its rope ladder, climbing to the top deck with his violet-blue cloak flapping behind him in a light breeze. Everyone else was already aboard and waiting.

He never looked back. Soon, the long black ship was lifting away, and before long it was gone.

About an hour later, Gaye took a ragged breath and wiped her eyes on the hem of her dress for the last time. "I guess that's that, then," she said. "Everything comes and goes. Life is a pain sometimes, isn't it? Maybe we should do something so I can keep busy for a while. I appreciate you letting me stay here and help out around the place and learn something new. I love to learn." She sniffed and wiped her nose on her sleeve. "I feel like I've got so much to learn about life."

You wish to begin your lessons? queried the fal.

Gaye's head bobbed rapidly. "Now, please," she said, blinking and looking away for a moment to where the gnomes' ship had gone. There was nothing there now, and nothing inside her, either. It was best to stay busy.

Come with me, then, said the fal. The image of One Six Nine faded into the air—and so did the black-haired kender, with a shriek of surprise. *If you wish to learn, I have much to teach you, Gaeadrelle Goldring.*

* * * * *

"The gnomes' ship is departing, Captain Kilian."

The one who was addressed made no movement away from the forward window on the bridge, through which he peered at the distant landscape. Perhaps a minute passed. The aide cleared his throat, preparing to repeat the statement.

"I am aware of that," said the silver-armored elf at last,

without turning around. "When it is gone, we will go, too, and return to the Rock of Bral."

The aide blinked in confusion. "If you will forgive me for saying so, Captain, it might be wise to make one last attempt to recover the cloak from Teldin Moore."

"No," said the captain. He still didn't move. "We must not pursue him. Our duty is to inform the Imperial Fleet of the enemy's presence and actions, and of our own losses. We are the last of the Rock of Bral's fleet, and we are responsible for the safety of our people first. We have nothing more to gain by chasing unicorns."

The aide frowned. He had expected a different answer. "But the gnome ship is not effectively armed, Captain. We would have no trouble in capturing it and taking . . ."

The aide's voice faded as Kilian turned. A cold blue gaze stabbed out from the older elf's sharp-featured face.

"That path was already attempted, with grave losses," the captain said. "There was no honor in our hunt. We paid for our arrogance with our comrades' lives. Would you have us now bargain with our own?"

The aide caught his breath. "I meant, Captain, that . . . that we . . ." Seconds passed; he flushed with embarrassment. "The admiral wanted us to get the cloak," he finished.

The captain stared at his aide a moment longer, then turned back to the window of the man-o-war, looking down at the swirling clouds a thousand miles below him. "The admiral is dead, and we have other considerations now," he murmured. "Teldin Moore cannot be our concern. Perhaps the grand admiral will feel differently, but it is of no matter to me for the moment. We must warn our people of real dangers, not make sacrifices to legends." The elf seemed about to say more, but stopped.

Another minute or two passed before Kilian heard the door close behind him. He let out his breath in a long sigh and searched the vista before him for any sign of the gnomes' black ship. He saw nothing, but he had expected that.

"You are free for now," he whispered to the window. "I will let you depart in peace, but others will not. May the wind carry you wherever you run, Teldin Moore. May the wind be fast and sure. You cannot run forever."

BOOKS

The Cloakmaster Cycle

Beyond the Moons   David Cook

When a spelljamming ship crashes into Teldin Moore's home on Krynn, a dying alien gives him a mysterious cloak that makes him the target of killers and cutthroats. The young farmer must find answers to the cloak's mystery before the monstrous neogi can find him. On sale now.

Into the Void   Nigel Findley

Teldin is plunged into a sea of alien faces when his ship is attacked by space pirates. The mind flayer who rescues him offers to help him learn how to use the powers of the cloak--but for whose gain? On sale now.

The Radiant Dragon   Elaine Cunningham

A radiant dragon who also possesses a key to control of the *Spelljammer* joins Teldin in his search for the legendary ship, but the quest is interrupted by the advent of the second Unhuman War. Available November 1992.